RAVE REVIEWS FOR CHRISTIE CRAIG!

DIVOR...

"This sequel to ... *...icious* is another delightf... ...triguing mystery. Peopled ... ...familiar old ones, it also ... ...dd a lot of humor and w...

—*Romantic Times BOOKreviews*

"I was simply delighted by this breezy, snappy, good-time story....This book is sure to brighten your day."

—Beyond Her Book Blog, *Publishers Weekly*

"Christie Craig is the jewel of my finds when it comes to new authors to add to my favorites list. Her characters draw you in immediately, make you care about them in no time flat, and her humor is to die for."

—The Good, The Bad, and The Unread

"Ms. Craig seems in touch with the readers' desires. She does a great job of blending and sifting all the elements we love (heat, emotion, wit, and action) into one great story."

—Once Upon a Romance

WEDDINGS CAN BE MURDER

"Although the plot is threaded with sassy humor, a lighthearted touch, and misaligned lovers hinting strongly of Shakespeare, a deranged psychopath, a trail of murdered brides, and threats of real danger keep the story on the suspenseful side."

—*Library Journal*

"Once again Craig brings a wonderful story to life with a number of likable and interesting characters. There's quite decent mystery, a fair amount of suspense and two lovely romances."

—*Romantic Times BOOKreviews*

"If you want a sexy romance that will put a smile on your face, a Christie Craig book is the way to go!"

—Night Owl Romance

CRITICS LOVE CHRISTIE CRAIG!

WEDDINGS CAN BE MURDER

"A story that twines emotions and feelings with sizzle and steam, all wrapped around bits of humor... *Weddings Can Be Murder* combines passionate and intense characters with a plot that's well-balanced and fast-moving. It's edgy and fun."

—Once Upon a Romance

DIVORCED, DESPERATE AND DELICIOUS

"Christie Craig delivers humor, heat, and suspense in addictive doses. She's the newest addition to my list of have-to-read authors....Funny, hot, and suspenseful, Christie Craig's writing has it all. Warning: definitely addictive."

—*New York Times* Bestselling Author Nina Bangs

"Readers who enjoy Jennie Crusie and Janet Evanovich will fall head over heels for *Divorced, Desperate and Delicious*, a witty romantic adventure by debut author Christie Craig....A page-turner filled with humorous wit, sexy romance and just enough danger to keep you up long past midnight."

—*New York Times* Bestselling Author Dianna Love Snell

"Suspense and romance that keeps you on the edge of your seat ...until you fall off laughing....Christie Craig writes a book you can't put down."

—RITA Finalist Gemma Halliday

"This is an entertaining, fast-moving mystery and romance peopled with interesting, likable characters, as well as warm and cuddly animals. The main romance, as well as the secondary ones, are delightful, and the suspense is well done. This is an all-around enticing and fun story to read."

—*Romantic Times BOOKreviews*

"*Divorced, Desperate and Delicious* is funny, witty, suspenseful, and very entertaining....This is a wonderful book. The characters are charming, and there are enough twists and turns to keep the reader guessing. Christie Craig has a winner."

—Romance Reviews Today

JUST THE RIGHT PRESCRIPTION

He unbuttoned his shirt and tossed it onto her dresser. Macy blinked. The man looked downright edible without it. The golden lamplight showcased warm, melt-against-me skin. His chest, dusted with dark hair, appeared even more muscular.

An innie belly button, the cutest little dimple she'd ever seen, was centered among hard abs. His jeans fit snug around his narrow waist, and a trail of hair disappeared under the snap of his jeans. A treasure trail—wasn't that what the thin spray was called? Because it led to...

He unsnapped those jeans.

Macy's gaze shot up and found him studying her. "Uh, what are you doing?" she asked.

"I got on boxers," he said. His cocky grin proved he'd noted her appreciation.

She tried to wipe all approval from her expression. "Okay, I had you down for a white briefs kind of guy, but you don't have to prove me wrong." She sat the rest of the way up. "Now, back to my original question. What are you doing?"

"Getting in bed." He heel-kicked off his shoes.

She pointed to her bedroom door. "The sofa is thataway, big boy."

He picked up the folded piece of paper from the nightstand and handed it to her. "Doctor's orders."

Gotcha!

CHRISTIE CRAIG

LOVE SPELL NEW YORK CITY

To my daughter, Nina, and her husband, Jason, who when this book is released will be living a new chapter in their lives as parents. May you two be blessed with a child as easy to raise as you were, Nina. Love you—all three of you.

LOVE SPELL®

June 2009

Published by

Dorchester Publishing Co., Inc.
200 Madison Avenue
New York, NY 10016

ISBN 10: 0-505-52797-9
ISBN 13: 978-0-505-52797-4
E-ISBN: 978-1-4285-0688-6

The name "Love Spell" and its logo are trademarks of Dorchester Publishing Co., Inc.

Printed in the United States of America.

10 9 8 7 6 5 4 3 2 1

Visit us on the web at www.dorchesterpub.com.

ACKNOWLEDGMENTS

I'd like to give credit to all those who have supported me. To my husband who reads my galleys faster than he reads any other books, who recommends my books to all his friends and rightfully takes credit for being my inspiration for all the good stuff. (Seriously, babe, those are your abs.) To my son, Steve Craig Jr., who said, "Next time, can you please put my name in the acknowledgments so people will believe you are my mom?" To Faye Hughes, the kind of friend who will stay up most of the night proofing revisions, and only complain for a few months . . . and counting.

To every fan who has ever e-mailed me and used the word/ words, "wow," "great," "love it," or "can't wait to read the next one." Seriously, thank you. And Mom and Dad, if that's you getting different IP addresses, you can stop now. To Betty Hobbs and her daughter Tina Soltesz who pimp my books to everyone they meet and let me know when they spot one in a Goodwill store. (Hey, someone used me to get a tax write off. Cool!) To Val and Pat Sturman, for nothing less than a stomach virus keeps them away from an autographing, and whose own personal love story inspires my sense of romance. To Katy Budget Books for supporting me and so many Houston authors. You rock girls. To the real Faye Moore, another fan and friend whose zest for life is an inspiration to so many. To friends who believed in me as a writer before I did: Francyne, Nita, Leah, Linda and Janece—at one time or another you've all held my hand and given me just the right nudge—or shove—onto the correct path.

Thanks to my editor Chris Keeslar and to my agent Kim Lionetti for continuing to put up with me. (It isn't easy, ask my husband.) And finally, to Renee Yewdaev, Cindy Johnson, and Tracy Heydweiller in the Dorchester Production Department for taking my editor's handcuff idea and making it look awesome.

Gotcha!

CHAPTER ONE

"You lucky bastard."

Sergeant Jake Baldwin looked up from his desk and found Mark Donaldson, the new detective in the department and his sometime partner, leaning his head inside the office door.

"Why am I lucky?" Jake asked and shouldered back in his chair.

Donaldson's chickenshit grin widened. "She says she *needs* you, and only you will do." He looked down the hall, then shot off as if someone chased him.

"Hey, who needs . . . ?" Jake's question tripped over his lips as a blonde, a dead ringer for Marilyn Monroe in her chubbier years, sashayed into his office. She didn't walk. She sashayed.

About a foot from his desk she stopped moving, but her body didn't. Her breasts, squeezed into a low-cut red tank top, continued to bounce. Up. Down. Up. Behind her, two Houston police officers paused, their tongues dangling out like hounds'. Jake's tongue remained in his mouth. He'd never been a Monroe fan.

His visitor leaned over to pull out a chair, and he got a peek at her cleavage—which led him to realize maybe you didn't really have to be a true fan to appreciate a look-alike. He glanced away. Gawking was crude. Besides, he'd stopped letting women know they had the upper hand. They still had it, of course. He was, after all, flesh and blood, but he refrained from giving them the leverage that came with knowing. His ex-fiancée, now sister-in-law, had taught him better.

"What can I do for you?" he asked, but his male mind was

already considering options. Then he gave her another once-over. She was twenty, maybe? At thirty-one, Jake refused to date anyone who might still believe in Santa.

Miss Monroe opened her mouth to speak, and Jake waited for her sweet husky voice to flow over him, sound effects to add to the fantasies that no doubt he'd have later on. His fantasies had no problems with a twenty-year-old. And lately, fantasies were all he had.

"My name's Ellie Chandler." Her voice, some would call it cartoonish—a really bad cartoon—came out two octaves above chalk screeching across a blackboard. "You're Jake Baldwin, riiiight?"

Jake jerked, knocking over his coffee mug. God help him. No, God help *her*, he thought, grabbing the cup and saving his files from the spill. No wonder the Almighty gave her that body. He'd been trying to make up for the voice.

She continued talking, and Jake would have done almost anything to shut her up. Anything but be rude. For the son of a Baptist preacher, rudeness wasn't an option, even for a religious backslider like himself. He finger-locked his hands in front of him and forced his attention on her. Every spoken syllable was like bowel surgery.

"I'm here to report a murder."

He sighed. "Then you need to talk to Homicide. I work Robbery." *Please God, let it be that easy.*

God wasn't listening.

"I want to talk to you."

"Why me?" he asked both the blonde and the Almighty.

"Because you know what he's like. You're the one who put him away."

"Put who away?"

"David Tanks. My ex-boyfriend."

Jake remembered Tanks. Too many tattoos. A dealer with a mean streak and a drug habit of his own.

"And because I love Billy now, David's threatening to kill him. He's even threatened Billy's sister. He called her one *dead* bitch."

Jake shook his head to clear her voice from his ears. "Tanks is still doing time, isn't he?"

"Yes." Ellie Chandler nodded vigorously, and her tank top strained to contain the jiggling. Up. Down. Jake had to force his eyes from lowering.

"So, the murder you want to report . . . It hasn't happened? No one's dead yet?"

"He cut the man's head off. I'd say that killed him."

Jake stiffened. "Whose head?"

"I don't know."

"Where did this happen?"

"I wasn't there"—her green eyes rolled—"so how would I know?"

Okay. She wasn't making a ton of sense, but he'd give it one more shot. "When did the murder happen?"

"Last year, I think. David got drunk and bragged about it. I want you to pin it on him and then get him moved in with the dangerous prisoners—away from the good ones."

Good prisoners? Unlocking his fingers, Jake pressed his palms on his desk. Suddenly, the pieces of the blonde's story began to fit together. "Where's Billy?"

"In prison with David. But don't murderers get moved away from people who accidentally rob a convenience store?"

"*Accidentally* robbed a store?" Jake tried to keep the disrespect from his voice.

The blonde started chattering again, and Jake listened. His eardrums throbbed. At last he reached for a yellow notebook and wrote down her contact info. Then he jotted, *Tanks—threatened to kill Billy's sister.* Glancing right at her, and for the sake of politeness, he said, "Miss Chandler, I'm glad you came in." Sons of Baptist preachers occasionally lied, but only when politeness was on the line.

She blinked, and something close to intelligence flashed in her green eyes. "You're not going to do a thing, are you?"

Okay, he'd try one more time to reason with her. "Honestly, you need to talk to Homicide." He then watched her storm out.

Though the view was nice, his gaze dropped back to his pad. *Tanks—threatened to kill Billy's sister.* Sadly, if a cop jumped every time one inmate threatened to hurt another's mother or sister, the whole damn force would be too busy playing leapfrog to do its job.

"You're his sister."

"No!" Macy Tucker said, dropping her veggie burger onto her plate. She should have guessed something was up when her mother served a lunch entrée that didn't include butchered livestock. Macy had been a vegetarian since she was sixteen. Twelve years later, her mother still felt it was a passing fad. Of course, her mom, clueless at times, also waited for Macy's dad to walk back in and yell, "I'm home. Get me a beer, would ya?" Never mind he'd been gone for fourteen years; she kept waiting. Not that Macy would want him back.

"Siblings are supposed to—"

"It's not happening, Mom."

Macy's chest clutched when her mother's blue eyes filled with tears. Not that Faye Moore's crying would surprise anyone. In the last three years, she had taken her part-time job of hysterics and made it a full-fledged career. Hundreds of trees had fallen to make the facial tissues to dry her eyes. The doctor said it was menopause. Macy decided it was *men.* Macy sympathized, because she'd almost succumbed to the malady herself.

"He said he needed to see you."

"I'm not his fix-it fairy anymore." But Macy's chest ached watching her mom dry her tears. Crying could be contagious.

"You've always been there for him." Her mom snatched another Kleenex from a box on the counter and went to work with it.

"Maybe that's where I went wrong. If he'd faced the consequences—"

"It's been months since you've seen him." The used tissues got pocketed.

"I've been busy. Between work, school, and getting a divorce, my plate's been a bit full." And the thought of seeing her baby brother behind bars was horrifying.

"Just because you're . . ." *Sniffle.*

Her mom glanced at the Kleenex box again. Macy glanced at the door. Two tissues were her limit. Any more heartfelt sobs and she'd need her own box of tear catchers.

Faye continued, "Just because you're mad at your husband, you can't take it out on your brother."

"He's my *ex*-husband, and I'm not mad at him." What Macy felt went far beyond anger.

"Your brother thinks you're embarrassed by him," her mom suggested.

"Well, when Father Luis asked what Billy was doing, and I said, 'Three to five in the pen,' I wasn't exactly beaming with pride."

"Oh, Mace. You can't be this way."

"What way?" The self-control Macy maintained around her mother was starting to slip. She was tired of sugarcoating everything. It didn't help. She had tried all sorts of ploys to curb her mother's tears, biting her sharp tongue among them, but all had failed. And lately, Macy was tired of failure.

Her mom sighed. "He loves you."

He should have thought about that before he borrowed my car to hold up a Stop & Go. And wrecking it didn't help, either. "I love him, but I can't fix this."

"He said he was sorry." Emotion filled her mom's face.

Anger at Billy's selfish actions and their consequences shot through Macy like blue fire. She embraced it, because anger felt better than helplessness. But as her mom reached for a third tissue, Macy reached for her purse. No third tissue! "Gotta go. Thanks for lunch." And with a quick kiss to a damp cheek, Macy fled her grandmother's kitchen.

Her mother's words chased her across the living room. "Mace! You weren't raised to turn your back on the people you love."

Macy kept walking. "It's called tough love, Mom." The

front door was Macy's target, and not crying her immediate goal. Not turning into her mother? That was a lifelong challenge.

"All love is tough," her mom snapped. Then: "*Men.*"

"Yup. We should all become lesbians," Macy countered. And she never looked back as she hit the screen door with her open palm.

Tears did spring to her eyes, however. *You weren't raised to turn your back on the people you love.* The lump in her throat grew as she headed for her car. Macy hadn't been raised that way, but it sure seemed all the men in her life had. First her father—no, first was Grandpa, *then* dear ol' Dad. Next her husband, now Billy. Of all the stupid, idiotic things to do, the brother she loved more than good chocolate, the brother she'd sworn to protect, had gotten himself a prison sentence. How could Macy take care of him now? She couldn't, and she was tired of trying.

No, trying wasn't the issue. But trying and failing was breaking her heart. And she'd obviously failed Billy, failed to teach him right from wrong.

She'd almost made it to her green Saturn when she heard the distinct clearing of a throat. Blinking the watery weakness from her eyes, Macy turned to face the music.

The music was dressed in purple biking shorts and an orange T-shirt that read BITE ME. It was Macy's grandma, who flipped the bird at the world's view of a senior citizen. No rocking chairs, no matronly house dresses or quiet home life. At sixty-eight, she biked six miles a day, taught yoga and, as Macy had recently discovered, did a few other things, probably in yoga positions.

"Your mom has a point." Nan stood beside her new ten-speed.

Macy quirked an eyebrow. "Her having a point is fine. It's when she starts jabbing me with it that I get out of sorts."

"He *is* your brother. Would it hurt to just see him?"

"Yes. It would hurt me." The thought of seeing Billy behind bars brought back the lump in her throat. Didn't everyone know it was easier to be mad? She couldn't start feeling sorry for him. That would hurt too damn much.

A sympathetic smile deepened the laugh lines in Nan's face. "You'll do the right thing. You always do."

"I'm *not* going." Macy suddenly remembered the package in her purse. She pulled out the plastic bag and said, "Here. And you can buy these yourself. They aren't illegal."

Nan's smile vanished. "I . . . It would be . . . embarrassing."

"Embarrassing?" Macy stalked to her car and opened the door. The smell of yesterday's pepperoni wafted from the vehicle—one of the drawbacks of delivering pizza for a living. But going to law school full-time had left her with limited job choices. Never mind that her ex, Tom, was supposed to put her through college, just as she'd spent the first years of their marriage doing for him.

Nan looked at the bag. "You're young. People know you're doing it."

"I haven't done it in two years." Giving up men meant giving up sex.

Nan smiled. "Mr. Jacobs has a nephew. . . ."

"And he's welcome to keep him." With one foot inside her car, Macy swung around and hugged her grandmother. "I love you," she said. And she meant it, too. As much of a nutcase as her sexually active relative was, she'd been the glue of their family since Macy's father walked out. She had cocooned them in her nutty life. It wasn't Nan's fault that the glue hadn't been enough. What *did* keep families like hers together? Macy wondered. She'd let her marriage fall apart in less than five years. How sad. Heck, even her mother had stayed married to her dad for fourteen.

"I know you love me," Nan said. "Just like you love Billy."

Macy jumped behind the wheel of her Saturn, shut the door, and drove away. "I'm not going," she muttered. "I'm not."

She hated being proved wrong, but the next day Macy sat behind the wheel of her pizza-scented, fender-dented, convenience-store-robbing Saturn, driving toward the prison. Her mom's "you don't turn your back on people" speech and Nan's "you'll do the right thing" lecture had done her in. However, she'd postponed the trip until today because she didn't know the proper attire to wear to a prison. Visions of all the men ogling her, running tin cups along the bars, had been daunting. Not that she was the type who warranted a tin cup. Men preferred bouncy blondes. Macy was brunette, and her size Bs didn't bounce without the help of a bra that pushed up, pulled in, and captured jiggle mass—and she'd burned those bras the day she found her husband in bed with his blonde, bouncy secretary—but prison inmates were desperate.

In the end, she had decided to wear her pizza uniform. How sexy could Papa's Pizza's polyester be? Plus, she had to hurry back to Houston, go to the library to do some research, and then go straight to slinging cheese pies. Then she had to study for exams. There was no time to cry tonight about the emotional havoc this visit was sure to bring. No. Not tonight. A vision of Billy behind bars popped into her mind. Dread pulled at her stomach.

Spotting the sign proudly announcing the prison, she pulled into the parking lot and mentally scheduled herself a pity party this weekend. But only two tissues. What was good for the mother goose was good for the . . . goosette.

Oh Lord, she didn't want to do this.

Do what, exactly? Why had Billy insisted she visit? All night, Macy's fitful tossing had given her mattress springs a workout, and she'd half dreamed, half imagined her brother begging, *Macy, you've gotta break me out of jail.*

Her chest ached as she got out of her car. She stuffed her long, unruly hair up under her pizza cap and approached the desolate building that was to be her brother's home for the next three years. He'd only gotten three to five, thanks to the fantastic lawyer she'd hired to defend him. That was one credit card that would be maxed for a while.

Like her mom, Macy had wanted to blame Billy's downfall

on his bad group of friends, on the fact that he had grown up without a father. But the pain of it all had forced her to pull her head out of that pile of kitty litter. Billy had done this to himself. He'd done it to their mom and to Nan. And, God help Macy for being angry, he'd done it to her, too.

Chin up, she entered the prison. No tin cups or bars. The impression she got was minimalism meets drab: all was linear, sterile. The only warmth in the place came from the old red-brick walls.

A guard snagged her purse and locked it away, another wanded her for weapons, then a serious-faced geezer led her into a gymnasium-type room to wait. After a few minutes of her finger-tapping the metal table, the door opened and inmates rushed through.

Tears sprang to her eyes as her brother approached. She knew it was too much, but Macy didn't see Billy the nineteen-year-old. She saw the five-year-old kid with big blue eyes fringed in black lashes, the kid who'd sneaked into her bedroom at night with his teddy bear because he was afraid of trolls under the bed. He looked scared now. All her anger vanished in a big puff of smoke. And without the anger, the anguish of knowing she'd failed him ripped at her heart.

"Hey, Sis." His voice shook as he lowered himself into the chair across from her. Once settled, he touched her hand, carefully, almost as if he feared she'd pull away.

Didn't he know she loved him with every ounce of her heart? Didn't he know the reason she hadn't come until now was because this was going to kill her, and perhaps the only way to teach him to deal with the messes he created was to leave him on his own? Tough love wasn't easy. Not for the giver or the receiver. She felt a few tears trickle down her cheeks. This visit might take three tissues.

"Hey back at you." The ache in her throat doubled as she turned her palm over and threaded her fingers through his.

"You look good. Mom said you finally got your divorce."

"Yeah. And I sure showed him. I got custody of most of

his bills." Swallowing, she fought for control. Billy probably got all the tears he needed from their mom. "How are you?"

"I'm . . . making it." He gave the room a glance then met her eyes. "I know you're mad," he whispered. "You deserve to be mad. But I . . . There's trouble."

Macy braced herself for the whole break-out-of-prison request. This visit would definitely require three tissues.

Billy leaned in. "I need your help."

"What kind of help?" she whispered back.

"There's this man. He's real bad." Billy's big blue eyes grew wide. "He cut this guy's head off. Now he wants to kill me and—"

"Why?" Macy gasped. "Why does he want to kill you?"

"Well, I sort of stole his girl."

Macy's mouth fell open. "You did what?"

"Her letter to him got caught inside my magazine in the mail room. I thought it was to me . . . from you, Nan, or Mom." He glanced away. "It wasn't to me, but . . . She wrote this poem about her grandma, and it was so beautiful. I wrote her and told her I'd accidentally opened her mail, and I told her how beautiful her poem was. I never dreamed that she would write me back. But she did, and . . . we fell in love."

"You stole a murderer's girl?" she asked. "Couldn't you have, I don't know, gone after a deadbeat dad's? Or someone less violent, like a white-collar criminal?"

Billy's forehead wrinkled. "I'm serious."

"I'm not? What the hell were you thinking? You don't steal a murderer's girlfriend. Didn't they teach you anything in school?"

"I didn't know he was a murderer."

"Wait!" Macy held up her hands. "I don't need to know this. Because I can't fix it. I mean, if you think this guy who just happens to cut people's heads off will listen to me, why, I'll be happy to read him the riot act, but something tells me—"

"I don't want you near that freak. I want you to talk to Ellie."

"Ellie?"

"My girlfriend." Billy bit down on his lip.

Macy blinked. "The same girl who dated the murderer?" When Billy nodded, Macy dropped her head on the table. Her pizza delivery hat flipped off and her hair scattered. The cold metal on her forehead was bracing, but everything else felt surreal. Damn, if it still didn't hurt, though. It might take four tissues.

Billy rested his hand on her shoulder. "Between the two of you, maybe y'all can fix things."

Macy raised her head. "Fix what?"

"Maybe you could talk to the cops. Anyone but Jake Baldwin—don't go to him. Maybe they'd listen to you. Ellie's not like you. She's too pretty. Men don't listen to her."

Macy was suddenly a frog's hair away from committing her own murder. "But they'll listen to homely-looking girls like me, huh?"

"I didn't mean that. It's just she's blonde and—"

"Big boobed?" It would be justifiable homicide.

"Yeah." Her brother smiled, then frowned when he looked at her. "What I mean is, men don't think she's smart."

"Of course she's, like, megaintelligent, right? That's why she was dating a man who chops people's heads off." Macy knew she was being catty, but how much could a girl take?

"It's not like that. She just got mixed up with him because of her stupid brother."

Because of her stupid brother, huh? Well, *that* was an excuse she could understand. Macy dropped her head back on the table. She even gave it a good thump.

"She's not stupid. Okay, she's not smart like you. . . ." Her brother nudged Macy up. "I know you'll think I love her because she's pretty, but I didn't know what she looked like. I fell in love with her in her letters. We wrote every day—still do—and she comes to see me four times a week."

Only the fear in Billy's eyes kept Macy from grabbing her pizza hat and getting her homely butt home. Or was it the memory of the one time Billy hadn't been afraid? Four years old, teddy bear in his arms, he'd stood up for her, stood up for her when no one else had been there. *You're not hurting my sister.* Macy could still hear his little-boy voice saying those words. She could still hear the sound of her father's fist knocking Billy across the room.

Another tear rolled down her cheek. "You need to talk to someone here. If they know—"

"They won't do crap," Billy interrupted. "Even the guards are afraid of him. And some of them . . . he does things for them. He's got people on the outside, too. He's the head of some big gang. I heard he has some cops doing things for him. Ellie even thinks that cop, that Baldwin guy who arrested him, is in his pocket now. He wouldn't even listen when she tried to tell him about the murder."

"Talk to someone above the guards," Macy suggested. What was she supposed to do?

"Please, Mace. Her name's Ellie Chandler. She lives a couple of miles from you. I gave her your number. Promise you'll see her. I'm scared for her. But it's not just her. Look, the main reason I needed to see you is . . . I'm scared for you, too."

"For me?" Macy's blood ran cold.

"I wrote you a letter, addressed and everything. I wrote to tell you how sorry I was about your car and all." Guilt shadowed Billy's eyes. "But it came up missing before I could mail it. The next day, Tanks told me he knew where my family lives. He's got people on the outside and . . . he's got your address. You need to get with Ellie. She'll explain." He placed a scrap of paper in Macy's hand. "This is Ellie's information. Promise me you'll call her, Mace. *Promise* me."

The bell announcing that the visitation was over rang. Macy didn't make Billy any promises, but she took the paper he'd pushed into her hand.

After his sister left, Billy waited in his cell for a guard to collect him for work duty. If anyone would have told him he'd someday be excited to weed petunias, he'd have called them a friggin' liar. But it was true. He loved the chance to get out from behind the prison walls. It was a tiny taste of freedom.

"You going on garden duty?" his cellmate Pablo asked, sitting in the room's one chair, his face hidden behind a book.

"Yeah." Billy dropped down onto his bed. Some days, he thought he'd go nuts being in here. Then he would remember that he deserved it.

"Your sister come to see ya?" Pablo lowered his book.

Billy only nodded, not wanting to get into a conversation.

How many times had Mace told him he was going to get himself into trouble if he didn't start thinking about his actions? He'd let her down, and she didn't deserve it. That's why he'd decided to turn his life around. He hadn't told her about the college classes; he wanted to surprise her when he got out. He wanted to show her, his mom, and Nan that he was better than his ol' man. And he would.

"I heard she was really pretty," Pablo said.

"Drop it." Billy closed his eyes.

What really hurt was Mace being disappointed in him. Again. But Billy refused to see Ellie as another of his mistakes. She was too sweet, too good-natured, and yeah, too pretty to be a mistake. Sure, he regretted getting Mace mixed up in this, but he hadn't meant to do that.

Someone down the hall coughed, and it echoed along the gray concrete walls. Billy hated the echoes in here. God, he prayed Mace would do like he'd said and talk to Ellie. His girl might not be intelligent like Mace, but she had street smarts. And if Tanks went after his sister, Ellie would know better how to protect her.

Billy heard footsteps and remembered garden duty. Eager to leave the cramped room, he jumped up. He could almost smell the outside air.

"You ready?" Hal, one of the day guards, asked. The cell door clicked open.

"Yeah," Billy said.

Of all the guards, Hal was the only one Billy liked. In his

fifties, Hal reminded him of what a father should be. Once Hal had even shown him pictures of his grandkids. Billy wondered if the man's family appreciated him, or if they took him for granted the way Billy had done with Mace. No more, though. Somehow he was going to make his sister proud.

Hal's gaze shot to the stack of books. "School going okay?" he asked.

"Fine," Billy grunted.

He and Hal made their way down the prison halls, their footsteps echoing. The thrill of leaving for a few hours stayed with Billy until he crawled into the van and saw a tattooed forearm resting on the back of a seat. David Tanks glanced at him over a shoulder. The man's sneer had 24-karat evil stamped all over it.

"Heard your sis came by today," the murderer whispered. "Heard she's hot. I can't wait to get me some of that. I'm going to fuck her hard, Billy boy—right before I slit her throat."

CHAPTER TWO

It was five on Tuesday evening when Jake leaned back in his chair and tried to clear the paperwork from his desk. He spotted the pad where he'd written down Ellie Chandler's info. It had been a whole day, and so far he hadn't done a thing with it. Yes, he'd told her she needed to go to Homicide, but his gut told him she hadn't done it. He supposed he should follow up.

He grabbed his cell phone and dialed. Ripping off the sheet of paper, he tossed it in the trash. He wouldn't learn anything, but for his conscience's sake he'd do it. Then he could forget the whole incident.

"Sergeant Anders," his buddy in Homicide answered.

"Stan, it's Jake. Look, I had this girl come in yesterday. . . ." He gave Stan the short version, about arresting

Tanks and adding a bit of male color commentary, including, "Gorgeous. Stacked. But the voice!"

Stan laughed. "I don't see a problem. Keep your tongue in her mouth or keep her mouth busy."

Jake grinned, finished his story, and asked if they'd had any headless corpses show up.

"Didn't you hear about the John Doe case?" Stan asked, the earlier humor missing from his tone.

"Don't yank my chain." Jake leaned against his desk.

"No chain yanking here. The body washed up in the Houston Ship Channel about six months ago. Clear Lake's handling things. They still haven't ID'd the guy. The body was in bad shape."

"Great." Jake snatched the crumpled notepaper out of the trash can. It looked as if he and Miss Squeaky Voice were destined to meet again. Damn if he probably didn't owe her an apology, too. Sons of Baptist preachers always apologized when they made mistakes.

"Baldwin!" Donaldson barged into his office, his posture rigid.

"I'll call you back, Stan," Jake said, and disconnected. He turned to his coworker. "What's up?"

"There's been a prison break. A guard and an inmate were shot. Doesn't look good for either one. Three other inmates escaped. Captain said you know one of them—David Tanks."

Jake sighed. Oh yeah. He'd definitely be seeing Miss Squeaky Voice again.

Leaving the library, Macy realized her day was about to get worse. She'd forgotten her cash bag, so she had to swing home to pick it up. The stop would make her five minutes late for work, which meant the assistant manager, Mr. Prack—the employees referred to him as something funnier, if a bit obvious—was going to give her hell. Ever since she'd turned him down for beers and a night in the sack, he'd been particularly hard on her. Yeah, she could slap a sexual-harassment charge on him, but it would mean losing a job—a job close to home and with perfect hours. As long as the pervert kept his hands to himself, the verbal hell wasn't enough to make her jump ship.

Of course, he was the least of her worries. Macy's heart and mind were stuck on Billy. Stuck on her inability to change his circumstances.

Unlocking the door to her house, she stepped inside. A thump sounded. She paused and listened to the eerie hum of the old home. "Elvis?" Her voice vibrated in a strange silence. "Here, kitty, kitty." She stepped farther into her living room, but the silence still felt too loud. Then she saw him. "Elvis?"

Her long-haired gray tabby stood beside the sofa, near the coffee table. A candy dish and a few peppermints lay on the floor beside him. Macy had a big desire to fall on the couch, hug her cat, and have herself a good cry. And a peppermint.

The blinking on her answering machine caught her eye. She gave Elvis a scratch, glanced at her watch, then hit the play button.

"Hey, this is Ellie Chandler," a voice screeched from the machine.

Elvis hissed and darted out of the room. Macy flinched, but it was for a different reason than the squeaky, high-pitched tone. She hadn't decided if she would or wouldn't contact this woman. All that talk about danger had to be Billy's overactive imagination, didn't it? Then again, maybe she'd give the prison warden a call tomorrow. Just to give him a heads-up.

Ellie's voice continued. "Billy said to call. I think David is up to something. I went to talk to that cop, Jake Baldwin. . . . He's the cop who put David away. I thought maybe he might help, but he seemed more interested in my boobs than what I had to say. I wouldn't be surprised if he's working for David. What a jerk. Not like your brother." She paused. "I know you don't know me from Adam, and it probably sounds crazy me falling for him while he's in prison, but I just want you to know I love Billy. Really love him."

What kind of woman fell in love with inmates? Macy wondered. She herself had made some mistakes in her life, but none like that.

Grabbing her money bag, she darted out the door for work. She'd worry later. There was no time for it now.

It wasn't until *much* later that night that Macy had time to breathe, but she'd worried the whole time. She parked her Saturn back at Papa's Pizza and sat listening to the final minute of the tape she'd recorded, her notes about constitutional law. Listening to tapes while she delivered pizza had saved her butt on finals before. Tonight, however, her heart wasn't into it. She'd been preoccupied with Billy, with the fear she'd seen in his eyes. Her mind kept replaying images of pulling her four-year-old brother into her lap and saying, *There aren't any trolls, Billy. Really, they don't exist. You don't have to be scared.* But had she been wrong?

A knock at her window had Macy jumping off her seat. Sandy, the other female driver, smiled through the window. Macy got out.

"Was I right?"

Sandy, a single mom and college student, always wore a smile. If Macy had time, she figured they might actually become friends, but between school, work, family, and a few hours of volunteering at the church garden, time didn't exist.

"Yup. He was a big tipper. Ten bucks." Macy adjusted her baseball cap, which advertised Papa's Pizza.

Sandy nudged her shoulder. "Told you. Did you loosen your buttons like I said?"

"No. But I fluttered my lashes at him," Macy teased. In truth, flirting didn't appeal to her these days, not even for a big tip. They walked to the front door of Papa's Pizza, where the smell of yeast and spicy tomato sauce hung thick.

"Macy!" a voice called out.

"Prick alert," Sandy muttered.

Macy dropped her pizza warmers on the counter. "Yes, Mr. Prack?"

"Your mom's called six times, said it was crucial you call her."

Macy remembered her cell phone was temporarily out of order. No money, no service.

"Then some squeaky-voiced female called," the restaurant manager snapped. "Seven messages altogether—and you know we don't allow personal calls."

"Sorry," Macy said. She turned to the cook, who slid a pizza onto a rack to cool. "Where am I off to now?"

Mr. Prack leaned in. "Nowhere. Declare your bank and clock out. Call your mommy on your own time. And fix your hair, it keeps falling down. If you want to look sexy on the job, go work at a bar."

Macy ground her teeth. The more she considered, maybe this job wasn't worth it.

"I thought I got off first," Sandy spoke up. "But I don't mind working." The last hour could gain a runner big bucks, and as a single mom she had it tough.

"I'm fine with it if you are," Macy said.

As she wrapped things up, she thought about calling her mom. Or about not calling. Her mother would want a verbal report on the visit with Billy, but Macy hadn't figured out how much to divulge. All her mom needed was another reason to cry.

Just as she stepped toward the door, Anthony the cook called out, "Macy, I got two cheese pies we had to redo. Want 'em?"

"Thanks," Macy said. She hadn't had dinner yet, so she took the boxes and said her good-byes for the night. Maybe it'd be nice to go home early. Maybe catch the late-night news. Maybe she could catch up on last night's lost sleep.

But as she got into her car, she saw the scrap of paper she'd abandoned on the passenger seat: Ellie's address.

"I didn't *promise* I'd go," she muttered, gripping the steering wheel. Then again, what would it hurt to just talk to the girl? Maybe she could get some info that would help in her conversation with the warden tomorrow. And yeah, she had definitely decided to talk to the warden.

As she pulled out of the lot, two cop cars pulled in. She hoped it was the Rude Police, arriving to arrest Mr. Prack.

She soon parked in front of her brother's girlfriend's old frame house. The place looked about as "reasonably priced" as Macy's rental. It was an old, not-so-good residence in a not-so-good neighborhood, where some not-so-good things happened to good people. Taking a deep breath, Macy remembered the squeaky voice on her answering machine.

"You're going to owe me big, Billy," she muttered.

As Macy stepped out of the car, she caught sight of the boxes in the back. An idea arose: if Ellie's voice grew to be too much, one of these pizzas might shut her up.

The night's silence thickened as Macy walked up to the front door. In the back of her mind she heard Billy saying, *I'm scared for Ellie—and you, too.* The hairs on her neck did a little dance. Ignoring a tingle of fear, she knocked. No answer.

Macy moved to the window and peered inside. A light beckoned from a room in the rear. Seeing it, she moved down the steps and ambled toward the back. The inky blackness reminded her of every horror movie she'd ever seen. Her foot banged into a metal trash can, sending up the smell of rotting fruit. A cat shrieked in the bushes next door. A dog barked. Fear fluttered in her stomach.

Macy bit her lip and moved around a few flowerpots. "It's nothing," she muttered. Balancing her pizza in one hand, she put one foot in front of the other. The hairs on her neck did another prickle dance. The chorus of noise exploded again, only louder. A dog. A cat. Something like a kicked trash can. And . . . was that a man's voice in the middle of the chaos?

She darted up onto the back porch. Footsteps echoed behind her. *Right* behind her. She screamed. The pizza box flew up in the air. She jammed her elbow back and hit a solid male mass that didn't budge. But she hit it hard enough that an *oomph* of air struck her neck. Chills tap-danced down her spine. She bolted off the porch and away.

She'd barely hit the ground when someone snagged her arm. Her second scream pierced the night. No stranger to a man's weak spot, she hiked up her knee. The mass she hit this time wasn't so solid.

"Son of a . . ." Her attacker's grip weakened.

Macy yanked free, and her hat went flying. Her assailant's hand latched onto the front of her shirt. She heard her uniform buttons rip. She hiked her knee up again and hit pay dirt one more time.

Her attacker cursed and started to crumple. But he didn't fall alone; he took her down with him. Her body hit the ground with a thud. Hard. And before she could react, the man rolled over, pinning her to the ground with his body.

"Police!" A voice yelled from the side of the yard. "Hold it right there."

Thank God! "Get him off me," Macy screamed. Her attacker's weight and warmth continued to suffocate her.

"Don't move," her assailant hissed with puzzling authority.

She stopped jerking and gasped for air. The man on top of her pushed up onto his elbow, allowing her breathing room. She focused on his scowl until the beam of a flashlight hit her eyes. The orb of light then lowered, and her attacker glanced down, following it. Macy's own gaze shifted, and she saw what had drawn his attention. Her shirt lay open, her blue bra and chest spotlighted. She jerked to sit up.

His hand shot out and pushed her back to the ground. "I swear, you knee me again and . . ."

"You okay?" asked the man who'd claimed to be a cop. He'd walked up to the two of them.

Was he blind? No, she wasn't okay! "He attacked me!" she shrieked. She gave the self-proclaimed cop a quick once-over. He was blond, about six feet. He wasn't in uniform, but he had a gun and an official-looking flashlight. However, neither the gun nor the flashlight was aimed at her assailant.

Nope. They were aimed at her.

"Fine," muttered the man on the ground beside her. He sat the rest of the way up.

Macy reached to close her shirt, but the cop yelled, "Freeze!"

Her attacker, who she was beginning to believe might also be a cop, shifted forward and pulled the garment closed. While the movement didn't seem hostile, or sexual, his words weren't exactly friendly. "You got any weapons on you? Any needles?"

She managed to squeak out a *no*.

He ran his big hands firmly down her black polyester pants to check for weapons. "She's clean."

The flashlight moved from her eyes. Macy's gaze flickered from the blond with the gun to the dark-haired man she'd just kneed twice. Still grimacing, he pulled out a badge. She scanned it.

"I didn't know. You grabbed me and—"

"I *said*, 'Police.'" He spoke between gritted teeth.

"Maybe at the same time the dog barked and the cat howled." She started to sit up.

"Not so fast!" He pressed a palm on her leg. "Until I can stand up, you're not moving."

The heat of his hand on her thigh zipped through her, and her breath caught. A cool April breeze hit her breasts, and she realized her shirt had fallen open again. His eyes shifted down. In spite of his orders, she yanked her shirt closed.

"Who are you?" He raised his hand from her leg, and his gaze darted to her hat on the ground. Picking it up, he eyed the cap, and then his gaze shifted to her uniform. "I asked you a question," he snapped.

"Macy Tucker." *The idiot who just assaulted a police officer. I guess my brother's not the only criminal in the family.*

As Macy sat up, the blond cop stepped closer, his gun and light still in his hands. "You okay, Baldwin?" he asked.

Baldwin? Ellie's message rang in Macy's head. Surely not Jake Baldwin?

"You delivering a pizza to this address?" the dark-haired man asked.

Macy's panic inched up a notch. Had something happened to Ellie? Is that why the cops were here? "What's going on?"

"I ask the questions," he replied. "Why were you sneaking—?"

"I wasn't sneaking." But her heart skipped a beat.

He eyed her hat again. "So, you were delivering pizza?"

She hesitated. She needed time to think, to rationalize. *I wouldn't be surprised if he was working with David.* That's what Ellie had said about Baldwin. What if she and Macy's brother weren't crazy? What if this was a dirty cop?

"There's a pizza over here," the blond officer said, flashing his light across the ground.

Baldwin eyed her. "It's late for a delivery, isn't it?"

Still clutching her shirt, Macy pondered the wisdom of lying to the police. "We're open until midnight," she responded. Not a lie.

"Kind of strange that no one's home," he accused. "Who ordered it?"

"I . . ." Something about his eyes bothered her. They were either dark blue or brown, she couldn't tell which, but she didn't like the way they analyzed her or the way his gaze had shifted to her chest. And she remembered the feel of his body pressing her against the hard ground, causing things to tingle that hadn't tingled in a long time, a not-so-subtle reminder that she hadn't been close to a man in a long time. She definitely didn't like this and didn't want those tingles.

More uncomfortable than ever, she stated another truth. "I wasn't doing anything wrong."

"Really? What's your name again?"

"Macy Tucker. And yours?" *Don't let it be—*

"Sergeant Jake Baldwin." The cop pressed a fist to his thigh.

Her hopes dashed, Macy's heart pounded with indecision. *Tell him the truth. Don't tell him. What if he's a dirty cop?*

"I'm sure you've got identification on you," he said.

"It's in my car." Her gaze shot back to the house. "Something happen here?"

"Why don't you get me your ID?" The cop got to his feet and motioned for her to do the same. Either she hadn't hit her mark perfectly or he had balls of steel.

Standing, blouse held tightly together, she walked to her car. There she used her right hand to dig her wallet from her purse. Her left hand kept her shirt closed. The blond cop, standing under the spray of a streetlight, watched her with a keen eye, while Baldwin walked around her vehicle and studied the license plate, her hat clasped in his hands. He met her at the driver side door and took her driver's license.

"Why did you try to run, Pizza Girl?" He studied her license before returning it.

"Because you scared the crap out of me," she answered.

"I told you I was police."

"And I told you, I didn't hear you identify yourself. I heard the dog, the cat, and the trash can. Didn't you hear the commotion?"

"Maybe I did." He set her hat back on her head and gave it a playful little twist. The action matched a suddenly playful look in his eyes.

Ugh. She didn't want "playful" with a man, and her body's response to his nearness didn't matter. She tossed her wallet back in her car and readjusted her hat. "Can I go now?"

Instead of answering, he dipped his head inside her car, eyed the second pizza box, and sniffed as if he'd caught wind of the old pizza scent. Pulling back, he met her gaze. "Looks as if you might be telling the truth. I'm sorry I scared you. You okay?"

"Yeah."

His apology rang sincere. Could she trust him? She wanted to, but Ellie hadn't and Billie hadn't. What if they were right?

She glanced back at the house and asked one more time,

"What happened?" She hoped he'd give her a reason to trust him. She needed a reason. Her time studying legal philosophy had taught her that cops were not above breaking the law. Her time on the Earth had taught her trusting men could get her hurt.

"What do you mean, what happened?" A sudden suspicion pulled at his eyebrows. "And why do I get a funny feeling in my gut about you?" He leaned his arm on her car roof. His blue shirt stretched taut across wide shoulders.

"Could be because I kneed you." But now wasn't the time to showcase her smart mouth, so she added, "Er, which I'm very sorry about." She met his eyes. They were blue. Dark blue. And instead of the anger she expected, they almost held amusement. Taken aback, she asked again, "Can I go?"

He nodded. "If I need you, I know where to find you, Pizza Girl."

"But you won't," she said before she thought.

"Won't what?" he asked.

She hesitated. "Need me."

His eyes crinkled into that almost smile again. "I might. I really like pizza."

Not answering, she got in her car and took off. She didn't look back. Okay, she looked one time in the rearview mirror. But not because he was male, or gorgeous, and not because she could still remember how his hand had felt on her thigh, how his body had felt pressed atop hers. She looked back because . . . just because.

She hadn't made it all the way down the block when his almost smile flashed again in her mind. She switched on the radio to chase away her thoughts. Disturbing thoughts. Downright gorgeous—

The radio announcer's voice pumped through the airwaves. "Continued breaking news: three Huntsville Prison inmates have escaped."

Macy immediately slowed her car, shocked.

"A guard and an inmate were shot during the escape," the broadcaster continued. "Both are listed in critical condition.

Police—Wait. We've just received another report. The inmate has died."

The inmate died?

Died? Died! Macy told herself it wasn't Billy, but all she could hear was her brother saying, *And now he wants to kill me.*

Then she remembered her mother calling work. She remembered the police pulling into Papa's Pizza.

Slamming on her brakes, she turned the car around and headed straight to Nan's.

CHAPTER THREE

Macy came to a tire-screeching halt in front of her grandmother's house. Tears dampened her cheeks. She'd passed the two-tissue limit about four stop signs ago, but that hardly mattered. Nothing did but Billy. She needed to know her baby brother was okay.

She bolted out of her car and raced to the front porch. Intent only on talking to her mom, she didn't even jump when someone caught her arm. She swung around and came face to face with a uniformed Harris County deputy. Breathing became almost impossible.

"Slow down," he commanded. "Who . . . ?" His eyes widened.

She ignored the commanding grip, disregarded his awkward expression, and yanked open the door. "Mom? Nan?"

The grasp on her arm tightened. Swerving, she glared at the officer. She'd brought one cop to the ground tonight. What was one more?

"Macy?" her mom called from inside.

The cop released her but followed her inside. Another man, dressed in a suit, stood beside her crying mother. Nan jumped up from the green sofa. The look of anguish in her eyes wrenched a sob from Macy's throat.

"Tell me it's not him. Tell me!" She made her hands into fists. Her nails cut into her palms.

Nan rushed over and placed a hand on each of Macy's shoulders, but she didn't say a word. Pain exploded in Macy's chest.

"No." She dropped to the floor and buried her face into her knees. "Nooooo."

Behind her closed eyelids, she saw her brother as a boy standing at the foot of her bed, teddy bear clutched in his arms. *I'm scared Daddy will come home.* She heard his whispered words and knew she'd failed him for good this time.

Macy's mom joined her on the carpet. "Go ahead and cry," she said.

"Oh, Mace." Nan plopped down beside Macy. "It's gonna be okay." Her grandma's voice cracked with emotion, and Nan never cracked. She was strong, together, everything Macy wanted but often failed to be. As she'd failed Billy.

Images of him sitting across from her at the prison flashed in Macy's mind. He'd been so afraid. Why hadn't she done something? This was her fault. He'd asked for help and she hadn't done a damn thing. Gripping two handfuls of the faded green shag carpet, she rocked back and forth. "No."

"Listen." Nan brushed a hand over Macy's back. "Billy's not totally brainless. He'll turn himself in."

Macy hiccupped and stared at her grandma. "He's alive?"

"As far as we know," someone answered. "I'm assuming you're his sister?"

Macy looked up and saw a middle-aged man in a suit. "Yes."

"Oh goodness, you thought—" Nan didn't finish her sentence before starting another. "He's fine. Of course, we're going to kick his ass when this is over."

The realization of it all hit Macy with sweet relief, but it left a bitter aftertaste. Billy wasn't dead, but he'd broken out of prison? Why hadn't she realized how desperate he sounded, how afraid? Now the police would chase him down, shoot him dead if he did something stupid. And Billy was notorious for doing stupid things. Nan was right. As soon as they got him safely back behind bars, Macy was going to kick that boy's ass.

She glanced at her mother, wrapped in her faded pink terry-cloth robe, then at Nan, who appeared strong in her purple Cinderella pajamas. God, she loved them both. And Billy. She loved her brother—who was alive. Alive!

Another sob escaped Macy's lips, and she hugged her mom. Nan moved in, and it became a group hug. "I'm sorry I didn't call," Macy said. "I thought you wanted to ask about the visit."

A deep clearing of a male throat made Macy glance up.

"I'm Peter James, FBI," said the middle-aged, suited guy who'd spoken earlier. His expression implied that his training hadn't handled whimpering females who sat huddled on the floor. And yeah, right now Macy fit that profile. Not that she cared what he thought.

Macy stood, then offered a hand up to her mom and Nan. Drawing in a shaky breath, she hugged her mom again. "I love you," she whispered. Turning, she gave her grandma a watery smile.

"Mace?" Nan's eyes widened.

"I'm okay," she replied. Then, willing herself to be strong, Macy walked over to the coffee table and snatched a tissue. Feeling more composed, she gathered her wits and blew. Nose clean, dignity intact, she faced the two lawmen. "I want to know everything. For starters, why is the FBI involved?"

It wasn't until both men's gazes lowered that Macy remembered the state of her attire. She jerked her shirt closed over her blue bra, realizing that maybe it would take a few more minutes to gather her dignity. But that didn't matter—Billy was alive. Now all she had to do was figure out how to keep him that way.

It was pitch dark out as Billy paced the trailer's living room, uncomfortable in the borrowed clothes and with the gun tucked inside the waist of his pants. He watched out the window for Ellie's car. The sixteen-year-old boy who had picked him up, Andy Canton, now sat with a bag of potato chips in his lap. The kid's black Lab lay beside him on the lopsided sofa, which was missing a front leg.

When the boy had first pulled over and asked Billy if he needed a ride, Billy worried the kid was either high on something or one of those "special" kids. But he didn't seem to be either. Not that it mattered. Billy got in the car.

When Andy had asked him where he was going, Billy asked if the kid could spare him a change of clothes. At first, he thought Andy was going to say no, but he'd nodded and told him he'd take him to his place—that no one but him lived there.

"You think your girlfriend is gonna come?" Andy shoved a handful of chips into his mouth. The dog sniffed at the boy's jeans for crumbs.

Billy gazed around the home—if it could be called one. Take-out boxes and junk mail littered the floor. He'd heard the term *trailer trash*, and he suspected this was an example. Not that he judged Andy. Nope. He couldn't blame Andy. The boy had explained that his parents just up and left. That was hard to grasp. Sure, fathers tended to run off— Billy's own had—but mothers weren't supposed to do that. Yeah, his mom could be pretty crazy, but she would never have left him. It was a shame that Andy didn't have a sister like Mace, or maybe a grandma like Nan. They'd have taken care of him. Of course, Andy said he didn't need anyone. He worked at a fast-food place where they fed him on his shifts and let him bring home any mistakes from the kitchen. Pride had filled the teen's eyes when he'd claimed to make enough money to pay the utilities, his cell phone, and to buy dog food for Spike.

Why had Andy picked him up? The question still jumped around Billy's confused brain. If it was for money, the kid hadn't asked yet. Maybe the boy was just lonely. He sure as hell didn't have anyone else in his life. Then again, it was probably because he thought it was cool to help an escaped prisoner. There might have been a day when Billy believed that, too. But right now, nothing felt cool about this. And when Andy asked Billy why he'd gone to jail, Billy's answer had been short. "I made a mistake."

The dog stirred beside Andy. "It's been four hours since you called her."

"She'll come." Billy refused to think that something had happened. Ellie had been so scared when he'd told her that Tanks had escaped. Somehow, Billy had managed to calm her down and tell her what to do. At least he hadn't screwed that up. He'd almost reminded himself of his sister: taking care of situations, telling others what needed to be done. Not that Mace would ever have gotten herself into this jam. Why did he always get messed up in things?

He wanted to call Mace to see if Ellie had gotten there yet, but he was afraid the police had tapped her phone. And while he wanted to see his sister, he knew she would try to talk him into turning himself in. That wasn't an option, not until he fixed this.

Stepping over a pile of dirty clothes, he bit the inside of his lip. He could almost hear Mace saying, *Don't bite your lips raw—it's just gonna hurt.* She was right.

His sister had always taken care of him. But now it was his turn to take care of her. Especially when this was his fault. He wouldn't let Tanks hurt Mace or Ellie.

He thought about Hal. Was the guard alive? Images flashed in Billy's mind of the man lying on the ground, blood oozing from his chest. Then he saw the other inmate, Brandon, his prison uniform soaked in red. Billy wanted to puke.

The gun tucked into the waistband of his pants felt heavy and cold against his hip. Part of him wanted to throw it away, but another part wouldn't let him. He'd messed up. He wouldn't be a coward again. David Tanks had to be stopped, and it no longer mattered what happened to Billy himself. Hadn't Mace told him that he had to grow up, to stop thinking about himself and start thinking about other people?

A spray of light danced across the blinds, followed by the sound of a car pulling down the gravel street. Billy ran to the window, praying it was Ellie and that she'd brought Mace. But the car drove past, its red taillights winking in the darkness.

"That's my neighbor," Andy said. "He works second shift . . . when he works. Mostly he just hides from his ex-wives."

Billy bit down on the inside of his lip so hard he tasted blood.

It was midnight when Jake pulled his car into the precinct parking lot. "You can head home," he told Donaldson, who sat in the passenger seat. He opened the car door but didn't look forward to getting out; he was still sore from his run-in with a certain brunette's knee. "I'm just going to see if the reports I requested on the prison breakout were faxed."

"You want me to go over them with you?" Donaldson asked.

"Nah. I'll probably grab them and head home myself."

Donaldson's orthodontist-straightened teeth gleamed in the dark. "Wait until I tell the guys that you got taken down by a pizza girl."

"Wait until I tell everyone you get your ass waxed."

While Jake only had a year of experience on the other detective, it felt like more. Probably it was because of Donaldson's background. His daddy was a bigwig in Washington. Donaldson, an only child, had spent his childhood traveling the globe—first-class, no doubt. Not that Jake had anything against rich people, but he and this kid came from two different worlds. Of course, while he didn't relate to Donaldson, he'd grown to respect him. No matter how much razzing the unit gave him about being a golden boy with Washington ties, the new detective took it on the chin and continued to prove he cared about his job.

"My ass has never been waxed," Donaldson laughed. "But you buy me breakfast in the morning and I'll keep this to myself."

"What'll it be, caviar?" Jake's parents had raised him and his brother on a preacher's salary. They'd never gone hungry, never gone without clothes, though hand-me-downs and meatless casseroles had been a way of life. Still, he'd never considered them poor until his dad got cancer and the insurance had covered only a portion of the medical expenses. He doubted Donaldson had ever experienced that sort of glitch.

"A ham omelet will do—with a side of caviar." The new detective chuckled and got out of the car.

Jake, bruised balls and all, followed suit. He groaned. "How about a Pop-Tart?"

"Still hurting?" Donaldson asked.

"Hell, no."

"You got more pride than balls." Donaldson smiled.

Jake took a step. It wasn't the first time he'd been accused of having pride to spare, but some things were hard to forget. Like the humiliation of watching church members drop change into the Baldwin donation tin every Sunday. It wasn't that he didn't appreciate help, but he hated being at the mercy of others.

Donaldson took the keys to his Mustang Cobra out of his pocket, tossed them up in the air, and caught them. "I like my Pop-Tarts with icing."

Jake kept walking. "See you tomorrow," he said over his shoulder.

After limping to his office, Jake found the ten-page report on the fax machine. He dropped the papers on his desk, placed his gun and handcuffs in a drawer, curled back in his chair, and ran his hand between his legs. Pizza Girl could fight, he'd give her that. He would've been furious if he hadn't believed it was panic that sent her into attack mode.

"Macy Tucker." He'd memorized her name, address, and descriptive information from her driver's license. And of course there was his visual inspection and their physical contact. Twenty-eight, five feet four, brunette, blue eyes. A full B or a small C cup. And while he'd bet she didn't weigh a hundred pounds in wet shoes, what she lacked in mass she made up for in spunk . . . and in hair. He remembered pinning her to the ground, burying his nose in all that hair. She'd smelled like pizza. He loved pizza. Give him the meat lover's special, a beer, and . . .

Closing his eyes, he intended to visualize a pie with extra sausage. Instead, his mind conjured up an image of Macy Tucker, her long dark mane spread around her head and her shirt open. Damn, he'd always been fond of colored underwear. Did she wear matching panties? Maybe a thong, or something lacy?

He moaned as he realized where his mind was taking this. Hell, the woman had kneed him in the balls, twice, and he was lusting after her? He really needed to start working on his personal life. Meaning, he needed to get laid.

Rummaging through his desk drawer, he found an unused address book. He took a moment to jot down her info, hoping that after doing so he could let it go. Then, forcing her image from his mind, he focused on the prison report.

All they'd gotten from the guard before he'd lapsed into unconsciousness was that a gun was buried in the flowerbeds where the prisoners were working, and a couple of boot prints had been found that didn't appear to match those of the inmates. CSI had taken images. They'd release any information as soon as they had it, yet it was obvious the inmates had help from outside. Someone had either picked them up or left a getaway car.

Jake tapped his pencil's eraser against his desk. Was Ellie Chandler's showing up at his office yesterday a coincidence? Hell, no. He'd learned not to believe in coincidences. Like the coincidence of his ex-fiancée announcing her engagement to his brother six months after she'd broken up with him. Yeah, that was a coincidence.

Why the hell was he thinking about that now? The answer rolled over him like a sputtering 18-wheeler. His mom expected him to attend the celebration that she was hosting in a couple of weeks for his grandfather's hundredth birthday. He'd been a no-show last year, managed to avoid the newly-weds altogether. But this time his mom had made her feelings clear: *You will be there.*

Gritting his teeth, he pushed back in his chair and focused on work. He had escaped-convicts and a different co-incidence to figure out. Not that this was his case, but having ties to David Tanks, his captain would expect him to contribute. Jake prided himself on exceeding people's expectations. He was no one's charity case—not anymore.

Elbows bracketing the report, he focused on reading. Had Tanks orchestrated the breakout alone, or were all the inmates involved? The bullet that killed the fourth prisoner appeared to be from the same nine millimeter that had shot the guard.

Scanning the page, Jake digested what he'd read about the murdered inmate: Brandon Stafford, grand theft auto, five years down on a seven-year sentence.

"Why were you killed, Brandon?"

Thoughts about the guard, Hal Klein, raced through Jake's mind. The last report that came in said the guard was still in surgery. Doctors weren't optimistic, which meant that every law officer in Texas would be out to bring in the escapees. Jake stared at the guard's name, remembered hearing that Klein was a father and a grandfather.

Hang tough, old man.

The next page contained the data about Tanks and the other two escaped inmates, Chase Roberts and Billy Moore. Jake's eyes caught on the second name, and Ellie Chandler's words echoed through his brain: *I love Billy now.*

It couldn't be, could it?

Thumbing through the pages, he searched to see if he had the most recent visitors log of the escaped inmates. He found it. The list went back three weeks, and the names were easily legible. *Faye Moore, mother. Bo Gomez, friend. Ellie Chandler*—

Crap. It was the same guy.

But if these two criminals were in a dispute over a woman, why would they run off together? Something didn't fit. He'd feel a lot better if he could find Miss Chandler. Where was she? Had she been part of the breakout? Before he'd gone there tonight, he'd called her home and cell phone. He'd left messages saying he wanted to help. She hadn't called back.

He scanned the pages again. Ellie visited Billy at least four times a week. Then Jake's gaze caught the last name on the visitor's log: Macy Tucker, sister.

Pizza Girl.

"Son of a . . . That little liar!"

His gut had tried to tell him. Why the hell hadn't he listened?

Because you were too busy listening with your dick.

He grabbed his gun and his handcuffs and headed for his car.

Suddenly conscious, all Hal Klein could think about was his chest pain. Was this a heart attack? He tried to remember things, important things, like what had happened. Yes, something had gone down. But what? Or was it still happening? He tried to open his eyes, but they felt glued shut—or maybe just heavy.

"Daddy?"

It was his daughter Melissa's voice. But Hal couldn't concentrate.

Danger. Fear. Emotions ran chaotic in his mind, fragments of dreams or perhaps reality. He didn't know. The pain kept him from thinking clearly. He worked harder to open his eyes. He couldn't. Words formed on his tongue, but he couldn't spit them out. He tried to swallow, but his mouth was too dry.

He heard a soft cry. His daughter's. Was something wrong with Melissa? The feeling of danger pulled at his mind. Was someone hurting her? He had to help her, but—

"Don't talk," Melissa whispered. "Doctors say you'll be fine. Steve's here, too."

His son was here? Where was here? The smells of the room began to register: rubbing alcohol, pine cleaner. Hospital smells. Yes, Melissa had said something about doctors. The pain in his chest registered again. Heart attack? No. Now he remembered David Tanks rising up from the flowerbed.

At first Hal thought he'd spotted a snake, because the inmate moved so fast. He should have been more suspicious. Tanks came for him, and there was no time to go for his gun. The bullet hit Hal, and Hal hit the ground. He almost passed out but fought it. If these were the last minutes of his life, he wanted them. Flat on his back, he watched Tanks aim his gun again. Hal tried to pull his weapon, but his arms were dead weights.

Then the kid—Billy—tackled Tanks. The two prisoners rolled around. Hal almost reached his weapon, but the inmate Roberts snatched it from his holster and took off. A bullet was fired. Not by Roberts, but from the gun Billy and Tanks fought over. The fourth inmate, Brandon Stafford, crumpled to the grass.

Billy broke free, gun in hand. He looked at Hal, and then at Stafford, who lay screaming. "I didn't do that," he said. "I didn't shoot him."

Tanks got up and moved forward. Billy raised the gun.

"Don't," Billy ordered, but his voice quavered.

Hal wasn't the only one who heard. Tanks laughed. "You won't shoot. You're a coward."

Right then, a car squealed to a halt beside them. "Get in!" yelled a man from the car.

"Give me a gun," Tanks said to the driver.

But they had to go, said the man. Tanks yelled things at Billy, ugly things about what he planned to do to the kid's sister, then the car pulled off.

"Daddy? Daddy?" Melissa's voice rang out.

The pain in Hal's chest grew worse. He heard beeping noises and more voices.

"You're going to have to go," someone ordered.

"What's happening?" Melissa asked, fear and panic ringing in her voice.

Hal wanted to say something, something to let her know he was okay, but he couldn't talk. Could hardly think, if not for the pain, then that damn bright light. "Get her out of here! We're losing him! Losing . . ."

CHAPTER FOUR

It was two in the morning when Macy pulled into her driveway. Exhausted, she grabbed her purse and the remaining pizza box and crawled out of her Saturn. She didn't have a clue how to go about finding Billy or how to get him safely back to jail. She hoped that tomorrow she'd be thinking clearer and would come up with something.

As she crossed her front lawn, a blue van coasted past. Was it Billy? Hope rose in her chest, but the van kept going.

Looking at her house, she wondered if Billy had called. Eager to check her messages, she increased her pace. She got to her porch, key in hand, when she heard footsteps.

Not again.

"Gotcha!" A hand landed on her shoulder. "Police." A cheek pressed close, a five-o'clock shadow scraped her skin, and a voice said, "I repeat, *police*, Pizza Girl. Did you hear me this time? If you throw that elbow back, or try anything with your knees, I'll have cuffs on your wrists in two seconds flat."

Macy's mind flashed a mental picture of this cop's almost smile. Somehow she didn't think he was smiling now. But while her pin-prickling fear began to fade, wariness followed. Was Ellie right about Baldwin? On the heels of everything that had happened, Macy didn't know what to believe. All she knew was what she'd repeated dozens of times to the FBI: *Yes, Billy manages to get himself into messes, but he's not a murderer. He'd never kill anyone.*

Squaring her shoulders, clutching her box of cold pizza, she tried to sound calm. "What are you doing here?"

"I don't like to be lied to." Sergeant Baldwin's hand stayed on her shoulder.

She turned to face him. "I never lied." She kept the pizza box between them.

He moved forward, nudging the box to the side. "So, Miss Chandler ordered a pizza tonight? Do you think I'm an idiot?"

Macy tilted her chin up. "Your intelligence is not for me to judge. As for your first inquiry, you're right that Ellie never ordered a pizza. But I never said she did. You assumed it."

He leaned in, his face inches from hers. "You said—"

"I said, 'We're open till twelve.' I never said I was delivering a pizza there. It's not my fault you do shoddy police work." Damn. She shouldn't have said that. Gritting her teeth, she vowed to keep her tongue in check.

His expression tightened, but he didn't speak. Not that she minded. Backpedaling in her mind, she tried to think and speak rationally. Not easy. "I've had a bad day," she said at last. "I just want to go to bed." She fit her key into the front-door lock.

"Oh, hell no. You've got some explaining to do, lady." The cop's hand found her elbow.

Macy forced herself to speak calmly. "I've filled my quota of explaining for the night. Come back tomorrow."

"You haven't explained shit," he argued.

"Not to you I haven't. I spent the last hour with the FBI."

"Try again," he growled. "The FBI aren't involved with state-prison breaks."

"I know that," she replied with a sigh. "And they wouldn't say why they were there. But they were, so you've been outranked, and I'm tired."

"Tired? Then let's get this over with." He motioned to the door as if they were both going inside.

"*No.*" She backed up. "I know my rights, and I don't recall inviting you in."

He scowled. "Let me tell you how it's going to be. You can either invite me inside, let me look around to make sure you're not hiding your brother, then you can explain what's going on, or"—he pulled out his cell phone—"I'm going to make a call, and I'll have three patrol cars here in about five minutes. We'll tear through your place while you sit hand-cuffed in one of those cars, waiting to be carted downtown to have your pretty face photographed."

Pretty?

She ground her teeth, then snapped, "First, you'd need a search warrant. Second, you can't arrest me. I haven't done anything."

"First, I don't need a warrant when I have reasonable cause to believe there might be an escaped convict hiding out in your home and putting someone's life in jeopardy. Second, you've lied and assaulted—"

"I didn't lie. And the assault was only because—"

"Quit stalling." He waved his cell phone. "Do I call or not?"

He was serious—she saw it in his eyes. "I've already talked to the FBI," she complained.

"And now you're going to talk to me."

"About what?"

"About why you weren't up-front with me tonight. Why you're so dead set against me coming in." His right brow arched up. "Did you help your brother escape? Is he here?"

"No."

"Prove it. Let me in." He stared at her and waved the phone again. "Call, or not call?"

"Fine. Come in." Fighting with him was more trouble than it was worth. She stormed inside and into the living room. The red light was blinking on her answering machine, making her heart pound. She dropped her purse on top of it, then set the pizza box on the coffee table. Weak-kneed, she collapsed on her sofa.

"Look around," she suggested. "You'll see no one is here.

Ask your questions, but don't expect drawn-out answers. I gave those to the FBI."

The cop lingered outside, clearly wary. Finally, he came in and shut the front door. He scanned the room.

"You live alone?"

"With Elvis." She looked around for the feline.

Baldwin's gaze speared her. "Elvis. Does your smart mouth ever stop?"

A thump sounded from behind him. The cop swung around, his right hand dipping inside his shirt as if for his gun. Then his gaze met the cause of the thump. He froze. Elvis, on the ground in front of him, hissed and flicked his tail.

Satisfaction poured into Macy's chest. She'd have to give the feline a treat for perfect timing. "Sergeant Baldwin, meet Elvis."

Baldwin's gaze cut to her, and she bit back a laugh. Then she saw her cat's tail flicking in discontent.

"Elvis doesn't like strangers," she said. The cat's ears flattened back and his gray fur fluffed out. He crouched down, hissing, and his yellow eyes rounded. Macy knew what came next; the question was if she would warn Baldwin. He didn't deserve it. Then again, she really didn't like the sight of blood.

"If I were you, I'd move back. Because in about two seconds, he's going to jump. And I haven't had him"—the cat sprang up in the air—"declawed."

"Damn!" Baldwin yelled as Elvis caught his shoulder and used the cop to propel himself up onto a bookshelf. A moment later he jumped down and disappeared down the hall.

"I warned you." Macy curled back on her sofa, fighting amusement.

Hand clapped to his shoulder, Baldwin swung around. Macy waited for him to lash out, to claim he'd have the cat put down for slashing him. Not that he could do it. She knew the law, but she still expected the guy to try to bully her. She waited, counting to ten, but he didn't prove her right. Okay, so maybe he wasn't *that* big of a bully.

"I'm bleeding." He yanked his shirt away from his shoulder.

"Maybe you should seek medical attention. Cat scratch fever can be deadly."

His blue gaze locked on her. "You never ease up, do you?"

"I'm tired. I've had a hellish day." *Plus PMS*, she didn't say. She cut her eyes to her purse-covered answering machine. *And a brother who needs me.*

His gaze shot down the hall. "Well, I'm going to look around."

"Go for it," she said, wishing he'd hurry.

"Is Elvis going to attack again?" he asked as he walked off.

"I wouldn't suggest you stick your head under the bed. Of course, someone could be hiding under there. So maybe you should."

Surprisingly, she could have sworn she heard him laugh. Slumping back, she raked her palms over her shirt. Nan's emergency safety pins now served as buttons.

Eyes closed, Macy suddenly realized her fear of Baldwin, and even her suspicions, had evaporated. Was she just so tired that she was forgetting to be afraid, or was she beginning to trust the guy? It hadn't been very long. But she remembered him threatening to bring out more police. If he was working with David Tanks, would he do that? Not likely. Of course, nothing else made sense. Why had Billy run off with a man who'd threatened to kill him? Why was the FBI involved?

Baldwin's footsteps sounded in the hall. As Macy opened her eyes, he walked past the living room and into the kitchen. Letting her eyelids flutter closed again, Macy leaned her head back. *Where are you, Billy?*

Baldwin cleared his throat, and Macy snapped her eyes open to find him standing in front of her.

"Finished?" she asked.

"Just getting started."

The cop wore a dark blue, long-sleeved shirt, unbuttoned.

Under it, he had on a white T-shirt. His jeans were well-worn, and were faded where they hugged his body as he lowered himself into a green recliner. Oddly enough, Macy compared how he fit the piece of furniture to how her ex had filled the chair. Baldwin's hard frame, wide shoulders, and long legs made the chair look smaller. She figured him to be taller than her ex's six feet. Baldwin probably weighed in around—she appraised his flat stomach, the snug fit of his jeans—maybe 210.

She stopped appreciating the man's form as her gaze found his eyes, eyes that seemed to find her survey amusing.

"I'm tired," she said. She wished he'd leave. She was feeling antsy, and the feeling grew as he glanced around the room.

"Where's your phone?" he asked, rubbing his shoulder.

She fought the tightness in her voice. "Use your own."

"Where's your *phone*?"

She debated whether or not to lie, but she knew when she was beaten. Well, she almost knew. Throwing in the towel had never been easy. "Can't you just call the FBI?"

"Where is it, Macy?"

Something about the way he said her name made her even more eager to see him gone. Accepting defeat, she yanked her purse off the end table.

He stood and eyed the machine's flashing red light. "Did you really think I wouldn't ask?"

She shrugged. "Actually, I did."

"And your cell phone?" He pointed to her purse.

"Dead. Out of minutes. Out of money."

"Convenient," he said as if he didn't believe her.

She pulled the phone from her purse and tossed it at him.

He caught it. Eyeing her suspiciously, he opened it, pushed a few buttons, and tossed it back at her. Then his gaze went back to the blinking red light on her answering machine.

His face was like granite. "Before I listen to this, is there anything you'd like to tell me? I'll say you gave the information voluntarily."

"Voluntarily?" She stiffened under his scrutiny. "I don't know where Billy is or who's on the machine. I'm not guilty of anything but loving my brother."

He settled down on the couch, between her and the recorder. She scooted over, away from his body warmth. She expected him to hit the play button, but instead he shouldered back in the sofa and watched her squirm.

"Why were you at Ellie Chandler's tonight?"

"I went to talk to her, but I didn't know Billy had escaped. I went to see him today. He begged me to go see Ellie. And . . . I told all this to the FBI."

"Where were you the rest of the afternoon?"

"I had a five-thirty shift. I went straight to work. It wasn't until I left Ellie's that I heard about the prison break. My mom had called me several times tonight at work, and that's probably her on the answering machine. I didn't call her back, and when I heard—" Emotion crowded her throat. "When I heard about the inmate who was killed, I thought it was Billy."

"Why would you assume that? Did he tell you he was going to try to escape? Ask for help?" Suspicion thickened the policeman's tone.

"No! He told me that another inmate wanted him dead. He said that the guards were afraid of this David Tanks person. He said Tanks has people on the outside who do things for the guards, and—"

"What kind of things?" the cop interrupted.

Macy shrugged "He didn't say. And then Ellie said—"

"You talked to Ellie?" Baldwin leaned forward. "When did you talk to her?"

"I haven't actually spoken with her. When I came home today, she'd left a message on my recorder."

"I thought you went straight to work." Suspicion again tightened his voice.

"I came home to get my money bag. After I went to the library."

He nodded, but she couldn't tell if he believed her or not. "What did Ellie say?"

"She said she was afraid Tanks was going to do something."

Sergeant Baldwin's eyebrows pinched together. "Did it occur to you to come to the police with the information?"

"I might have, if Ellie hadn't already tried, but she said some cop was too busy staring at her boobs to listen. You wouldn't happen to know that jerk, would you? Someone named Jake something?"

She could swear he flinched, but he didn't comment. "And, that's all you know? I'm not going to learn something else on this tape? They'll go easier on you if—"

"That's all I know," she snapped.

He looked over at her answering machine. His gaze lowered, then froze. Leaning down, he picked up her gardening boots from under the end table. He turned them over. A clod of dirt from the church garden dropped onto her carpet. He stared.

She frowned, a little unnerved. "Don't tell me. Boot fetish?"

The cop stared at her. "Did you wear these to see your brother today?"

"No."

"They found boot prints at the prison, in the flowerbed where the gun was planted. When I take these in to be checked, the guys in the lab will know if they match," he warned.

Macy clenched her jaw, furious, though unsure why his suspicions bothered her so much. Then understanding dawned: she'd been the one with reasons to distrust him, and she'd pushed those reasons aside. Had he? No.

"Take the boots. Have them tested," she snapped. "But when those size sixes don't match, I can promise—"

A resounding knock on the door brought both of them bolting from the sofa.

Baldwin stared at her. "Expecting anyone?" His hand reached inside his shirt and drew out a weapon.

"No!" She hurtled between him and the door. "Put the gun away."

"Move aside," he ordered. His focus stayed on the door.

"I'm not going to let you shoot my brother."

"I won't shoot unless—"

"No!" More tears threatened. Just like her mom. She hated it. "Let me answer. You can stand beside me. I just . . . I don't want Billy hurt. He's not a bad kid. Even if he's done some things wrong, he—"

The knock sounded again.

"Please," she begged.

The policeman wavered. "Ask who it is."

Macy stepped closer to the door.

"Wait!" He pulled her back into the living room from the hall and whispered, "Ellie said Tanks threatened to kill Billy's sister. That's you. This could be Tanks."

"And it could be Billy," she snapped. She tried pulling free, but he held on. "Let me answer!"

"Calm down," he said in her ear. "Ask who it is."

She took a deep breath. "Who is it?" she said. The knocking thudded harder. "He can't hear me." She looked back at the door. "Who is it?" she yelled, and prayed her brother would answer—prayed Baldwin wouldn't hurt him.

The knocking stopped. Baldwin released her. The doorknob rattled, and from the corner of her eye she saw Sergeant Baldwin raise his gun.

"No!" she screamed.

"Mace?" a deep voice called from outside the house.

The timbre of the voice filled Macy's ears. It rang all sorts of bells—familiar bells, though not Billy ones.

"Is it your brother?" Baldwin asked.

"No." Her mind tried unsuccessfully to wrap around the voice.

"Mace?" the man called again from outside. "I heard what happened."

Recognition hit. It hit with a resounding thud. Not a positive thud, either, but an ex-husband, cheating-louse kind of thud. She looked back at Baldwin, gun drawn.

"What the hell," she said. "Go ahead and shoot."

CHAPTER FIVE

Shoot? Had he heard right? Jake latched an arm around Macy Tucker's abdomen. "Who is it?" he growled.

She looked up. "My husband."

He jerked his arm back. "You're married?" While he hadn't meant the hold to be personal, it suddenly felt personal—at least too personal for a married woman.

"We're divorced," she said.

He breathed a sigh of relief. "Then I think the correct terminology is *ex*-husband."

"Didn't I say that?" She stared at the door.

Jake shook his head. "No. You didn't." He didn't have a clue why the thought of her being married made him flinch, but . . . Oh, hell. Yes, he did know why. Macy Tucker, ball buster and conniving twit, had snagged his interest the moment he laid eyes on her. Lust at first sight. It had been too long since he'd felt real lust. Too long since he'd wanted—

The knocking grew louder.

"Mace?" the voice called again. "I thought you might need some company."

Jake studied the woman before him. "If you're lying to me . . ."

She rolled her eyes. "I'm not. It's Tom, my *ex*-husband."

He stared into her baby blues and, just like that, he believed her. Believed the man behind the door was her ex-husband, believed that she hadn't helped her brother escape prison, believed her boots weren't the ones that had left the prints at the breakout scene. The doorknob rattled again, only this time it came with the clink of a key and the click of a lock. Jake tucked his gun behind his shirt right before Macy's ex-husband stepped inside.

An ex-husband with a key. What did that say about their relationship?

Then he saw Macy staring at the keys in the man's hand. The ex was busy staring at him.

"Why do you still have—?" She reached for the keys just as her ex reached for her. Macy skidded back so fast that she banged up against Jake.

"Who are *you?*" the ex asked him.

Jake just smiled and watched Macy.

Emotion flashed in her gaze, and not a good kind. Pain, really. Maybe he was reading more into it than he should. Maybe his own issues were affecting him. Or maybe not. Either way, his protect-and-serve instincts took over. He wrapped an arm around Macy's waist.

She felt good against him. This time, his touch was meant to be personal, or at least to appear personal. Or maybe it wasn't just for show.

Macy flinched and took a quick few steps away. Then her gaze shot to her ex, as if she realized the movement had brought her closer to him, and she frowned. She divided the distance, moving to stand equally between the two men. As crazy as it seemed to him, Jake hoped she'd scoot back closer to him.

One step. Come on, Pizza Girl.

"What are you doing here?" she asked her ex.

"I heard about Billy." The man scowled at Jake. "But you've got company."

She did it. She took a step toward Jake, and he couldn't help but smile.

"You should try calling first," she said. "How did you hear—?"

"Don't be rude, Mace," the ex insisted. "Introduce us."

Macy looked back at Jake as if debating what to say.

Without thinking, Jake took the decision from her. He

brushed a lock of her hair off her shoulder. "No need for introductions. I know who you are. You're Tom."

"Now, if I only knew who *you* were . . ." Tom glared at him.

"I'm Jake Baldwin." He winked at Macy. She opened her mouth as if to speak, but not a word escaped.

"And what are you doing here with my wife?"

"I think that's *ex*-wife," Jake responded.

"Okay, let me rephrase. What are you doing with my ex-wife?"

Jake smiled again. "Macy invited me in."

The woman's eyes widened.

Her ex looked at her. "Can I have a minute with you, Mace? *Alone?*"

Jake shrugged. "Don't mind me," he said. "You two go ahead. Just pretend I'm not here."

The ex's posture tightened, but he seemed to resolve himself. "You're already bringing guys home?"

Macy appeared shocked by his question, but she recovered quickly. "Well, I guess I didn't think you'd mind, considering you brought girls home while we were still married."

Jake laughed, and they both stared at him as if he were crazy. He spoke his mind. "She sure has a way with words, doesn't she?" Then he raised his hand. "Oh, carry on. Sorry."

Macy faced him. "Can you give us a minute?"

Jake saw the ex smirk, but if Macy's expression was any indication, he shouldn't exactly have been planning any victory parties. He winked at Macy. "Anything for you. I'll just wait in the bedroom. With Elvis."

Macy watched Sergeant Baldwin walk toward the rear of her house, but something told her he didn't go as far as the bedroom.

Bedroom? How suggestively he'd said it. Had he purposely, shamelessly, tried to give Tom the wrong idea? Was he so cocky, so bold, that he would really try to deceive her ex-husband into believing that—?

Oh, heck, she didn't have time to admire or be grateful to the cop right now. She refocused on Tom.

"How did you hear about Billy?" She worked at keeping her tone casual, because she was just a bit touched that her ex-husband was worried about her. Not enough to accept his offer of company, of course. His shoulder to cry on would no doubt come with a price. A flat price—as in, she'd be flat on her back. She'd heard that his fling had flung itself out.

"Your grandma's neighbor called my mom. When I got the message, I knew you'd be upset, so I came to—"

"I appreciate your concern." A tiny part of her did. Then again, she would have appreciated a lot more his not having had an affair with his secretary, and especially not in her own bed. "But we're divorced. You should go."

"You're really seeing that clown?" he seethed.

She shrugged, not willing to lie. "What? You don't like his sense of humor?"

"I suppose you do. My God, we've only been divorced a few weeks!"

His words landed with a bruising bump on her heart—a heart that had suffered too many blows today. Too many blows in the last five years, mostly thanks to Tom himself.

"We'd have been divorced almost two years ago if you'd signed the papers."

He took a step forward. "Don't be hardheaded. Tell the guy to leave. I'll fix you some hot chocolate, just the way you like it." He opened his arms as if he expected her to melt into his embrace and rejoice because he remembered her culinary dependency.

She didn't move into his arms. The hot chocolate sounded good, but Tom's embrace didn't tempt her. Not even a smidgen. That felt pretty damn good, too.

He puffed out his chest. "Come on Macy, it's him or me."

That clinched it. "Him."

"You would choose—?"

"Definitely." Her gut had always told her Tom was an idiot, and now she knew for sure. She pointed to the door. "You need to go."

His green eyes widened. "You're obviously upset. You're not thinking clearly."

"You're right about me being upset. I'm worried about my brother. As for thinking . . . ?" She pushed a finger to her temple. "Seems pretty clear." She opened the front door. "'Bye, Tom."

He didn't budge. She could tell from his expression that he was struggling to find a new approach. That did a little something for her ego. Other than doing everything he could to delay the divorce, he hadn't once seemed to regret their split. But why now?

The answer hit her: Baldwin. Tom didn't want her. Not permanently. But he didn't want anyone else to have her, either. Especially when he didn't have anyone. The dog.

It still felt good. What woman didn't want a man to regret his mistakes?

She spotted the red blinking light on her answering machine. "Door's open," she said. "Good-bye."

"Look," he begged. "I was wrong to get involved with Tammy, but I said I was sorry."

His words brought back her anger. "No, what you said was, 'Can't we just forget about this?' And I recall telling you that I would do that just as soon as hell turned into a snowy winter wonderland that Santa lists among his top ten favorite places to visit." Macy thought she heard a chuckle from the hall.

"Okay, it's obvious we need to talk." Tom's gaze darkened with anger. "Ask the bozo to leave." He grabbed her.

She stared at his hand on her arm. "Let me go!" Tom had never hit her, but he had a bad habit of being grabby. She wasn't his to grab anymore. One glance at his crotch, and she locked in on her target.

She didn't get a chance to strike. Baldwin came hotfooting it into the foyer and tucked her to his side. "That's it," he said.

Normally, Macy would have resented the implication that she couldn't take care of herself, but the resentment didn't come. The policeman's surprising action felt nice. Kind of.

With one arm around her waist, Baldwin said, "I've counted four times that she's asked you to leave, Tom. In my book, that's four times too many, because you shouldn't be here in the first place. So do yourself a favor and go."

"And if I don't?" Tom snapped. "You gonna fight me? What are you, some tough guy?"

Baldwin's body tensed against hers. The cold shape of his gun pressed against Macy's ribs. Anger seemed to ooze out of him, though he appeared to purposely hold it in. She could tell he was a man who depended on his wits before his fists—but she'd hate to see what he'd do to Tom with his fists. Maybe.

"Fight? Oh, no. I'll just sic Elvis on you." His hand tugged Macy a little closer and he smiled, though not a flicker of warmth filled the expression.

"Oh, hell," Tom gritted out. "I'm out of here."

"Wait," Baldwin said. "Macy meant to ask you for something."

"I did?" She looked up at him in surprise.

"You said I was to remind you to get your key back."

"Oh. Yeah." She held her hand out to Tom. The knowledge that she should move away from Baldwin played havoc with her sanity, but the strength in his touch, the sense of being protected, seduced her for just a few more seconds.

"I'll mail it." Tom left, slamming the door in their faces.

Baldwin's palm sank deeper into the curve of Macy's waist. "You want me to get that key?" he asked.

No, she needed to fight her own battles. "I'll get it later," she said.

His arm felt so solid around her, and his touch reminded

her that she was female and normally most females found the opposite sex appealing. But she didn't want normal, so she stepped out of his embrace and shuffled back to her living room. She dropped onto the sofa. Sighing, she pulled a pillow into her lap and hugged it, purposely ignoring the blinking light on her answering machine. Maybe she'd get lucky and Baldwin would leave.

Jake Baldwin stood there, studying her, as if he expected her to say something. But, what?

"You're welcome," he finally said. He reached down, flipped open the pizza box, and snatched out a slice. "Just cheese?" he groused.

"I didn't say thank you," she snapped. She watched him eat. She hadn't offered him pizza either.

He spoke around the food in his mouth. "Yeah, but I could tell you were thinking it. You wanted him gone."

She didn't deny it. However, the fact that this stranger could read her so easily made her uncomfortable.

Pulling her knees to her chest, she watched him inhale the entire slice. "Thank you," she said, accepting she owed him that much. He winked. Emotionally, she felt that wink all the way to the pit of her stomach—the kind of flutter that got women in trouble. "You should go," she said.

He snagged another slice. "I haven't forgotten the messages."

Thoughts of hearing Billy's voice, and Jake Baldwin's hearing it too, tightened her stomach. She asked something she needed to know. "If he's on here and he tells me where he is, what are you going do?"

"The only thing I can do. Go pick him up."

A knot formed in her throat. "You won't hurt him . . . ?"

"I'm not into hurting people, Pizza Girl."

He didn't offer guarantees. She'd known he wouldn't. Then she recalled how he'd handled himself with Tom, and a part of her realized she trusted him.

Scooting over to the arm of the sofa, she hit the play

button on her answering machine. The recorder stated in its monotone computerized voice, "You have ten new messages." There was a pause, and then: "Tuesday, 4:48 p.m."

Macy tightened her hold on her legs as she awaited the first message.

"Mace. It's your mom. I was"—sniffle, sniffle—"just wondering how the visit went."

"Tuesday, 4:57 p.m."

"Macy. It's Father Luis. Sister Beth told me you were wavering on joining us full-time. It's a lot to ask, but you belong here. It's God's work. I know this is your calling. Sister Beth won't be leaving until next month. We really need to fill her position."

Baldwin choked on his pizza. "What position?"

Macy just quirked an eyebrow.

The phone messages continued. They were all her mom, time and again. "Mace, baby, please call me." And there was a lot of sniffling. Then there was a hang-up. Finally, they were at the last call. Macy didn't know whether to hope it was Billy or not.

"Wednesday, 12:03 a.m."

"Hello, bitch."

Macy flinched. Sergeant Baldwin moved closer. The message played on.

"Just wanted to let you know I was thinking about you. If you talk to your brother, tell him David Tanks always makes good on his promises. You and I are gonna have us a fucking good time. You do like to fuck, don't you?" Then the machine clicked off.

Silence filled the room. Macy sat frozen, staring at the phone.

Suddenly, it rang.

"You have a speakerphone?" Baldwin asked in a rushed voice.

"Yeah."

"Use it."

Gulping, Macy hit the speaker button. "Hello?" she said.

"Glad you're home finally, bitch. Get pretty for me and wait. It might be tonight or tomorrow, but I'll be there."

Then the escaped convict hung up.

Billy's patience had cracked about an hour before. At least a dozen times he'd picked up Andy's cell phone to call Mace or try Ellie's number, but he'd never followed through. Every police show talked about tracing phone calls. He didn't want to be traced, but damn it, where were they?

It was almost four o'clock in the morning before the next set of headlights flashed across the window. Billy pushed back the dirty drapes, praying to see Ellie. Instead, a blue van pulled to a stop in front of Andy's trailer. Ellie didn't drive a van.

Jake's phone, set on vibrate, jarred him awake. He sat up and almost tumbled out of his seat; the footrest on this green recliner had snapped forward. In the light spilling through the window, he saw a brunette and a cat curled up on a sofa. Not his sofa. Not his brunette or cat either. Where the hell was he?

The cat's ears pulled back. Hissing at him, the animal darted off the sofa and disappeared down the hall. Jake's memory returned.

He stood, snatched up his phone, and ducked into the kitchen. Checking the number, he saw it was Donaldson. As he pressed it to his ear, he spotted the clock on the wall. Damn. He was two hours late for work.

"I'm on my way," he said without preamble.

"Good," Donaldson replied. "The brown stuff the lab boys refer to as shit is nearing the fan. The Feds are looking for you."

Jake ran a hand through his hair. He should have called in last night, reported the phone call, but damn it, he knew what would have happened. They'd have brought someone out, sent him packing, taken Macy in, but not a damn thing would have been done to investigate the call until this morning. "The Feds? It has to be about Tanks. I just don't know why—"

"Why Internal Affairs is with them?" Donaldson said. "Me neither."

Jake's palm tightened on the back of his neck. "IA's with them?" That was a surprise.

"Yep."

Last night, he'd played all of Macy's messages, including the earlier one where Ellie accused him of being in cahoots with Tanks. He wondered if IA had heard something similar, and if so, who'd told them. Glancing into the living room he said, "I'm on my way."

Snapping his phone shut, he walked into the living room and reached for his gun, which was lying on the floor beside the recliner. Macy was rousing. She propped herself up on her elbow and stared.

"So, you sicced the Feds on me?" He holstered his gun.

She lowered her feet to the carpet and pulled her hair back with two hands. "Lovely day to you, too." Her voice was husky from just waking up.

Damn, but he liked her. He didn't have a clue why. In less than twenty-four hours, she'd committed two of the greatest sins a woman could against a man: interfering with his job and messing with his family jewels. Well, a man's jewels could and should be messed with, but gently. For a split second his mind conjured an image of the two of them naked and—

"I only told them what Ellie said." She frowned.

Was that guilt? Well, even the woman's grimace was cute and sexy. "I guess you didn't have a choice," he admitted. "But you'd better get moving." He pulled the tape out of the answering machine. "We're leaving in five minutes."

She stared droopy-eyed at the television. The ten-inch tube was still on, the volume muted. He'd cut the sound last night after she'd dropped off. Sleep hadn't come so easily for him. He'd sat in the chair and watched her, and somewhere around four in the morning he'd finally decided she was beautiful. Not drop-dead gorgeous, exactly, with legs up to the neck and knockout boobs. But she was more than girl-next-door pretty. She had one of those faces you just wanted to study forever. And her body? Yeah, about four thirty, he'd decided a closer look at that was high on his wish list.

Visions of tattooed Tanks suddenly flashed in his head. Maybe it was his attraction to Macy, or maybe it was because he felt guilty for not listening to Ellie Chandler, but he felt personally responsible for this whole mess.

"Come on. Up and at 'em. Get ready," he told her.

"Ready? For what?"

"You're coming in with me. Five minutes."

"Why?" Macy asked.

"First, because you've got an escaped convict after you and I don't want to leave you alone. Second, because I'm certain that the Feds will want to chat."

"I already talked to them," she grumbled.

"Yeah, but that was before they knew Tanks had a thing for you and . . . well, it was when you had me down as a bad guy."

"And you think I've changed my mind about that?"

"You chose me over your ex."

"You were listening?" She frowned. "I don't have time—" Her gaze shot to the clock. "My test!" She buried her face in her hands. "Oh, crap! How could I miss my test?"

Jake shrugged. "Five minutes. I'm serious."

Macy took thirty. Five minutes were to politely suggest that she could meet him at the precinct as soon as she pulled herself together, but polite didn't work, and she'd never had a surplus of early-morning patience. The other twenty-five minutes were needed to shower, brush her teeth, comb her hair, and then find her very last emergency tampon under the sink. Every time he'd yell from behind the bathroom door, she'd give herself permission to dawdle for another five minutes. She wasn't his prisoner, his wife, or his girlfriend. And while she didn't enjoy being mean, she didn't believe in rewarding bad behavior.

Banging on the door when a PMS-stricken woman was trying to insert her last tampon? That definitely fell into the category of bad behavior. Oh, and when he screamed, *What are you doing in there?* she'd been tempted to tell him the truth. That would have shut him up.

But she also had begun to feel a few things other than annoyance for the man.

Staring at her image in the mirror, Macy made one of those face-your-fears kind of confessions that are supposed to help your mood. "Hi, I'm Macy Tucker, and Jake Baldwin scares me. He tempts me. Being with him is like driving a bike too close to the edge of a cliff." A cliff with great scenery, of course. But Gawd have mercy, she hadn't thought there was a man alive who could make her want to risk falling off that cliff again. Hadn't she fallen too many times, only to find herself bruised, battered, and broken?

She blinked at her image and waited for the confession to offer her some relief. None came.

She gave her reflection another once-over. "You look like hammered poo on a bad hair day." It all showed on her face: lack of sleep, stress over Billy, that missed exam for a teacher who swore he wouldn't give retests, an escaped prisoner threatening to rape her, the realization that she still had a weak spot for a pair of wide shoulders and a sexy grin. Throw in PMS, and the world wasn't ready for her.

"You've got one minute. Then I'm coming in," Baldwin yelled.

She glared at the door. "I wouldn't do that if I were you."

If the world wasn't ready for her, Jake Baldwin sure as hell wasn't.

Chapter Six

Billy woke up as Andy trotted through the living room to let the dog out. Though the boy never glanced over, Billy pulled the sheet across Ellie, who slept beside him on the lopsided sofa.

He remembered the fear he'd felt at seeing the blue van stop in front of the trailer last night, but then Ellie had crawled out. She'd explained how she'd loaned her car to someone else and was now using their van. Then she'd told him about finding that cop, Jake Baldwin, at Mace's house. She'd parked down the street and waited for the guy to leave, and when he didn't, she'd peeked in the windows only to find the two sitting on the sofa together.

"I think I was wrong about him," Ellie had said. "I don't think he's working with David. He even left me messages saying he wanted to help."

Billy still didn't like it. He had to know Mace was safe.

Andy walked back inside, his dog trotting behind him, and both disappeared back into the one and only bedroom.

Ellie's backside brushed up against Billy's crotch. He hardened. Last night she'd told him she was willing, if he wanted. God, he wanted, and having her soft body next to him had been a torment. But taking her for the first time on a broken sofa, with no privacy and garbage all over the place, didn't feel right, so he'd kissed her and insisted they wait until they were alone. And while he'd never share this with his sister, he bet Mace would say he'd done the right thing. He liked thinking Mace would be proud of him.

Ellie rolled over. "Morning," she said in her cartoonish voice.

He kissed her nose. He bet people teased her about her voice. Not around him they wouldn't. If people couldn't look past her voice and see her beauty, then they were stupid. And he didn't mean her beauty on the outside. In a lot of ways, Ellie reminded Billy of Mace. Like Macy, Ellie loved with all her heart. She loved him that way, and she'd been totally devoted to her grandma, who'd raised her. Ellie even got a job at the nursing home so she could keep an eye on her granny. The woman had died, but Ellie hadn't left her other patients, even though she could make more money waitressing.

In the letters, she'd written all about the people she cared for. Some of their stories were funny. Some were sad, about how no one ever visited. Ellie did things for those patients—things like cutting out pictures from magazines to hang by their beds. Sometimes she'd sneak candy or cigarettes to those who could have them.

Ellie rose up and eyed the trailer in daylight. She frowned. "He really lives by himself?"

Billy sat up, pushed his gun under the sofa with his foot. "Sad, isn't it?"

"Yeah." She yawned and covered her mouth.

Billy studied her face without makeup. He knew she liked wearing it, but she didn't need any. She had beautiful skin. He didn't know how old she was—probably a year or so older than him? He didn't care.

Her green eyes met his. "What are we doing today?" Concern tightened her voice.

"I've got to find a way to talk to Mace. To make sure she's okay." Billy had heard on the radio that Hal was alive. Brandon hadn't been so lucky. Billy remembered leaning over him and yelling, *Where are they going? Tell me!* The address the dying inmate had given was his only lead, so he hoped like hell it was correct.

Billy shuddered. The memory of Brandon lying helpless on the ground was horrible. He wasn't sure if he was the one who'd shot him. If so, it had been an accident. Not that it mattered in the long run.

Ellie stirred beside him. "Then what?"

"I . . . don't know," he said. He couldn't tell Ellie the truth. She wouldn't like it, but he couldn't think of any other way out of this mess. Yesterday he'd been a coward. Not today. As soon as he made sure Mace was okay, he'd do what he should have done yesterday. He'd go and kill Tanks.

Jake and Macy arrived at the precinct an hour later than he'd planned.

"They're waiting in the captain's office," Donaldson said.

Jake gave Macy a nudge toward the other detective. "Watch her." As much as Jake had started to like her, he'd begun to second-guess his attraction. The woman had argued about everything this morning—about getting ready, riding with him instead of following, about her rights as a civilian, about the sausage and biscuit he'd ordered at the drive-through. Well, she hadn't argued about that. She'd simply refused to eat it. Jake eyed the bag containing her breakfast.

"I don't need a sitter," Macy remarked.

"In here." Donaldson motioned Macy into Jake's office, then followed Jake into the hall. "What's going on?"

"Pizza Girl is Billy Moore's sister. He's—"

"The other escapee," Donaldson said. "Shit."

"Yeah. And I'm serious—watch her. She's likely to skip out."

"You think she's in on the breakout?"

After her attitude this morning, Jake had actually considered it again, but . . . "No, I don't. But she doesn't want to be here. Which, to her way of thinking, gives her the right to leave."

He remembered her spouting off about citizens' rights and wondered where the woman got her information. It wasn't just info she'd picked up on television shows; she'd sounded like some fancy lawyer. And everyone knew what cops thought of fancy lawyers.

He ran a hand through his hair. Macy Tucker was a

mystery. One that frustrated and intrigued him all at once. He watched her move to the window in his office and stare outside.

His gaze lingered on that heart-shaped backside encased in faded denim. Oh hell, he'd always loved a good mystery. What was a little frustration? Especially when he suspected her attitude stemmed from her concern over her brother. He could only imagine how he'd feel if the shoe were on the other foot. Then again, he had his own brother issues.

Donaldson chuckled. "She'd better not go for my balls."

"Just watch her." Jake turned to go, then remembered. "Here."

"What?" Donaldson took the bag, looking shocked. "You really bought me breakfast?"

"Sort of." Jake headed down the hall to meet with the Feds and IA.

Jake, the FBI, and the Internal Affairs suit had been at it over twenty minutes and suffered long bouts of silence.

"I haven't seen Tanks since I testified at his trial." Jake shrugged. He was irritated as hell for having to be here, but he'd be damned if he'd let them know. It wasn't that he didn't intend to tell them what he knew, it just pissed him off that IA had been brought in. But years of sitting in the front pew, pretending that he loved every moment of the sermon, had prepared him for every IA questioning he'd suffered through.

On one side of the table sat Agent James, FBI. On the other sat Officer Clayton. Clayton, the weasel from IA, did all the talking. "So, you don't know anything about this prison breakout?" Clayton asked.

"Only what I read in the report." Jake leaned his chair back on two legs, hoping it annoyed them the way it annoyed his mom. He then dropped his chair forward and sat with arms open, posture relaxed. He could tell his lack of anxiety pissed off Clayton, but not Agent James.

He glanced at the Fed. "Why is the FBI involved?"

James closed the file he'd been reading. "Heard some allegations of prison corruption. It seems prison officials were taking payoffs from inmates for favors. Drugs and prostitution. Your name came up."

"Interesting," Jake said.

"Interesting?" Clayton snapped. "Is that all you have to say?"

Jake leaned in. "My only drug use is an occasional aspirin, and as for prostitutes . . . Well, I've never paid for sex. So knock yourself out looking for something. Besides, I'm the one who put Tanks in the slammer. Why the hell would I be doing him favors?" He turned back to Agent James. "Huntsville isn't a federal prison, so why are you guys really looking into this?"

The government man didn't look put off by the question. "We're looking at Tanks for the murder of an FBI agent. Due to our special request, as of today I've been assigned to the Gulf Coast Violent Offenders Task Force. We'll be working the case together."

Hearing honesty in the man's voice, Jake decided to reciprocate. He pulled the tape from his shirt pocket and laid it on the table.

"What's this?" Clayton snapped.

Jake spoke directly to Agent James. "I don't blame you for questioning me. I *do* blame you for bringing IA into this before you spoke to me. As for my name being mentioned, Macy Tucker was only—"

"How do you know we spoke with Ms. Tucker?" The Fed's eyes narrowed.

Jake went through everything for the agent: Ellie's visit, the headless corpse, finding Macy at Ellie's place, how he discovered Macy's name on the report. He left out the family jewels business.

He pointed to the answering-machine tape. "You'll find two messages of importance on this. One is from Ellie

Chandler. I'm not sure how she plays into it all, but she seems genuinely scared of David Tanks. The other message is from Tanks—threatening Ms. Tucker."

"She didn't mention Tanks's call last night," James said.

"She hadn't gotten it when she saw you." Jake also left out that he'd been there when Tanks had called back. No reason to bring more wrath down on himself.

"I need to speak with her." James sounded annoyed that Jake knew more than he did, but there was also a hint of grudging respect.

"She's here." But he didn't want them strong-arming her. "She's a victim in all this."

"You sound sure of that," James said.

"Yes, I am."

"Then she doesn't have anything to worry about."

James made a call and started spouting orders to someone to get a rundown on Macy and a log of incoming and outgoing calls made on her home phone in the past forty-eight hours. Macy Tucker might not be guilty, but that wasn't going to stop the FBI from ripping her life apart. Which was never fun. A wave of guilt and sympathy hit Jake.

"Sounds as if the two of you have *bonded*," Clayton suggested, lending sleaze to the word.

"If you mean I don't want Tanks to get to her, well, yeah, we've 'bonded,'" Jake answered.

Agent James closed his cell phone and eyed Clayton. "Baldwin's right. I jumped the gun asking for IA's involvement."

Clayton's expression soured. "We can't have our officers screwing—"

"This isn't Baldwin's case. If he's friends with Ms. Tucker, I'd say that's his business." The Fed turned back to Jake. "I'm planning on talking to her, but can I assume you're planning on keeping an eye on her?"

She won't like it, but . . . "I've pretty much decided to do that. As much as I can." The moment the words were out, he knew he'd committed himself. Just how close that commitment brought him and Macy was still up for debate, but a sliver of anticipation shot all the way down to his bruised balls. Anticipation he hadn't felt in years.

"We'll check in, but it's nice to know you'll be around." James reached for the tape. "And I'm sure you'll keep us informed. Unofficially, of course." He shot Clayton a glance.

"You can count on it," Jake agreed.

He wondered how Macy Tucker would react to knowing he'd unofficially been assigned to keep tabs on her.

He felt pretty damn good a few minutes later as he left the meeting. But nearing his office, he heard laughter—Donaldson's deep rumble, followed by a soft female chuckle. Arriving at the door, he saw Donaldson with his feet on the desk and his head thrown back in mirth. Pizza Girl sat in the other chair, her knees pulled up to her chest and her arms wrapped around her shins.

God, she was beautiful when she smiled. And Jake wasn't the only one who noticed. Golden Boy looked at the dark-haired spitfire, and Jake saw the man take it all in: the way Macy's lips twisted in amusement, the way her dark hair framed her face just right, the way her blue eyes crackled with fiery intelligence. Without warning, he felt the bite of an ugly and all-too-familiar emotion—jealousy. His mind summoned the image of the wedding photo on his mother's mantel. In it, his brother stood decked out in a tux, his arm around his bride. Lisa, Jake's ex-fiancée, dressed in a white gown, gazed lovingly at him. The hurt hadn't gone completely away.

More feminine laughter brought him back to the present. He stared at Donaldson, whose gaze was riveted on Macy. "Something funny?"

Donaldson and Macy turned at the same time.

Moving in, Jake sat on the edge of his desk and gave the other detective's shoes a nudge. They hit the ground with a thunk. "Has this bozo offered you something to drink?"

Macy picked up a can of juice. "He's been very accommodating. Thank you." But the smile she'd worn minutes earlier had faded.

Damn, if he didn't feel cheated. Okay, so they hadn't gotten off to the best start this morning, but considering she was the first woman to spike his interest in two years, he had to try to salvage things. "Can I get you something else?"

"A pass to leave."

Jake shrugged in apology. "Right after the FBI talks to you."

Annoyance filled her eyes. "Fine, let's get it over with."

She shot up from the chair. Her sweater gapped and gave him a peek of her smooth midriff. Jake's mouth went dry. All he could think about was running his hand across that naked skin, letting his touch move up—The vision of her blue bra flashed in his head.

He met her less-than-pleasant expression with a smile. Okay, convincing her wasn't going to be easy, but he'd never minded a challenge. He put some calm into his voice and said, "Agent James is taking some calls, and—"

"I don't have all day." One eyebrow shot up.

Jake countered with his own, and put a touch of sweetness in his tone. "Won't be long."

"Why don't I take her to lunch?" Donaldson offered.

Macy smiled. "That would be—"

"Not a good idea," Jake interrupted.

Macy sat back down and crossed her legs. For about the hundredth time since she'd walked out of the bathroom this morning, Jake admired the way her soft denim pants fit. That pizza uniform hid a lot of secrets. Curves. Dips. Interesting places a man ached to explore. Her foot rocked back and forth. Her pink-painted toenails peeked out from the leather straps of white sandals. Even her toes were sexy.

"How long?" she asked, drawing Jake's attention. Their eyes met and held. He felt it again—the soul-deep attraction, the sizzle of anticipation.

"An hour at the most. Maybe you'd like me to grab you a snack from the lunchroom."

"No. But I do need to run to the store."

"For what?" he asked.

She nibbled at her lower lip. "Aspirin. Gotta headache."

"I've got some." He rolled Donaldson, chair and all, aside—farther from Macy—and pulled out his desk drawer. Taking the bottle, he leaned across the desk and dropped it in her hands.

Donaldson stood up. "I'll get you some water."

Jake shot the detective a glare. "She's got juice."

Macy stared at the aspirin. After a moment she said, "I prefer my own brand."

"I could run to the store for you." Donaldson pulled a set of keys from his pocket. "I needed to run an errand, anyway. What kind—"

"I'll do it," Jake insisted, irritated by Donaldson's play at Macy. And that's exactly what the boy was doing.

He focused on the other detective. Suddenly the Golden Boy looked more like competition and less like a kid. He fired Donaldson the age-old "back off" glare. Hell, he'd been the one to get kneed in the balls by the woman. He had dibs.

Donaldson obviously recognized the look. "Well, I'll go . . . catch up on something."

Jake watched him leave, then faced Macy. "Now, what kind of headache medicine do you need? You name it, and I'll get it."

"I'd rather buy it myself."

"Agent James specifically asked to have you wait here. But I can make a quick run." He was putting his best foot forward. Heck, he was a preacher's son. He knew all about being nice. Sunday manners and polite behavior had been instilled in him before potty training.

Her eyes got that particular gleam that meant she didn't want nice. She didn't want Sunday manners or politeness. She wanted a fight.

He crossed his arms over his chest. "Are you purposely trying to be difficult?"

She didn't deny it. She didn't say anything.

"Just tell me what you need," he pressed.

"You can't hold me here against my will," she snipped.

He shook his head. "I'm not—Don't be stubborn. Tell me what you need, and I'll get it."

She tilted her head back, and along with what he'd swear was a flash of defiance in her eyes, she smiled. "Fine."

Relief swept him. "Now, was that so hard?"

"Not at all."

Something in her tone warned him, much too late.

"I need tampons," she stated—loud enough for anyone passing by to hear. "The kind with the plastic applicator. They come in a pink box. You'll find them in the aisle of the grocery store that men avoid, beside the yeast-infection medications and feminine-deodorant products. Oh, and don't get the cardboard-applicator kind. They're not nearly as comfortable. Women already feel bloated this time of the month. We don't like to feel uncomfortable, too."

He opened his mouth to speak, but freaking hell, what could he say?

"And make sure you get the pack that has a variety of absorbency. For slow days, medium days, and heavy days. And, oh yeah, pick me up some panty liners while you're at it. You know this time of the month can be a little messy. I like the kind of liners that have those wings."

Macy wished she had a camera. The look on Sergeant Baldwin's face was priceless. But she wasn't finished. She yanked open her purse, pulled out her wallet, and handed him a ten spot.

"This should cover it. But wait. I have a coupon." She shuffled through several, then dropped the tampon coupon in his hand. In her experience, men hated using coupons almost as much as discussing feminine protection. Oh, and buying it.

She plopped back into her chair and smiled. "I'll just wait right here."

She pretended to be surprised when he caught her by the elbow and practically dragged her out of the chair. As they passed the front desk, he spoke to the female attendant. "If Agent James asks, tell him we'll be right back."

Macy grinned all the way to the store. Eyeing Jake as she moved down the feminine-protection aisle, she couldn't remember the last time she'd had so much fun. He hadn't said one word the whole trip. Not one.

Then, somewhere between enjoying his silent comeuppance and paying for her items, the warm fuzzy feeling that teasing Baldwin seemed to bring out in her faded. She returned to reality. Her baby brother's life was on the line. Somehow she had to figure out how to help Billy, how to get him safely back in jail before he ended up dead. Pleasurable or not, verbally sparring with Jake Baldwin wasn't going to do that. She had to get the FBI interrogation over and get back to her life.

It took longer than she would have wished. It was almost two before Sergeant Baldwin drove her home. The interview with Agent James had been a nail-biting experience. He'd asked her the same four or five questions in about a dozen different ways—trying to catch her in a lie, no doubt. She'd managed to keep her head and answer each question without telling him to go climb up an elephant's butt. Oddly, the only man she couldn't seem to control her tongue with today was the one sitting next to her. Cutting him a quick glance, she decided to blame everything on PMS.

As the interview was coming to a close, Baldwin had come inside the room and handed both Macy and the federal agent coffee. For some reason, Agent James seemed to respect him. Of course, Macy recalled how Baldwin had dealt with her ex, how even after her being difficult, he'd been nice—and protective. That had garnered some respect from her as well, in spite of the other emotions he evoked. The realization caused a little hiccup in her chest. Maybe because she'd never met a man she could respect other than Father Luis, and the priest didn't count.

"I know that wasn't easy for you," Baldwin said as he pulled into her drive. His silence had ended right after they got back from buying the tampons. A part of her felt guilty for teasing him.

"I'll be okay."

She would be. Jake Baldwin had offered her a helping—if exasperating—hand for the last eighteen hours, but it was time for her to stand on her own. Besides, even Jake's partner seemed to believe Tanks was halfway to Mexico by now. The car had hardly stopped when she jumped out. Feet on her driveway, she dipped down to look at him. "Thanks for . . . everything."

He looked over at her as if he didn't want to leave. "There's going to be a cop driving by here every few hours. You've got my number." He pointed to her purse, where he'd put his card. "If you need anything, call me."

"I won't need anything," she said, holding fast to the belief that Tanks was long gone.

He took a deep breath. "I want to help, Macy."

"You did." *But all things must come to an end. And this is it. Sayonara. Adios.*

The seriousness in his eyes changed to a teasing twinkle. "I want to do *more*. But if you start spouting off again about feminine protection, I'm out of here."

She smiled. Their gaze met, held for one second. She really did respect him.

Two seconds. She could really like this guy. She already liked him.

Three seconds. Crappers. This wasn't just PMS.

She couldn't look away. His smile tugged her emotions tangled them tightly around her heart.

Enough! She didn't need to start counting on a man to make her feel better. Hadn't everyone in her life proven that?

Heaven help her, the cliff loomed way too close. Jake didn't loom quite close enough.

"Let's have dinner tonight," he suggested. "Somewhere nice. I could—"

"Nope." She slammed the car door and stepped back, expecting him to drive off. Instead, he cut the engine, got out, and started around the car toward her.

"You're not getting rid of me that easy."

She took a backward step and held up her hand. "Yes, I am."

He kept coming at her, like a man who knew what he wanted and planned on getting it. The way his masculine form swaggered closer brought more emotions banging around her heart. Her lungs: she couldn't breathe. Her brain: she couldn't think. Nerve endings throughout her body responded to his smile.

She started walking backward around the car and, swallowing, forced herself to speak. "What are you doing? Um . . . if I gave the wrong impression, I'm sorry, but I'm not interested in any—"

"Liar."

He stopped when he was almost on top of her, and she had the craziest feeling he might actually try for a kiss. All sorts of mental voices were screaming *Run*, but part of her wanted this, craved it. *Needed* it.

"Seriously, I don't . . ."

He looked into her eyes, and she could have sworn he saw things she'd never intended another man to see. That she was a woman hungry for a man's touch. A woman aching to lean on someone. A . . .

A woman just like her dear ol' mom. "I mean, if you got the impression—"

He brushed a finger over her lips. "The impression I get is of a girl who's scared. One who can be very difficult to put up with. But I think you're worth it, and I think—" His attention shifted over her left shoulder and his face went stone cold. She tried to turn and see what had brought on the change, but he caught her by the arm.

"Get back in the car."

"What?"

He pulled out his gun. "Get back in the car. Don't argue."

He pushed her behind him, yanked his phone out of his front pocket, snapped it open, and hit a button. "This is Baldwin. I'm at 417 Jackson Street. I'm going to need backup."

CHAPTER SEVEN

"I think he's going to be fine. Aren't you, Mr. Klein?"

Hal nodded at the doctor and at his daughter standing beside his bed. In truth, he felt like roadkill opossum. Twenty-four hours out of surgery, and he still had tubes in places where no tube should go on a man. Not to mention the friggin' backless hospital gown. Every time he tried to get comfortable, he ended up mooning someone. At fifty-six years old, he felt certain no one cared to see his ass. That FBI hotshot, Agent James, who had ten minutes ago rushed out after getting some important summons, hadn't seemed too thrilled by seeing it. But between hurting like hell and the drugs, Hal didn't give a rat's ear.

The doc patted his leg. "I'll get you moved out of ICU."

"Thanks." Hal watched the man leave, then looked at his daughter. "Maybe you can pick me up some pajamas."

She smiled for the first time today. "You saw my bare bottom when I was little. It's only fair I get to see yours."

Hal arched his eyebrow, amused. "If your mom were alive, she'd call you on talking to me like you did."

Tears filled her eyes. "I was so scared. I'm not ready to be an orphan."

"Oh, fiddlesticks, girl. I'm too stubborn to die."

She leaned over and kissed his forehead. "Love you."

"You too, pumpkin." He patted her arm. "Now go home and take care of my grandbabies."

Melissa left, but Hal bet his bottom dollar she'd gone straight to the waiting room. Closing his eyes, he knew, stubborn or not, he'd come close to dying. The memory still floated in his head. He'd seen Judy, his wife, standing in the door of a bright corridor. "It's not over for you, ol' man," she said. She'd started calling him an old man when he'd turned fifty. A year later, she'd been the one who'd aged. Cancer did that to a person.

"Go back and live, Hal," she'd said. "And I mean *live*."

"I don't know how to live without you," he whispered. Four years had passed since her death, and he'd done nothing but think about his job.

His mind returned to the prison break as he fingered the bandage on his chest. He'd heard Billy Moore had run off. He'd told the Feds and the prison officials that he thought Billy ran because of Tanks's threats to hurt his sister. The kid had saved his life, which Hal had told the Feds, too. But it didn't mean shit. Billy Moore was in a whole heap of trouble. It would be nothing less than a miracle if they brought him in alive.

Morphine ran through Hal's veins, making him woozy. He sighed and bent his knee, and his catheter shifted. Hal scowled. From the corner of his eye, he saw someone walk by. "Nurse?" he yelled, with all the frustration of man with a tube up his pecker.

The woman stopped at the door. Hal yanked the sheet off him, accidentally bringing his gown with it. "I want this removed."

The woman's mouth dropped open.

"I mean the tube!" He tried to grab for the edge of the gown but couldn't find it without rising. And rising up hurt, damn it, so he simply lay there, his tubed pecker bared for the world to see.

The woman's face grew beet red. "I'm . . . just a volunteer.

Someone asked for some ice chips." She sniffled as if she was about to cry.

Although drugged, he wasn't blind. He'd embarrassed the socks off of her. If he weren't feeling fuzzy, he'd have laughed. Though that would have hurt like hell, too. Nevertheless, he hadn't seen a beautiful woman blush in a long time. He found it refreshing.

"I'm sorry." She pulled a tissue from her uniform pocket and patted her eyes.

A nurse appeared beside the volunteer. "Sorry, Faye. Looks as if Mr. Klein is feeling better."

Faye, still teary eyed, stepped back. "His . . . name is Klein?"

"Yeah," the nurse continued. "And when they start complaining"—her eyes moved to Hal, and she grinned—"and exposing themselves, it's time for them to leave ICU. And I've got the doctor's orders to do it." She looked at the volunteer. "Would you help me gather his things?"

The volunteer pressed a hand to her lips. "I shouldn't be here," she said. And with that, she ran off.

Jake looked over Macy's shoulder toward her front door. The words *Dead Bitch* were written across it in red.

Macy turned to see. "Is that . . . blood?"

He snagged her arm. "I said to get in the car."

"Elvis?" she breathed, and her eyes filled with fear.

Oh, she acted tough . . . but he had her figured out. She used her sharp tongue and wit to cover up a lot of pain and vulnerability. Someone had hurt Macy Tucker. Maybe several people. Jake recalled her ex-husband last night, and wished he'd followed the jerk outside and taught him a lesson.

"I'll check on your cat." He opened his car door and pushed her inside. "Get in and stay."

Sirens blared in the distance; there must have been a few units nearby. He heard them pulling onto the street behind him. Macy bounced back up and opened her mouth to argue. He didn't know why he did it, or even how he knew it would work, but he leaned in and touched his lips to hers. She dropped back in her seat, touched her mouth, then slammed the door closed.

It wasn't a kiss. Not by his standards. Hell, now wasn't the time to even think of kissing. Two minutes earlier he'd wanted to pull her against him and lose himself in her mouth, to run his tongue between her lips, to taste, to savor, to move past the barriers she'd seemed to build around herself. But not now. Not now, dammit.

He shot her a warning glance to stay put. The glare she returned said he'd pay for the half kiss, but if it kept her in the car until he knew it was safe, until he found out how bad things were inside, then he'd willingly pay that price.

He refocused on the door. It did look like blood. He wasn't exactly fond of Elvis, but for Macy's sake he hoped like hell it wasn't the cat's.

Billy and Ellie had spent the last hour cuddled on the sofa, talking. Earlier, she'd gotten some crackers and cheese she had in the van. They'd eaten. Now, as much as Billy hated doing it, he knew it was time to go. He picked up the keys to her van from the coffee table.

"Why can't I go?" Ellie asked, watching. "Maybe he'll listen to me."

"I don't want you near him." He'd lied, telling Ellie he was going to find Tanks and warn him to stay away from her and his sister.

"But what if he hurts you? He's not like you. He's mean."

Her lashes were webbed with tears. Those watery eyes reminded Billy of his mom. He bet she was crying right now.

"I can be mean if I have to." And he had to.

"I'm scared." She buried her face in his shoulder.

"Me, too," he admitted. His chest swelled with an ache he'd never known. He loved Ellie. Really loved her. For the last few months, she had been his link to sanity. Her letters and her visits kept him from falling into some deep place in his mind.

"It's gonna be okay." He whispered the lie into her soft blonde hair. He knew it wouldn't be okay. This morning, as he'd watched Ellie cleaning up Andy's trailer, he'd forced himself to see things clearly. Even if everything happened the way he planned, if he got to Tanks and made sure that scum wouldn't ever be able to touch Ellie or Mace, even then things wouldn't be okay. The cops were looking for him. They wouldn't hesitate to shoot. And if he took Ellie with him . . .

When he'd first planned on Ellie's helping him, he hadn't thought about what it would do to her. How many times had Mace told him he didn't think things through? There had been a second when he'd considered taking Ellie and running to Mexico. But he couldn't let Tanks do something to Mace. And what kind of life could he offer Ellie? Always running, always afraid.

Turning himself in was the right thing, and he wouldn't lie about killing Tanks either. Not that it much mattered. He was probably already going to be accused of killing Brandon. And maybe he had.

"I love you," Ellie said in that squeaky voice of hers.

"I know," Billy answered, but he didn't say he loved her back. Because somehow, when this was finished, he had to convince Ellie to stop loving him. Before, when he'd thought about her waiting on him for two and a half more years, he hadn't felt so bad. Now he would be in prison for a long time. Ellie didn't deserve to spend her life loving a jailbird.

He'd almost told Ellie to leave that morning. Maybe it was selfishness, but he hadn't been strong enough to do it. Until he got Tanks, he wanted her here. When it was over, he'd find a way to make her forget about him.

"I gotta go. I'll be back as soon as I can." He pulled away. "You got that cop's number?" After trying to decide how to make sure Mace was okay without getting caught, he'd decided to trust Ellie's instinct about Jake Baldwin. Billy would tell him about Tanks threatening his sister. Hopefully, the cop would watch out for Mace.

"Yeah. He called me." She grabbed her cell phone from her purse, found the number, and wrote it down.

Billy touched her cheek. "Remember, whatever happens, you say I forced you to help me. And don't use your cell phone; they might trace it."

"I'm not going to lie." That beautiful mouth of hers pouted. "I love you and I don't care who knows."

Frustration swelled in his chest. "If they know you helped me willingly, you could go to jail."

"But you escaped because you were scared David would do something to me and your sister. If you tell them the truth, they'll understand."

Ellie might believe that, but he knew better. Sometimes even doing the right thing came with a price.

"I've got to go."

Jake had his badge out when the four officers appeared at his side.

"One of you stay here and watch her," Jake ordered. "You two cover the back door." He pointed to two officers. "We'll go in the front," he said to the last. "I haven't seen any signs that anyone is still there, but if it's who I think it is, and he's in there, he plays hardball."

Jake heard his car door open. He pointed a finger at Macy, who was emerging. "Don't!"

Her gaze spat blue sparks, but she lowered her butt back into the seat.

"Watch her," he reminded the officer he'd left in charge of Macy. "If you have to, handcuff her to my steering wheel."

"I got her," the officer said.

Jake started toward the door. The other two patrol cops headed for the back, their Glocks held ready.

As he approached, Jake eyed the words *Dead Bitch* and caught a whiff of paint. His gut relaxed. The fear of finding Macy's cat lying in a puddle of blood lessened. But the smell of the paint jarred a sense of déjà vu.

"Houston police. Drop your weapons!" He pushed the

slightly open door with his foot. He and his backup barged inside.

The words *Wanna Fuck?* were sprayed on the wall. Gritting his teeth, gun held high, Jake cut the corner into the living room.

His gaze shifted left, then right. More obscenities. Glass from the shattered back window covered the brown carpet. He heard the officer behind him. A thump sounded to his right.

Adrenaline shot through his veins. He swung around, finger on the trigger of his pistol. Elvis! His breath caught. The feline crouched down, gold eyes bright, tail twitching. Jake remembered in the nick of time and ducked. Elvis flew into the air.

Gun clutched firm, Jake motioned the officer behind him to move into the kitchen. He himself followed the cat down the hall.

He passed the bathroom, where Elvis had disappeared. He passed the computer room. More obscenities plastered the hallway walls. The smell of spray paint filled his nose. Scowling, he poised his foot to nudge open the bedroom door, when he heard a sound. It wasn't a thump. It was an aerosol hiss. He pushed back against the hall wall, listened to get an idea of the location of the intruder, then barged inside.

CHAPTER EIGHT

Macy sat tapping her sandals against the car floorboard. She closed her eyes and in her mind saw her front door blazing with the message DEAD BITCH. It looked like blood. Had Tanks broken into her house and hurt Elvis? Fear backed with fury knotted her stomach. What kind of a person would hurt a helpless animal? The kind who would cut people's heads off, of course. The man who wanted to hurt Billy . . . whom Billy had run off with? None of this made sense.

Not a fan of being ordered to stay put—damn that Baldwin—she clutched her hands in her lap and gazed at the uniformed officer who stood outside the car. His gun held high, his gaze flickered from the house to her. Macy looked away.

That's when she saw it—the ten-speed bike parked on the other side of the porch.

"Nan!" Macy bolted out of the car. The armed officer followed inches behind.

Jake's finger tapped the trigger of his gun, but stopped the moment he saw his elderly suspect. The woman swung around, paint still spewing, and sprayed him across the chest.

"Police," he said.

The old woman stared at him.

Her thick gray hair held in a ponytail, she wore an orange T-shirt that read BIKER CHIC. Jake looked at the wall where the half the *F* of *FUCK* was sprayed over. He didn't lower his gun. She didn't lower the paint can. But at least she'd stopped spraying him.

Jake had been in a several standoffs, but never like this. "What are you doing?"

"I don't want my granddaughter to see this."

"Granddaughter?" He lowered his gun and stared at the red stripe across his chest.

"Nan!" Macy's scream filled the house.

"In here," the woman answered. "Don't read the walls."

Macy, handcuffs dangling from one wrist, flew past Jake and wrapped her arms around the old woman. "I thought . . ."

The officer from the kitchen ran into the bedroom. "I nearly shot her!" he said.

"I'm still considering shooting her," remarked the officer he'd left at the car. The young man's pained expression and fisted hand on his upper thigh told the rest of the story. She really had to watch where she threw her knee.

Not that Jake doubted that she'd been aiming for any place but where the knee had landed.

An hour later, Macy sat on her sofa with Nan. "Don't tell Mom about this," Macy said. She snatched a pillow and hugged it. "Where is she?"

Nan frowned. "She wanted to stay home and cry today, but I talked her into going to the hospital. She can cry there just as good as she can cry at home." When Macy slumped against the sofa, Nan patted her leg. "Your mom's gonna be fine. She just needs to cry it out."

"Duh? She's been crying for over a decade."

"Yeah. I figure she should be stopping any day now."

Pillow still hugged close, Macy watched the cops skitter around like roaches. They were everywhere, different cops in different uniforms, and some in plain clothes. Every few minutes, one of the roaches—the one with a red stripe across his shirt—would wink at her. Why was he doing that? And why had he kissed her? Just what sort of idea had she given him?

Mark Donaldson plopped down beside her on the couch. He introduced himself to Nan, then focused on Macy. "You okay?"

"Dandy." She tried to smile. Mark seemed like a nice guy, and for some reason she found him harmless. At least, he was harmless compared to how Sergeant Baldwin made her feel.

She raised her right hand and the handcuffs danced in the air. "Got a hacksaw?"

Donaldson chuckled. "They're thinking about having your knee declared a lethal weapon and making you register it."

Grimacing, Macy stared at the painted words on the wall: *Fuck* and *Die*. Fear played a slow tune on her heart.

As Baldwin appeared, fear vanished. Or really it just changed tempo. She'd already admitted that this man scared her.

Jake nudged Donaldson aside—not physically, but with a look. The blond cop moved to a chair, and Jake lowered his six-feet-plus frame next to Macy. His jean-covered thigh pressed warm against hers. She scooted closer to Nan.

"Give me your hand," he said.

"Why?"

He dangled a key in front of her. "I talked Thompson into forgiving you."

"He's a wuss. I didn't hit him half as hard as I hit you."

"Hold your tongue," Nan commanded. "And give him your arm." Her gaze went to Baldwin. "She gets mouthy when she's scared."

"I figured that out." Baldwin winked at Nan. His smile oozed charm, and Nan responded with a grin of her own.

Great. Now the man was flirting with her grandma.

Nan leaned in. "The ball busting might be my fault. I taught her to do it."

"You taught her well." A smile filled Baldwin's blue eyes. He removed the cuffs, then gently rubbed Macy's wrist.

She jerked away and glanced at the clock. "How much longer will this take?"

Jake glanced around. "I think they're almost done. I've never seen CSI move so quick."

Donaldson sat forward. "That's because of the FBI."

Macy looked back at Jake. "I've got to leave in an hour."

"Where to?" Baldwin's brow wrinkled.

Macy scowled. "I have to clear my schedule with you?"

"Since an escaped convict is trying to kill you," he said in tense voice, "yeah."

The front door swung open, and two men wearing suits crossed the threshold as if they owned the joint. Macy recognized one of them. "What, my doorbell isn't working?" she asked.

"Behave," Baldwin snapped.

Agent James's gaze moved from wall to wall before focusing on Baldwin. The look in the FBI agent's eyes predicted bad news. "Can I have a word with you?" he asked.

Baldwin rose from the sofa. Macy popped up beside him. Nan shot up, too.

Macy and Nan asked in unison, "Is Billy okay?"

Hal had just settled into his new room and got the damn tube out of his pecker when the urge to pee hit. He almost called the nurse, but hated feeling useless. Pulling himself up, he managed to get his legs to the side of the bed. He inched off the mattress, tested his footing, and found himself shaky but mobile. One hand on the bed, he reached for his IV pole.

Cold air breezed over his bare ass. The door squeaked open, followed by a soft yelp. He'd just mooned himself another victim.

"Goddamn it." He looked over his shoulder. The same volunteer from the ICU stood in his doorway, her blue eyes zeroed in on his behind. His knees weakened. "Could you give me a hand? Before I fall on my ass?" he grunted.

She rushed forward and wrapped her arm around his waist. His naked waist. She nudged him toward the bed.

"I'm not getting in," he growled. "I'm getting out."

She sniffled. He glanced up. The woman had tears in her eyes. *Again.*

"I know my ass isn't pretty, but I didn't think it could bring a woman to tears."

She blinked. "You need to get in bed."

"I *need* to go to the bathroom."

"I'll get you the bedpan," she said in a hiccupping voice.

"I'm not using a damn bedpan. Help me to the john."

"I'm not a nurse," she argued.

"It's not surgery," he countered. "I just want to take a piss."

She sniffled but moved toward the bathroom. "You shouldn't be so stubborn."

"I'm sorry," he seethed. "But getting shot by a damn jail-bird put me in a piss-poor mood." Hearing her take a sharp breath, he studied her face again. "Do I know you?"

She opened the bathroom door. "Can you manage from here?" Her voice trembled.

He continued to study her nice, familiar face. Right then he became aware that he held her waist, aware that her arm pressed sweetly around his hip. His naked hip. It had been a long time since he'd touched or been touched by a woman, and damn if a tightness didn't stir low in his belly. He almost jerked away, but he knew he'd land flat on his face, bare ass up. So he grabbed the doorjamb. "I'm fine."

He shut the door and rolled his IV pole to the toilet. Too weak to do his business like a man, he sat down. Down was easy. Getting up would be hell. He heard a door squeaking as if she'd fled. Great. He was stuck on the pisser until someone came in. Or until he got desperate enough to ring the dang buzzer.

A nurse poked her nose in the door. "You should have called someone," she chided.

"I had someone, but she ran off."

I'd like her back, too. The thought came out of nowhere, but it was true. He wanted to see that woman again, to figure out if he knew her. To figure out why her touch had stirred things he'd thought were all through stirring.

The corners of the nurse's lips tightened. "You're going to be a troublemaker, aren't you?"

He thought about it. "Probably."

"Baldwin?" Agent James nodded toward the front door and motioned.

Macy's grandma grabbed the Fed by the arm. "Is Billy okay?"

"As far as we know," the man replied.

Jake gently pulled the old woman off him. "I'll be right back." He sent Macy a look that he hoped promised he'd explain.

He followed Agent James outside. "What's up?"

The agent stared at the painted door. "This guy needs to be caught."

"Tell me something I don't know," Jake replied. "You guys taking over the scene?"

James waved away an insect. "Let's just say we'll be looking over Harris County's shoulder." He leaned back on his heels. "You said that when Ellie Chandler came to see you, she appeared afraid of Tanks?"

"Yes."

"And you believed her?" he asked.

Jake considered the question. "Didn't you hear the message she left on Macy's recorder?"

James handed the tape back. "We made copies." He paused. "You think Miss Chandler was telling the truth."

"Yeah, I do." Jake paused. "Why?"

"We spoke to Hal Klein, the prison guard."

"He's awake? He gonna make it?" Jake asked.

"Looks like. You were right about Moore. Klein says Moore and Tanks didn't run off together. Moore stopped Tanks from shooting the guard a second time. They fought. The gun went off during the scuffle. That's how the other inmate took a bullet."

"So that's why Billy ran. He got scared."

"According to Klein, Tanks threatened Moore's sister. Klein thinks Moore left to protect her."

"I believe that." Jake had been hit with the overwhelming desire to protect her, too.

Skepticism etched the agent's face. "Or maybe he just decided to take advantage of the opportunity. He hasn't contacted her yet, has he?"

"No." Jake studied the paint-chipped house. "My gut says this kid isn't bad. I read his sheets. Nothing really serious until the convenience store, and he swore up and down he didn't know they were robbing the place."

"Don't you think every driver of every getaway car says the same thing?" Agent James asked.

"Maybe, but perhaps this one is telling the truth." Jake brushed a fly away. "Why the questions on Ellie Chandler?"

"She cleaned out her checking account and hasn't shown up at work in two days."

Jake crossed his arms over his chest. "I assume she's with Billy. He probably contacted her after—"

"We assumed that, too. But we checked the recent calls Tanks made from prison. Her number showed up six times last week. According to the guard, the getaway car was a gold Cavalier. The same make and description as Chandler's."

That information bounced around Jake's head. "That doesn't make sense."

Another fly buzzed past the agent's face. "Neither does the fact that the boots we found at her place are a match for the prints found in the flowerbed where the gun was buried."

"She helped with the breakout?" Jake was shocked.

"Looks like it," James said. "Sure as hell looks like it."

Jake recalled his visit with Ellie. He had her pegged as a ditz, but he didn't think she would have done this. "It doesn't fit."

"It seldom does." The agent shifted in place.

The words *Dead Bitch* caught Jake's eye. His gut clenched. "You're going to have someone on her, right?"

"If we knew where Chandler was—"

"Not Ellie. Macy Tucker."

The agent frowned. "We don't have the manpower to put someone on her full-time. I thought you said you were going to watch her. You and your department can—"

"I can't be here all the time. And he's after her. And having a car ride by isn't—"

"He *was* after her. He has to know that the law will be on to him after this. If he's got half a brain he'll be trying to get out the state. I've got most of my men at the borders now."

"The guy's meaner than he is smart," Jake said.

Agent James swatted at another bug. "We'll do what we can. But our first priority is catching Tanks, not protecting

Miss Tucker. If you can keep watching her, I'd do so. But I don't think this guy is stupid enough to hang around."

"That's what everyone thought this morning, too."

"Then make her your personal project. I can only do so much."

CHAPTER NINE

Macy stepped into the shower. She felt even more vulnerable when she reread the vulgar graffiti on the wall. Frantically scrubbing a washcloth over it, she felt panic drum through her ears. Soap and water wouldn't fix this. But while fear crawled like fuzzy spiders along her spine, she knew that if she let herself be consumed by it she was letting that bastard win. Better to just get mad. He wasn't going to win!

Adjusting the water temperature, she stood under the hot spray and willed herself to relax—willed herself to believe Billy was still okay. Was he with Ellie? What if Agent James was right? What if Ellie had helped with the escape?

"That doesn't make sense," she'd told Baldwin.

"I know," he'd said, and then launched into a dozen reasons why she shouldn't go to work. She'd just as quickly launched into a dozen reasons why she should.

"Are you always this stubborn?" he'd snapped.

"No. It gets worse on weekends."

He'd looked as though he didn't have a clue how to deal with her. Admittedly, she didn't have a clue how to deal with him. She was also completely at a loss as to why Baldwin cared. She'd been shocked that he'd told her what he and Agent James had spoken about. When had the cop decided to trust her?

Not that she was complaining, but—Okay, she was complaining. She didn't want to like this man, and she already did. If he started trusting her, she was a tiny baby step away from trusting him in return. Really trusting him. And trusting someone led to depending on them. She'd learned the hard the way that depending on men could land you in a world of hurt. Look at her mom.

Fifteen minutes later, freshly showered and determined to avoid harm from murderers and hunky cops alike, she stepped into the living room wearing her Papa's Pizza polyester. Baldwin stood up from her recliner.

"You're really going to do it?"

"If by 'do it' you mean rob a bank, no, I've reconsidered. I found out I don't deal with cops very well."

He frowned.

She frowned back. "I've got to go to work."

"Take the night off." He spoke between gritted teeth.

"And what about tomorrow, or the next night? What if you don't catch him this month?" She imagined getting axed by Mr. Prack, unable to pay her bills, crying her eyes out and living with Nan. She was her mother's daughter after all, so an unending tearfest wasn't farfetched. "I'll be fine. Besides, I heard that FBI guy tell someone he bet Tanks has already left the state."

"What if he's wrong? Have you read the messages Tanks left you? That isn't love poetry."

"They're just words," Macy said. Fake courage was better than no courage at all. "I appreciate this"—she waved to the plywood he'd nailed over her broken window—"and you staying last night. Which, for the record, I never asked you to do."

He pinched the bridge of his nose between his thumb and forefinger. "CSI needs to run one more check for fingerprints. I told them someone would be here."

"Well, this someone has to go to work. Make yourself at home." She pointed toward the kitchen. "There's beer in the fridge." She pointed back to the entryway. "Please, lock the door when you leave. 'Bye."

She was almost out the door when she heard him talking.

"She's leaving." His voice held buckets of frustration. "Make sure you do."

Macy two-stepped it back into her living room. Hit again by how darn gorgeous Sergeant Baldwin was, she had to fight to remember why she'd stomped back. "Make sure who does what?"

He snapped his phone shut. "The FBI is following you."

She started stuffing her hair under her hat. "They're not following me because of Tanks, though, are they? They think I know where Billy is."

Baldwin shrugged. "Doesn't matter. Are you stupid enough not to want the help? Are you too dumb to be scared?"

I'm scared, she admitted to herself, *but I'm not going to let that freak win.* "If I don't go to work, I'll lose my job," she reminded him. And it was true. Mr. Prack would do cartwheels at the chance to fire her. That wasn't going to happen. "Besides, everyone but you seems to think he's long gone."

Billy waited outside the empty house for three hours, watching the shadows deepen and waiting for Tanks to show up. Where was he? Had Brandon lied about the address?

Exhaling a puff of stale air, Billy ran his tongue along the inside of his lip. The taste of blood lingered. Mace was right. He needed to stop biting himself. Gripping his fist, he swore he'd stop. He wasn't going to continue to do stupid things.

The walls of the van seemed to close in on him. He slipped out of the vehicle and ducked into the shadows lining the house. If he could just get inside, maybe he'd find a clue that would tell him where Tanks was. The sound of his footfalls echoed in the empty street.

The golden glow of the sun had faded to gray. With his back against the house, he reached under his shirt and wrapped his hand around his gun. Fear fogged his mind as he peeked into the window. He'd checked earlier to see if anyone was home, but better safe than sorry. Better safe than dead. Tanks wouldn't think twice about killing him. Billy only hoped to kill the bastard first.

Cheek pressed against the cool glass window pane, he studied the kitchen's peeling linoleum floors and scarred pine table. When he saw no one, heard only the hum of the refrigerator, he tried to lift the window. The heavy frame wouldn't budge.

He moved to the door and grasped the knob. It twisted. He pushed it open, the hinges squeaking. Dead still, he waited and listened. Time seemed suspended. The hum of the fridge grew louder. A drip of sweat rolled down his forehead. Did he have what it took to kill Tanks?

He moved through the kitchen into the living room. The whole place smelled like dirty socks, as if only men lived here. Women always made things smell good. Ellie smelled good. It was hard to keep his mind off her.

Just enough gray-dusk light came in through the window so he could see. A pizza box lay on the coffee table. The idea that Macy delivered pizza to people like Tanks made his gut twist. He thought again about calling that Baldwin cop. And he needed to call Ellie, too.

Beside the pizza box lay a book of matches with the silhouette of a naked woman. GIRLS GALORE was printed across the front. A titty bar. He and one of his friends had sneaked into one once with fake IDs.

On the end table lay a pad with a number scratched across it. Billy picked up the phone and dialed.

"Girls Galore," someone answered.

Billy hung up.

Girls Galore. Was Tanks there? Billy took a step toward the door, but the unnatural silence beckoned him to stop. He walked down the hall. The first bedroom held only a bed and a pile of dirty clothes. He made his way to the second bedroom. Pitch darkness swelled inside.

Using the barrel of the gun, he hit the light switch. "Fuck!" He jumped back but didn't look away. He couldn't. Bile rose in his throat. A man lay faceup on the floor, eyes open. They were empty eyes. The man's throat was slashed, and blood, a lot of blood, soaked the beige carpet. Its coppery smell filled Billy's nose.

Gagging, Billy ran back to the living room and threw up on the carpet. When he stopped puking, he saw the phone book lying open on the sofa. He blinked and stared at the number underlined in red. *Papa's Pizza.*

"You got it bad for her, don't you?" Donaldson asked.

"Just hold the glass." Kneeling in Macy's living room, Jake removed a piece of the broken glass. CSI had called and said they'd gotten several good prints and wouldn't need to come back. They hadn't gotten the results yet. Not that Jake needed proof who'd done this.

Unlike Agent James and the Gulf Coast Task Force, Jake wasn't sure Tanks would be satisfied with spray painting Macy's walls. Not when his intent had obviously been to do more. He wasn't the sort to give up. Jake recalled why he'd put the man away in the first place.

"You can pay people to fix windows, you know," Donaldson said.

"What? You don't like getting dirty?"

Donaldson shot him a go-to-hell look. "She doesn't know you're doing this, does she?"

Jake squirted the glazing compound into the window seal. "Just helping her out." The task force wasn't going to take it upon themselves to watch Macy full-time, so she was stuck with him. He didn't mind one iota. The problem was, Macy didn't share the sentiment.

Donaldson watched him. "Where did you learn to do this?" he asked.

"Habitat for Humanity."

"You worked for them?" Donaldson asked.

"I volunteered." Sons of Baptist preachers always volunteered. And wasn't that what he was doing now, being a Good Samaritan and fixing Macy's window? Without her permission?

Oh, hell, Donaldson was right. He had it bad. Then again, she had said for him to make himself at home. At home, if something was broken, he'd—

"Did you ever meet President Carter?" Donaldson asked.

"We have lunch once a month," Jake retorted.

"He's a friend of my dad's, too."

Jake glanced up. "I was being sarcastic."

"Oh." Silence fell while he worked. "I'm surprised you aren't following her."

"When Agent James found out she was going to work, he decided it might be worth his while to have her tailed in case her brother tried to contact her." If Jake thought Macy wouldn't have fought him, he would have insisted on being the one watching her.

"Is that who you've called? Twice?"

Yeah, he'd called the Fed. He was just making sure the guy was doing his job.

"Okay, I'm interested in her," he admitted to Donaldson. "Does it matter?" He moved away from the window pane. "Unless you'd like to hit on her yourself."

"Hey. I backed off when I got the look," Donaldson replied.

Jake finished securing the window. Satisfied that the other detective was really backing off, that Macy would be okay, and that his handiwork was sufficient, he folded his arms over his chest. Would this get him brownie points with Macy, or would she accuse him of overstepping his boundaries? Brownie points would be nice. He knew exactly how he'd spend them.

"What now?" Donaldson asked.

"You know how to use a brush?" Jake picked up a can of Kilz.

"You're joking. You want us to paint her house, too?"

"Not paint it all, just cover the graffiti with some primer. Why, you scared of a little manual labor, Golden Boy?"

Donaldson reached for the can. "I'll help, but only because you brought me breakfast," he grumbled.

"I guess now wouldn't be the time to tell you that I actually bought it for Macy."

Both men laughed, then they positioned several plastic drop cloths and started splashing primer on the walls.

Dipping his brush into the can for the fifth time, Jake looked at the other man. "You must really be bored."

"Why? Because I'm helping your sorry ass get lucky instead of trying to get lucky myself?"

"Yeah." Jake grinned. "What's with that?"

"I've only been here a month. I haven't met anyone yet." Donaldson dropped his brush and picked up one of the beers they'd raided from the fridge.

"Don't tell me you're shy."

"Just picky."

An hour later, they had the graffiti covered. Jake grabbed them each another beer. He'd have to refill Macy's fridge, he realized, but he'd been planning to do that anyway. Dropping into a recliner, he faced Donaldson, who sat on the sofa. The memory of watching Macy sleep there filled his mind. Anticipation of seeing her tonight brought a stirring low in his belly.

Not wanting to start down that road, he shot Golden Boy another question. "What was it like growing up rich?"

Donaldson raised an eyebrow. "Fantastic." He didn't offer any other comment.

"So even the rich and famous have ugly childhoods."

Donaldson cut him a sharp look. "Why would you say that?"

"If rumors are true, you've got more money than God and an education to match. I figure your becoming a cop was a way of throwing all that fancy schooling back in your parents' faces."

The tightness in Donaldson's eyes told Jake he'd tapped a nerve. "What? Are you trying to save my soul and stop me from disrespecting my parents, preacher's boy? Guess I've heard a few rumors, too, huh?"

Jake leaned back in the recliner. "That's fair. Who told you my dad was a preacher?"

"It's common knowledge. Rumor is you never go to church, but you still pray before you pull your weapon."

"Doesn't everyone?" Jake palmed his beer.

Donaldson eyed the bottle in his own hands. "We should." After a moment, he looked at the clock. "What time is she due home?"

"Midnight."

"And you're going to be here?"

Jake grinned. "You think I did this for nothing?"

"You believe you'll get lucky because you played handyman?"

"No. Just to second base."

Both men laughed. Macy didn't seem like the kind who jumped into bed with a man very fast. Jake wasn't above trying to change her mind, though.

He eyed the walls and decided he'd share his suspicion with Donaldson. "Remember those home-robbery cases that were tagged with red paint?"

The other cop's eyes widened. "You think this is connected?"

"I don't know. I mean, Tanks was in prison. And I know he did this, but . . ." He let his thoughts run around his brain. "Maybe whoever helped him was involved with those."

"Sounds like a long shot," Donaldson said.

Jake's cell phone rang. He said, "That's why I didn't mention it to the task force." Then he answered the call. "Hello?"

"Baldwin?" It was his buddy Stan, with Homicide. "You called. What's up?"

"I needed someone to give me a hand replacing a window. But I found someone else."

Stan snorted. "I'm glad I missed your call. Hey . . ." The man's tone changed. "Did you get with the Clear Lake detectives about that headless floater?"

"We talked," Jake admitted.

"Good. So where you at now? It's after work. Tell me you're out with a woman for a change."

Jake glanced at Donaldson, who picked up a book off Macy's end table. "Maybe soon." If he didn't get his ass kicked by said woman for trying to help her.

He explained to Stan about Macy's house being broken into and spray painted. He also mentioned the coincidence of the other robberies tagged with red paint.

"Is this the squeaky-voiced Monroe chick?" Stan asked.

"No. She's the sister to the one of the escapees."

"Ah. Well, good luck with that family."

Jake said good-bye and hung up, then told Donaldson, "Stan Anders, from Homicide."

Donaldson nodded and looked at the books on the table again. "Macy in school?"

"Yeah." Jake remembered her mentioning a test. It hit him suddenly how little he knew about her. Well, he planned to remedy that. In about three hours, when she came home.

"So she's studying to be a shyster." Donaldson held up a constitutional-law textbook.

Crap. *That* would explain her citizens' rights speech. Lawyers weren't his favorite people. Then Jake remembered her smile, her never-ending wit, her body, and how the whole package made him feel whole again. He supposed not all lawyers had to be bad.

Donaldson stood and glanced down at his paint-speckled jeans. "Well, I've reached my quota of manual labor for the day."

"Rich kids," Jake teased. He stood as well. "Thanks for everything."

"Anything to help a guy get lucky." Donaldson hesitated. "Actually, I enjoyed it." He started out the front door and then glanced back. "Tomorrow I want cheese on my biscuit."

Macy pulled up to the condo gate and punched in the apartment number of her final delivery. She'd already paid for the pizza out of her own money and turned in her bank so she wouldn't have go back to the restaurant. Since she'd gotten off a little early, she planned to swing by and visit Nan and her mom. If she couldn't stop thinking about Billy, she suspected her mom and Nan couldn't, either. While Macy wasn't eager to hear her mom cry, family stuck together—but only through two tissues.

"Pizza delivery," Macy said into the gate phone. A buzzer sounded and the gate opened. Macy pulled inside.

She drove to the second building and parked. She was out of her car before she remembered she was being followed. When she looked back to see if her tail had made it through, she saw he hadn't; the agent was standing by the iron gate. He yelled something in an angry voice.

Macy waved, smirking. "Guess FBI agents need to work on their tailing skills as well as their manners," she muttered, remembering his unkind comments about her driving when he'd accosted her between deliveries. She considered pulling back to let him in. But she'd be out in a snap.

Two minutes later she was back in her car with a five-dollar tip. She glanced around to see if her tail had made it into the complex, but it seemed he hadn't; the sedan was nowhere to be seen. Exiting the lot, she drove around the block to see if he'd waited. Nothing. So she headed towards Nan's. It wasn't her fault she'd lost the guy. Well, not *all* her fault. Besides, Tanks was probably halfway to Mexico right now. She just hoped Billy wasn't with him.

Jake had gone to his place to grab an overnight bag and a quick shower. Convincing Macy to let him stay would be tricky, but if he had everything already collected, she might be more inclined to give in. Though the idea of Macy giving in to anything seemed farfetched. For that reason, he'd also tucked a blanket and pillow in the backseat of his car.

Yep. He had it bad. And this wasn't about being a Good Samaritan. This was about a man wanting to protect a woman. And about getting her naked—provided she wanted him to, of course.

Returning to Macy's, he tossed the used drop cloths into the garage. They could use them again when he helped her paint over the primer. *If* she let him help. Even he had to admit his sudden possessiveness seemed too much, especially when he hadn't had any real interest in women since Lisa. He shook his head, determined not to do a Sunday drive down memory lane. Plain and simple, he liked Macy, wanted to see where that could lead. Now, what could be wrong with that? Not a damn thing.

He snatched new locks out of his bag. No, he hadn't forgotten about the key-toting ex-husband. And after making fast work of the installations, he went to the shower. Earlier he'd spotted the painted messages on the shower walls. Staring at them now, he couldn't believe Macy had bathed here.

He scrubbed off most of the paint. As he headed out of the bathroom, Macy's phone rang. The answering machine caught the call. He listened to her recorded message. "Hi, this is Macy . . ." She sure had a sexy voice.

"Macy. It's Father Luis. I hate to call you again, but I wanted to talk about you replacing Sister Beth. I know you're concerned about how it will fit into your life, but I know it would work. The church needs you, Macy. God needs you."

What? Jake remembered hearing the message last night. Was Macy . . . ? Was he lusting after a woman who was about to take vows? No! She was divorced. Then he recalled reading that the Catholic Church was desperate for new nuns and priests.

Dropping onto the sofa, he ran a hand through his hair. While he didn't like competition, he could handle the normal kind—but he hadn't planned on taking on the Catholic Church. Before he made any serious moves, he'd have to get to the bottom of this.

As he stood up, his cell phone rang. He snatched it from the table, and he couldn't keep the frustration of imagining Macy Tucker garbed in a nun's habit out of his voice. "Yeah?"

"Jake Baldwin?" the male voice asked.

"You got him. Who's this?"

"This is Billy Moore."

CHAPTER TEN

Jake gripped the cell phone tight. "Where are you, Billy?"

"I'm only going to talk for thirty seconds, so listen." The kid sounded scared.

"Tell me where you are, and we'll talk in person."

"I need a favor."

"Tell me in person." Jake searched for a pen and pencil.

"I need you to watch my sister Macy. David Tanks doesn't make idle threats. He—he's already killed someone else."

"Billy, your sister is worried. Let me—"

"He's capable of anything. Watch her. Don't let him get to her. And about Ellie . . . I made her do everything."

"Do what, Billy? What did you make her do?"

"Tanks knows where Mace works. He had her work number and address circled in a phone book. I drove there to make sure she was okay. I saw someone following her, like a cop or something, but . . . she went to a gated apartment to deliver a pizza, and the man following her couldn't get in. Then I think she left. I couldn't find her." There was the sound of a scared hiccup. "And Tanks knows where she works. Find Mace and make sure she's okay."

"Billy, look—"

"Find her. Do it now!"

"Is Tanks near Macy? Where are you?" Jake demanded. The line clicked. He hit his callback button, but though the phone rang, no one answered. He hit memory keys until he found Agent James's number. It rang again—once, twice. No answer there, either.

"Damn!" He grabbed his keys and bolted out the door.

He drove like hell and parked in front of Papa's Pizza. Through the restaurant's glass doors, he saw the agent who'd been following Macy talking to another employee. Jake jumped out of his car and hurried inside.

"Where is she?"

"She got away!" Agent Mimms snapped back. "She pulled—"

"How the hell could you lose her?" Jake bellowed.

"She did it on purpose. And I swear to God, I'm going to teach—"

Another female employee came out of the back and interrupted. "Are you guys talking about Macy? She mentioned going to her mom's place."

"Where's that?" Jake asked, frustrated that he knew so little. He prayed he still had a chance to learn more.

The moon vanished behind clouds just as Macy got out of her car and headed across Nan's lawn, and the night went black. A spray of light caught her as a car turned down the street, and at the same time, the bushes rustled. Macy swung around. Spook, the neighbor's golden retriever, tail thumping, came swaying up to her, hoping for a handout.

Macy willed her heart to stop racing. "Sorry, no pizza tonight." She gave the dog a rub behind his ear and cast another glance around the darkness, then hurried to the porch.

Macy tapped on the door at the same time as she opened it. One step inside, and she found everything was the status quo. Nan sat on the floor, her body pretzeled in yoga. Her mom burrowed deep into a recliner, sobbing into a tissue.

"Oh, Mace!" her mom cried, hugging her nubby robe closer around herself. "I've done a terrible thing." She sniffled.

Macy looked at Nan, who unwrapped her left leg from around her neck. "What did she do?" She shut the door behind her.

"I visited that guard who accused Billy of shooting him."

Macy stopped short of Nan's yoga mat. "You did what?"

Nan swung her right leg around her neck. "He's at the same hospital where she volunteers." She took in a deep breath and held it.

Macy plopped down on the sofa. "You can't do that, Mom! You can't start accusing—"

"She didn't do anything." Nan unfolded her body.

"But I wanted to," her mom cried out. "I wanted to ask him how dare he say my son shot him when . . . when we know that Billy could never do that. He's a *good* boy."

Nan shot Macy a smile. "It's a funny story." She stood and brushed off her Little Mermaid pajamas. She had a thing for Disney.

"Then why am I not laughing?" Macy snapped. She turned back to her mom. "The guard never said Billy shot him. He told the FBI that Billy saved his life." Sergeant Baldwin had told her that.

"He did?" her mom and Nan both asked at the same time.

"How do you know this?" Nan asked.

"Baldwin told me. After you left."

"Who's Baldwin?" her mom said.

Nan grinned. "That cop who has a thing for your daughter."

"He doesn't have a thing for me," Macy said. She regretted saying it, because she knew it was a lie. But he could take his thing somewhere else.

"And bears don't do the hanky-panky in the woods," Nan answered.

Macy shook her head. "Mom, what did you say to this guy?"

"Nothing." Faye dropped her face into her hands. Snorting sounds leaked through her fingers.

Macy had never heard her mother cry like that, and she blamed it all on Billy. Then her mom raised her face. She wasn't crying.

"It was terrible!" A full-blown giggle escaped her lips.

"What was terrible?" Macy asked, confused.

Nan snickered. "He flashed her."

Macy leaned forward. "What?"

"She saw everything," Nan said. "The full monty."

Macy's mother talked around her giggles. "He thought I was crying because I didn't like what I saw!"

"I think she liked it." Nan reached her hands to the ceiling in one last stretch.

"I didn't say that." Faye snickered again. "I said it wasn't *that* bad."

"Wait," Nan said. "If you're going to tell the story again, I'm going to get us some wine coolers. You're going to love this, Mace." They all moved to the kitchen table.

Macy did love it. Well, she loved seeing her mom laugh for the first time in years. They all laughed.

Macy stopped laughing when Nan brought up Sergeant Baldwin again.

"So, you and that cop have got the hots for each other, huh?"

Macy felt her face flush. "Are you joking?"

"She hit him in the balls," Nan explained to Macy's mom.

"Macy!" her mother scolded. "Didn't you learn anything when you got expelled from school for doing that?"

"That creep was stealing panties from my gym locker. He deserved it."

"Did Baldwin deserve it?" Nan asked.

"How did you meet this guy?" Her mom looked at Nan. "And how do you know about him and I don't?"

Macy glanced at Nan. "I just mentioned it to her this afternoon. But he's not important. He's sort of working with that task force, and sort of came to see me about Billy."

"And you sort of hit him in the balls?" her mom asked.

"I didn't know who he was at the time." Macy sipped her wine cooler, then flicked the bottle label with her fingernail.

"He's good-looking," Nan remarked. "Dark and sinful."

Her gaze switched from her daughter to her granddaughter. "I think you should go for it."

The image of Jake Baldwin flashed into Macy's head, but she sent it packing. "I'll go for it right about the time they start serving Baskin-Robbins in hell."

"Why wouldn't you go for it?" her mom asked. "You're divorced now."

"Please. Do I really have to explain?"

"Yeah," Nan said. "Explain."

Macy rolled her eyes. "Look at us, all three. Where has a man gotten any of us?"

"I loved your father," her mom sniffled.

"Yeah. And Dad left you so he could go pan for gold in Nevada." *And screw showgirls*, she didn't say. Hearing that would have hurt her mother. "Then there's Tom. He brought his bimbo to my bed." And the sofa. And probably the floor.

Macy looked at Nan next. "You've had two husbands. Where are they?"

Nan's brow furrowed. "It's hard to blame them for dying."

"That makes it even worse," Macy snapped. "Because even if by some grace of God you find a decent man who makes you feel safe and loved, he gives you nickels for candy, promises to take you to the circus, and then spoils everything by falling dead into a plate of spaghetti."

"It was lasagna," Nan corrected.

"I think it was spaghetti," Macy's mother said and sniffled.

Macy sighed. "Lasagna, spaghetti. I was five. All I remember is tomato sauce everywhere. My point is, all men end up hurting me. Hurting *us*."

"This is my fault." Her mom started crying.

"No, it's Dad's fault. It's Tom's fault. It's Grandpa's fault for croaking during dinner. It's all men, even Billy." Tears filled her vision. "Look what he's done to us. You're getting flashed and I . . ." *Have a murderer out to rape me.* But she couldn't say that.

"You what?" her mom asked, still sniffling.

Macy was saved from answering by the bell. Well, not a bell, but a loud, whacking knock at the door. One thought hit Macy like a brick.

Tanks.

And from the look on Nan's face, Nan thought the same thing.

Macy and Nan hotfooted it to the door. Nan got to the peephole first.

"Oh, crappers," she said.

"Who is it?" Macy glanced around the room for a weapon. The lamp, her grandma's purse . . . Hey, the thing weighed a ton.

"It's your boyfriend, but he doesn't look happy."

"I don't have a boyfriend," Macy spat out.

"You really shouldn't have hit him in the balls." Her mom stepped up behind them. "Men are really funny about that."

"He's not my boyfriend!" Macy repeated. She gripped her wine cooler as Nan started to open the door.

"Don't!" Macy didn't want to face Baldwin right now. Then again, maybe he was here about Billy.

"What?" Nan asked. "You want me to holler that no one's home? Tom might have been stupid enough to fall for that, but I don't think this guy will."

Macy bit down on her lip. "Fine. Open it."

Nan did, and Baldwin charged inside. No *Hello, how are you, can I come in?* He barged in, not shutting the door, and his eyes alighted on her like fruit flies on a gone-bad banana.

"You ditched him on purpose," he accused.

"No, I forgot he was there."

Macy's mom stepped forward. "Forgot who?"

Macy ignored her. "I didn't mean to do it. I went into the apartment complex. He didn't follow. I looked for him before I left."

"Do you have a death wish? Are you stupid?"

"You must have hit him really hard," her mom remarked. "Tell the man you're sorry, Mace."

Nan stared at Baldwin. "What did my granddaughter do?"

Her mom spoke up. "You said she hit him in the balls."

"She did." Nan looked at Baldwin. "Did she hit you in the balls again?"

Macy tried to ignore the tangent the conversation had taken and focus on the angry man in front of her. "I drove around the block looking for that guy."

"He was supposed to follow you. You knew that. Why make it hard on him?"

Suddenly, bolting through the open door came the FBI man himself. He glared at Macy. "I want to talk to you," he growled.

"Did she hit *everyone* in the balls?" her mom asked.

"Maybe," Nan said. "It does give a woman a rush."

The FBI agent stepped closer. "You need to be taught a lesson," he said.

Macy stepped back.

Nan and her mom moved forward, each taking a protective stance beside her. What a picture, Macy thought: Nan in lemon yellow Little Mermaid pj's, Macy herself in drab Papa Pizza polyester, and her mom in a faded pink nubby robe. All three of them were clutching fuzzy-navel wine coolers.

Nan and her mom's protectiveness didn't surprise Macy. But Baldwin joined the defense. He stepped between her and the angry agent. "*I* deal with Miss Tucker."

Nan snickered. "Told you he had a thing for you."

The FBI agent started smarting off to Baldwin. Baldwin gave back in kind. Macy decided to be smarter than both of them, and snatched her purse and left.

Billy sat in the van and watched the cars pull in and out of the Girls Galore parking lot. Was Tanks here, inside and watching naked girls? Billy considered trying to get in, but without an ID it would be impossible.

"Damn!" He looked down at the loaded gun resting on the passenger seat and wished this was over. He almost bit his lip, but stopped himself.

He drew in a deep breath of pure frustration. The sound reminded him of his grandma doing yoga. He missed Nan and his mom, missed Mace. What he wouldn't give to go back eight months and tell the Harp brothers no. No, I'm not going to be a part of your game. All they were supposed to do was score some beer. Billy hadn't known the Harp brothers carried knives and had robbed stores in the past. Sometimes what you didn't know cost a hell of a lot. His whole friggin' life was screwed up because he hadn't said no.

For a while, Billy had wanted to blame the Harp brothers. Then he'd wanted to blame his lawyer and the judge. After a week behind bars, a week of hearing all the other inmates blaming someone else for their being there, Billy had accepted the cruel, cold truth. He had no one to blame but himself.

His focus stayed on the front entrance of Girls Galore until, when he least expected it, the van's passenger door swung open.

Billy went for his gun.

CHAPTER ELEVEN

Almost home, Macy wanted nothing more than to bury herself under her covers, to snuggle with Elvis while indulging in a good two-tissue cry, but ever since Baldwin had caught up with her and ridden her bumper, she had a feeling he entertained the idea of continuing his are-you-stupid lecture. It was a lecture she might deserve, because she remembered feeling half guilty when she'd waved at the agent from behind the gate. However, deserving or not, she really preferred being in tip-top shape for a chewing out. Tonight she wasn't tip-top.

She parked in her driveway and bolted out of the car, hoping her pace alone would encourage him to leave. No such luck. The slam of his car door echoed hers almost instantly. She got to her front porch, then heard him talking—not to her, but on the phone.

"It was Billy?" he said.

She turned around.

"I know. She's difficult. Hardheaded. Stubborn." His gaze slapped into hers.

Now, who could he be talking about? Macy rolled her eyes.

"I simply said it was my job to handle her." Baldwin paused. "Put a trace on it. I don't care."

Realizing she was obviously eavesdropping, she started to look away but then decided she didn't care. Her brother was more important than manners.

"He said he'd seen your guy." Pause. "He was right. So, what does that tell you?"

Still listening, Macy attempted to fit her key into the lock. It wouldn't go. She turned the key over, listening more than paying attention to the door. She tried again. No fit. She studied the knob, perplexed.

Something was wrong. Her doorknob had long ago tarnished. It had white paint speckles from three years ago when Tom had done a lousy job painting the house. This knob was shiny and new. Her gaze shot up to the door. The extra-white door.

While her mind tried to work out the color issue, Baldwin stepped up on the porch. He slid a key into the lock and pushed open her front door. Her front door? His key? Something didn't compute. Yes, this was *her* extra-white door, but where and why . . . ?

It hit her then. Not the reason the door was so white, or why her knob looked new, or why Sergeant Baldwin had a key, but what she was returning to. "Home, Sweet Home" didn't feel so sweet anymore. David Tanks had been here, had left his mark on the walls. Somehow she'd managed to forget.

Her gaze shot back up to the door. Tanks's mark was gone.

Extra-white problem solved. She touched the wood panel. The tacky feel met her fingertips at the same time as the smell of wet paint tickled her nose. She looked back at Baldwin, who was still on the phone. He'd painted her door?

"Yes, I agree," he said. His gaze met hers. "Can we discuss this tomorrow? I realize that. Tomorrow at nine." He closed his phone and motioned for her to go inside. She didn't need an invitation to enter her own home, but she took it.

Inside, the smell of fresh paint grew stronger. She turned on a lamp, dropped onto the sofa, and gazed from wall to wall. The words were gone, replaced by splotches of primer. Her attention shot to the window. Fixed. She looked at Baldwin. Standing with his arms crossed over his chest, he stared at her with a scowl on his handsome face. Not GQ handsome, but manly. She hugged her knees to her chest and wished he was gawd-awful ugly.

"Do you have any idea how stupid you were tonight?"

She tightened her arms around her shins and emotion clogged her throat. The are-you-stupid lecture was about to begin. "Yes. It was wrong."

He looked baffled. "It was stupid."

Her sinuses stung, a precursor to tears, but she refused to cry. "I said I was wrong. And generally the word *wrong* can be translated to mean stupid. But how about cutting me an itsy-bitsy break? This is new for me."

"What's new?"

"All of it. Having my baby brother do time. Having cops tackle me. Having an escaped convict trying to rape me— and who knows, he may even fancy the idea of cutting my head off. And . . . oh yeah, having the FBI follow me and threaten to have my driving license yanked because he couldn't keep up with a dented Saturn."

Sergeant Baldwin's arms tightened across his chest. "He threatened to have your license yanked?"

"Yeah. I'm not saying it made what I did right. But—"

"Good, because neither am I." Silence followed his words.

She looked around again. "You do all this?"

He inhaled. "I'm not finished raking you over the coals."

"Why?" she asked.

"Because you scared the shit out of me."

"No. Why did you do this?"

He got an odd look on his face. "I like fixing things. It's not a big deal."

But it was. "Thank you."

Spotting the discarded package that had held the new doorknob, she unwrapped her hold on her legs and grabbed it from the table. The price tag was stickered on the front. Frowning, she looked up. "There was nothing wrong with my old doorknob."

"Nothing except your ex has the key." Baldwin's right eyebrow arched.

Macy sighed. "My ex is the least of my problems." She reached for her purse and pulled out some money.

"You should have changed the locks when you kicked him out."

"If we're summing up my mistakes, it began when I married him. Or better yet, when I slept with him. Here." She tossed money on the coffee table.

"I'm glad we agree on something." He ignored the money and dropped into her green recliner.

She grabbed a throw pillow, hugged it, and tried to think of a clever way to find out about the phone call. When nothing came to mind, she just spit it out. "I heard you on the phone. Has something happened?"

Baldwin leaned forward. Their gazes met and held. Interest filled his blue eyes. "You scared me."

So, you and that cop have got the hots for each other? she remembered Nan saying.

"What about Billy?" she asked, determined not to think about this man as anything but a source of information.

He let out deep breath. "Let's make a deal."

"What kind of a deal?" What did she have worth bartering

for, anyway? Nothing except what every man wanted. What Mr. Prack wanted. What Tom had wanted with the bimbo, and what he'd wanted when he'd come over last night, allegedly to help her.

The fact that Baldwin might want to barter for sex should have had her feeling repulsed, and it did. A little. But lying to herself wouldn't change the fact that a spark of excitement shimmied down her spine. And that spark came with a message: *Welcome back to the real world, where women want men and men want women, a world where people put their hearts on the chopping block and wait for the ax to fall. You can only hide from it for so long.*

Oh, hell. She didn't want any part of the real world.

Sergeant Baldwin continued. "I'll tell you what I know, but only if you promise not to pull any more stunts like tonight."

"Deal." She answered before he could add, *And if you let me take you to the bedroom and have my way with you.*

He didn't say that. Instead, he studied her. "Your brother called."

"Billy?" She glanced at her answering machine. The red light blinked. She reached over to hit the play button.

"No. He called me. On my cell phone," Baldwin corrected.

Macy froze, her finger poised. "You?"

"Yeah." He told her about the call—or about *part* of it. The suspicious way Baldwin cut the conversation short seemed to mean he held something back.

"What else did he say?" She glared, daring him to lie.

"He mentioned he knew the cops were following you, that you managed to lose them. He must have been there watching you."

"Why didn't he talk to me? Why . . . ?" Questions floated up to the top of her head like a school of dynamited fish. "Why did he call you and not me? How did he even get your number?"

"Ellie," Baldwin said. "I left my number on her cell."

"But is Ellie on my brother's side, or with that creep who cuts people's heads off?"

"I don't know. It appears she helped with the escape."

Emotion tightened Macy's throat. "I don't understand."

"I know," Baldwin said. There was a pause, then: "You want some hot chocolate?"

She stared at him. "How do you know—?"

"Your ex mentioned fixing you hot chocolate."

"Oh." She laced her hands together, uncomfortable with the sympathy she saw in his eyes. Wasn't that the way most people looked at her mom? "I'm fine, but thanks."

Jake decided Macy Tucker wasn't fine. She looked like a woman on the verge of a meltdown, so he ignored her and went into the kitchen.

"What are you doing?" she called.

"You'll see."

When he pressed the mug of freshly made hot cocoa into her hands a few minutes later, he wished he could also offer a shoulder. Something warned him she'd decline melting onto it. Instead, she sipped her steaming drink, and the silence drifted toward the awkward stage—to the point where he feared she might ask him to leave. He hoped like hell she wouldn't. While driving back tonight, he'd noticed that Macy's house backed up onto a strip mall. Even if he slept out front, someone could easily come in the back.

Giving the window a quick glance, he said, "Tell me about your brother."

Cup to her lips, she said, "You think he's all bad."

Jake shrugged. "I think he's managed to get in a lot of trouble."

"Trouble and Billy go hand in hand," she admitted.

"Then why do you keep trying to protect him?"

"He's not a bad kid. He just doesn't think things through. But he's loyal and . . . he stood up for me." Tears brightened her eyes. "Four years old, and he was willing to take on a two hundred–pound drunk." She shook her head.

Jake figured there was a story behind that, and he almost asked, but the way she looked away told him she regretted divulging even that much. "So, you're close?"

"Aren't all siblings?"

Until they steal your fiancées he thought. "I guess." His gaze caught the schoolbooks on the end table. "What are you taking in school?" he asked, though he already knew.

"Law. And no wisecracks." Her tone was lighter; she clearly appreciated the change of subject.

"Hey, I've met a few lawyers I liked," he replied. "For a few minutes. Well, a second. Okay, I'm lying, but it *could* happen." He grinned, and when she laughed he remembered hearing her laughing with Donaldson. He liked it better now when it was just him and her.

The blinking red light on the answering machine caught his gaze, and he recalled the message from the priest. Was there a good way to approach *that* subject? For some reason, *Hey, before I make a move on you, are you really considering entering a convent?* didn't sound too smooth. But he needed to know.

"You got a call tonight," he remarked.

Nodding, she pressed play.

Her expression remained unreadable. The priest's words rang out, then the message clicked off and Jake waited for her to say something, to offer an explanation.

"It's late." She stifled a yawn.

"Father Luis sounded as if that was important."

"Yes." She hugged her pillow closer, her gaze finding the clock.

"So, you're Catholic?"

"Why? You have something against that, too?" Smiling, she drank some more hot chocolate.

"No. Just curious what was so important."

"It's not about Billy."

"I didn't think it was."

She studied him. "One of the sisters is leaving, and they want me to take over her job."

Damn. "And you're actually thinking about it?"

Her brow furrowed. "I . . . yeah. But what does that have to do with Billy?"

"You're really considering it? You're joking, right?"

Elvis pranced into the room and jumped up on the sofa. Macy smoothed her hand down the cat's back. "And you have an opinion on this because . . . ?"

"No. I don't." He took a deep breath, then admitted, "Oh, shit. Why lie? Yeah, I have an opinion."

She looked shocked, and he wished he'd kept his mouth shut. Religious beliefs were not something he questioned. Each to his own, he'd grown up believing. Nevertheless, celibacy wasn't something he grasped, and from what he'd heard, celibacy was a biggie for nuns.

Her brow crinkled in puzzlement. "And what's this opinion?"

"You don't seem the type."

Real smooth. His gut told him to bow out now. "I shouldn't have said anything," he apologized. He shut his mouth, planned to keep it shut, but then his gaze went back to her mouth, to that mouth with which he wanted to get up close and personal. To the body he wanted to get next to while naked.

Damn it to hell and back, he was actually lusting over a soon-to-be nun! He let out a groan. "I didn't know they accepted divorced nuns. And, personally, I don't think you have the personality for it."

Her eyes widened. Her cat rose and tapped her chin with his nose. Then the dang animal rubbed himself against her breasts and purred. Hell, Jake would be purring too if she let him get that close. But no, she had no intention of letting him.

Was she smiling?

"The personality?" she asked.

He shook his head and decided that since his damned foot was already in his mouth, he might as well continue. "You knee men in the balls. You're hardheaded, stubborn, sassy, and . . . well, sexy as hell. You—" Wait, that was definitely a smile on her lips. "What?"

"You haven't been around a lot of nuns, have you?"

"No."

"They can be pretty stubborn. Opinionated. And sassy."

"But not sexy, right? You're gonna tell me you won't miss sex?"

An unreadable twinkle lit in her eyes, and she snorted. "I pretty much live a nun's life anyway."

He shook his head. "By choice, or because some jerk hurt you?"

"Both. And . . . well, some people speculate that all nuns are lesbians."

He shook his head, and it took a second for him to clear it. He pushed a hand through his hair. "Er, are you lesbian?"

She stood up. "I . . . Restroom."

Macy had herself a good laugh in the bathroom. Now, sitting back on her sofa, she watched Sergeant Jake Baldwin's fingers thread through the dark strands of his hair. She pulled the throw pillow back to her chest and buried her mouth in it so he couldn't see her smile.

Wow, the man was easy to tease. Fun to tease. Even when she was half sick with worry over her brother, she enjoyed Jake Baldwin's company.

"So, you're going to be a nun with a law degree? Wear a habit into the courtroom?" he asked. "Sounds like a sitcom to me."

"Mmm, a man-hating, lesbian nun with a law degree. Bet I could intimidate my witnesses." Laughter caught in her chest.

His eyes narrowed. "You're pulling my chain."

"Why would I do that?" Why *was* she? She was toying with herself, too. She didn't want to get any closer to this man. Didn't want to continue liking him. "Well, it's late, Sergeant Baldwin. And I have an early morning."

His expression changed from suspicion to concern. "I think my sleeping here again might be a good idea."

"Here?"

"On the sofa, of course—since you're considering a convent." His smile said how ludicrous he felt that was, and it made her heart beat a little faster.

"I don't think . . ."

He leaned forward, elbows propped on his knees. "Tanks knows where you live. If what Ellie says is true, this guy would just as soon slit your throat as—"

He was just trying to push her buttons. "I'll keep the phone by the bed. And remember, the FBI thinks Tanks has taken off." That was right, wasn't it? They wouldn't leave her unprotected if the convict was expected to return.

Baldwin shook his head. "They've been wrong before. Do you know how long it takes for someone to break into a house? A person can be inside in sixty seconds. Guess how long the response time is for a patrol car."

Macy stared at him. "Do you really believe he'd stay in town just to—"

"I think it's a stupid risk to take, when you have me here. I'll sleep on the sofa. You won't know I'm around." He smiled. "So your virtue's safe—unless you don't want it to be." The heat in his eyes had returned.

"But—"

He lifted his hands in a display of mock fear. "You think I'd try something with a soon-to-be man-hating lesbian nun working on her law degree?"

She almost grinned, but the humor of the situation faded as the bright patches of white paint on her walls caught her attention. *He'd just as soon slit your throat as*—Baldwin's words echoed inside her head. She met his eyes.

The truth? She was afraid of Baldwin, too. But who frightened her more, a man who would cut off her head . . . or a man who could rip out her heart? But Baldwin couldn't touch her heart unless she let him, and she wasn't letting him.

"Just one night." She could trust herself for one night. Couldn't she?

"It might be over tomorrow," he agreed.

Might be? Then he'd leave and she wouldn't have to see him anymore. The thought didn't make her nearly as happy as it should have.

Macy stood and collected a blanket and a pillow from the hall closet before she had a chance to change her mind. She dumped them in the detective's lap and said, "There's only one bathroom. The lock's broke. So when you're in there . . . sing."

He grinned and warned her, "Can't sing worth a damn."

"Then hum." She took three steps.

"Macy?"

She turned and faced him. He looked at her with a mixture of concern and heat—not the way a man should look at a wannabe nun. But then, she wasn't a nun, and the way her body responded made that all too clear. "Yes?"

"You were joking about the nun thing. Right?"

She crossed herself as she'd seen Father Luis and Sister Beth do. "Bless you, Baldwin." Then she headed to her bedroom, adding over her shoulder, "Thanks for the hot chocolate."

God help her, she was smiling again.

Jake refluffed a pillow that had no fluffing capacity. He could live with a lot of things, but a wimpy pillow wasn't one of them. Finding the sofa pillow instead, he stuffed it behind his head. A whiff of Macy floated up, a feminine scent with traces of pizza, and his body tightened. Just his luck! The one woman who would tempt him to resurface in the dating world, and she was a wannabe man-hating lesbian nun out to get her law degree. But, staring at the ceiling, he recalled that twinkle in her eye. She'd been playing him. Hadn't she?

A divorcée couldn't become a nun, could she? Then again, Catholics were famous for annulling marriages. Well, he didn't know one way or another, but he knew someone who would. His brother. Religion was his brother's thing, just as it had been their father's.

Jake sat up and grabbed his cell phone. He punched in the numbers before he remembered he didn't talk to his brother anymore—and if he did, he wouldn't be calling this late. "Damn!" He shut the phone off and dropped it.

Right then, it hit him. He missed Harry, missed the late-night conversations and religious debates. He missed the Saturday nights when Harry would call to practice his Sunday sermon. Jake seldom attended church, but he'd heard Harry's sermons. They were good.

Night and day, day and night. As brothers, the Baldwins were different. But they'd also been as close as two brothers could be. Until Lisa.

For two years, he and Lisa had dated and made plans. They'd marry in June; she'd be pregnant in two years; they'd have a house in the suburbs in five. None of it had happened. *Be happy you got out of the ball and chain*, friends had told him when they heard the wedding was off. He'd laughed and said he was dancing to the tune of freedom. That was a damn lie. He'd loved Lisa—he'd wanted the ball and chain. His parents' love had filled the house with laughter and taken the couple early to bed many nights. Jake had wanted the same thing.

Yeah, he knew he'd not been the picture-perfect fiancé during those last months. Watching someone you love die isn't easy. His father's cancer had returned with a vengeance, and Jake had taken off work and helped his mom care for him. Jake still hadn't gotten over the grief when Lisa returned his ring, and within a few months, she'd started wearing his brother's. Within seven months, he'd lost his father, his fiancée, and his brother.

Jake would have recovered from losing his father. One has no choice but to accept death. Losing Lisa had stung. He could have gotten over that, too. But *losing Harry to Lisa* had cost too much. It cost him pride and it cost him his brother. He'd thought he could deal with that, eventually, if he never had to see them. But that was the problem. The family reunion was weeks away. Knowing he'd have to see Lisa and Harry together . . . Damn, he didn't want to be reminded of all he'd lost.

For an hour, he juggled the problem in his mind. Then, eager to switch gears away from his family issues, he thought about Macy's family. He recalled the report he'd read on Billy. The kid had used her car to rob the convenience store. Jake wasn't sure Billy deserved Macy's devotion any more than Harry deserved Jake's. However, in the short conversation he'd had with Billy, he'd certainly heard the boy's devotion for his sister.

Take care of my sister, Baldwin. Billy's words vibrated through Jake's head, and he pulled the pillow to his nose to breathe in her scent again. "I plan on it, Billy. I plan on it."

Rolling over, he tried to shut off his mind and sleep. It worked. His eyes finally drifted shut. But he hadn't slept five minutes when a loud noise jarred Jake awake.

CHAPTER TWELVE

Jake grabbed his gun and, realizing the sound was a knock on the front door, bolted from the sofa into the entryway. As his bare feet hit cold tile he heard someone call his name from the other side.

"Jake? It's Mark."

Jake sucked air into his lungs. Relief surged, then vanished. Donaldson would only come for a reason. Chances were, the reason wasn't good.

He opened the door, trying to shake off his sleepiness. From Donaldson's tousled appearance, the Golden Boy didn't fare much better.

"What's up?" he asked.

"I got a call from your friend in Homicide—Anders. He's at a case and wants you there."

"Why didn't he call me?"

"He tried your cell. I tried your cell. It's not on."

"Shit!" Jake remembered he'd turned his phone off when he'd almost called his brother. "What's this about?"

"Don't know. But if it's his case, there's probably a body."

Was it Macy's brother? Jake fought back a wave of fear, for both what he'd find out and what might happen if he left Macy alone. He pushed a hand over his face and thought about options. Then his gaze alighted on Donaldson.

"Come in," he said.

"So our effort was worth it?" the blond cop asked in a low voice as he entered. He smiled.

Jake sighed. "I'm sleeping on the couch. And that's exactly where you're going to be until I get back." He went to collect his things.

A little while later, Jake parked beside a patrol car and took out his badge to help cut his way through the barrage of cops and press. The small white-framed house that was his destination had "rental property" written all over it.

He spotted Stan Anders in a corner of the living room. From the man's rumpled appearance, he appeared to have been dragged from bed. Jake nodded at both Stan and the officer beside him.

"You made it," his friend said. "Give me a sec."

Jake's gaze drifted around the room. A hubbub of voices, mostly cops', and the smell of dirty laundry filled the room. No body—not in here. Not that he looked forward to seeing a corpse, but Stan had brought him here for a reason. Considering that a body was usually why Stan showed up, Jake could add one plus one. He just hoped "two" wasn't Macy's brother.

As Stan talked, Jake continued to assess the situation. A robbery maybe? That would explain his being summoned.

When his friend approached, Jake said, "What's up?"

"In here."

Jake followed. As he walked past, he noticed a busty red-headed woman sitting on the sofa, sobbing on an officer's shoulder. She wore a skimpy cocktail dress that left little to the imagination. The officer looked all too happy to be assisting.

"She works at Girls Galore, if you're interested," Stan whispered.

Jake frowned. "You better have another reason for getting me out of bed."

"Hey, she's hot!" Stan moved into the kitchen. "I know how much you need your beauty rest, but I remembered what you said about your gal's place. I know it's a long shot, but . . ." He pointed to a box on the floor beside a humming refrigerator.

"Okay, you got my interest." Jake knelt down beside the case of red spray paint—the same brand and color that had been used at Macy's. Two cans were missing from the box.

"The near-naked woman didn't intrigue you, but a box of spray paint does?" Chuckling, Stan shook his head as Jake got to his feet. "I worry about you."

"Is there a body?" Jake's gaze moved around the room.

"Yup. Scantily clad women and a murder. Do I know how to throw a party or what?"

Jake focused on his friend. "You like this too much."

Honesty deepened Stan's tone. "It's laugh or cry. Now come on, I'll give you the tour. The vic's a male. Young. Too young."

Jake created a mental picture of Billy Moore from his mug shot. He dreaded explaining this to Macy.

Passing the sobbing redhead and opportunistic patrol officer again, Jake recalled he'd wanted to hold Macy in just the same way, to comfort her. Yeah, it was happening fast. And fast wasn't Jake's style. Not when it came to emotions. He'd dated Lisa a month before she'd gotten under his skin. While he damn well wasn't backing away from Macy, maybe he should chill out a bit. He'd been pursuing her a bit hard.

Stan led him to a bedroom. Cops, uniformed and plain-clothes, milled everywhere. Jake stopped in the doorway and stared at the corpse sprawled out on the carpet. The boy's lifeless eyes stared up at the ceiling. A deep slit gaped across his throat. Blood haloed his head. The smell of death filled Jake's sinuses, but he studied the face with relief. It wasn't Billy.

"How did you find him?" Jake placed a hand over his nose.

"Red did. He's her boyfriend. He was supposed to pick her up from work. When he didn't show, she caught a ride home with someone else."

"Does . . . did the guy have a record?" Jake asked.

"She said he was on parole, but she doesn't know what for. I've got someone checking."

"Hey, Anders." An officer motioned for Stan from the other side of the room.

Having seen enough, Jake went back into the living room. A pizza box on the coffee table caught his gaze, and his thoughts shifted to Macy. The idea of her delivering pizza while Tanks was loose didn't sit well. He wondered if she even carried pepper spray. Hell, the woman didn't even have a working cell phone. Of course, he didn't have to worry about that. Pretty soon she'd trade the pizza uniform in for a nun's habit.

He blew out a breath and shifted his focus back to the sexy redhead. Definitely not nun material. But neither was Macy, damn it! She'd been joking. Hadn't she?

Forcing his mind off Macy, he watched Red tug at her skirt. It confused the hell out of him why women wore something too short and tight, then tugged at it. Either show off your assets or don't! Red had a very nice pair of legs.

His focus caught on what lay beside those legs: an open phone book with something circled. His brain started playing connect the dots. Billy's words rang in his memory. *He's killed someone else. Tanks knows where Mace works. I saw . . . he had her work number and address circled in a phone book.* Jake edged closer. Papa's Pizza was circled.

"Damn!" The guy or guys who'd done this were the same ones after Macy. He jerked out his cell phone and dialed Donaldson's cell.

Answer, damn it! One ring. Two . . .

"Hello?" Donaldson's voice came out sleepy.

"Everything okay?" Jake asked.

"Yes. Something happen?"

"Just keep an eye out. Looks like Tanks might be mixed up in whatever happened here, and it's ugly. I'll fill you in later."

Shutting his phone, Jake considered his next call and glanced toward the bedroom. Stan wasn't going to be happy. No cop liked having another agency nosing around. But the Gulf Coast Violent Offenders unit was already sniffing out Tanks and would want to know about this.

Raking a hand though his hair, Jake headed back to the bedroom. The least he could do was give Stan a heads-up before he made the call.

Billy watched the lights go off in Girls Galore, and his thoughts went to the young woman who'd crawled into his car—one of the establishment's dancers who'd been angling for a little side trade. He'd been able to hide his gun beneath his shirt before she saw it. Six months ago, he would have unzipped his pants and taken her up on the ten-dollar special she'd offered, girlfriend or no. Was it prison or Ellie that had changed him? Maybe both.

Growing impatient, he waited until the last car left the parking lot. No Tanks.

"Shit!" What was he going to do if he couldn't find the man? He sucked on his bottom lip, catching himself right before he bit down. Closing his eyes, he wondered what Mace would tell him to do.

Turn yourself in now, Billy, he could hear his sister say. But, he couldn't do that. Even if Tanks was caught and put back in prison, he had people on the outside. People who could hurt Ellie and Mace. Billy would be helpless in the joint, unable to protect the people he loved.

"I can't turn myself in," he mumbled. "I gotta do this."

Starting the van, he drove back to the house with the dead man. Maybe Tanks was fool enough to return.

When he pulled down the street, however, he saw flashing blue lights. The police! Whipping his van into a neighbor's driveway, he squeezed air into his tight lungs and put the vehicle in reverse. Slowly he pulled away. He had to figure a different destination.

An hour later he parked in front of Andy's trailer. He noticed the boy's car was gone, but he supposed that didn't mean anything. Billy crawled out of the van, wanting only to pull Ellie against him, to hold her and forget about all the terrible images flashing in his head. Images of Hal, the guard, bleeding; of Brandon gasping for air while blood oozed from his lips; and now of that dead guy with his throat slashed. For just a few minutes, he wanted to see the world as Ellie did, through rose-colored glasses.

The light glowed yellow from the front window as he stepped up on the trailer's wobbly porch. Had Ellie waited up? The door creaked open. The smell of pine cleaner filled Billy's nose. The trailer looked different, with no trash, no dirty clothes. Even the old sofa sat level, thanks to two phone books tucked under the missing leg.

"Ellie?" The silence hung thick. Billy's heart began to thump. He ran to the bedroom, searched the bathroom.

Nope. Ellie wasn't there.

While CSI loaded the body on a stretcher, Jake stepped onto the back porch. The task force had arrived, and Agent James had insisted he hang around, though all Jake wanted to do was get back to Macy.

The door slammed behind him, and Stan stormed out. "Tell me again why you felt the need to call those jerks."

"They're after Tanks."

"And you think they're more capable of catching the guy than we are?"

"I think they've got a leg up on the case."

"And you're working with them. Why?"

"I'm not working with them. I'm just . . . It's the girl. The one whose house was broken into. Tanks is after her."

"Well, that explains it. There's always a piece of ass involved."

Jake flinched. "Damn, Stan! You know I'm—"

His friend held up a hand, rescinding his previous comment. "I just don't like it," he admitted. "Why is this Tanks guy after her, anyway? And why are the Feds in on it?"

Jake hadn't been sworn to any secrecy. "The Feds are looking at Tanks for the murder of one of their agents. I'm guessing that's the reason Gulf Coast got involved so quickly. As for the reason he's after Macy . . . It's revenge. Her brother Billy stole his girl."

Stan folded his arms across his chest. "Women are at the root of every problem."

Jake scuffed his shoe against the slatted wooden porch. "You get anything in there?"

"Lots of prints. No murder weapon. One of the guys recognizes him. Name's Mike Sawyer. He did three years for grand theft auto, and a few breaking-and-entering charges. He was—probably still is—part of a gang. They call themselves the Wolves."

"I've heard of them." Jake's mind returned to the red paint. Agent James didn't seem convinced that Tanks had been here, but Jake's gut said different. He knew the escaped convict had offed Sawyer.

Silence reigned, and a few lightning bugs floated across the yard. Jake glanced back at Stan. "You know anything about the Catholic religion?" he asked.

Stan wrinkled his brow. "Not really. Why?"

Jake shrugged. "Nothing."

Agent James, wearing a task-force jacket, walked out of the house. His gaze found Stan. "Sorry about what happened in there. Sometimes the kitchen isn't big enough for two cooks."

"Your cook is an ass," Stan said.

"I just told him that myself," James agreed. "Look, I'd like to work together, not fight over who's in charge."

"So you believe Tanks was behind this?" Jake asked.

Agent James nodded. "Never disbelieved it, but I wanted more than a circled phone number and a can of paint."

"And you found it?" Stan asked.

The FBI man motioned them inside. As they entered, Mike Sawyer's body exited. Agent James slipped on a pair of gloves, went to the answering machine, and hit a button.

"Hey," a shrill voice said. "This is Ellie. Call me."

James's lips tightened. "I'm willing to bet there's not another Ellie with that voice."

"God, I hope not," Stan said. "That hurt my ears."

Agent James nodded. "We've gotten a trace on her home phone and are working on her cell."

Jake remembered Ellie's phone call to Macy. It didn't make sense that Ellie would be calling Tanks. . . . "We're missing something," he said.

Agent James raised an eyebrow. "When you figure out what it is, you be sure to let me know."

CHAPTER THIRTEEN

Billy paced the trailer living room. Where was Ellie? It had been over an hour since he'd arrived, and she still wasn't back.

Lights flashed across the blinds, and he bolted to the window. Ellie got out of Andy's car before it drove off. Billy met her at the door. She ran to him. Furious, he wrapped his arms around her.

"Where the hell have you been?" When he heard her hiccupping breath, he regretted his tone. "I was worried." He pulled back so he could look at her. "What happened?"

"Fred died." Tears filled her eyes.

"Who?" Billy thought about the man with his throat slashed.

"My patient. Remember the one I told you sneaked into Mrs. Kelly's room?"

Billy recalled Ellie talking about the two old lovebirds. "What happened?"

"A stroke." She buried her face back in his chest.

"How did you find out?"

"Nancy, the other nurse's aide, called me. She knew how close we were. He died an hour after I arrived."

"Damn it, Ellie! I told you not to use your phone."

She stiffened. "I just checked my messages. I used Andy's phone to call"

"Don't even check your messages. They could trace it."

She walked over to the sofa and dropped down on it. "Don't be mad. I'm hurting too much—"

"I'm not mad," he interrupted. "I just . . . don't want you getting into trouble." He sat down beside her. She leaned against him. Her soft weight felt good.

"I feel so bad for Mrs. Kelly. They loved each other. She stayed with me by his bed and held his hand. She called him the love of her life and kept saying it was unfair that she had only met him in the last year. It was so sad."

"I know," he whispered into her hair, holding her. Neither of them spoke, but it wasn't a bad silence. Just two people holding on to each other.

"I'm scared," she finally said. "I think we should leave. Get in the van and just go."

Billy shook his head. "I can't. I've got to make sure Mace is okay."

Ellie glanced up. "Did you call that cop like you said?"

"Yeah. But I don't know if he'll protect her. I've got to find Tanks."

"But, how's talking going to change things? I don't see him promising you anything, and even if he did, that doesn't mean he'll keep his word."

"I'll make him understand," Billy said. He didn't want to talk about Tanks. Even exhausted, his body knew what it wanted. It wanted Ellie. "Where did Andy go, anyway?"

"He's going to stay with a friend. I think . . . I think he thought we'd like to be alone."

"Do we?" Billy asked.

She smiled and some of the worry left her eyes. "I do if you do."

Billy's gaze shifted around. Thanks to Ellie's work, it didn't seem like such a terrible place anymore. He felt her soft breasts against his arm and his body responded.

"I asked Andy why he was helping us. He said that he heard a preacher on television say that the next person you don't offer to help, they might be Jesus."

"He thinks I'm Jesus?" Billy laughed and then sighed as Ellie shifted to sit in his lap.

"No. But he said he needed to help others so he'd be a better person."

"Why does he think he needs to be better?" Billy asked. But maybe he understood. Both Andy's parents had left, and for years Billy had blamed himself for his dad leaving. Maybe Andy was trying to make up for whatever he believed he'd done wrong.

"I don't know," Ellie said. "But he's a good kid. He wouldn't even let me put gas in his car for taking me to the nursing home."

Billy gazed into his girlfriend's pale green eyes. "You're beautiful," he said. And the soft weight of her bottom against his crotch was delicious.

Her smile widened. "I love you, Billy. Just like Mrs. Kelly loved Fred. I'll love you forever, and I'm glad I found you now instead of when we're in an old-folks home."

Billy's gut clenched as he remembered that somehow, after he'd taken care of Tanks, he had to convince Ellie to stop loving him.

She leaned in and kissed him. Was it wrong of him to take tonight, when tomorrow . . . ? Her tongue entered his mouth, and suddenly wrong and right didn't seem so important. He kissed her the way he'd dreamed of doing it for five months. His hand shook a little as he slid his palm up under her light-blue T-shirt to cup her breast.

"You feel good," he mumbled, rubbing his fingers over her bra, feeling her nipples harden. He didn't have a lot of experience with women, but he knew enough to know that they liked to take this sort of thing slow. He'd go as slow as Ellie wanted.

"So do you." She shifted her bottom against him, then grabbed her T-shirt and pulled it over her head.

Her bra was white with lots of lace. Her nipples pebbled against it. He ran his hand over one tight, satin-covered little bud, and then Ellie said words he'd been dying to hear.

"Love me, Billy. Help me forget what a crazy mess we're in."

At seven, Macy slapped her alarm silent. Sleep offered escape. She didn't want to worry about Billy, about getting her head chopped off, about the guy stretched out on her sofa who thought she was entering the convent. *You won't even know I'm here,* he'd said. As if.

Crappers! Turning over, she buried her face in her pillow and mumbled a few more unladylike words. She'd known he was there, all right. She'd lain in bed for over an hour, listening to hear Baldwin roll over, listening to see if he snored. She'd hoped he did. Big, ugly, honking snores. Anything to stop her from thinking about what it would be like to have his body next to hers.

For almost two years she'd gone without sex. Sure, every now and then her body would ask, *Hey, remember orgasms?* Her brain would answer, *Yeah, I remember. But the last one I experienced wasn't mine. It was my husband's secretary's.* She still couldn't believe she'd let them finish before interrupting. Then again, it hadn't taken very long. Tom had never had staying power.

Generally, thinking about Tom and his secretary was enough to trot her hormones back to the ice age. Last night, her hormones had refused to take the hike.

Remembering she had to work in the church garden, she sat up. She hadn't gotten her eyes all the way open when someone knocked on her bedroom door, and before she could say *Go away*, Baldwin walked into her bedroom carrying two steaming cups.

"Got you coffee," he said.

She wanted to scold him for walking in, to refuse the caffeine fix, but it smelled as good as he looked. A frown twisted her lips.

"Somebody isn't a morning person," he said. He winked, then had the audacity to sit on the edge of her bed. "A little birdie told me you take it with cream and sugar."

"What little birdie?" she asked. "Where is it? I'm pretty sure I still have Billy's old BB gun and I could take it out."

"You wouldn't shoot your grandma, would you? She called."

Jake handed over a coffee. The warm, scented steam rose. Macy curled her hands around the cup.

Jake drew his own cup to his lips, and his gaze, as steamy as the coffee, swept over her. "There goes my fantasy that you sleep in a red silk nightie."

Macy tugged at the front of her cotton pajamas. "Would you mind getting out? I need to say my morning prayers. It's what soon-to-be nuns do." She didn't think he'd have been so brave as to ask Nan about that.

The heat in his eyes faded. Which told her she was right. Now, if she could just do something about the heat in her belly. Why did he look so natural sitting on the edge of her bed? Oh yeah, she'd imagined him here last night. Imagined him crawling under the covers with her, without clothes, to touch places on her body that hadn't been touched in—

"What are your plans today?" he asked. He sipped his coffee.

"I'm going to church," she replied. Not a lie, either. The nun excuse wasn't going to last long, of course—he was bound to wise up sooner or later. But she'd milk it as long as she could.

"And then what?"

Then I'll find some other excuse to keep you at arm's length.

"I usually go visit my mom and Nan at Yoga Works." Seeing Baldwin's pinched brow she explained, "Nan runs a yoga school."

"Biker girl, spray-paint grandma? She does yoga, too?"

Macy shrugged. "Teaches it." She wouldn't tell him what else Nan did.

"You don't go to school today?"

"Not on Thursdays."

"Work?" His face wore an odd expression.

"Not until tomorrow."

"Yeah, well, you should hold off going to work until Tanks is caught." He arched an eyebrow as if knowing she'd challenge him.

She didn't disappoint. "So, you're paying my rent this month?" she asked. "That's sweet of you." She set her coffee down and laughed.

He frowned. "If it'll keep you alive, yeah."

Macy scootched off her mattress, shaking her head. "Actually, I can take care of myself." She then headed for the bathroom, ignoring him as he called her name. She hoped this was one room he'd consider sacred.

Slamming the door behind her, she came to an instant, heels-on-the-linoleum halt. Her eyes alighted on the broad chest and then lowered to—She yelped at the same time as the naked man, and only then did she look up at his face. She scrambled out of the bathroom.

Baldwin stood in the hall. Seeing her horror, his blue eyes danced with humor.

"What's your partner doing naked in my bathroom?" she shrieked.

Baldwin grinned. "I forgot to tell him the singing rule."

* * *

Today Hal felt . . . not better, but clearheaded. He'd cut back on the pain medication, but thinking clearly came with a price. Now he *really* knew how it felt to be shot in the chest.

When the nurse popped in and announced it was time for a walk, he'd told her to go on without him, and if he changed his mind he would catch up. Obviously, she thought he was joking. Now, one hand around his IV stand, he shuffled through the gray hospital halls like an old man. At least his ass was covered, thanks to the pajamas Melissa had brought this morning.

Hal had just cut a corner when he heard a familiar voice from one of the hospital rooms with the door ajar. He listened. The volunteer? What was her name? Faye, wasn't it?

"You're welcome," the woman was saying. "I'll come by and see you later."

Hal stopped walking, if you could call his shuffling a real walk. Was it her?

"You okay?" his nurse asked, looking harried.

"Yeah." He didn't move.

The door opened, and Faye almost ran him over on her way out. She bumped his IV pole and sent the dang thing rocking. As she caught it, her blue eyes found him.

Desire to suck in his gut rolled over Hal. He didn't have a large one, but a man his age came with a toolshed. Funny thing was, he hadn't thought about his toolshed—or his tool—in years. Ahh, but *she* made him think about it.

"We meet again." Hal smiled. "At least I got my clothes on this time."

Faye's gaze darted to his nurse. "Hospital-gown problems," she explained, blushing. Then she met Hal's eyes. "You look better," she offered, though she looked nervous.

"Because I've got clothes on?" he asked.

"Healthier." She was probably in her early fifties, he realized, noticing the gray strands in her dark curly hair, but as her cheeks brightened, she reminded him of someone a lot younger.

The nurse looked back and forth between them. "Great, Faye. You two know each other? Could you finish walking Mr. Klein?" She didn't wait for an answer before she made tracks down the hall.

"Looks like you're stuck with me." Hal glanced at Faye's name tag to see if it had a last name. It didn't.

The woman nodded. "So it seems."

Hal held out his arm, even though a few minutes ago he'd told the nurse he could gimp better without her clinging to him. But the idea of touching Faye . . .

She looped her arm through his, and a warm tickle, the one a normal man gets when he touches a beautiful woman, washed over Hal. Thing was, Hal hadn't felt normal in a long time.

"So"—he purposely kept his pace slow, but began to walk—"how long have you volunteered here?"

"Four years." She kept her eye on the passing doors, as if she couldn't wait to dump him in his room.

"You do anything else besides volunteer?" His hip brushed against hers. It felt good. He caught her fresh, clean scent, too. Not perfumed, but something familiar. Baby powder?

"I . . . work part-time at my mother's yoga school."

He looked at her, to make sure he wasn't hitting on a woman way too young. But nope, there were definitely some signs of age around her eyes. "Your mother runs a yoga school?"

She stopped. "This is your room, isn't it?"

He glanced at the door. "The nurse said I needed to do two laps," he lied, and set off walking again. "It's not often I get escorted by a pretty woman."

When he saw her frown, Hal got a bad feeling. Shit, he hadn't been in this business so long that he'd forgotten to consider she might be married. But when his gaze darted to her left hand, he saw no ring.

She fidgeted with something in her pocket. They took several steps in silence.

"I'm Harold Klein," he said at last. "People call me Hal." He hoped she'd tell him her own full name. He still got the strange feeling he'd met her before.

"Hal's a nice name," she said, but she didn't look at him.

"Doing good, Mr. Klein!" one of the nurses called out, walking by.

He smiled at her, then focused on Faye again. "So, what do you do at the hospital?"

"Run errands, help with the food trays." The woman still didn't look at him.

"Walk old men around the halls," he suggested.

She glanced up. "You're not old."

"I feel old right now." *Or I did until you walked up.*

"You'll feel better in a few days."

"I might if . . . you'll come visit me." It was a horrible come-on line, but Hal lacked practice. Not that he hadn't whispered sweet nothings to his wife, but those had been different, not first-time nothings. "Will you? Come visit me again?" he asked.

Her eyes widened and she glanced away. "I'm pretty busy."

He frowned, realizing he'd failed. "I guess I'm bad at this."

"Bad at what?" she asked.

"I haven't flirted in thirty years. I guess a man gets rusty."

He'd forgotten what it was like to be rejected by a woman. His chest felt heavy, and not because of the bullet he'd taken. He let go of her arm as they reached his room and she stopped. "Sorry if I made you uncomfortable."

"I need to see you to your bed," she said. She wouldn't even look at him.

He shuffled in and pushed himself up on his mattress. She gave his legs a little lift. Then she pulled his house slippers off and dropped them on the floor.

"Thanks," he said.

He expected her to run out, but instead she stood there, staring at her hands. And, damn it, he could swear he saw tears in her eyes.

"I've got my clothes on," he joked. "You have no reason to cry."

She half grinned. Then, raising her tear-filled eyes she said, "Maybe it's not that you're bad at flirting. I'm probably rusty at being flirted with."

Hope fluttered to life in his aching chest. "Then maybe you'll give me another shot. Come back this afternoon?"

"I—I'm leaving in just a bit."

"Tomorrow, then?" he tried.

She stood there, clearly debating with herself. Finally: "For a short visit."

"I'll look forward to it."

She didn't say, *Me, too,* but he could swear he saw it in her eyes. For the first time in eons, Hal found himself smiling for no apparent reason.

Jake sat in his office, thumping his pencil against his desk and studying the recent unsolved-robbery files. Donaldson sat across from him, his nose in his own stack of documents. Jake's mind kept jumping from his work to the sweet way Macy's mouth tilted when she smiled. To the taste he'd had of that mouth. To how sexy she'd made pink cotton pj's look.

"So, we have six burglaries that were tagged with red paint and four that weren't," Donaldson said.

It took Jake a minute to pull his thoughts away from pink flannel being unbuttoned, of imagining his hand running along feminine dips and valleys. "Yeah, there're ten," he said.

"You're right. There are major differences between those houses that were tagged with paint and those that weren't." Donaldson pointed to one file. "For example, the cases that had graffiti took only the big items, were grab and go. No searching for the harder-to-find valuables." He picked up another file folder. "The others, the perps either knew where things were or took time to look."

"My thoughts exactly." But Jake's thoughts were actually

on Macy. Would he ever get a chance to remove that pink flannel, or would it be replaced by a nun's habit?

"You know anything about the Catholic religion?" he asked.

Donaldson's brow furrowed. "I'm Methodist."

Jake looked up as Evelyn, an older female clerk, walked by his open door. She looked Catholic, didn't she? Not that he had a clue what a Catholic looked like.

"But I met the pope once," Donaldson continued. "In Italy, in—"

"Evelyn?" Jake called, interrupting.

She stuck her head in the door. "Yeah?"

"You Catholic?" he asked.

She smiled. "Buddhist."

Tired from his lack of sleep, and frustrated, he asked, "Do you *know* anyone who's Catholic—a friend, a neighbor, your mailman?"

"Why?" Evelyn and Donaldson both asked.

"No reason. Never mind."

Jake ignored Donaldson and Evelyn's shared look and gazed at his watch. Eleven o'clock. Macy had said she'd be at church until afternoon. Hell, instead of looking for a Catholic person, why not go directly to the church and ask there? And while he visited, maybe he could talk Macy into having lunch with him.

Besides, he had to explain to her why she wouldn't be delivering pizzas for a while. He hadn't told her about finding her work address circled at the murder scene, because he hadn't wanted to scare her. But if scaring her was a way to get her to see reason, he'd do it.

He stood. "I'll be back after lunch," he said. Turning to Donaldson he added, "Do me a favor. Call the victims of the robberies and see how many have painted over the graffiti. Let's get chip samples from those who haven't, see if they match the stuff on Macy's walls."

He'd just made it to his car when his phone rang. Checking

the number, he smiled. "Hello, Mom. Nice day, isn't it?" He looked around. Blue sky. Green grass. Even the birds chirped. What more could a person ask?

"I wanted to ask you if you'd do me a big favor," his mom said.

He got in his car. "A favor? What?"

"I've ordered some chicken salad from that deli by your house for your grandfather's party. I was wondering if you would pick it up and bring it when you come."

The day suddenly lost its appeal. Jake knew this was his mother's way of finding out if he seriously planned on coming. And . . . he seriously didn't. But each time he'd start to tell her so, he'd recall the last conversation he'd had with his dad. He'd promised his dying father he'd make sure his mom was always happy.

"Let's talk about this over lunch tomorrow," he suggested. "How about the deli you like on Fifth Street?" If he was going to break her heart and his promise to his father, he could at least do it over the pasta salad she loved.

"Lunch is great. But son, I expect you to be at your grandfather's party. It's time to make amends. I swear, if I have to personally snatch your dad from Heaven to talk with you, you will be at that party!"

He didn't get to reply. His mother had hung up.

CHAPTER FOURTEEN

Jake spent the drive over to the church worrying about his mom's doggedness to reconcile the differences between him and his brother, differences Jake wasn't so sure were reconcilable. What did she expect him to do, go shake his brother's hand and say, *I'm glad you're happy and found yourself a great little wife—never mind that she was supposed to be mine?*

Parking in front of the church, Jake popped a lid on those thoughts and went back to his original problem: Macy. While he didn't have a clue how to ask if the church allowed divorced women to become nuns, he'd be damned if he left without knowing Macy's availability.

A warm breeze stirred as he stepped out of his car. Everything smelled and looked green. Spring fever—the world was changing and he didn't mind one bit, because for the first time in two years, Jake felt like changing. He wanted . . . more. He wasn't ready to make amends with Lisa and his brother yet, but he wanted to move past the emptiness in which he'd wallowed for the last two years.

As he started up the church steps, he spotted the black sedan parked across the street. Agent Mimms, he suspected. He was pleased the task force had continued Macy's sometime protection, but he suspected they would be pulling the tail if Tanks didn't try something soon. The idea of Tanks trying something didn't appeal to Jake, but neither did the idea of Macy being left unguarded.

As he reached for the church door, it swung open. A man in his early fifties wearing mud-caked overalls barged out. "You're going the wrong way, aren't you?" the man asked in a cheery voice. Then, startled, he gave Jake a second look.

Jake hesitated. "Well, I was—"

"I'm sorry. I thought you were someone else. I'm Father Luis." The priest held out his hand. "Can I help you?"

Jake shook, ignoring the dirt.

"Excuse my muddiness. I'm working in the garden."

As the priest zipped off down the steps, Jake followed. "I'm Sergeant Jake Baldwin, with the HPD."

"Ah." The priest chuckled. "You should keep your naked partner out of Macy's bathroom. Or at least tell him the singing rule."

Jake fought back surprise. Macy had told the priest about that? "I . . . Mark swore he wouldn't wake up if he didn't take a quick shower, and I didn't think Macy would mind. I tried to warn her."

The priest just laughed. "Walk with me. Macy's in the garden. I'm assuming you're here to see her."

And to get some answers, Jake silently vowed. "The garden?"

"She didn't tell you about her garden?" Father Luis continued walking.

"*Her* garden?"

"Well, God's garden. But Macy's brainchild. We were going to simply plant roses, and she said, 'Roses don't fill bellies.' Girl's got a way with words, doesn't she?"

"I've thought the same thing, myself."

"Anyway, it's been an amazing success for three years." The priest talked at the same speed as he walked; Jake had to walk fast to keep up. "Sister Beth has been tremendous at heading it up after Macy got it started, but now she's being called away, and we're stranded. There's a shortage of help within the church, you know." Father Luis shook his head. "Then one morning God told me to offer the position back to Macy."

Position? That doesn't sound like joining a convent. "Give it back to Macy? You mean . . ."

"Macy told me about the prison escape. Poor girl."

Father Luis kept walking and talking. He and Jake darted across the street, dodging traffic, and passed in front of the black sedan where Mimms probably waited. Jake gave the dark windshield a nod, then saw a two-acre garden. He almost tripped over the sidewalk at the sight of Macy.

Instead of the jeans she'd worn out of the house this morning, she had on a pair of khaki shorts. Not too short, not too tight, but what he could see sent every bit of his blood south. Slender legs, shapely calves, and the way the shorts fit her backside . . .

She raised her hands and stretched. The pink T-shirt she wore pulled across her breasts. Jake's body, not caring that a priest stood nearby or that they were fifty feet from a place of worship, responded with about two years of stored-up desire. He wanted those legs wrapped around his waist, to feel those breasts in his hands and up against his naked chest. Damn it, he had to know if she was off-limits!

He took some fast steps to catch up with Father Luis. "We're tying up the tomatoes," the clergyman said.

"Sir . . . uh, Father?" Jake interrupted before he lost his nerve. "About Macy's position . . ."

"Listen to Father laugh," Sister Beth said. "I'm going to miss him." The Sister looked up from the tomato plant and glanced over Macy's shoulder. "What's he doing here today? I thought his crew comes tomorrow."

"Who?" Macy turned around to see, but the sun hit her eyes. All she could see were two male shapes. Looking back at the plant, she pulled out the small branch so it wouldn't get tied along with the stem. The smell of earth and the verdant scent of tomato vines flavored the air. Working in the garden brought her peace. Here, at least, she felt what she did produced positive results. Face it, she hated failing, and lately she'd tallied up too many failures in her life.

"Oh. That's not Pastor Harry." Sister Beth went back to knotting the strip of material around the plant. "But he's the spitting image of him."

"I've never met him," Macy said.

A couple of shadows fell over them. Macy looked up at a smiling Father Luis, but the other man was still indistinguishable in the sun's glare.

"Did you two know that Macy is considering entering the convent? A Methodist nun!" The clergyman's brown eyes danced with humor as he asked.

Baldwin.

Macy knew the nun story would fall flat sooner or later. She just hadn't planned on having witnesses when it fell.

"Really?" Sister Beth chuckled and gave Macy a nudge on the arm. "Must have been seeing that naked man this morning."

Macy regretted sharing that story, too.

"Sister Macy Tucker." Father Luis laughed again, but managed to make introductions. "This is the detective watching out for her."

Sister Beth stood. "Oh, my. I hope you weren't the one in—"

"No, ma'am," Baldwin answered and shifted into a spot where Macy could see him better. "It wasn't me."

Father Luis spoke up. "How about we check on the baby corn and leave *Sister* Macy with the detective to talk about her entering the Methodist convent."

Sister Beth said good-bye to Baldwin and made footprints in the moist dirt as she hurried after Father Luis. Macy watched her go.

Feeling the same disconcertment she usually felt around Baldwin, Macy stood, dusted off her hands, and faced him. His grin made her want to step back, but she thought she might trample the baby cucumbers. So she held her ground in midrow.

"I never actually told you I was entering the convent. You just assumed. . . ."

"More of my shoddy police work." He chuckled. "For some reason, I don't do my best work when you're around." His gaze lowered to her legs. "Too many distractions."

She ignored the heat in his eyes and the sexy tone of his voice, and heard Father Luis laughing again.

"Exactly what did you say to him?" she asked.

Jake's left eyebrow quirked upward. "Let's just say it wasn't one of my finer moments." He paused. "So you're not even Catholic?"

She shook her head. "I met Father Luis at a shelter where I volunteered a couple of years ago. We hit it off."

"I can see why. He seems like a nice guy."

Yeah, sort of like you. Their gazes met, held, and Macy felt the pull between them.

A war of instincts battled inside. One screamed *Run*, while the other cheered *Jump his bones right here in the tomato patch.* Her hormones had no shame! However, she didn't plan on listening to either voice. On the drive over this morning, she'd given her situation some serious thought. Basically, she needed Jake Baldwin. Not Baldwin the man, but Baldwin the detective. Not just for her safety, but to keep her posted about Billy.

Billy.

Her gaze shot to Baldwin. Did he have news? "Is everything okay?"

"Yeah. I just thought I could buy a soon-to-be nun lunch."

Her gaze moved over him. He wore jeans and a green polo shirt that hung loose, average clothes that didn't look average on him. Sex appeal oozed from him like honey out of an overstuffed beehive.

No. She had to put her raging hormones on hold. There was no time for men. She had tomatoes to tie up, a brother to save, a law degree to get, and oh yeah, she'd sworn off men for the next two lifetimes. It had originally been six lifetimes, but after her reviving hormones made their presence known, she'd decided to be reasonable. Two was more reasonable.

"Can't. I need to finish here," she said.

He glanced around. "So this was your brainchild?"

Macy shrugged. "I read about one like it in a magazine. It just seemed . . . doable."

"He told me about the produce donated last year to shelters. You should be proud."

"It's done well, but not because of me. The community rallied behind it. We've got about eight churches that volunteer, even . . ." She brushed a mosquito from her face and looked up at him, remembering. "Sister Beth said you looked—"

"Did you take the church's job offer?" he interrupted.

"I couldn't say no. Father Luis said he'd work with me on my school schedule. They're turning it into a paid position."

"So, you're quitting the pizza-delivery business?"

"Not exactly. With what the church can pay, I'll still have to work part-time."

"How about cooling it for a while? Just until Tanks is caught."

"You make it sound as if you think he'll be caught soon."

"I do. Escapees are usually taken down . . ." He paused. "I mean—"

The fear for Billy that she'd been holding at bay hit full force in a wave. "What's going to happen to my brother?"

She didn't need to ask. Even the best-case scenario said Billy's prison sentence would be drawn out considerably. But maybe she wanted someone to lie to her.

"If we can get him to turn himself in, it'll go easier," he replied.

Okay, so Baldwin was one of the honorable types who wouldn't lie. But at least he'd tried to sound positive. She dropped down on her knees beside the next tomato plant. Its smell flavored her frustrated gasp of air. Snatching up a strip of material, she wrapped it around the stem.

"I feel helpless," she said. "He doesn't call me, and if he did . . . He's stubborn."

"Must be a family trait." Baldwin's knees popped as he bent down on the other side of the tomato plant. Slipping his hand into it, he held the stem to the stick for her to tie. "I don't want you delivering pizzas right now."

"Why? Tanks knows where I live. I'm probably safer at work than home." She wrapped the strip of yellow cotton around the stake and tied it.

"He knows where you work, too."

Baldwin's tense tone had her studying him through the green tomato leaves. "How do you know that?"

His eyes narrowed, but he didn't speak.

"What are you not telling me?" She fell back on her bottom. "Is Billy okay?"

"I haven't heard anything about Billy." Baldwin stood up.

"Tell me what you know. It's our deal. Remember?" She raised her gaze. The sun came from behind him, making her blink. Her eyes began to water, and she blamed it on the glare. Then she blamed it on herself. Everything on herself. If she'd visited Billy from the beginning none of this would have happened. He wouldn't have been so lonely that he got involved with Ellie. Tanks wouldn't have threatened him.

It was all her fault.

Jake looked at Macy. She had tears in her eyes and a smudge of dirt across her cheek—and he'd never wanted to kiss a woman so badly in his life. "I got called to a case last night. Which is why Donaldson was at your house and—"

"What does that have to do—?"

"A man was murdered last night."

Her eyes widened. "Billy?"

"No. I told you I didn't know anything more about him. It wasn't Billy." Jake stepped between the rowed plants and knelt down beside her. "But when Billy called me, he said that Tanks had killed someone else. And the reason your brother went looking for you at work was that he found a phone book with the address of Papa's Pizza marked."

"My work address?" Her face lost a little color.

He watched her struggle not to cry, to not be afraid. She looked back at the tomato plants, snatched up the strips of material, and moved to the next plant. He'd never seen a woman work so hard to hide her vulnerability. Right then he knew he'd never met a woman like Macy. So yin and yang. So sweet yet sassy. So soft yet hard. So self-reliant but ready to embrace the needs of others. So afraid but courageous.

"You okay?" He moved next to her.

"What choice do I have? I have to be okay. Just tired of being freaking helpless!"

He dropped down and reached in to hold the plant close to the stake. She tied the stem. Then she moved to the next.

For thirty minutes, they worked together. He held. She tied. They seldom spoke. But whenever their hands met inside a tomato plant, he felt the power of their touch. She felt it, too. He knew because she'd raise her gaze to his. Once he even brushed his thumb over her knuckles. As they worked, he found himself thinking that his father would have liked her. It was, Jake realized, the measuring stick he judged women by when they crossed the line from just somebody to somebody special. Macy was special. How she'd moved to this level in such a short time, he didn't know. He hadn't even slept with her. While his first instinct was to search for his mental brakes again, his second instinct brought him up short.

Go for the ride, a voice whispered in his head.

They finally came to the end of the row. Jake stood and knocked the dirt from his knees. "You need to eat some lunch. Let me take you somewhere."

"I'm not hungry," she insisted.

"Did you eat breakfast?" he asked.

"I grabbed a yogurt."

"That's not enough. Let me take you out for a burger."

She tilted her chin back. "You're not my keeper, Baldwin."

"Yeah, but I'm considering the position." He wiped his thumb over the mud on her cheek. Then he let his hand move behind her neck. She was sweating, and all those soft moist curls of her hair rested on the back of his hand. He fought the desire to press his lips to her neck, to taste her with a hint of sweat on her skin, knowing she'd taste just like that when he got through making love to her.

"I'm not taking applications," she growled.

"Good, because I don't much care for competition."

"You're not listening to me." She brushed his hand from her neck. "I don't want . . . this." She motioned between her and him.

Jake had never lacked confidence, but her words dinged his ego. Thankfully, his ego was pretty thick. "You need me, Pizza Girl."

"I need your protection. Agreed. I need someone who'll keep me informed about my brother. But that's all I need, Baldwin. Do you understand what I'm saying?"

"Yeah." He smiled. "I just don't believe it. We've got something between us. Chemistry, fate—I don't know what to call it. I don't even know where it's leading; but I'd like to take the ride to find out."

"I've been on that ride, and I don't like where it leads." She turned to go.

"You didn't go with me."

"You're all alike," she said over her shoulder.

"That's not fair."

"Who told you life is fair?" She started walking.

Jake decided not to push. "What time will you be home?"

"You're not my keeper," she repeated. She didn't look back.

He let her go. For now. But not for long. This ball-busting, conniving, sassy gardener who worried about feeding the poor had gotten under his skin, and he planned to keep her there.

Jake stood in the middle of the garden for a few minutes thinking about how his dad would have liked Macy, and then he started for his car. The black sedan of Agent Mimms caught his gaze. He walked over and motioned for the FBI man to roll down the window. It stayed up. He gave the dark glass a tap. Nothing.

His gaze caught the back door on the other side, which had been left ajar. Damn! He grabbed his Glock from his shoulder holster and raced around. Hit with an adrenaline rush, he jerked the door open. Agent Mimms lay slumped over the steering wheel. Then Jake saw the blood.

The smell and sound of bacon frying woke Billy up around noon. Ellie stood by the stove. Andy's dog Spike sat beside her.

"Okay, one more." Ellie dropped the dog a piece of bacon. "But no more, or there won't be enough for breakfast." The dog cocked his head and she chuckled. "You're too cute. I guess I didn't need any anyhow." She gave the dog another piece.

Billy smiled. How a person could be so miserable and exhilarated at the same time, he didn't know. But that's what he was, caught in a tug-of-war of emotions. His gaze shifted to Ellie's backside, which was encased in a pair of cutoff jeans. The memory of last night took his normal morning hard-on up a notch.

Sex with Ellie had been the best he'd ever had. He knew why, too. They hadn't just had sex. They'd made love. Twice. Billy dropped his chin on the pillow. There wasn't a place on her body that he hadn't kissed and tasted. And he'd done it slow, the way he'd heard women liked.

Oh, she'd liked it. A sense of pride brought on another smile. Too bad it had to end.

He flung himself over and stared at the ceiling.

"You're awake?" Ellie dashed across the room and wriggled that soft body down beside him. "You hungry?" She kissed him.

"Yeah, but you've fed Spike all the bacon," he complained with a smile. "Is Andy here?" Curling his hand around her waist, he thought that maybe they could postpone breakfast.

"Yeah, he's in his room, and he went by the store. We've got eggs and bacon and toast!"

Billy's stomach ached with the hollowness of hunger, but his heart ached from knowing his time with Ellie was almost over. "It smells good."

"Then come eat." She shot upright and tugged on his hand.

He pulled her back to the sofa, and she fell against him. Chasing away thoughts of getting her naked, he concentrated on what he needed to ask—things he'd thought about last night after she'd fallen asleep.

"How well did you know David?"

She frowned. "I never loved him. We never even . . . you know."

Relief washed over him, but that wasn't what he needed to know. Billy ran his hand up her arm, wanting to memorize how she felt. "Where do you think he's at? Where would he go?"

"I thought you said you knew where he was going."

He hadn't told her about last night, except that he'd waited for David to show up, and he hadn't. The less she knew the better. "I'm thinking he might have gone somewhere else."

She hesitated. "He might go to his ex-girlfriend's house. I think her name is Jamie Clay. I don't know where she lives, but she works at Girls Galore. The strip club."

Right then Billy knew he had to find a way to get into that club. He recalled the fake IDs he'd stuffed under his mattress at home. Would they still be there? Would the cops be watching Nan's place?

There was only one way to find out.

His gun gripped tight, Jake touched Agent Mimms's neck to check for signs of life. The skin felt warm. Warm was good. A slight flutter danced beneath the man's skin. A pulse! Thank God. Maybe it wasn't as bad as it looked.

Jake cut his eyes around, looking for the person who could have done this, but the streets stood empty. He grabbed his phone from his pocket and, hitting the button, spat out his name and badge number, and then: "Officer down. I need an ambulance and backup." He gave the names of the cross streets, then moved out of the backseat and opened the front door to get a better look at Mimms. Blood covered one side of his face, but at least the man was breathing.

Jake could think of only one reason the man had been attacked: Macy. His gaze zipped back to the church. Where was she? His heart slammed against his rib cage. Then he spotted Father Luis jogging down the steps.

Jake stepped back and yelled to the priest, "Find Macy. Get her inside!"

Instead of listening, the priest bolted over. "What? Macy left. She went to Nan's yoga place. What's—?" His gaze shifted to Agent Mimms. "Dear God, what happened?"

"She left?" Jake stared up and down the street. "When?"

"A few minutes ago. Is he okay?"

"I've called for help."

Jake snapped open his phone and hit buttons until he found Agent James's number. He made the call. "Answer, damn it!" Beside him, the priest knelt down next to the injured FBI man—to pray or check on him, Jake didn't know. He hoped both.

"Agent James," the Fed finally answered.

"It's Baldwin. Someone got to Agent Mimms."

Agent James started spouting questions, but Jake cut him off and told him their location. "He's alive. I've called for backup. Got an ambulance on its way. Macy Tucker has driven away, however. They probably followed her. I'm going after her."

"Is the scene clear?" Agent James asked.

"Looks clear." He straightened and took in his surroundings again.

"Not good enough! Don't you dare leave my man alone."

Jake hung up. Police procedure demanded he stay. His heart said go. In the distance, sirens blared. Music to Jake's ears.

"I'm going after Macy," he yelled to the priest after he'd run halfway across the street. "Where's her grandmother's yoga school, anyway?"

"Two miles down on the right. Past the second light, beside the Target."

A patrol car squealed to halt and an officer jumped out. Jake held out his badge and pointed to Agent Mimms's sedan. "He's FBI," he called, dashing for his car. "Medics are on their way."

He crawled into his vehicle, ignoring the backup officer's questions, then sped off. He kept a lead foot on the gas pedal. God, let him get there in time.

CHAPTER FIFTEEN

When Macy walked into Nan's yoga studio, all the lights were off and the blackout shades were down. The smell of burning incense and a lone jasmine-scented candle flickering in the darkness told her a class was about to begin.

She slipped through front area to peek into the back, into the yoga room. Inching open the door, she expected to give Nan just a little wave. Before she could peer inside, someone caught her elbow.

Tanks?

Macy swung around, knee raised and ready, when . . . "Nan, you scared—"

"Thank heavens you're here." Her grandma pulled Macy across the room to the stairs to the second level. She ascended.

"What's up?" Macy bounded up the steps to keep pace.

"Your mom's up. *Really* up. Not that I'm not happy about it, but I have a class." She opened the door at the top of stairs, and the sunlight pouring in the room beyond made Macy blink. Today Nan wore lime green leggings paired with a purple shirt that read DON'T WORRY. JUST HIDE THE BODY.

"She's what?" Macy glanced away from Nan's shirt into the empty office and makeshift lunchroom. The door from the small bathroom creaked open and her mom stepped out, humming. See? Even her mother knew the singing rule.

But, something wasn't right. Faye Moore didn't hum. She normally was too busy crying.

"Mace!" Her mom said, sounding like a giddy teenager. "Oh, goodie. I need your help."

Goodie? Faye Moore didn't hum, and she didn't say goodie either.

Okay, an "up" mom would require some getting used to. But seeing her mom smile, Macy decided she could deal with it. "Help with what?" She glanced at Nan for a hint.

Her mom spoke. "I didn't know what color would look good, so I got them all. Except the blonde. I don't see myself as a blonde."

Macy's gaze fell to a nearby table where at least ten Nice 'n Easy boxes lined up like soldiers. "You're dyeing your hair?"

"Why didn't anyone tell me I'd gone gray?" Her mom ran her fingers through her grizzled curls. "You'll help, right?"

"Me? Don't you remember the time I did Nan's hair?"

Macy's grandmother chuckled. "I liked that shade of purple." Then she pointed to the bags crowding the room's love seat. "She bought clothes, too."

"Clothes?" Macy plopped down in a chair. Her mom *never* bought clothes. Whenever Macy would say something about tossing out a blouse or a dress, her mother would say, *Your dad loves this.* Loves! Not loved.

Her mom picked up a box of hair dye. "I think all we have to do is mix bottle A with bottle B, after we decide what color."

"I have a class," Nan reminded them. "I leave you in good hands." On her way out, she whispered to Macy, "No purple."

Nan bounced down the stairs. Macy's gaze flickered from the table of Nice 'n Easy to her mother. "Why are you doing this?"

Instantly, Macy wished she could take back the words, scared her mom would back out and, in a small way, also scared she wouldn't. Change was frightening, even good change. For some half-baked reason, Macy's thoughts shot to Baldwin, to their hands touching in the tomato plants to the possibilities of where those electric sensations could lead.

No! She didn't want change. Especially not that kind.

She'd tried that lifestyle on for size, hadn't she? It fit like a too-tight thong. She'd married Tom, believed in love, honor, and "until death do you part." In her case, death had been his secretary.

"You don't think I should dye my hair?" her mother asked with a sniffle.

No, not the tears. "Yes, I do." Macy tossed Baldwin into the darkest corner of her mind, where no doubt she'd return to him later.

Her mom's eyes continued to tear. "Your dad wouldn't like it, would he?" Sniffle.

Macy frantically searched for the right words, something short that encompassed her exact feelings. Advice from the heart.

"Screw that bastard!" Faye Moore snapped, taking the words from Macy's lips. Her mom scrubbed a tear from her cheek. "Screw him and his gold panning. Screw him for walking out on his family. I'm dyeing my fucking hair. And look!" She pushed back her curls. "I even got my ears pierced with a second hole. I'm considering doing my belly button next."

Macy's mouth dropped open. Then, realizing her mom needed positive reinforcement, she pulled herself together. "Go, Mom!" She paused. "But don't ever say 'fuck' again. Mothers don't say that. And your belly button is fine without holes."

Her mother laughed—a deep, soulful, contagious laugh. The kind that hinted at newfound freedom. The kind that came with so much emotion, it brought on new tears. Good tears. And while they giggled and cried together, Macy saw strength in Faye Moore that she hadn't known existed. Her mom really was Nan's daughter.

"I love you." Macy gave her mom a hug. Then she turned back to the table and eyed the various boxes before she cratered and they had to arm themselves with tissues. "Do you want to be a sexy redhead or a sassy brunette?"

"Do men find redheads sexy?" Faye's smile was sly.

"Probably."

Macy wondered what had nudged her mother into recovery. It couldn't be a man, could it? No, not after she'd spent the last fourteen years trying to get over what the last one had done to her.

The sparkle in her mom's eyes had Macy rethinking. "Let's do red," Faye chirped.

It was on the tip of Macy's tongue to warn her mother against jumping back into the fire, but then her mom started humming again. Her mom deserved to hum, didn't she?

"Red it is." Macy opened the box. And as she mixed the supplies, she refused to dwell on the fact that maybe her mother wasn't the only person who deserved to hum.

Jake pushed open the door to Yoga Works. His heart hadn't slowed. The lights were off, and the silence shot adrenaline through his veins. He reached for his Glock and took another step, heard a murmur of voices in the back, and pushed open another door. The smell of burnt herbs filled his nose. Then he saw it: someone facedown on the floor. Was he too late?

"Police!" Blinking his eyes, he needed another second to adjust to the dimness.

Light suddenly flooded the room. Many people were spread out on the floor, their knees over their heads, asses in the air. Jake's gaze shot around the room, looking for a certain heart-shaped posterior.

"What are you doing?" The voice came from behind him. He turned and stared at Macy's grandma, who was standing by the light switch. She eyed his gun. "No fair. I didn't bring my paint."

He ignored that. "Where's Macy?" he asked.

"Upstairs." The humor in her expression faded. "What happened?"

Jake darted back to the front, where he'd seen a staircase. His gut now told him she was okay, but he needed to see her.

He bounded up the steps and slung open the door at the top . . . and stopped short. Macy stood behind her mom, who sat in a chair. Macy's startled gaze shifted from where she'd been squirting something onto her mother's hair.

"Oh, *goodie*," Macy said, sounding anything but pleased. "We've got company." Then she seemed to spot his gun. "What's wrong?"

Jake tucked his Glock into its shoulder holster. Macy's grandma appeared beside him.

"Is my son okay?" Macy's mom clutched a green towel to her chest, and something dark red dripped down her brow.

"It's not Billy." Jake met Macy's concerned gaze. "I need you to come with me."

"It's not Billy?" Macy turned his words into a question. Fear danced in her blue eyes.

"No. I promise."

She looked at her mom's hair. "Let me finish this first."

He tapped his watch. "I don't have time—"

"She can't leave!" her mom insisted. "I'll end up purple."

"And I've got a class to teach." Nan bounded back down the stairs.

Jake cut his gaze to Macy. "This is important," he said.

"So is this," Mrs. Moore replied. "If she messes up my hair, I'll cry. And I'm really trying hard not to do that anymore. Except if it's about Billy. I can cry about my son."

Macy started squeezing the dark substance faster into her mother's locks. "One minute."

It took two. Jake timed it on his watch.

"What time is it?" Macy set the bottle on the table.

The vision of Agent Mimms slumped over the steering wheel flashed in Jake's head. "Time to go." At her frown, he looked at his watch. "One fifteen." He'd been gone ten minutes from a scene he should never have left.

Macy looked at her mom. "Wait forty-five minutes and then rinse."

Frowning, Mrs. Moore pointed a finger at Jake. "I don't care if you *are* Macy's boyfriend. If I'm purple, it's your fault."

"I understand." Jake looked at Macy and waved toward the door.

"He's not my boyfriend," Macy snapped. She grabbed her purse from the floor and hurried out and down the stairs.

Jake followed, his gaze fixed on Macy's backside. With each sway, he became determined of two things: hurrying back to the scene, and making a liar out of Macy. He was going to be her boyfriend.

The moment she exited the building, Macy stopped. Jake didn't. He wrapped his arm around her waist and forced her to keep walking.

"What happened?" she asked.

After hitting the clicker on his key chain, he opened his car's passenger door. "I'll explain while I drive."

"But my car. I'll just—"

"No," he insisted.

"Yes!"

She opened her mouth to speak again, and with no time to argue, he did the only thing he could think of to shut her up. He kissed her. He expected nothing more than a chaste touching of lips that would surprise her enough to get her into his car. His expectations were more than matched. She melted into him, soft breasts to his abdomen. Her lips, warm and pliant, met his with enthusiasm. Damn, if she wasn't kissing him back!

But he had to get back to the church. He pulled away. "I . . . I need a rain check."

She blinked, dazed. "Why do you keep doing that?"

"It shuts you up." And with a nudge, he settled her into the passenger seat. Leaning inside, he buckled her in. As he started to draw back, he paused to stare at her mouth, which was still wet from their kiss. "And because I like it. A lot."

Billy sat on Andy's porch so that he could breathe the fresh air. It smelled like trees and nature. The birds sang and the squirrels rustled. The thought of going back to only echoes—

to a life regulated by guards and steel bars—made Billy want to hit something. But a good man didn't hit things. That was a lesson he'd learned from his no-good dad.

The door behind Billy opened, and Andy and his dog Spike stepped out. The porch wobbled as the boy sat down on the steps.

"You gonna stay here tonight?" he asked.

"If you don't mind. Just for a few more days." Or so Billy hoped. Last night he'd sensed it was a race: find David Tanks before the cops did . . . or before Tanks found him. Every time he left Andy's trailer Billy knew he chanced getting caught. "I'll make it up to you somehow." He thought again about telling Mace and Nan about Andy. They'd help the kid.

"I don't mind." Andy scratched his dog behind the ears. "It's nice having company. And besides, Ellie cleaned my place. She cooks good, too." The dog settled at Andy's side.

"That's women for you. Cooking, cleaning . . ."

"Yeah, women." Andy stared off into the trees. "My mom didn't cook, but she did get mad when I'd leave my schoolbooks everywhere."

"My mom fussed about my dirty underwear on the floor," Billy admitted, wishing he could go back to the old days, when leaving clothes around was his biggest sin. Then again, he supposed not appreciating people was a pretty big sin, too.

"Where's your mom now?" Andy asked.

"In Houston." Billy watched a bird soar through the air.

"Did she come to see you in prison?"

"Every week."

Billy saw two squirrels chase each other up a tree. He listened to the scratchy sound of their nails clinging to the tree bark, and reflected on how free they were. A breeze stirred, and Billy thought about flying a kite. His mom bought him one every Easter. He'd bet he had three of them in his closet, never opened. Crazy, but now he'd give anything to fly one.

"And your dad, he come to see you, too?"

Billy shook his head. "He left."

"Mine, too." Andy petted his dog. "You miss him?"

Billy almost said no. "I barely remember him, and what I remember isn't good. But . . . yeah, I miss him. Or at least I miss having a dad."

"Me, too." Andy paused as they were interrupted by a chattering squirrel. "What did you do to get put in prison?"

Billy winced. "I let my friends talk me into doing something bad."

"What did you do?"

Even the wind grew quiet, as if to listen. "They robbed a convenience store. I was in the car. I didn't . . . I thought they were just going to shoplift some beer. It was still wrong. You need to be careful who your friends are."

"I just have one friend," Andy said. His dog nosed him. "Nobody got hurt, did they? During the robbery?"

"No. But it was wrong, and I'm paying for it."

Andy waved a bee away. "Ellie said you met her while you were in prison. So maybe going to jail wasn't a bad thing."

"She's the best thing in my life, but what I did was still wrong. And prison *is* a bad thing." Billy looked back at the door. "What's she doing?"

"She's using my phone to call someone."

"Damn." Ellie obviously didn't understand how important it was to keep a low profile. "To call who?" Billy watched Andy shrug, so he got up to go find out.

"What happened?" Macy nipped at her bottom lip that still tasted like his kiss and watched Jake zip through the afternoon traffic.

"I found Agent Mimms in his car in front of the church. Someone attacked him."

"Is he . . . is he going to be okay?" Questions ran through her head. "They don't . . . they don't think Billy did it, do they?"

"It's too soon to name suspects, but my money's on Tanks. Whoever did this wanted to get to you."

Macy's chest clenched, and she laced her hands together. "It's my fault."

Jake moved a hand from the steering wheel to her shoulder. "You can't control what Tanks does."

"I know, but—"

"It's not your fault." He parked in front of the church just as two medics jumped into an ambulance. The sirens began to blare.

"Was he shot? He's not going to . . ." She couldn't say it. The idea someone might die was horrible.

"He didn't appear shot, but I'm not positive." He faced her. "Macy?"

Their eyes met, and she fought the odd desire to throw herself against him and cry. That's when she realized how dangerously close she was to depending on him. Depending on him emotionally.

"It's *not* your fault," he repeated. "You got that?"

Taking a deep breath, she watched the ambulance drive off.

"Stay here and I'll find out about Mimms's condition and come back and tell you." Jake leaned over and kissed her forehead. "You going to be okay?" Tenderness filled his voice.

She glanced up to see the concern in his eyes. "Yeah."

He moved in to kiss her again. Her hand shot out, but he smiled. "I've got a rain check."

"I didn't give you one."

"I took it when you weren't looking." He touched her cheek. "Stay in the car. I can't have you running around a crime scene."

"But—"

"Macy . . . Please?"

She watched him get out and walk away. He went to talk to someone. Then, keeping his promise, he headed back to the car.

She opened the door to meet him, started to get out, but he pushed her back into the seat. "Mimms wasn't shot, just hit with something from behind. He's regained consciousness. They think he's going to make it."

"Thank God." She let out a breath.

"I've got to finish up here. It could take a while. I'll check on you in a bit." He tucked a strand of her hair behind her ear. The tenderness in his touch made her heart ache.

"Is this really necessary?"

"What?" His hand lingered against her neck.

"My having to wait here. Can't I just go home?"

He frowned. "I've seen what this guy does. I'm not going to let that happen to you. We're going to be spending a lot of time together." He studied her. "Am I such bad company?"

"No." She wished she didn't like his company at all. Or his kisses. "I don't get it."

A breeze sent his brown hair stirring. "Don't get what?"

"Why you're doing this. We're not even friends."

He leaned in until his breath touched hers. "We're more than friends. We both know it."

Her denial, like hope, sprang eternal. "I don't know anything."

He stared at her mouth and his lips tilted into a warm smile. "Really? Then why did you kiss me in the parking lot? Why is it that when I get close to you, I can see your pulse fluttering in your neck?" He put a finger to the spot and lowered his mouth to hers—not to kiss her, but just to whisper the words, "You *want* me, Macy Tucker, as much as I want you. Don't fight it."

"I'm a fighter by nature," she replied.

He grinned. "That's why I like you so much."

Hal raised his hospital bed a few inches. "And bring my razor and aftershave when you come back," he told his daughter, who shouldered her purse.

"Aftershave?" Melissa's smile was so much like her mom's

that, seeing it, Hal always thought of Judy. "Why, Daddy? Are you trying to pick up one of the nurses?" There was teasing in her tone, but for the first time Hal wondered how Melissa would take it if he actually considered being with someone other than her mother.

Melissa's grin widened. "Are you getting sweet on a nurse?"

His first inclination was to deny it, but he asked, "Would it bother you if I was?"

The teasing glint in his daughter's eyes vanished. "I . . . Well, I . . ." She stepped closer.

"It would make you uncomfortable?" Hal's chest grew hollow at the thought.

"No. I'm just shocked. Honestly, Mom wouldn't want you to be lonely."

Thinking of Judy, Hal wondered if he could do this. "I loved your mom more than—"

"I know." Melissa smiled again. "However, you know the dating rules, right?"

"Dating rules?" He studied his daughter and missed his wife so much his throat tightened. Then, deep inside, he heard Judy's words from his dream. *Go back and live, ol' man.*

"No dating anyone with tattoos or strange hair color. No French kissing—and she'd better not have ever seen the inside of a jail. Aren't those the rules you made me live by?" She grinned. "Oh yeah. No piercings. You made me ditch a really hot guy because he had his ear pierced."

CHAPTER SIXTEEN

"I really do like you." Jake's lips were so close that Macy could taste him.

She remembered his question. *Then why did you kiss me in the parking lot?* She answered with, "Temporary insanity. That's why I kissed you *back*."

Humor brightened his blue eyes. "It does kind of feel crazy, doesn't it? But we'll find the answers . . . together."

"I'm not looking for answers. Believe it or not, I wasn't looking for a romp in the hay when I kneed you in the privates. I don't go around busting balls so guys will like me. As a matter of fact, it generally works just the opposite."

Laughter rumbled from his chest. "Well, you make me laugh, Pizza Girl. And it's been too long since I laughed." He shook his head. "I'll try to hurry." He walked away.

Making him laugh was not necessarily a good thing, so why did she feel giddy? Why did his sexy smile make everything wrong in the world feel a little righter? She didn't want this.

Okay, she *did* want it, but that's where the temporary insanity came in. "Crap!" She had to put a stop to this.

Minutes passed with the speed of a three-legged turtle. She had nothing to do but worry—worry about Billy, about Ellie perhaps setting up her brother, about . . . that kiss. *You want me.* The memory of his dark voice kept tiptoeing through her mind.

She glanced out the window, antsy. Agent James, wearing a Gulf Coast Violent Offenders jacket, motioned Jake aside. She couldn't hear either man, but the agent's expression radiated anger. Had coming after her instead of staying with Agent Mimms gotten Jake into trouble?

If so, he didn't look too nervous. The FBI agent finally jerked up his arms and stomped off.

Jake walked over to the edge of the garden, alone. The way he stood, shoulders squared, a tad defensive, told her more than anything he'd ever said to her. Detective Sergeant Jake Baldwin played life like some people played poker. He didn't show his cards. Or his emotions. Sort of like her.

"You can't fool me, Mr. Tough Guy," she murmured.

Seeing his frown, she was tempted to go to him. But he studied his watch, started toward his car and toward her. Even his walk struck her as sexy.

He opened the driver side door and handed her his phone. "Here. It's been forty minutes. Call your mom and tell her to wash her hair or do whatever it is she needs to do."

Was he for real? "You remembered that?"

He shot her a charming smile. "I don't want a purple-haired woman coming after me."

He *was* for real. And she studied his eyes for the remnants of emotion he tried to hide. "You okay? Agent James looked mad."

"I'm fine. Call your mom."

Yup, he was fine—except he was getting harder and harder to push away.

Who was Ellie talking to?

Billy walked into the trailer. She wasn't in the front room, so he followed the sound of her voice down the hall and stopped outside the bathroom. The door stood ajar.

"I'll try," he heard her say. "It's hard. We'll talk later."

He pushed open the door. "Who were you talking to?"

She swung around. "You scared me."

"Who were you talking to?" He frowned. "I've told you that you shouldn't talk to—"

"I was talking to Mrs. Kelly, my patient at work. She wants me to come to Fred's funeral."

Billy shook his head. "You can't go, Ellie."

Her eyes grew bright, the way his mother's did before she cried. "I told her I couldn't promise, but it's just . . . She really wants me to come."

"You shouldn't be talking to her. And going there last night was crazy. The cops are probably looking for you, too." He shook his head. "I should have never gotten you into this."

Anger sparked in her green eyes. "Fred was dying. I had to go. And don't you dare say you shouldn't have gotten me into this. I love you. How can you regret what we—?"

Andy called from the kitchen. "I'm going to work."

"Do you need your phone?" Billy asked, and pulled Ellie against him.

"Nah, keep it tonight," Andy said. "Watch after Spike."

When the front door shut, the whole trailer shook. Ellie stayed where she was, her head pillowed on Billy's shoulder. He buried his nose in her hair. She smelled like cotton candy, and something about having her this close made him feel stronger, important. He'd miss her more than he'd miss anything when he got back to prison, more than the outside air, more than having a dad. He'd miss her even more than his family. Ellie was . . . special. She didn't make him feel bad about the mistakes he'd made, and at the same time she made him want to be a better man for her.

"I know you want to be there." His words were whispered against her wispy blonde locks. "I just don't want you to get into any trouble. If they caught you, even if you didn't get into any trouble, they'd watch you. We wouldn't be together anymore."

She raised her face. "Then, don't leave tonight. I'll fix us some dinner and we'll stay here."

He hated disappointing her, but he had to deal with Tanks. To protect her and Mace.

"We've got the trailer to ourselves again," she whispered. She brushed her hips against his.

"I have to go." But he felt himself grow hard, wanting to be with her again. And again.

"Then let me come with you."

"No." He reached for her wrist to see her watch. "We got an hour." He slid his hand under her shirt. Her nipple grew hard at his touch. "How many times do you think I can get you to come in an hour?"

She looked up with pleading in her eyes. "Don't go tonight."

He ached to give in, to give her anything she asked. He couldn't. Instead of arguing, he kissed her and decided to make use of the time. Because, face it, time was running out.

Macy shifted in her seat, growing more and more impatient. *Wait here, leave your car there, let me kiss you.* Jake was super bossy, and she was getting tired of it. Fidgeting, she shifted in her seat and saw a receipt beside her shoe.

She picked it up and noticed where it was from. Home Depot. She read off the list of items: primer, glass, doorknob, caulk, caulk gun, doorknob. *Two* doorknobs? Had he replaced the back doorknob, too? She looked at the sum on the bottom and subtracted the money she'd already paid him for the front door lock, even if it was still sitting on her coffee table. That still left ninety-eight dollars. Wonderful! Lovely. With her rent due next week, it would be at least two weeks before she could pay him back. Then she recalled him telling her that she shouldn't go to work, that Tanks knew all about Papa's Pizza. That meant no tips, no money to pay rent. Panic swirled in her gut. Hadn't Baldwin ever met anyone that lived from paycheck to paycheck? She had to work, didn't she?

More edgy than ever, feeling almost claustrophobic, she practiced yoga breathing. "In. One, two, three . . . Out. One, two, and three. In. One . . ."

Turning, she eyed the backseat. A pillow? The heck with yoga—a nap sounded good. Hoisting herself up on her knees and bending over, she reached for it. But as she snatched at the pillow, a thick manila file dropped to the floor.

She might have ignored it, might have taken the pillow, napped, and forgotten all about snooping. Might have, if Billy's mug shot hadn't landed faceup on the floorboard behind the driver seat.

Hal stared at the hospital's white walls. He'd refused another pain shot and turned on the news. Moore's mug shot flashed across the screen. Hal let out a sigh of regret. The kid didn't stand a chance.

The anchorman spoke into the camera. "Early this morning our reporters went out to visit the home of one of the escaped convicts." The picture changed to one of a reporter standing in someone's front yard. An elderly woman wearing a black T-shirt and biker shorts walked out.

"Are you Billy Moore's mother? Could we have just a few words with you?"

The woman turned and faced the camera. "No comment," she said. The focus on the screen went to her shirt, which read DON'T ASK.

"Have you heard from your son?" the reporter pressed.

The old lady frowned, and Hal felt a wave of sympathy. He blinked and looked closer at the screen. He recognized Mrs. Moore. She'd probably been out to the prison to see Billy.

"I said, 'No comment.'" The woman pushed past.

The reporter dogged her tracks. "Just a few words?"

"I have words for you, but do you have your bleeper ready?"

Hal grinned. The camera shifted. Stepping out of the door was a purple-haired woman wearing . . . a candy striper's uniform? Recognition hit. Faye! *His* Faye. His volunteer.

* * *

Jake watched Agent James pace beside the black sedan while CSI went over it a second time. "How could no one have seen anything? It happened in friggin' daylight!"

Jake didn't answer. Internally, he waged his own war with frustration.

James stopped pacing. "Nothing? You saw nothing?"

"I was in the garden."

"You're a damn cop, Baldwin, not a friggin' farmer!"

Jake intentionally kept his expression blank. "I wasn't aware I needed to babysit your guys while they did their job." Even as he said the words, guilt knotted in his belly. It was a knot that wouldn't go away until he made this right, until he personally slapped a pair of handcuffs on David Tanks. If he'd been more aware of what was going on, Agent Mimms wouldn't be at the hospital.

Donaldson stepped forward. "Who would have guessed this idiot would try something in the middle of the day on a busy street?"

I should have. The words zipped around Jake's head at the same time Agent James spoke them.

"I should have!" Guilt echoed in the FBI agent's tone. "Tanks is suspected of taking out one of our other guys. He has no boundaries. He's one sick motherfucker. I should have known."

And the sick fucker is after Macy. Jake cut his gaze to his car and let Agent James simmer for a minute before asking, "You get anything else on Ellie Chandler?"

"Just that she turned her cell on for about forty seconds. Not long enough to get a location. We're still working on it."

Jake remembered the info he'd dug up on the Marilyn Monroe look-alike. Deceased parents. No siblings. No family. Raised by her grandma, who had died about a year ago. "Have you checked with her work again?" He'd read in the reports that they'd questioned her boss. "Talked to neighbors?"

"Got a man working it," Agent James said.

But they weren't getting anywhere. Jake decided he'd do his own checking. He *would* find David Tanks. First, because he wanted to stop the bastard from hurting Macy. Second, because when he screwed up, he always set out to make things right. He saw letting an officer of the law get hurt when he was within yelling distance as a major screwup. Nothing short of hauling David Tanks back to jail would make this right.

Macy crawled over the seat, picked up the file and photograph, then hoisted herself back. She stared at her brother's mug shot. Maybe she saw him through rose-colored glasses, but this wasn't the face of a criminal. Too much youthful innocence. She ran a finger over the image and tried to see his smile. All she could see was the frightened little boy who'd stood up for her against their father. *You're not hurting my sister.* His long-ago words echoed in her head.

"Where are you, Billy?" As the first hot tear slid down her cheek, she opened the folder.

While snooping in Baldwin's file wasn't illegal, it wasn't exactly ethical. She didn't give a damn. This was about her brother.

The file wasn't just about Billy. It contained information about David Tanks, Ellie Chandler, and the other escaped convict, and mug shots were included. Macy read everything. Then she reread Ellie's information. Something felt amiss. But, what? What did she know about Ellie?

Too antsy to do much thinking, Macy found a pen and notepad in the glove box and took down names, phone numbers, and addresses. She didn't know what she would do with the information, but one thing was for sure: she was tired of doing nothing.

Almost an hour after speaking to Agent James, Jake eased into his car so he wouldn't wake Macy. She'd found the pillow he'd thrown in his backseat. Now, with it beneath one cheek, she slept cuddled against the passenger door.

Damn, but she was beautiful. He studied her profile. Her nose had a slight tilt, her thick lashes rested on the tender skin beneath her eyes, and her mouth . . . Her lips were full—not Julia Roberts full, but close.

Protectiveness, desire, and something softer filled his chest. That trio of emotions had propelled him to leave the scene to find her in the first place. When an officer was down, protecting him or her took top priority. While one patrol car had arrived before he'd taken off, he'd been the first on the scene, and his leaving had left the arriving officers in the lurch. James had reminded him of this. Jake's captain would no doubt read him the riot act, too. He deserved it, and yet if the same situation happened again, he'd do the same thing. How had the petite brunette sleeping next to him become more important than his job?

As he sank deeper in his seat, the sun spilled into the car, making it warm but not too hot. Jake yawned. Running on less than four hours of sleep for the last two days, he needed a bit of shut-eye himself. Macy stirred, and his gaze veered to her again. What he wouldn't give to take that nap with her in his arms after they reached exhaustion from making love a couple of times. He let himself enjoy the view—the way her breasts pushed against her shirt, the way . . .

Why was she so adamantly against them becoming something more? The answer shot back with clarity: the same damn reason he'd been celibate for two years. Her ex had hurt her. From the conversation he'd overheard between the two, Jake gathered Tom had run around on her. Some people didn't know what they had until they'd lost it.

He remembered Tom showing up the other night, acting possessive. Jake would be damned if he'd let the man walk back into the picture now. What was that childhood saying? Losers weepers, finders keepers. He'd found Macy Tucker, and he planned on . . .

Keeping her?

The words bounced around his brain. Just how serious was he about her?

Serious enough.

Her eyes fluttered open, her gaze met his, and she shot up, blinking the sleepy look away. "I really need to get back to my car," she said.

From the stubborn tilt of her chin, he knew she was going to try to get rid of him. He also knew it wasn't going to work.

Dusk had turned everything gray as Billy exited the freeway and headed toward Nan's house. *Toward home,* he thought. He could hardly remember living anywhere else. Sure, there were a few mental snapshots of times before his dad left, mostly of his dad hitting things. Hitting his mom. Hitting Mace. Billy recalled telling Andy that he missed his dad. Funny, how you could miss people you hardly remembered and weren't even sure you liked.

At last he pulled into Nan's neighborhood. The hairs on the back of his neck stood up as if someone was watching. He forced himself to keep driving. He needed the fake ID. His mom and Nan would be at Yoga Works. Nan had classes on Wednesday evenings.

He turned onto Nan's street, the street where he'd tossed the football with his friends, the street where Macy had taught him to ride his bike. Memories assaulted him. Bittersweet memories. He eased off the gas as the van rolled closer. Nan's house was dark except for the porch light. He'd almost pulled over, when he noticed a sedan parked across the street. Shit! It had to be the police.

Billy drove past and prayed the car wouldn't follow. It didn't. He let out a breath. He drove two more blocks, checking the rearview mirror constantly. Finally, he pulled to a stop.

What now? His palms had started to sweat. He clenched and unclenched them around the steering wheel. *Leave.* That one word echoed inside Billy's head. He put his foot on the gas. But without the fake ID he'd never get into Girls Galore. Without getting in and talking to Jamie Clay, Tanks's ex-girlfriend, he might never find Tanks.

He cut off the engine. He had to get that ID.

Getting out of the car, he looked at the elderly Mrs. Perry's house, located one block behind Nan's. He could jump her fence and the cops in front might not even notice.

Might not. But if he got caught . . .

He walked past Mrs. Perry's front porch. Not seeing anyone, he ducked between the two houses. A German shepherd warming a doormat on the back porch barked and lunged.

Crap! Billy hauled his ass to the back fence and hurled himself over. He landed hard. His hand came down on a rock that cut into his palm. The fence beside him wobbled as the dog clawed the aged wood, and his shrieking bark warned the whole damn neighborhood.

"Smoky?" Mrs. Perry called. "What is it?" Her question mingled with the scratching of the dog's claws on the fence. The sound of footsteps kept Billy from stirring. "Who's there? Somebody there?"

Macy settled into her pizza-scented vehicle. Her gaze shot to the parking lot of Yoga Works. She was curious to see her mother's hair, but her mom's car—and thus her and her hair—was already gone.

She pulled her Saturn out into the street and watched Jake's Monte Carlo follow. He flashed his lights as if to remind her to turn hers on. Great, now the man was telling her how to drive. She shot him a quick scowl in her rearview mirror and then hit her lights. Stopping at a yellow signal, she dug into her front pocket to make sure she hadn't lost the names and addresses she'd taken from his file.

She slipped out the folded paper and stared at it. Tomorrow, she would do her own investigation. Hopefully, somehow, one of the addresses or phone numbers would lead her to her brother. Then by the grace of God, she'd talk Billy into turning himself in. She'd worry about what his prison escape would do to his sentence once she had him off the streets. With the help of a good lawyer, maybe . . . maybe it wouldn't be too bad. She could hope.

Fighting back the feeling of doom, she tucked the paper back into her khaki shorts and stared up at the stoplight. From the corner of her eye, a movement in the car next to her caught her attention. She turned.

"Crappers!"

Jake spotted the end of the gun. "Son of a . . ." His breath hitched.

No time to go for his Glock. No time to think. He slammed his foot on the gas, rear-ending Macy's Saturn. The screech of crashing metal came at the same time as the blast of a gun. Panic crushed his chest. Macy's green Saturn shot into the intersection. A white Honda smashed into the front of it. The impact sent the Saturn spinning.

Jake yanked out his gun. He shoved his car into park, aiming his Glock at the gunman's car. The car burst forward, ran the red light. A garbage truck swerved to miss it and crashed into the side of a hearse. The sound of brakes, of metal slamming into metal, and the smell of hot rubber were terrifying.

Jake leapt out of his car as a coffin flew out of the back of the hearse. The casket spun across the road, slamming into Macy's Saturn, bounced off, and kept spinning. Jake managed to get his phone out as he ran. He dodged cars and the still-twirling coffin to get to Macy. He screamed into the phone, "I need backup. Shots fired. Several automobile accidents." He added the name of the intersection into the phone as his gaze riveted on Macy's car. The sight of the shattered driver side window caused air to lock in his chest. He remembered the sound of a bullet being fired.

"A gold Cavalier," he added, and forced himself to spout out the license plate number. "Going southwest on North Banks. Suspect is armed." He called out his location again. "Get some ambulances here. Now, damn it!"

CHAPTER SEVENTEEN

Macy couldn't breathe. She forced her eyes open and felt blinded by white. Memories flashed. A gun. Getting hit from behind. Being thrown against her seat. Slamming her head against the steering wheel. Careening into the intersection. Another bone-jarring jolt, then the car spinning. And . . . a coffin?

A coffin? Oh, God. Was this *the* white? As in, The White Light? As in, The End? If so, why wasn't it beautiful? Why didn't she want to go into it? Or did she want to?

No!

She opened her mouth to scream and got a mouthful of a chalky substance. Her mental fog started to lift. And she saw . . . not the path to the afterlife, just the freaking air bag. She sat back, gasped, and that's when she saw red. Red all over the white air bag. Red, as in blood.

Her vision blurred. Black spots started popping up like fireworks in front of her eyes. She recalled another car hitting her. People could be hurt!

She opened the door. It creaked in protest but complied. She got one foot out of the car, and it landed on the street with a heavy thud. She saw more black spots.

"Macy," someone called. She twisted, got her second foot out of the car. Between the black splotches, she saw Baldwin dodging a spinning coffin to get to her. Yup, it was really a coffin. Damn, he looked . . . hot? Good thing she wasn't dead, because she'd have regretted never . . . Never what? Seeing him naked? Doing the naked Hokey Pokey? Okay, obviously she wasn't thinking straight.

She heard a car door open. A man stepped out of a wrecked

Honda. He looked okay. No blood. She recalled the blood smeared on her air bag and then felt something warm drip down her forehead. She pulled herself upright and felt more blood. Her knees buckled, and . . .

She felt herself being lifted, pulled close. Baldwin? Okay, maybe she should start calling him Jake now. Her cheek found his masculine chest a perfect pillow. Black fireworks floated across her vision again. She inhaled. "Jake, you smell . . . good." Then her whole world went black.

Billy didn't move until Mrs. Perry's back door shut. Then he ran across the yard toward the window of his bedroom.

Please, let it be unlocked.

He pushed himself up, his bleeding palm stinging. When the window rose, relief filled his chest. Hoisting himself over the sill, he fell inside and smacked against the dresser.

Damn.

He crawled to his feet. His heart throbbed as he listened, expecting someone to bolt into the room. Nothing but the empty-house hum met his ears. He started toward the bed but slowed down long enough to enjoy the smells: Nan's incense that she burned when practicing yoga. Residual scent of his mom's breakfast, two slices of bacon and one egg every morning. He'd bet the cast-iron skillet sat on the gas stove now, shiny because his mom always greased it after use. After all these years, the smells had simply infused the home.

His next breath came flavored with the baby power that his mom used after showering. God, he missed these people. Walking to the door, he creaked it open and fed his lungs a breath of home.

The gas stove gave off a tiny hiss, the water heater an occasional creak. Then a grandfather clock chimed and reminded him he had to hurry. He inched back to his bed, dropped onto his knees, and sandwiched his hand between the mattress and box springs. His fingers brushed the edge of a fake ID.

Yes.

He stood. Then he swung round when he heard the sound of the front door opening. Damn! Dropping back to his knees, he eyed the window.

"Thank you for helping me," his mom's voice echoed from the other room. "Unloading groceries can't be in your job description."

"You'd be surprised what the federal bureau assigns us sometimes," a man answered.

Federal bureau? Billy's mind started chewing on options.

"Let me get you a glass of tea," his mother offered.

"Tea would be great."

Billy's gaze flew to the bedroom door he'd left ajar. He saw someone pass outside the door. Falling flat on his back, he squeezed himself under the bed.

Holy hell. He was stuck in the house while his mother fucking entertained an FBI agent.

Jake arrived at the hospital only a few minutes behind the ambulance. They saw the blood on him and thought he was hurt, but he assured them he wasn't. They'd tried to stop him from coming back; he hadn't listened. He stalked into the emergency room, peering into all the rooms until he found Macy. She lay stretched on a bed, blood streaming down her face. He tried to go to her, but the nurse moved between them.

"Why don't you step outside?" the nurse asked.

"It's okay," he gritted out through his teeth. "I'm her boyfriend."

"He's *not* my boyfriend," Macy mumbled.

Jake's gaze shot up. He pushed the nurse aside to get to her. "You okay?" When she'd passed out, he'd been frantic. "You hurting anywhere?"

"No," she said. It sounded like a lie.

He shot the nurse a look. "Get the doctor in here."

This is my fault, damn it! He'd pushed her right into on-coming traffic. He could have killed her, though he'd been trying to save her life.

"Calm down," the nurse said. "Move out and let me do my job. The doctor's on his way."

Macy's blood continued to flow. Guilt took another tumble around his chest. The nurse put a hand on his arm.

He jerked out his wallet and flashed his badge. "I'm a cop."

"And I'm a nurse. Out!" She pointed to the door.

He took a step but didn't leave. The nurse glared. "Get out while I undress her."

Did she think he was here to get a cheap thrill? "Look—"

"If I'm arguing with you, I can't take care of her." The statement slapped Jake back to the right side of logic.

Get a grip.

Relenting, he stormed out into the hall. The smell filled his nose, his mouth. What little control he had over his emotions started to slip. This was the smell of hopelessness. He hated hospitals. Memories flooded him: Sitting beside a skeleton of a man who'd stood behind the pulpit preaching about God's mercy. Watching his father face a painful and humiliating death. Where had God's mercy been then?

Fear curled inside Jake's chest. Yesteryear's emotions—the feeling of despair, the ugly acceptance that someone he loved was dying—all mingled with the present.

"No." He inhaled. Damn it, he had to calm down. Macy was going to be okay.

He moved up and down the hall. Finally, able to think, he pulled out his phone and hit Donaldson's number. "Tell me you got him," he growled.

"Not yet. We've put an APB out on the car. If he's still around, we'll get him."

"Damn it to hell! I want this creep."

"I know." Silence. "How's she doing?"

"She's conscious. The doctor hasn't seen her yet." Frustration sang in his voice. "Hold on." He snagged a white-coated man by the arm and pointed to Macy's door. "The patient in there needs to be seen. She's bleeding."

"That's where I'm heading," the doctor answered in an even tone. But when he stepped toward Macy's room and

Jake followed, the doctor turned around. "Let me examine her. Then I'll give you a personal report."

Taking a deep breath, Jake backed up and collapsed against the hospital's white wall. *Let her be okay*, he prayed. Then, remembering Donaldson, he pressed the phone back to his ear. "Did you call the Gulf Coast Task Force?"

"Yeah. I think Agent James is on his way there."

"Good." Jake closed his eyes. James would be pissed at him. Shit, Jake was pissed at himself. The second time in one day, he'd been within an arm's reach of the escaped convict and had let him get away.

"Was anybody hurt besides Macy?" Donaldson asked.

"No." Jake filled his lungs, trying not to taste the anesthetic-scented air.

"Good," Donaldson said. "Is it true that a dead guy got spilled across the median?"

"He didn't fall out of his coffin, but the news will have a field day."

Jake looked up to see his captain and Agent James walking down the hall. Neither of them looked happy, but they could just join him in the not-happy club. He wouldn't be content until he knew Macy was okay. "Gotta go," he told Donaldson. "Keep looking."

Billy tried not to breathe too loud and stared up at the gauzy material covering the box springs of his old bed. He wondered about his chances of making it out the window without anyone hearing.

A phone rang—not the home phone, but a cell phone. "Excuse me," the agent said.

Billy heard steps move closer to the bedroom door. Angling his head, he could see the man's suit pants through the crack in the door. God, don't let his mom notice the open door.

"Who?" The agent's voice carried. "I'm talking to her mother right now." A pause. "Is she going to make it?"

Make it? Macy? No! Billy's heart drummed in his chest.

"Good. We sure it was Tanks?" Silence. "Really? Damn, I sure as hell wouldn't want to be Baldwin when Agent James gets hold of him." Another pause. "I'll tell her."

Billy gripped his fist as panic scratched his chest.

"Ma'am . . ." The agent's tone came out unsure. "That call was about your daughter. She's been in an accident."

The empty pit of Billy's stomach got rock hard.

"Is she okay? What kind of accident?" Tears already sounded in his mom's voice.

"A car accident. I'm told she's stable right now. She was taken to Memorial Hospital."

Billy closed his eyes and visualized Macy sitting across the table from him at the prison. So smart, so full of life. Now she lay in a hospital, hurting. She could die.

I'm going to kill you, Tanks. I'm going to kill you, and I'm going to enjoy doing it!

After a few minutes, he heard the front door close. Billy climbed out from under the bed. He paced the bedroom once, then twice. He had to know if Macy was okay. But how?

"Are you okay?" both men asked, looking at all the blood on Jake's shirt.

Jake assured them he was okay and that he had a clean shirt in his car. Shortly thereafter, the ass chewing began.

"You could have gone after him!" his captain snapped.

"I did what I had to do. Macy was hurt." Jake kept his eyes on the door of Macy's room, waiting for the doctor to finish. His mind flashed on the image of the gun sticking out of that window. Pushing Macy into the intersection had been his only choice. Hadn't it?

"You're too close to this. I'm taking you off the case," his captain said.

Jake looked at him. "I'm not officially *on* the case."

His captain shook his head. "Well, if you were, I'd take you off."

"If I was, I'd take myself off," he admitted. Taking care of

Macy had become personal. He looked from one man to the other. "Nothing would make me happier than seeing Tanks's ass back in prison, and I'll do anything I can to assure that, but Macy Tucker is my priority. And if I have to take some time off to—"

"That reminds me, what were you doing there, anyway?" his captain asked.

"It was my lunch break."

Agent James ran a hand over his face. "We should have had a man on her twenty-four-seven. After Mimms . . . Well, there will be one on her from here on out."

The doctor walked out of Macy's room, and Jake swung around. "How is she?"

"Nasty cut and concussion. I'm going to have her X-rayed. She's going to need stitches. I'd like to keep her overnight, but . . ."

"You keep her," Jake snapped.

"She's not willing." The doctor frowned. "Anyway, unless something shows up on her X-rays, she'll go home. Who'll be taking care of her?"

"I will," Jake said.

"You're the husband?"

"Boyfriend," Jake said.

"He's not the boyfriend," the nurse said, walking out of the room.

Jake frowned. The nurse frowned. The doctor frowned and said, "Does she have family?"

"Shit. I need to call them." Jake pulled out his cell phone.

"I had someone talk to the mom," Agent James said. He was giving Jake an odd look, probably because of the claim of being Macy's boyfriend. Jake's captain was doing the same.

The doctor glanced back at Jake. "I'll have the nurse go over the care instructions. You'll need to keep a close eye on her."

"Can we talk to her now?" Agent James flashed his badge.

The doctor's eyebrows rose. "Only for a minute or two. I'll be back in a few to stitch her up."

Jake, followed by the two men, walked into Macy's room. She was sitting up.

"You okay?" he asked.

Her color had improved, but she didn't seem happy to see him. He didn't blame her.

"My head hurts, but I'm fine," she said.

"Can you tell us what happened?" the captain asked.

Jake took her hand. "If you don't feel like talking now—"

She looked at his captain. "I was going home. I stopped at a light. I saw the gun, then . . ."

"Then I ran into you," Jake confessed, hoping it would lessen the guilt building in his chest. "I saw the gun. It was the first thing I thought of." Tension vibrated through his body.

"*You* caused the accident?" the captain bellowed. "Jesus! Three cars and a hearse were wrecked and . . . and that damn casket! When the press gets a hold of this—"

"I was trying to save your life." Jake kept his eyes on Macy. He didn't give a rat's ass what the captain thought. It was Macy he'd hurt.

She glanced at the captain. "He may have hit me, but I ran the light. It was the gun or that white Honda. I decided to take the Honda."

Jake's mind replayed the moment his car had rear-ended her. The jolting impact. He'd heard her tires burn into the asphalt. She hadn't been moving forward. She was lying to protect him.

"No, I—" His cell phone rang. He pulled it out of his pocket, praying it would be Donaldson with good news. "Tell me you got the bastard."

"Is my sister okay?"

The voice sent red flags flying up everywhere. Jake's gaze darted to Agent James. The man's eyes widened with a silent question. Jake nodded. The agent pulled his cell phone out and started punching in numbers.

"What do you mean?" Jake spoke the question while looking at Macy. Oblivious that he was speaking to Billy, she'd sunk deeper into her bed and closed her eyes.

Agent James stepped outside the room, but Jake heard him and he figured so could Macy. "Moore's on Baldwin's line. Get a location, now!"

Jake's line crackled, and he watched Macy sit up.

"You *know* what I mean, damn it!" Billy said. Static buzzed, then: "Is she okay?"

"She's fine," Jake said.

Macy grabbed his arm. He saw the questions in her eyes as his own questions bounced around his head. How did Billy know about Macy? There hadn't been time to get it on the news. Had Billy been at the scene of the accident?

When Billy didn't speak, Jake asked, "Do you want to talk to her?"

"I told you to watch her."

"I'm trying. Billy, if you turn yourself in, it would—"

"I want to talk to him!" Tears welled up in Macy's eyes.

Billy continued, "Well, you're doing a piss-poor job. He"— the phone crackled again—"didn't he?"

"I'm losing you, Billy." Jake looked at Macy, but focused on the conversation. "Where are you?" The line went dead. Jake lowered the phone.

"Where is he?" Macy asked.

"Was that who I think it was?" the captain asked.

Jake hit the redial button to display the number. Agent James stormed back, his phone still attached to his ear. He grabbed Jake's wrist to see the small screen on Jake's phone.

"Damn it!" James snapped. "He's at the grandmother's place."

"He's at Nan's?" Macy kicked off the sheet draped over her.

Agent James punched in more numbers on his phone and

pressed it to his ear. "Billy Moore is there." James's scowl deepened. "In the house. Get him. Now!"

"Lie back down." Jake jerked the sheet over Macy.

She swung her legs over the bed and got up. "No. I'm going with you."

CHAPTER EIGHTEEN

"The hell you are coming with me." Jake put a hand on Macy's shoulder and watched as blood trickled down her forehead. "You're bleeding again."

"He's my brother. Where are my clothes?" She looked around the small room.

"You need stitches. They've got to do some X-rays. Lie back down," Jake seethed.

A voice came from the hall. "Where's my daughter?" A sniffling sound followed. "I want to see her!"

Jake glanced at the door just as Faye Moore walked in. Her eyes were wet. Mascara smeared her face, and her hair . . . Oh, damn! Her hair was an odd shade of purple.

"Get me my clothes, Mom," Macy snapped.

Macy's grandma bounded into room. "Thank God you're okay," she said.

Macy, focused on the FBI agent, pushed off the bed. "I'm going."

Jake's gaze, along with the gazes of the two other men in the room, shot down to Macy's beautiful and exposed backside. He snatched up the thin blanket and wrapped it around her. "Get back in bed."

"I'm going!" Macy shrieked. "He'll listen to me."

"Going where?" her mom asked.

Agent James spoke into his cell. "Because we traced him on their home phone." Pause. "Damn! But he has to be close. Find him!" The Fed snapped his phone closed. Everyone looked at him. "He's not there. The phone is missing. He must have taken it."

"What's going on?" Nan asked.

A drop of blood fell from Macy's forehead and landed on Jake's shoe. Losing it, he scooped her up in his arms and set her on the bed.

Billy tossed his grandmother's phone onto the floor of the van. Macy was okay. For some crazy reason, he'd believed Jake Baldwin when he said that. But for how long would she be okay? Tanks wouldn't give up. He'd try again. And the next time, he might succeed.

Taking a curve at a fairly moderate speed, Billy slapped his pocket to make sure he'd left with the fake ID. The feel of the rectangular piece of plastic did very little to calm his racing heart.He drove out of the neighborhood. In the distance, he could hear sirens. The temptation to punch the gas pedal dug deep into his gut. He fought it. He couldn't lose control now.

With his eyes on the road, he drove and ticked off his to-do list. Go to Girls Galore. Talk to Jamie Clay. Find Tanks. Kill him.

Macy opened her eyes to find Jake standing over her, brushing her hair from her forehead. He leaned down. She thought he intended to kiss her, and vaguely she recalled those few seconds after the accident, thinking how dying would have meant regretting things.

He leaned closer and studied her stitches. "You might have a small scar, but—"

"Damn. There goes my modeling career," she groused. Fabric slipped off her shoulder, and she pulled it back up, aware she had nothing on but a backless hospital gown.

A smile pulled at his lips. "I was saying, it's at your hairline and shouldn't show."

Macy shifted. "Any news of my brother?"

"No." His gaze moved to her shoulder and, with a soft touch, he pushed up her gown. It had fallen again.

She sighed and yanked her thin blanket up to her chin. Why had Billy been at Nan's? Why was Jake hovering over her as if he really cared? Why was it that every time she dyed someone's hair, it turned purple? The questions bouncing around her head made her dizzy. Or was that the concussion?

"Have the X-rays come back yet?" she asked, wanting to leave and feel less naked. Less vulnerable. Good God, someone had tried to shoot her today. She looked around for her clothes. "Has someone stolen my underwear?"

"I think the doctor is looking at them now."

Her gaze shot back to Baldwin. "My underwear?"

He laughed. "Your X-rays." He pulled a chair closer and settled in beside her. Seriousness chased the humor from his eyes. "You didn't run that red light. You weren't moving when I rear-ended you."

"If I wasn't moving, I was about to." She glanced away. It hadn't been a total lie. She had thought about running the red light; she just hadn't got around to doing it.

The silence was too big for the closet-sized hospital room, and her chest too small for the emotions crowding inside her. She was beginning to like Baldwin way too much.

He let out a breathy sigh. "I saw the gun and it seemed like the only option."

She squeezed her eyes shut, reliving the moment she saw the gun, feeling her car careening forward, hearing the loud pop. Seeing the coffin slam into the fender. She'd run over a dead guy. Sucky.

"Can we not talk about that?"

"Yeah, I just . . . I didn't mean to get you hurt." He touched her hand.

"You're sorry for trying to save my life?"

"No, I'm sorry you got hurt in my poorly executed attempt to save your life. I could have gotten you killed myself."

His cell phone rang, and he dug it out of his pocket.

"Yeah?" He looked at her. "Hey . . . Mark." He said his partner's name as if purposely letting her know who it was.

Thoughtful, courteous, good-looking, a sense of humor . . .

"You did?" He cut his eyes away. "I appreciate it."

"What?" she asked when he ended the call.

His dark blue eyes met hers as he tucked his phone back in his pocket. "It's nothing."

"Don't 'nothing' me. What is it?" She sat up, and her gown fell to show some cleavage. One of his brows arched and he hesitated.

"The wrecker driver said he thought your car would be ruled as totaled."

She studied his nonchalant expression. Nonchalant didn't work on him. "What else?"

"They recovered the bullet fired at you. It was in your headrest. It's the same caliber as the gun used to shoot the prison guard."

"Headrest?" The word was squeaked out. The bullet had come within inches of splattering her brains. "You really saved my life."

He grinned a bad-boy smile, and bad boy definitely worked on him. Winking, he pulled her gown up to cover her chest. "So, what does it get me?"

She dropped back in bed, exhausted. "How about the next time you tick me off, I refrain from hitting you in the balls?"

His chuckle filled the room, far too intimate for Macy's comfort. "That would be nice, but I was hoping for more." His voice dropped. "Maybe another peek at the back of that gown?"

She tucked her blanket around her. "In your dreams."

"In my dreams you're not even wearing a hospital gown. I like that blue bra better."

She tried to think of a comeback, but her wit must have been affected by the bump on her head. Instead, she folded and unfolded her legs—and missed the presence of her underwear.

"Did Nan and my mom leave?" she asked.

"No, they're waiting until you're released. I think your mom is busy planning her revenge against me."

"She can't blame you for this!"

Jake shook his head, rueful. "Not for this. She blames me for her hair."

"Oh." Macy sank back on her pillow. "Well, she did warn you about that."

Billy sat at a table in Girls Galore staring through the semidarkness, looking for Tanks and waiting to see if Jamie Clay would come over. He'd asked for her. So far, no one had been able to point her out, but they all said she was here.

His gaze shifted. He noticed the near-naked bodies of the girls, but mostly he noticed their for-profit smiles. Tight. Forced. None of them looked genuine. Sort of how everyone looked in prison. Was that what this was for these women? A prison?

A red-haired waitress, her black skirt cut up to her ass and her blouse cut down to her nipples, set a drink on his table. "You ordered a Coke?" Her smile appeared even more forced than the others'.

"Yeah." Billy tossed down a five. "Keep the change."

"I hear you're looking for Jamie." She studied him.

"You Jamie?"

"It depends." She hugged the tray. "What do you want?"

"To talk." Billy noticed she had bruises up and down one arm. Had Tanks done that?

"You a cop?" she asked.

No, I'm an escaped convict. "Not hardly."

She must not have believed him. "I told you guys everything I know." Her green eyes filled with tears, which unlike her smile appeared real. She blinked, and he saw another emotion. Fear. "I don't know who killed Mike. I told you guys last night."

Who was Mike? Was his death connected? Billy decided to go for broke. "I'm not a cop. I'm looking for David Tanks."

Her pupils widened. "Who are you?"

"Have you seen him?" Billy countered.

"I haven't seen shit!"

She turned to leave, and he caught her wrist, though not too hard. Billy didn't believe in hurting women. He'd never be like his ol' man.

"Jamie, please. I . . ." Suddenly something clicked. "Tanks slit Mike's throat, didn't he?"

She tried to pull away. "Let go or I'll scream."

"Tanks is threatening to hurt someone I love, too."

The waitress squared her shoulders. "That's not my problem."

"You saw what he did to Mike. You want him to do that to someone else? Just tell me where he's at."

"And then he comes after me," she said. "Do I look crazy?"

"No. You look afraid. And we both know what he's capable of. Tell me, and I'll make sure he never hurts anyone again."

"I'm taking you to my place," Jake told Macy as he gathered her things.

"No," Agent James, the commander of the Gulf Coast Task Force, and Macy all said together.

Jake shot a look over his shoulder at the two men who'd just walked into the room. "Tanks knows where she lives."

"I'm not letting him chase me out of my own house," Macy growled.

"Men will be watching," James stated. "It's safe."

Fury cut a course to Jake's gut. "You're using her as bait," he accused. His gaze swung back to Macy. "They're using you."

Agent James spoke up. "You're going to be there. My men will be there. If Tanks gets anywhere near Ms. Tucker, we'll get him. No one will get hurt, and we'll have this case solved."

"I want him caught," Macy said. "If I leave, he's won."

Jake let out a deep gulp of air. "If you stay—"

"They'll catch him," Macy interrupted.

Jake turned to Agent James. "I don't—"

"Stop!" Agent James's eyes narrowed on Jake. "She wants to stay, Baldwin. Let it go." Both he and the other man stormed off.

Jake stared at Macy. "I don't like it."

"Welcome to my world," Macy said. She dropped back onto her hospital bed.

CHAPTER NINETEEN

Hal lay in the dark, staring at the hospital ceiling and thinking about Faye Moore. The nurse had given him something to help him sleep. The medication gave him a buzz, but sleep evaded him. Disappointment bounced around his chest and reminded him he'd been shot.

Faye. That's all her name tag had read. She hadn't told him her last name, and now he knew why. Knowing she had some ulterior motive for visiting made everything feel different, somehow tainted. Something about her, about meeting her and having the dream, had made it all feel special, but now . . .

"You still awake?" A male voice came from the doorway.

"Depends. If you want blood, piss, or for me to breathe in that damn contraption again, I'm not."

"I see you're feeling good enough to complain."

Hal hit the light button and stared at the FBI agent—Agent James, if he recalled correctly. "Yeah." The electric motor hummed as he pushed a button to lift the head of his bed. "What can I do for you?"

"Just checking to see if you remembered anything else."

"You must be desperate if you're coming back to see me."

"Not desperate. I was here at the hospital anyway. Just thought I'd pop in."

"Good, because I'm sure I told you everything." Hal glanced at the silent TV. "You talk to Billy Moore's family?"

"Yeah. Why?"

"The kid saved my life." The silence grew thick. Then: "Does he have a big family?"

The Fed stepped closer. "A mother, grandmother, and a sister."

Shifting in bed, Hal felt his chest muscles pull and he remembered the older woman on the news. "They decent folks?"

"A little strange," the agent remarked. "But I'd say they're decent. Why?"

"Strange like how?" Hal's mouth tasted like cotton, and he reached for his water jug and shook the empty plastic jug "You'd think at five Benjamins a day to stay here, they could at least refill your water."

The agent laughed. "I'll get it."

Hal's earlier drug-induced buzz grew. He closed his eyes and wondered how Faye Moore was strange. The door squeaked again and he heard footsteps, but he didn't open his eyes. "I appreciate it," he said. His tongue nearly stuck to the roof of his mouth.

"Appreciate what?" a soft voice asked.

Hal's eyes snapped open. Okay, the buzz had really gotten him now. Agent James was gone. Faye Moore stood beside his bed, smelling like powder, and she still had . . . purple hair? He rubbed a hand over his face and looked again. Still there. Still baby fresh. Still purple.

"Were you asleep?" she asked.

"I think I'm dreaming."

The door swung open again behind her. "They said they'll bring . . ." Agent James reentered, his black dress shoes squeaking to a stop. His gaze darted to Faye, then back to Hal. Suspicion entered his expression. "You two know each other?"

"I . . ." Faye focused on Hal, and tears filled her blue eyes. "I'm sorry. I was going to tell you." And with a streak of purple, leaving a residual baby-fresh scent, she took off.

"Faye?" Hal tried to sit up, but he didn't have the strength to give chase.

Agent James looked torn between going after her or interrogating him.

"Shit," Hal bellowed. "Can you get her for me?"

"You'd better have a good explanation," Agent James said.

"Well . . . I don't!" Hal raked a hand over his eyes. "Was her hair really purple?"

The man fixed his brown eyes on Hal. "Are you involved in this? What's your relationship with Billy Moore and his family?"

When Hal didn't answer, James grabbed up a cell phone. "Mrs. Moore is leaving the hospital. Stop her. Yes, she's the younger one. Dammit! She's the one with purple hair."

"Hey, Pizza Girl . . ."

Macy stirred at the sound of Jake's voice. *Jake?* Not Baldwin. When had she gone over completely to a first-name basis? Oh yeah, right about the time she'd decided if she died she'd regret not . . . Not doing what? Images flashed in her head, images of her and a certain cop kissing her until clothes started falling off. Images of having someone to lean on, to . . .

She opened her eyes and became completely clear about one thing: a person should never trust their instincts when facing death. Nope, instincts one should trust were based on life lessons. She'd had enough of those to know that losing clothes and leaning on someone ended badly.

Jake stood outside the open passenger door, leaning in. His dark blue eyes and sexy smile sucked her in like a new, high-powered Hoover. "Are you going to sleep in my car all night or come inside?"

"I'm going to sleep in your car." She let her eyes drift back shut to avoid temptation. Maybe she should have accepted Nan's invitation to stay at her house. Maybe she should've accepted her mom's offer for company. Because right now, the idea of being alone with Jake . . .

One strong arm slipped under her legs and another eased between her back and the seat. "Whoa!" She pressed a hand against Jake's chest—his warm, wide chest—and winced from the soreness in her shoulders. "Down, caveman."

Did he listen? No.

He whisked her out of his car and cuddled her up against his solid, perfect-fit chest.

"Okay, you've proven you can pick me up . . . again." She vaguely remembered him doing this after the accident. "Put me down." She glanced at his face and his smile. And she felt herself being lulled back to quietude again.

"You sure?" His question was a husky teasing. "I kind of like holding you."

She pointed. "Down."

He lowered her feet to the ground. His hands circled her waist as if to steady her. "The doctor said you might get dizzy."

"What do they know?" She reached back into the car to grab her purse, lost her balance, and swayed.

"Apparently a lot." He pulled her against him. "Don't be stubborn."

Her cheek landed against the soft spot on his chest just below his shoulder. Inhaling, she breathed in the lightest traces of soap and perhaps a touch of spice-scented deodorant. He smelled good. He felt good. Someone must have brought him a clean shirt, because the one she'd bled over was gone, and in its place was a pressed, button-down, baby blue oxford that made his eyes look bluer than she'd ever seen them.

"I'm not stubborn." How long she could stay like this without giving herself away—without him knowing how much she liked being here. And it wasn't just the hormone kind of good. It was a *safe* good. Which meant this wasn't at all safe. "I'm a very reasonable person."

"Could have fooled me." His whisper stirred her hair. "Let me pick you up." His hands gliding down her back sent chills slow-dancing up her spine. Now, *that* was hormone good. It was the man/woman kind of good that led her back to the losing-clothes image.

She pulled away. "I can make it. Really." *Clothes intact.*

His dark blue eyes met her gaze and he pushed a flyaway curl from her cheek. "It's a good thing that you're as beautiful as you are stubborn."

"Beautiful? You into bloody clothes and stitches?"

"I think I'm just into you, Pizza Girl." His mouth brushed against her forehead. "Let's get you inside and settled on the sofa, and I'll help you get cleaned up. I'll bet you're starved, too."

He put his arm around her waist, firmly, as if he fully intended to catch her if she fell. And even though she'd sworn to never again count on a man being there, she found herself leaning against him as they moved forward. Tomorrow she'd be stronger, she promised herself.

A few minutes later, Macy had a hunch that tomorrow might be too late. Jake had placed her on the sofa, gotten her a blanket, and collected her pink cotton pajamas. "Sit up and I'll help pull your T-shirt off."

She rolled her eyes. "Is that how you seduce all your women?"

He grinned, sat down beside her, cupped her chin in his palm, and made her look at him. "I'm not going to lie. I fully intend to get you naked. To get naked with you. But you're safe tonight. Now, can I help you get undressed? I promise not to enjoy it . . . much."

She didn't have a comeback. Nothing except "I gotta go to the bathroom."

He stood and offered her hand. She got up on her own.

"Stubborn," he muttered.

"Am not," she muttered back and stubbornly made it to the bathroom alone. She slipped out of her bloodstained clothes there and took care of her feminine needs. The movements made her head throb. Surrounded with soft cotton, and only a bit dizzy, she opened the door. He was standing there waiting. His arm slipped around her waist and he walked with her.

"You rest. I'm going to fix us something to eat," he suggested.

Too tired to argue, she lay back on her sofa and closed her eyes, and tried to think about what she could do to help bring this nightmare to an end. Billy was still out there, and she hadn't done one useful thing about it. She remembered the paper in her shorts pocket where she'd written down all the information from Jake's files. Tomorrow she'd pull herself together. Tomorrow . . .

Something warm and wet brushed across her brow, and she jerked her eyes open. Jake knelt beside her, smoothing a washcloth across her forehead. "You've still got blood in your hair."

She pushed herself up, and Elvis, who'd settled at the foot of the sofa, jumped off.

Jake sat down beside her. "Dinner is almost ready."

He leaned in. She thought it was to give her brow another swipe, but instead his mouth melted against hers. It wasn't a heat-and-sex kind of kiss, but a sweet kind. And for some reason, that was even more disturbing.

"Tomorrow I'm going to stop you from you doing that." She frowned when she realized she'd spoken aloud.

A mischievous grin tilted his lips. "But not tonight?"

"I'm weak right now."

"I think it's because you like it," he accused.

After tucking a lock of hair behind her ear, he pressed the warm washcloth gently to her temple. "I found some tomato soup in your cabinet. I'm heating it now. I made us grilled cheese sandwiches, but we're desperately low on groceries. I'll stop tomorrow and grab us some things. Maybe some steaks. I can grill a mean fillet."

She hadn't gotten over the *we* part of his speech or the *meat* part, which she didn't eat, when he pressed his hand to her brow. "No fever. Good. The paper said you might get a little temperature."

"What are you? A doctor who plays cop? Or a cop who plays doctor?" She leaned back against the sofa.

"I like playing doctor." His kiss might have lacked sizzle, but not his tone.

"Seriously?" she asked.

"I am serious. And I'm good at it, too." He winked.

She shook her head. "I bet. You do this too well."

"What? Kiss?" He leaned in again.

She pressed a hand to his mouth. "Take care of people."

"Oh. Unfortunately, I had plenty of practice." The moment the words left his mouth, the teasing twinkle left his expression.

Macy found herself intrigued. "With who?"

He stood without answering. "I'll bet the soup's hot."

And she'd bet Jake Baldwin had secrets. "Jake?"

He stopped halfway across the living room and turned. She wasn't an expert on reading emotions, but she knew grief when she saw it. It was there in his eyes.

"You need an aspirin?" he asked.

"Who was it that you took care of?"

"You want milk to drink with your dinner?"

"You don't like talking about yourself, do you?"

He rubbed the back of his neck. "Some things don't warrant discussing. Try another subject."

It hit her then. The man had met her ex-husband, her mom, and Nan. He'd seen her underwear, seen her naked butt in a hospital gown, had done repairs on her house, slept on her sofa, gone with her to buy tampons, had a key to her house on his key ring, had sworn to protect her, saved her life, was now taking care of her like a mama bear, and yet she knew nothing about him. Zilch.

Try another subject. "You ever been married?"

"No." He walked into the kitchen, out of her view. The clink of silverware and the clatter of dishes filled the silence.

So it wasn't a wife he'd taken care of.

"Ever been in love?" She spoke just loud enough for him to hear.

The dish rattling stopped. His head popped out, then vanished again. "Once."

"What was she like?" Macy stared and waited. And waited.

"Beautiful," he finally answered.

"Blonde and bouncy?" she asked, frowning.

"Blonde, no. Bouncy, yes."

"And?" Macy asked.

"And what?" His head popped out again.

"What was she *like*?" She watched him disappear back into the kitchen.

"She had big brown eyes. Very loyal." More dish rattling. "And she loved to cuddle."

Macy would just bet she did. "She sounds nice. What happened?"

"Heartworm. She had floppy ears," he continued. "Part Lab."

Macy grinned, even though she knew he was avoiding her true question. "Seriously," she complained.

"I am. She thought I walked on water." He stepped back into the living room with two sets of plates and cups in his hands and a devilish smile on his face. "She'd bounce into bed with me at the least invitation. Men like that." He waggled his eyebrows. "She never complained when I left the toilet seat up. Oh, she even loved it when I left my dirty socks around!" He handed her a plate. "Do you know you have zero protein sources in this house?"

The smell of basil-tomato soup filled her nose and Macy's stomach grumbled. Her mouth watered at the sight of the toasted sandwich and the cup with swirling steam. She picked up the grilled cheese centered with gooey cheddar. "Cheese is protein."

"I mean real protein." He set his plate on the coffee table and walked back into the kitchen. "I poured us some milk."

Her stomach begged for her to start eating; her manners dictated she wait. She licked her lips, waited, and looked up to see him coming toward her. "Cheese *is* real protein. And milk."

The sofa sank as he settled beside her and placed glasses on the coffee table. "I mean meat." He scooted hip close. Balancing his plate on his lap, he picked up his sandwich. "Eat."

She was too hungry to worry about his nearness—but not too hungry to notice the warm sensation his jean-covered thigh sent swirling through her body. "There's no meat in the house because I don't eat it." She sank her teeth into the sandwich.

His eyes widened. "You're joking."

The warm toasted bread and the sharp flavor of cheddar cheese spilled over her tongue. "Oh, this is good. I didn't realize I was so hungry."

He stared at her. "You're joking about not eating meat, right?"

She took another bite. "No joke." A string of melted cheese landed on her lip, and she licked it off.

"Damn. This relationship is doomed. We'll never make it."

She swallowed, ignoring the spark of emotion that suspiciously felt like disappointment. But deep down she recognized this for what it was: an opportunity. Picking up her spoon, she pointed it at him. "I've been telling you that."

A frown puckered his brow. "No beef, chicken, or . . . No *bacon*?" He paused. "Screw that! How can you go through life not eating bacon? Bacon is part of American culture!"

She picked up her sandwich again, still warm, and before she realized what she was going to say, she'd said it. "Sometimes I cheat and eat seafood."

He smiled and seemed to contemplate.

She frowned and did her own contemplation. Why had she said that? Best to cut this off before it went any further.

He continued. "Well, I like seafood. So maybe there's hope for us." He scooped up his sandwich and took a big bite, then spoke around the food. "What kind of fish do you like? And could you . . . wrap it in bacon to grill it?"

She spooned some warm tomato soup into her mouth. "Save your ego and just accept that all we'll ever be is friends." Friends like her and Father Luis. Her chest filled with a vague achiness. Maybe it was the fact that he'd just put her second to a piece of pork.

"Close friends?" He leaned in.

She flipped the spoon up over her mouth. "I'm serious."

"So am I." He dodged her spoon to kiss her neck.

She pressed a hand against his chest but didn't push him away. He continued to kiss the curve of her neck. Using his tongue and teeth, he sent sweet vibrations through her body. "You've been . . . But I . . ." Oh, goodness, that felt so good. "I don't want a relationship," she blurted.

He tilted his head to look her right in the eyes. "Why does that sound like a lie?"

Because it *was* a lie. Instead of looking at him, she gave her soup her undivided attention. She gave the spoon a lap around the cup. Yeah, she'd admit it: she did want a relationship. But there were bad-hair, premenstrual days when she wanted to eat an entire box of Cocoa Pebbles, and she didn't.

Liar.

Okay, she'd eaten a whole box once, but the point was that wanting something didn't make it right.

She looked up. "I like you. But . . . no relationship."

"Okay, no relationship. We'll start with a fling, pure sex, and see where it leads." His blue eyes were full of laughter.

"I can't." She blinked and hoped he understood she was serious, hoped he understood that deep down she wished it could be different. But her heart just wasn't up for the risk.

He set his plate back on the coffee table as if she'd finally gotten through to him, and stared at the ceiling. She felt a little guilty. Okay, a lot guilty. He'd been good to her. He'd saved her life.

After several heavy, heartfelt seconds, he faced her. "I'm sorry, but this is really hard for me to understand. I mean . . . have you ever even tried bacon?"

Frustrated, she bit into her sandwich. "You're not taking me seriously, are you?"

"Yes, I am. Not eating bacon is very serious."

She rolled her eyes and chewed.

He grinned. "Oh, did you mean about the relationship?"

"Of course that's what I mean." She poked him in the chest.

"Then, no, I'm not taking you seriously." He leaned his head down again, his forehead touching hers. "Because you say one thing, Pizza Girl, but your eyes say another. And your eyes don't lie. I learned that with the whole nun story."

CHAPTER TWENTY

Billy drove by the house where Jamie had said Tanks might be. The lights were on. His heart thumped against his breastbone with fear. He parked a block up and, staying in the shadows, walked toward the house. Thunder rumbled in the distance, and the same feelings seemed to echo inside him. Moving to the side of the house, crowding the azalea shrubs heavy with blooms, he crouched down and edged closer to a window.

One step.

Two more. Swallowing fear, he pressed his palms against the gritty window ledge and raised up just enough to peer inside.

People. Billy's gaze went to a man who sat on the worn brown sofa. Facing the opposite direction, he wore a gray T-shirt and a cap. Was it Tanks?

The man leaned back and rested his arm on the back of a sofa, and Billy saw the snake tattoos. His heart jolted. It was Tanks.

Billy's gaze zeroed in on the man who had tried to kill his sister. His attention was so focused, he almost didn't see the blonde walking toward the window through which he peeped. Suddenly aware, he dropped down, pressing himself against the side of the house. At his angle, he could see the blonde with stoned eyes press her nose against the glass above him. There came a crack of thunder, then the sky lit up again, and the smell of rain grew heavier. He didn't move and prayed she couldn't see him.

"It's storming." The blonde's voice penetrated the glass.

Billy pulled the gun from the waistband of his jeans. This was it. Tonight it would be over. He'd kill Tanks. Protect Macy and Ellie. Even help Jamie Clay.

It had taken only slight persuasion for Jamie to tell him where David might be staying. She'd been scared. Now Billy was scared. His stomach churned with emotion, and in spite of the chill in the air his hand sweated around the grip of his gun.

When the taste of blood filled his mouth he realized he'd sunk his teeth into the side of his lip. *Don't bite on your lip.* Macy. Was his sister okay? Had Jake Baldwin been honest with him?

Soft rain fell on Billy's face. More light filtered through the window above, telling him the woman had stepped away. Trying to move silently, he scooted over to the right and cautiously lifted up to see inside again.

Two men milled around beside Tanks, and about four women . . . or girls. Two of them didn't look old enough to drive. Even from here, Billy smelled the marijuana. One of the younger girls went and stood beside Tanks. When she reached for his joint, Tanks shook his head and motioned to his lap. Obviously, the fucker expected a trade.

The girl, dark haired and pixie faced, pretty except for the black lipstick, crawled onto Tanks's lap. The man handed her the joint and then reached up and squeezed her breasts. She pushed him away. Tanks yanked the roach clip from her fingers.

Billy couldn't hear the words, but he could imagine them. The girl stared at the smoking weed as if debating whether being groped by this lowlife was worth the high. Then, nodding, she started unbuttoning her shirt. Billy saw the uncertainty and the revulsion in her eyes. The two other guys in the room turned to watch. Billy shook off his disgust.

The thought of Ellie being close to this man made his anger gnaw deeper, however. Tanks was trash.

And what are you? A crack of thunder seemed to punctuate the question.

Billy inwardly flinched and wished like hell he could have been a better man for Ellie. But did it really matter? After tonight, he'd have to pull away from her. Completely.

He ducked down again and fought the ache in his heart. "Focus," he muttered. He needed to concentrate on what was important: killing Tanks.

With his back pressed against the scratchy, paint-chipped siding, Billy tried to figure out how he could get to Tanks without hurting anyone else. And possibly without getting killed. He didn't want to die, though if that's what it took, so be it. But he definitely didn't want to hurt one of those girls.

Another flash of lightning filled the darkness. "Look." Voices came from the porch and Billy's breath hitched. "I told you it was storming," a feminine voice remarked.

Billy crouched down behind an azalea bush. The pink blooms hung in front of his face. A streak of lightning brightened the navy sky, and fear rose in his throat. If the pair came to the edge of the porch, they might see him. He needed the element of surprise to carry this off. The rain pattering against the leaves seemed to match the thumping of his heart.

A cell phone rang. "Yeah?" a male voice said.

Was that Tanks? Billy clutched his gun tighter. Slowly, he rose up to peer in through the window again. The young, black-lipsticked girl sat alone on the sofa dragging smoke into her lungs. Billy cut his eyes back in the direction of the porch. It could be Tanks there, or one of the other guys.

Billy inched over. The squish of his footsteps on the wet ground was covered by the storm's rumble. The man on the cell started talking again. Billy strained to listen, hoping to recognize Tanks's voice. If it was him, he could do this and maybe get away before anyone shot back. Thunder rolled.

"No." The man's voice became audible again, but Billy, still unable to tell if it was his quarry, edged closer.

"Damn it," the man snapped. "Listen to me, Ellie! I want you to get away from that Moore piece of shit and do it now."

Ellie?

Ellie? The storm roared around him, seeped into his blood. His hold on the gun tightened.

Light caught him, but not lightning. A car had pulled into the drive. Like an animal in the headlights, he froze. Then he fell to the ground, pointing his gun at the car. Had the driver seen him? The smell of wet earth filled his nose, soaked into his clothes, and Billy tasted blood again.

"You ready to do this?" the driver yelled, and there came the sound of other people stepping out on the porch. They hadn't seen him.

"Ready," a man answered. "This time, we do it right."

Billy's breath hitched as the rain fell faster. His death grip on his gun loosened. Then Tanks and another man walked past, crawled into the car's backseat. He'd been too slow to fire.

Billy's finger trembled on the trigger. He considered unloading bullets at the car, but what were the odds he'd get Tanks before one of them got him? And dead, he wouldn't be able to protect Macy or . . . Ellie? Who had Ellie been talking to?

The white Honda backed out of the drive. "Fuck!" Billy seethed. By the time he got back to the van, he'd never catch them. But he had to try. And then . . .

Then he'd go back to Andy's and find out if Ellie . . . If Ellie what? He'd find out why Ellie was talking to Tanks.

"Come on, Pizza Girl, let's get you to bed." The voice was a whisper in her ear, and her brain started downloading data. Gun. Hospital. Home.

A sexy man.

She remembered. They'd eaten. She'd washed up in the bathroom while Jake stood by the closed door in case she . . . what? Drowned in the sink? He took this nurse/protector thing a tad too seriously. Recalling that now reminded Macy of the question Jake refused to answer: who had he taken care of before?

"Can you walk?"

"Of course I can." After she'd washed up, they'd returned to the sofa and watched the *Tonight Show* . . . when, obviously, she'd drifted asleep—on his shoulder! She raised her head off that pillow of male warmth.

He had his hands around her forearms, easing her to her feet before she could complain. But whether she wanted to admit it or not, the coddling felt good. It had been a long time since she allowed anyone to take care of her.

Yeah! Because you don't want to turn out like Mom. Yup, that was the reason she needed to pull away. Depending on people could be addictive for codependent personalities. While Macy wished she could deny it, she'd learned the hard way that she was just too damn much like her mother.

His hand curled around her waist as he led her down the hall. She stepped out of his embrace.

"The blanket you used last night is . . . is beside the sofa."

He beat her to the bed and drew back the covers. He motioned for her to get in.

Macy slid between the sheets. The feel of the cool cotton on her bare feet reminded her that she hadn't slept well in over a week. Of course, she'd had good reasons: Billy running from the police, the rapist and murderer . . .

Her gaze went to the walls, primed with white where Jake

had covered the ugly messages. She owed him money. Tomorrow she'd have to go to work, after she made her insurance claims and got a rental car. Thank God she hadn't canceled full coverage.

"Here." Jake handed her a glass of water and shook out two tablets.

She sat up and swallowed the pills. "If you get news about Billy, you'll wake me, right?"

"That's our deal." He took the glass from her. "You don't do anything stupid, and I'll keep you updated on what I know."

She settled back on the pillow, remembering the information she'd gotten from his files. Yeah, they'd made a deal. All she had to do was figure out how to do what she needed to do, without it being stupid.

"Night," she said, looking up at him staring down at her. She really wished she didn't like him so much. "Thanks for saving my life."

"You're welcome." He turned to leave, and a little bit of loneliness crowded her chest. Yet instead of heading for the door, he went to the other side of the bed.

She blinked and pushed up on one elbow, watching him. He squeezed his hands into his jeans pockets and started unloading the contents onto the nightstand. His keys clanked against the edge of the lamp. Quarters and dimes did a shimmy on the polished wood. A folded piece of paper landed on top. He patted his pockets.

Then came his gun. Though gently placed, it clacked against her nightstand. *Her* nightstand, *her* bedroom, *his* pocket contents and gun, as if . . .

He unbuttoned his blue shirt and tossed it onto her dresser. Her dresser. His shirt.

She blinked. The man looked downright edible without a shirt. The golden hue of the lamplight showcased his warm, melt-against-me skin. His chest, dusted with dark hair, appeared even more muscular without a shirt stretched across it.

An innie belly button, the cutest little dimple she'd ever

seen, was centered among hard abs. His jeans fit snug around his narrow waist, and a trail of hair disappeared under the snap of his jeans. A treasure trail—wasn't that what the thin spray was called? Because it led to . . .

He unsnapped those jeans. His thumb and forefinger pinched at his fly, ready to unzip and unleash the treasure.

Her gaze shot up and found him studying her. "Uh, what are you doing?" she asked.

"I got on boxers," he said. His cocky grin proved he'd noted her feminine appreciation.

She tried to wipe all approval from her expression. "Okay, I had you down for a white briefs kind of guy, but you don't have to prove me wrong." She sat the rest of the way up. "Now back to my original question. What are you doing?"

"Getting in bed." He heel-kicked off his shoes.

She pointed to her bedroom door. "The sofa is thataway, big boy."

He picked up the folded piece of paper from the nightstand and handed it to her. "Doctor's orders. I'm to wake you up on the hour, every hour, and keep a very close eye on you. Hard to do if I'm sleeping in there."

He unzipped. The jeans dropped and a well-filled pair of navy-and-white-striped boxers drew her gaze. Thank God they had buttons, because something looked ready to come out and play.

Macy yanked her gaze up, and Jake pulled back the comforter. "You really need new pillows."

She fought a thrill. "What I need is for you to get out of my bed."

"It's not up for debate." He switched off the lamp. The darkness added more intimacy. "I'll wake you in an hour."

"I'm not—"

"Nothing is going to happen. Think of me as your doctor."

"My doctor doesn't strip down to his Skivvies and crawl in bed with me."

"Okay." There was a teasing quality to his tone. "I'm a

doctor that comes with perks, but I don't charge extra." He let out a deep sigh. "Now go to sleep and quit talking about sex before you get me worked up."

"I wasn't talking . . . I'm not sleeping next to you with nothing but a thin piece of cotton between me and—and your best friend."

He let a loud laugh. "He could be your best friend, too." He rolled to his side, facing her, and propped himself on his elbow. "Nothing's going to happen, Pizza Girl. Promise."

She blinked, her eyes adjusted to the low light.

His chest was close enough that she could feel the heat from his body. "I'm not having sex with you," she blurted. She *couldn't* have sex with him. And thank God she really meant it, because it was the wrong time of the month.

"You're right. Tonight we're not having sex. Now go to sleep."

"We're not having sex tomorrow night either." It would be two or three more days before she could even consider it, and hopefully, if God was on her side—*and please, please let Him be*—she would have found her runaway willpower by then.

He laughed again. "Okay, we'll shoot for Monday or Tuesday."

"Hmm, let me check my mental when-I-will-have-sex-with-you calendar." She pressed a finger to her temple. "Nope. Tuesday's out."

He didn't move. He just lay there, looking way too sexy, but at least he'd stopped smiling. "He really did a number on you, didn't he?"

She knew he referred to Tom, but it was her turn for silence. Falling back onto her pillow, she stared silently at the ceiling. Elvis leapt up on the bed, then jumped off.

"Crappers. I forgot to feed him," she muttered.

He caught her hand as she struggled to rise. "I did it."

"You fed my cat?" And why did his hand feel so good?

"I did it when I was fixing dinner."

Elvis hissed from below. Macy closed her eyes.

Jake gave her fingers a squeeze. "What happened?"

Macy laughed quietly. "He's upset because you're in his bed."

"I mean with your ex. What did he do besides cheat on you?"

Cheating wasn't enough? But deep down, she knew there was more. Tom's sin had not only shaken her weak belief in men; it had shaken her belief in herself. The situation had proven just how much like her mother she really was.

The cat meowed. Macy's eyes opened, but her gaze remained fixed on the ceiling. "Elvis wants his spot back."

"Come on. Talk to me."

She cut her eyes toward him and pulled her hand away. "Some subjects don't warrant talking about." And just in case he didn't recognize his own words, she added, "You should understand. You're the one who prefers to keep your secrets to yourself."

"What secrets?" he asked.

"I asked you earlier who you'd taken care of, remember? And you said, 'Some subjects don't warrant talking about.'"

"What does that have to do with us having sex?"

"It doesn't."

"Then why bring it up? We were talking about why you won't have sex with me!"

He confused her. "I'm just saying that, for a guy who doesn't want to share anything about himself, you sure do expect others to share." She paused. "And I don't have to tell you why I won't have sex with you."

"So I'm not the only one who's keeping secrets." He dropped back on the bed.

CHAPTER TWENTY-ONE

Jake couldn't sleep. First, the damn cat kept hissing at him. Second, he could smell Macy, the citrus of her hair products, the musky scent that was purely her . . . and every instinct screamed for him to roll over and introduce her to his "best friend." A few kisses on the sweet curve of her neck—she'd seemed to like that earlier—a hand passed slowly over her breasts to tease her nipples, a knee gently nudged between her soft thighs, and she'd cave. Macy wanted him. He knew and felt it with every surge of his blood—blood that right now was giving him the hard-on of the century.

Just in case she was still awake, he bent his knee to hide the tent pitched in the covers by his arousal. He looked at her. She lay on her back, looking angelic and asleep. Damn, he wanted her. But only a real cad would seduce a woman who had a concussion. He wasn't a cad. He was the decent, law-abiding son of a Baptist preacher.

But why the hell did she insist on not getting involved?

I'm just saying that, for a guy who doesn't want to share anything about himself, you sure do expect others to share. Her words replayed in his head. He vaguely recalled Lisa saying much the same thing. Didn't women know that men didn't enjoy spilling their guts?

His watch beeped, announcing it was one a.m. "Hey, Pizza Girl?" He brushed a lock of hair from her cheek.

"No sex," she whispered.

He chuckled. "I'm going to turn on the lights and check your eyes. Okay?"

"Bad idea." She pulled the blanket over her head.

He switched on the lamp. Then, tugging the blanket down, he kissed her nose. "Sleepyhead, open your eyes and look at me."

"I already know what you look like. You took your clothes off in front of me, remember?"

"And what do I look like?" he asked, remembering her appreciation.

"Like a man who won't talk about himself."

"So, this sharing thing is why you won't have sex with me?"

She opened her eyes. He leaned in to check her pupils, and her hand shot up to stop him.

Catching her hand, he frowned. "I'm just checking your eyes." He gazed deeply into those soft baby blues. Her pupils were the same size. Her lashes were long, her nose adorable. Her lips . . . "Now I want to kiss you."

She jerked the blanket back over her face.

"I guess that's a no, huh?" After setting his watch alarm again, he cut off the light and went back to staring at the ceiling.

Macy shifted beside him. "It was your wife, wasn't it? Who you took care of?"

"I told you I'd never been married."

"And men don't lie?"

"*I* haven't lied to you." He looked from the ceiling to her. Why the hell she needed to know about this was beyond him. She *didn't* need to know. He shouldn't have to tell her. But . . .

"My dad."

"What happened?" she asked.

"Cancer."

"Did he pull through?"

"No." Some memories were better left alone.

"I'm sorry."

She settled back on her pillow. He continued to stare at the ceiling.

"It was two years ago. I'm fine," he finally said.

She moved an inch nearer, and he wondered if she realized. "Were you close?"

"Yeah. We were different, but we respected each other."

"How were you different?"

Jake considered his answer. "He was a rule follower. Saw everything in black and white."

"And you aren't?" Disbelief rang in her voice. "You're a cop. I'd say you expect people to follow the rules."

"Those are laws. That's different."

"So what kind of *rules* did he follow?"

"Religious beliefs," he replied.

"Oh." Macy's hand dropped. It brushed his arm. "I'm assuming he wasn't Catholic?"

Jake heard the hint of humor in her voice, and remembered her whole nun charade. He turned his hand over and wrapped her fingers in his palm. "Baptist. Not a Biblethumper—he just looked to God to solve everything. Even if it meant taking handouts."

"And who do you look to?" she asked.

"Myself."

"So you're an atheist who doesn't believe in taking or giving handouts."

"I'm not against helping people," he argued. "I just prefer to take care of myself." Silence filled the room. "And I'm not an atheist. It's just . . . My father suffered more than any man should have been allowed. For a while I told myself I didn't believe in God. Then I realized that you don't get that angry at someone you don't believe in. So, yeah, I believe. I just don't think He's trying to solve my problems. He sure as hell wasn't watching out for my ol' man."

"I'm sorry," Macy repeated in a voice that held no judgment. "I can't imagine losing someone I love to something like that."

He threaded his fingers through hers. Thoughts of his father whisked through his head. Good thoughts. "He would have liked you."

"Because I'm going to be a Methodist nun?" she offered.

He chuckled. "He was a do-gooder like you."

"I'm not a *do-gooder*." She sounded offended.

"You volunteer at the garden, and didn't you say you volunteer at shelters?"

"That doesn't make me a do-gooder! I just like staying busy."

"Most people take a class or buy a book. They don't try to find ways to help others."

"It still doesn't make me a do-gooder. And I *do* read."

"So you're a humble, literate do-gooder." He chuckled. "But that's not the only reason my dad would've liked you. He had a wicked sense of humor. He loved to tease and be teased." Something he and his dad had in common, Jake realized. "He was a good man. That last month we talked more than ever. Even when he was hurting like hell, he loved to laugh."

"Then maybe that last month wasn't all bad." She gave his hand a squeeze.

Her words gave Jake pause. For two years he had refused to mentally revisit that time, worked hard not to remember. It never occurred to him until now that by blocking out those memories, he'd neglected to remember the good.

He turned his head and met Macy's gaze. "What about your dad?"

"He left," she said matter-of-factly. She tried to pull her hand away, but he held on.

"That must have stung."

"Please. His leaving was the best birthday present I ever got."

"He left on your birthday?" *Damn.*

"Yeah. But really it—"

"How old were you?"

"Twelve."

"Shit." He rested their locked hands on his chest, loving how her skin felt against him.

"He did us a favor by leaving."

"How's that?"

"He didn't want to be there." From the way she said it, he knew there was more to it. But unlike her, he wouldn't push. Not that he regretted telling Macy about his dad. But still.

Her hand shifted just a bit south, and his mind carried her touch lower. The blanket started to rise again. He bent his knee to hide it. "You'd better get some sleep." He let go of her hand, even though letting go was the last thing he wanted.

She rolled over, and he heard her sigh. "I keep thinking about Billy."

"I know." He reached over and touched her hair. God, it was soft. "He's lucky that you care so much."

Billy stepped onto Andy's wobbly porch around two a.m. He'd gone back to Girls Galore and driven around for an hour. No Tanks. He'd screwed up, let the bastard get away.

He pushed open the door, and Andy's dog growled from the back bedroom. Ellie slept on the sofa, perched on her side, her palms together, hands tucked beneath her cheek. The phone conversation he'd overheard was burned into his mind, yet denial begged to be embraced. He studied her. She wore a pink nightshirt with the word *Angel* printed across the front. And damn if she didn't look like one. Why had she been talking to Tanks?

"You're here." Her voice was sleepy but warm.

"We've got to talk."

She sat up. "What happened?"

"You called Tanks." It came out as an accusation.

Her brow furrowed. "Me?"

"Yeah." He dropped his gun on the coffee table.

"No. I didn't call Tanks!"

Doubt. So much doubt. Damn, he wanted to believe her. He wanted to pull off his clothes, pull off hers, and bury himself inside her.

"Where's your phone?"

She sat up straighter. "In my purse. Why?"

"I'm going to see if you're lying to me."

She sat there staring at him. He couldn't tell from looking at her if she was hurt or angry. Possibly both.

She got up and tossed him her purse from the chair. "Check for yourself." Anger brightened her eyes. "I'm going to sleep in the bedroom."

"Andy is in there." Billy stepped forward, but she stopped him with a look.

"I'll sleep with the devil before I'll sleep with a man who doesn't trust me." She bolted down the hall.

Three seconds later, Andy walked out, bringing a blanket and his dog. "That wasn't nice," he mumbled. He wandered sleepily into the living room, where he plopped down in the recliner and shoved a pillow behind his head. "Ellie's not the type that would be messing around with another guy," he added with a yawn.

Billy dug through Ellie's purse, found her phone, and hit the button to see if she'd made any calls. Not one.

He looked at Andy. "Did she use your phone again?"

The two a.m. alarm came before Jake realized. "I'm turning on the light," he warned.

"I really don't like you," Macy mumbled.

"Yes, you do," he said. Finding her pupils fine, he cut the light again, reset his watch, rolled over, and went back to sleep.

At the three a.m. alarm: "I'm positive I don't like you." Macy covered her eyes with her hand when the light flooded the room.

"You're a terrible liar," he said. "You so hot for me, you . . ." His gaze lowered, and his words tripped over his tongue. The top of her pajama shirt had come undone, exposing her soft breast and the better part of a rose-colored nipple. Swallowing a desire to lower his mouth and taste that sweet treasure, he focused on her face. Leaning in to check her eyes, he tried not to look at the open V of her shirt.

So close to her mouth he could feel her breath, he brushed his lips to hers. He seriously meant it to be just a quick kiss, but she slipped her tongue between his lips and her hand around his neck. Lost in want, he drank the flavor of her mouth. Lost in taste, he slipped his hand inside her flannel shirt and brushed his thumb over her nipple.

She moaned into his mouth and her hips rose up. And just like that, he remembered. He couldn't do this.

He pulled back, leaving them both short of breath. "Your pupils are fine." He rolled over.

"You shouldn't start something you can't finish," she growled.

"Do you want me to finish?" he asked, wondering if her okay was enough. He awaited her answer.

"No. But you still shouldn't have started it."

He hadn't started it! Well, not really. She'd been the one to deepen the kiss. But he didn't say that.

Thirty minutes later, he was still wide awake and fully aroused. He'd just checked his watch. That was how he knew the exact time the spray of bullets came through the window.

CHAPTER TWENTY-TWO

Macy heard loud popping sounds and shattering glass. Before she'd awakened enough to realize what they meant, she felt Jake's hard body on top of her. His oh-so-masculine weight brought a yelp from her throat. The next thing she knew, he had her in a bear hug rolling off the bed and onto the floor. She landed with a thud atop his naked chest, his arms locked around her, something cold and metallic pressed between her shoulder blades.

"Son of a bitch!" He flipped her over. "Are you okay?" Propped up on his elbow, he moved his left hand over her front, touching breasts, ribs, legs. "Macy?"

"Yeah." Popping sounds? "What was . . . ?"

Her eyes adjusted. The metal object he'd held to her back

now waved in his right hand: his gun. Clue number one that the popping noises hadn't been firecrackers.

Oh, sweet mother of earth. She tried to sit up.

"Stay down!" He forced her to the carpet and started crawling toward the door.

Her brain raced. Gun? Shattering glass? Someone had shot through her bedroom window. Someone could shoot again. Her sleep-hazed mind ricocheted from thought to thought and ended with the question *Where the hell does Jake think he's going?*

She arched her neck and saw him about to clear the edge of the bed. Hadn't he told her to stay down? That sounded like a darn good plan!

"No!" She jerked over and latched both hands around his hairy leg. "Are you an idiot? They've got guns."

"So do I!" He tried to yank free.

She held on like a hungry tick and butt-scooted in reverse, dragging him back behind the bed. "They could kill you."

He swiveled around and pried her fingers off his ankle. "Stay here!"

Before she could grab him again, he was on his feet and running out of the bedroom. She heard the thud of his footsteps, followed by the creaking of her back door. And then . . . more gunfire.

"No!" Macy jackknifed upright.

She cleared the hall, darted around the coffee table, and made it to the open back door, where she stopped dead in her tracks. People had guns out there! What the hell she was doing? One deep breath, and she crouched against the wall and peered around the doorjamb. Inky blackness clung to the wet night, and she prayed she'd see Jake. Prayed she'd see him standing. Walking. Alive.

She remembered the most recent gunshots. Her hands trembled at the thought that he lay out in the blackness now, dying.

Dead?

Damn him! She should have never let go of his ankle. "Jake!"

Nothing. No answer. Fear clawed at her throat. And—bam!

She was five years old, sitting at Nan's dinner table. Her grandpa was smiling.

"Eat up, sweetheart, and I'll take you to the—"

She was certain he'd intended to say circus. There was one in town, and she'd begged to go. But he never finished his sentence. He flinched, his eyes went blank, and he fell face-first into his plate of spaghetti.

Five years old, and she'd learned death nullified promises, that death was final, that loving someone came with a price.

"God, let Jake be okay," she mumbled into the night.

She jumped up and put her finger on the light switch, then hesitated. Her heart pounded against her ribs, and she hugged the doorjamb. Was he lying facedown on the ground, the way her grandpa had lain in his lunch? She wanted to turn on the light and see.

Before she could think about it any further, she hit the switch. A silver glow flooded the tiny patio, and her gaze flicked out, back and forth. "Jake?"

Nothing. No Jake. Oh, God!

Voices came from the alley behind her fence. She stepped past the patio and onto the squishy grass. The fence creaked, and two men hurtled over it, toward her. One wore a dark suit and tie. The other wore a pair of boxers.

Jake!

Macy's knees folded like chewed toothpicks.

"I don't give a damn. Goddamn it, I trusted that you guys had things covered, but—," Jake was saying. But after he and the FBI agent took the fence, he came to an abrupt stop when he saw Macy collapsing. His bare feet pounded the wet grass. By the time he got to her, she sat curled into a ball, her arms hugging her legs.

He squatted in front of her. "Hey, you okay?"

"Just dan-dy." She blinked, and her breath came out in quavering gasps. "I'm just . . . dandy." Moisture spiked her lashes, and a few tears dripped down her cheeks.

Guilt bored holes into his chest. He should have stood up to Agent James and taken her to his place. He'd known what they were doing. Setting a trap, using her as bait. They had underestimated Tanks. But damn it to hell and back if Jake hadn't overestimated their ability to do it. He hadn't liked the plan, but he hadn't assumed they'd screw up this badly. This wouldn't have happened if he'd listened to his gut. He wouldn't make that mistake again.

Macy leaned forward and placed a soft palm on each side of his bare shoulders. "You idiot!" She shoved him backward so hard that he landed on the muddy ground. His Glock thudded next to him.

"They had guns!" She crawled on top of him and pounded his chest with her tiny fist. "I thought they killed you!"

Jake heard a chuckle come from the agent behind him, but he focused on the tears streaming down Macy's face.

He took two, three blows, four, before he captured her wrists in his hands. "I'm fine." He pulled her down, wrapped his arms around her, and held her cotton-covered body against him. The cold mud oozed against his back, but she was warm on his chest, and nothing had ever felt so right.

Deep, heartfelt sobs bubbled from her throat.

"Shh," he whispered, and brushed his hands up and down her spine. "It's okay, baby. I promise. I'll take care of you." And he pitied the man who tried to get in his way.

He heard her catch her breath, felt her stiffen. "It's not"—sniffle—"okay."

She spoke between little hiccups, sounding just like her mom. And that woman scared him. But even the fact that Macy might be more like her mother than he'd suspected didn't lessen his desire. He didn't need perfection. He just needed Macy. Her sense of humor, her one-liners, her giving heart. And he'd take more of this, too—the holding, the closeness. Damn, he loved the way she fit against him. In spite of his height advantage, their bodies met in all the right places. Yeah, he wanted her in a forever kind of way.

She pushed up. Her chest raised off his. "I can take care of"—sniffle—"myself. Never wanted"—sniffle—"to go to the circus anyway!" She crawled off him and marched inside.

Two hours after the attack, Macy stood on the threshold of Jake's condo, physically, mentally, and emotionally exhausted. Before they'd left her place, she'd changed into a pair of gray sweats and a powder blue T-shirt. She'd forgotten to change out of her bright-yellow bunny slippers.

"You can come inside, Pizza Girl." Jake set down the litter box and bags of clothes, and he looked back at her. "I'll even let your three friends in." He motioned to the cat carrier and her bunny-slippered feet.

"You could have just taken me to my mom's," she said, too tuckered out to answer his joke.

He gently pulled her inside. "It's five in the morning."

"Nan's up doing yoga."

"Well, you're here now." He closed the door and then, taking the cat carrier from her, unlocked it to let Elvis free. The feline hissed and didn't come out.

Macy let her gaze move around his living room. If she weren't so zombified, she'd have enjoyed checking out his place, picking up clues about who Jake Baldwin really was. But right now, all she wanted was a place to get horizontal, to crash and forget the storm of emotions raging over her when she'd thought he was shot.

"This way." He led her down a hall and into a bedroom.

"Sorry. I never make my bed. But the sheets are semi-clean." He pulled back a rumpled blanket.

Semiclean didn't sound good. She almost insisted she'd sleep on the sofa, but sheer exhaustion left her devoid of energy. Elvis appeared in the doorway and darted under the bed. Maybe he had the right idea. A bed was a bed, semi-clean sheets or not.

She dropped onto the mattress. "If I get cooties, I'll sue."

He knelt between her knees and removed her slippers, as if taking off bunny shoes were part of his job description. Looking up, his gaze grew tense. "I'm so damn sorry."

She blinked, her lids almost too heavy to hold open. "For what? Being stupid enough to almost get yourself killed?"

"No." He put his palms on her knees. "For being stupid enough to take you back to your place. I had a feeling Tanks wouldn't quit. I let Agent James—"

"I'm the one who insisted I go home." Even dog tired, she saw the guilt he shouldered, saw his bloodshot eyes and the sad-little-boy look that she ached to chase away. Before she started questioning her feelings again, however, she collapsed back on the bed and stared at the ceiling fan. It was going around and around.

"I'm killing my brother when I see him," she muttered. Raising her knees, she slipped her legs beneath Jake's semi-clean sheets and rolled onto her side to face the wall.

"We both need sleep," Jake's husky voice said. "I don't have to be at work until after lunch. You're supposed to call and make an appointment to see your doctor later. Your grandma said she'd take you."

Macy heard the zipper of his jeans, but she closed her eyes, too tired to care that he was stripping down. The bed swayed as he climbed in beside her.

He wrapped his arm around her waist and pulled her into a spooning position. His chest surrounded her. His arms cradled her. His body heat melted through her T-shirt, and she felt safe—so safe that she didn't listen to the voice that said safe was dangerous.

"Macy?" Jake's voice pulled her from the fuzzy edges of sleep.

"Huh?"

"What did you mean tonight when you said that you didn't want to go to the circus?"

"Pick another subject," she muttered. Then she fell asleep, feeling safer than she had in years.

Hal glared at the clock. Ten, damn it! She should have been here.

He sat up, grabbed the phone, and dialed the front desk. "I need to speak to Faye Moore. She's a volunteer here."

The lady told him to hang on. He did so for five freaking minutes before the woman returned. "She's on the fourth floor. I'll connect you."

He let out a deep breath. It hurt less to breathe today.

A floor nurse answered his call. "Just a minute," she said after he asked for Faye. "She's passing out books."

He waited another four or five.

Finally Faye answered. "Hello?" She sounded concerned.

"Faye? It's Hal."

She didn't say anything, so he just jumped headfirst into the conversation. "You said you would come by today."

"I—I'm not working that floor."

His grip on the phone tightened. "And you don't get a break? You couldn't have stopped by before you started volunteering?"

More silence. "I'm not sure if . . . I think it's best if . . . They said I shouldn't see you."

"I don't care what they say," he growled, gruffer than he intended. "I think you at least owe me an explanation."

"I . . . I guess"—sniffle—"I could drop by during my lunch."

"I'll wait for you." He hung up and glanced at the clock. Patience wasn't his virtue.

A soft touch against her cheek stirred Macy from sleep. Warm, comfortable sleep. The growing hardness against her bended knee brought her closer to alertness. But not close enough. She shifted her leg over it.

Up.

Down.

Recognition struck. Her eyes flew open. A deep masculine inhalation sounded at her ear.

Oh, damn. She lay half on top of him, was giving him a knee job.

"Good morning," he whispered.

She didn't speak, didn't move. It had been forever since she'd dealt with such a "hard" issue. She wasn't sure if she should acknowledge the fact that she was aware of his condition or play clueless to the impressive situation arising in his boxer shorts.

"How do you feel?" He rose up to look down at her.

Clueless sounded better. She slammed her eyes shut, but too late—he'd seen her. She knew, because he chuckled. "I think it's time we get up," he said.

"Well, your Mr. Dudley seems to have gotten a head start." Inwardly she cringed. But what the heck, clueless had never worked for her. She rolled out of the cradle of his arm, sat up, but made the mistake of glancing back and down to his . . .

"Mr. *Dudley*?" Jake laughed. "Last night you referred to him as my best friend. Did you two meet and get acquainted when I wasn't looking?"

"No. That's what they're all called."

"Says who?" he asked.

She paused. "Says me." She stiffened. "And don't look so proud. He's not that impressive." It was a whopper of a lie, but she didn't want to give the guy a bigger head than he already had. Literally.

Jake's right eyebrow arched. The bright confidence sparkling in his gaze told her she was in trouble.

"Come back to bed and we could work on making him more impressive."

"I think I'll go pee instead." Macy scooted off the bed. Elvis appeared in the doorway.

"Macy?" Jake called. "I'm sorry."

She turned to him. He'd raised his knee to hide the evidence, but his smile told her he wasn't really sorry at all. Not that she deserved an apology. She'd started this conversation. Not one of her brightest moves, either. My God, she'd named the guy's penis! A *really* bad move. Because once introductions are made, men feel perfectly fine bringing them into conversations. *Mr. Dudley this. Mr. Dudley that.*

"You . . . you just seem to have that effect on . . . Mr. Dudley."

See? Big mistake.

She spent fifteen minutes in the shower of Jake's extra bathroom. Grabbing her purse, she took care of her feminine necessities, then wrapped a towel around her breasts. He'd suggested they shower and then go grab a bite to eat before he went to work. He'd suggested they shower *together.* She'd turned him down on that, but accepted breakfast.

Pulling her hair back, she gave the mirror a one-handed circular swipe. "Ugh!" she moaned. The image staring back had a semiblack eye and a bruised forehead, though the stitches were indeed high enough that any scar wouldn't be noticeable. Not that she was vain, but who wanted to be scarred? One stretch of her neck proved she wasn't as sore as she'd expected. Good, because she had a lot to do today. And it was already eleven.

Reaching into the plastic bag Jake had packed for her last night, she pulled out . . . a pair of muddy boxers and men's jeans. Damn. She'd grabbed the wrong bag. Glancing down at her sweats puddled on the floor, she saw the leaky shower curtain had doomed them.

Tucking her towel securely beneath her arms, she poked her head out into the hallway and listened. The sound of running water told her he'd already jumped into the other shower. She could wait and ask him to bring the clothes, or she could tempt fate and . . .

More of a fate tempter than a patient person, she stuck her bare feet back in her bunny slippers and stepped out of the steamy bathroom. She dashed across the adjoining study and got almost across the living room, when she heard the doorbell ring. Freezing, she tried to decide between darting back to the bathroom or running for her clothes. The sound of a key turning in the lock gave her a shot of adrenaline. She took off at a dead run toward the closest cover: the master bedroom.

She cleared the door but smacked straight into a freshly showered, naked Jake—well, naked but for the navy towel slung low around his waist. The feel of his skin against her nipples sent messages firing to her brain. The first message being that she really liked him undressed like this. The second message: *I lost my towel.*

His gaze dropped to her breasts, which were flattened against his lower abdomen. His hands went to her naked hips.

"Jake?" a female voice called. Then footsteps. "Sweetheart? Did you forget our date? Oh, my!" The last two words were said in panic.

Date?

Instantly Macy realized that "sweetheart's" date was probably staring at her naked ass. Her gaze shot to Jake's towel, and instantly she developed a plan. Since his date had probably seen him before, Macy took what she needed—providing everyone a good look at Jake Baldwin and the full monty.

CHAPTER TWENTY-THREE

Jake's gaze shot to the woman standing in his hall. He realized he was standing naked, now with a hard-on, in front of—

He snagged back his towel. Unfortunately, Macy fought him for it. It became a tug-of-war between them.

"Shit!" Finally coming to his senses, he slammed the bedroom door closed. He heard Macy dash for the master bath and close herself in.

As he stared at the door, laughter bubbled up in his chest.

Then, taking a deep breath, he opened the door an inch. "Mom, hold on. I'll . . . be right out."

"I'll just leave," his mom yelled, obviously shaken.

"Please don't." He knew it was best to handle this right away. The creaking of the bathroom door behind him made him turn. All he could see was Macy's nose, which was not nearly as nice as the view he'd gotten earlier.

"Please tell me I heard that wrong. Tell me it's not your mom who just saw me buck naked."

A laugh escaped as he grabbed a pair of jeans. "You weren't completely naked. You had on bunny slippers."

Hal stared at the lunch tray and waited for Faye. Ten minutes, and he'd be calling again.

A tap came at the door. She stepped inside, carrying one of those foldable lunch boxes. She wore khaki slacks and a striped smock. Her hair wasn't purple anymore, but a dark brown—her normal color, though missing the gray. Not that he'd minded the gray. His thick mop of hair had turned more salt than pepper a long time ago.

"I thought you weren't coming," Hal said.

"I almost didn't."

He started to ask why, but suddenly keeping her around seemed more important. "What did you bring for lunch?"

She looked down as if she'd forgotten what she'd packed. "Uh . . . a sandwich." Pause. "You haven't eaten?"

"I thought I'd wait and see if we couldn't trade."

A tiny smile brightened her eyes. "You're forgetting, I know how bad the food is here. Why would I trade for it?"

"Ah, but I got an ace up my sleeve."

"An ace?"

"You like chocolate?"

"What kind?"

"The good stuff. Expensive stuff. Swiss."

"Where would you get Swiss chocolate?" She took a step forward.

"My son works for a Swiss company. He always brings me

a box." He glanced at her lunch pack. "Let's see if what you've got is worth *me* trading."

She edged closer, bringing her baby-soft scent with her. Slowly she unloaded her lunch kit beside his covered tray. "Ham and cheese on homemade sourdough bread, low-fat baked potato chips, and . . . three Fig Newtons."

"I love Fig Newtons." He raised the top off his lunch tray to show a bowl of watery chicken soup capped with a sweating plastic top, a wilted and likely cold hamburger, and equally chill peas and carrots. "I say we split everything fifty-fifty."

She eyed his food and wrinkled her nose. "I don't know if your chocolate is worth it."

Carefully, so his stitches wouldn't pull, he retrieved the box from his bedside cabinet. He set the candy beside their lunches. "Some have nuts."

She hesitated. "Okay. But I think you're getting the better deal."

"You won't after you taste this chocolate."

She opened her sandwich and offered him half. She sat on the foot of his bed and they ate and shared small talk. Her sandwich and the chips disappeared, and they each ate a Fig Newton, leaving one cookie to accompany the untouched hospital food.

As Faye spooned a bite of soup into her mouth, tears sprang to her eyes. "I was going to tell you."

Hal forked up a few peas. "You knew from the beginning?"

She nodded. "I'd heard you were in ICU. When they called down and asked for someone to bring up some ice chips, I . . . just wanted to see you."

"Why?" He needed to know.

A tear slipped own her cheek. "The FBI said they thought Billy shot you, and I knew he'd never do that. I wanted to ask why you'd lie."

He dropped his fork. It banged against the lunch tray. "I never said Billy shot me."

"I found that out later."

"He saved my life," Hal remarked. "I told them that."

She met his eyes. "He's a good boy. I"—sniffle—"know he did a bad thing robbing that store, but . . . he's got a lot of good in him."

Hal picked up a box of tissues from the bedside table and passed it to her. She shook her head and reached into her pocket. "I bring my own." She dabbed at her eyes. "I'm sorry. You don't want to hear me cry. I'm trying to stop."

"I don't mind. I mean, I don't like to see you sad, but I understand. I'm sure you're worried about your son."

She nodded. "I am. And now I'm worried about Macy." She went on to tell about her daughter's accident and how someone had shot through her window in the middle of the night.

"I'm sure the police are watching out for her," Hal offered.

She nodded again. "There's some task force working the case along with the FBI. And there's this cop, too." She smiled. "I think he's sweet on Macy."

"If she's like her mom, I can understand why."

Faye gazed at the food tray. "I guess we're at the hard part. What do we do now?"

Hal inhaled, feeling slightly tongue-tied. "I know they said for you not to come, but I don't give a damn. I wanted to ask you out, but it's been so long since I've asked a woman for a date. I . . . don't know if I know how to date."

She looked surprised, and the slightest smile appeared on her lips. "I meant about the last Fig Newton."

He grinned, feeling better than he had in months. "I told you, it's fifty-fifty."

Her eyes crinkled with her smile. "You don't cut a lady a break? Not even when you're waiting to see if she'll go out with you?"

"Not when it involves Fig Newtons." But when he broke the cookie in two, he offered her the bigger half. Their hands touched and he got a little jolt. It was pleasant, and he wondered if getting shot wasn't going to turn out to be a good thing after all.

Dressed, laughter in control, Jake hurried out of the bedroom. His mom sat on his sofa.

"I'm sorry," she said. Embarrassment colored her face.

"It's okay." He stood beside her.

She blinked. "When you didn't show up for lunch, I called your office."

Lunch? Oh! "I forgot. I'm sorry. I had—"

"Your partner said you were at home," his mom continued. "I thought you might be sick." She started fumbling with her key chain. "I had your key from when I watered your plants last summer and . . . I never . . . I didn't know you were seeing anyone. Not that I'm not happy. Since you and Lisa broke up, I've worried. I mean, I know you loved her. But your brother never meant to hurt you, and—"

Jake held up his hand. When his mother got upset, she rattled on and on. She was midstream in a rattling that he didn't want to hear. "It's okay."

"I shouldn't have used your key." She dropped it onto the coffee table.

He sat down next to her. She didn't stop talking, but at least she changed directions. "That poor girl. I know she's humiliated."

"She'll be okay." The image of Macy with nothing on but her slippers filled Jake's mind. Curvy in the right places, that tiny waist, that dark triangle of black hair. . . .

His mom continued. "She'll never forgive me."

"She'll forgive you." Somehow he was certain Macy wouldn't hold a grudge.

His mother looked at him. "Are you two serious?"

He hesitated. Then: "Yeah, Macy's special." He'd have thought admitting it out loud for the first time would feel awkward. He was wrong.

"I should apologize to her." His mom jumped off the sofa. Before Jake could think of a reason for her not to go storming into his bedroom, she was doing just that. He bolted after her.

"Macy?" His mom tapped on the door.

"Mom, maybe this isn't—"

"Yes?" Macy's weak voice answered.

"Can I come in?" his mom asked.

Silence. "I guess." Macy sounded hesitant.

"Mom? Why don't—"

"She said I could come in." And his mom did just that.

Jake ran a hand through his hair, then followed her into the bedroom. Macy sat on his bed wearing her bunny slippers and the jeans and shirt he'd brought from her house. Her cheeks were flushed. Elvis sat beside her, looking skittish.

"I'm Brenda Baldwin," his mom offered. "I wanted to apologize for storming in."

Macy's gaze zipped to Jake and back. "You don't need to apologize."

"But I do, dear. I swear, I'm not a meddling mother. He didn't show for lunch, so I called his work. His partner told me he was at home, and I assumed he was sick. I panicked and came to check on him. I never dreamed that he'd be, uh . . . busy."

Jake bit back a moan. "We weren't 'busy,' Mom. We were getting out of the shower."

"Separate showers," Macy added. Elvis leapt off the bed and went to hide. Macy watched the cat as if she considered following suit. "I'm not . . . We're not . . . We don't *do* 'busy.' "

Jake put his arm around his mom's shoulder and tried turning her toward the door. "Let's reschedule our lunch?"

"That's fine. But . . ." She faced Macy. "You'll be coming with Jake to his grandfather's birthday party, won't you?"

Jake shot his mom a look. She ignored him.

"He has invited you, hasn't he?" she continued. "We're planning a huge celebration."

"Mother, I—"

"Jake, surely you've invited her. Haven't you?" His mom looked at him. Macy looked at him.

"We'll discuss this later?" Jake tried.

"What's to discuss? I want Macy at the party. My father will be a hundred."

Macy studied Jake. "I . . . work a lot, and—"

"Promise me you'll come. It will be the only way I'll know you've forgiven me." Jake's mother stared at Macy. "Oh, my. That's a nasty bruise."

Jake's cell phone rang. He went and snagged it off the bedside table. Recognizing Mark's number, he answered, "I'm running late. What's up?" But his attention stayed on the two people in the room. No damn way was he taking Macy to a party to meet the woman he'd loved, who'd dumped him for his brother.

"Another break-in. In North Houston," Mark said.

"Can you and Benton cover it?" What was his mom saying now?

"Sure, but it was tagged with red paint," Mark said.

Jake's focus changed. "I'll be right there. Oh, did the other samples come back yet?"

"No," Donaldson said. "I called. It's likely to be another few days."

CHAPTER TWENTY-FOUR

Jake's mother wouldn't leave until Macy promised she would consider accompanying Jake to the birthday party. Of course, Macy would keep her promise and consider it, but no way in hell would she actually go. Especially after seeing the way Jake had reacted. It was the first time she'd seen him look afraid.

Why had he been afraid?

Okay, so maybe she hadn't made a good impression on his mom, but did he not want her to meet his family? The thought gave Macy a little flutter in her heart. Not a big ache, it didn't even really hurt, it was just a little . . . a tiny, little hiccup.

The moment his mom left, Jake rushed into apologizing for her, then apologized for having to cancel their intended breakfast. Then he started getting dressed. Macy remembered he'd received a call.

"Is everything okay?" she asked.

He pulled some socks out of a drawer. "Another home robbery." His gaze shot up. "They used red paint to tag the place."

"Do you think it's Tanks?"

"Could be connected." He pulled a shirt from the closet. "Remember, Nan's driving you to the doctor. Oh, Agent James assigned a man to follow you. He's out front." He shot her a serious look while he buttoned up. "Don't do anything stupid, remember?"

"Nothing stupid," she repeated, and recalled the information she had on Ellie.

He grabbed his cell phone, called the assigned body-guard—one Agent Adkins, FBI—and gave the man the plan for Macy's day.

Since when did Jake Baldwin plan her days? The man didn't even want her to meet his family. She considered asking him about his new job description, but the kiss he gave her as soon as he hung up knocked her off track.

He grinned. "Mr. Dudley and I will miss you."

"Right." She waited for him to say something about the party. Not a word.

Not that it bothered her. It was his family. She had no reason to go. Didn't want to go, really—would have turned him down if he'd asked. Besides, she had her own family to worry about. Her mind went back to Billy, to Ellie. And then to the fact she'd been shot at last night.

"Hey." He caught her by the arm. "You okay?"

She nodded. "I . . . I was just thinking, maybe someone should talk to the nursing home where Ellie works. Maybe if I—"

"Stop." He glared down at her.

"Stop what?" She glared right back up and then wondered if he'd figured out she'd read his files.

"Stop trying to put yourself in harm's way."

"I just want to—"

"Let us take care of this. You go to the doctor."

He studied her, then eyed his watch. "Answer my home phone. I'll call you here."

Right at that moment, his cell phone rang. He pulled it out. "It's Mark again." He started toward the door. "Fix yourself something to eat."

So he thought he could tell her what to do, eh?

After Jake left, Macy found the paper with the information from his file. All she wanted to do was ask a few questions. Heck, she would take the FBI with her if he'd go. And that's when the idea hit. Macy grinned.

First she called to cancel Nan. "I'm fine," she told her grandmother.

"Now, little lady, the doctor said—"

"I'll go tomorrow."

"It's dangerous for you to be by yourself," Nan insisted. "What if this Tanks—?"

"I won't be by myself," Macy explained. "My bodyguard will be with me the whole way." She'd promised Jake not to do anything stupid, and, well, this wasn't stupid. Her plan was downright brilliant.

As soon as Nan agreed and hung up, Macy dialed a rental-car agency that delivered. Then she phoned Papa's Pizza to order her pizzas. And while she had the manager on the phone, she informed him she'd be back to work tomorrow night. Let the FBI earn its keep and follow her. She paid her taxes. Jake wouldn't like it, but a girl had to make a living.

Next she called her school counselor. She explained about her situation and asked if she could make up the work. Dropping those classes would cost her hundreds of dollars, hundreds she didn't have. The counselor promised to look into it.

Her calls finished, she fed Elvis and made herself some macaroni and cheese she'd found in Jake's pantry. It tasted like the box it came out of, but she ate it anyway.

Impatient for her rental car to arrive, she paced Jake's apartment with his cordless phone in hand. She took everything in, trying to discern the man's secrets.

She looked at her cat. "And we know all men have secrets. Don't they, Elvis?"

She eyed Jake's living room for clues. His furniture was contemporary—nothing too expensive, nothing froufrou that led her to believe a woman had pulled it together or anything like that.

She walked into his bedroom. No women's clothes hung in the closet, no hidden panties in his drawers, which indicated two things: there was a good chance he wasn't a cross-dresser, and he didn't have women showing up for midnight quickies and leaving articles of clothing. Not that she would have expected it, but she really wanted to know if there was something about Jake she wasn't seeing. It was hard to entirely trust any man. Not after Tom had lied to her.

Phone still in hand she darted to his bathroom. She had her nose in his medicine cabinet when the phone rang. Thinking it might be her rental car, she answered.

"Hello?"

"Hey." Jake's husky voice sang in her ear. An unexpected warmth filled her chest.

"Hi." She leaned against the bathroom counter. Was he going to ask her to the party now? She fought back hope.

"I can't seem to get the image of you naked in bunny shoes out of my mind." His cell phone crackled.

"I'll bet your mom is having the same problem," she replied. Just thinking about it made Macy's face hot. Remembering him in his towel and out of it made things worse. She focused on the medicine cabinet. Tylenol, Band-Aids . . . The man didn't even have condoms! Not that it mattered. She wasn't planning on having sex with him.

"Did you find something to eat?" Jake asked.

"I made some macaroni and cheese. Thank you."

"You're welcome." A long pause. "I heard on the radio that there's a circus in town. I remembered you mentioned something about the circus last night. You never did explain that."

Well, my granddad was going to take me to the circus, but chose to die in his plate of spaghetti instead. "It's nothing really," she said. She hadn't really wanted to go, any more than she wanted to go to Jake's granddad's birthday party.

"I could get us tickets if you like."

She closed her eyes. "Nah. I hear the elephant poop stinks."

"Okay." A pause. "What time is your doctor's appointment?"

"They haven't called to give me a time." It wasn't exactly a lie. Yes, it implied she had called them for an appointment, and that might be a stretch, but this was her brother she was stretching for.

She accidentally knocked over the Tylenol and it clattered down on the counter.

"What are you doing?" Jake asked.

Having already stretched, she went for the truth. "Searching your medicine cabinet for any STD meds."

His laugh echoed through the line. He probably thought she was joking.

"So, am I disease free?"

"Don't know. I haven't finished." She eyed the bathroom drawers.

"What else are you looking for, Pizza Girl?"

"You know . . . kinky stuff. Chains or whips."

He laughed again. "Don't look under my bed."

"Oh, Elvis already led me to that." She caught a glimpse of herself in the mirror, smiling, and with a heck of a lot of emotion in her eyes. Too much emotion.

He laughed again. "If you find I'm clean, is Tuesday on?"

"I never agreed to Tuesday!"

"But you will."

He sounded confident. Her heart hiccupped.

Someone called his name in the background, and he said, "I've got to go." Then, in a lower voice he added, "Miss you."

He missed her? Just like that, she remembered staring out her back door and being scared to death he'd been shot. Her heart jumped.

"Be careful," she said, realizing cop work could be dangerous, but the phone clicked silent. Had he heard her? What if he wasn't careful?

Her worry became something akin to panic, the same kind of panic she felt about Billy. Then she realized she was getting mushy over a guy who had freaked when his mom invited her to his grandfather's hundredth-birthday party. Not that she wanted to go.

She started out of the bathroom, stopped, turned, and went into his bedroom. She looked under the bed.

No whips.

No chains.

Not even a *Playboy*.

But while she was on her stomach, her breath making the dust bunnies quiver, she discovered something more disturbing, something waiting to be exposed. It lurked not under the bed, but within herself. Yup, she bumped noses with the truth: She wanted her brother to be okay, but she also wanted to go to the circus. She wanted Jake to ask her to his granddad's stupid birthday party. And she wanted to say yes to Tuesday, to a relationship with him.

Donaldson waited on the porch of the latest home robbery. Jake stepped out of his car. Almost two hours had passed since he'd left his place, but he'd gotten caught in his office by Agent James with some questions about Macy's mother and the possibility that she might be involved with the prison break. Jake just looked the man in the eyes and asked, "Have you *met* the woman?"

Only two hours he'd been gone, and he missed Macy like

the devil. He'd hated leaving her, even for a little while, but the sooner he could get Tanks back behind bars and Billy safely off the streets, the sooner he could focus on just her. The vision of her naked, tugging at that towel, made a lap around his mind. Want, desire, and a smile pulled at his gut.

Jake met Mark by the door. "What's up?"

"No one's answering," Mark said, and knocked again.

"Who called this in?"

"The owner," Donaldson offered. "A Mr. Brown."

"I'll go around back and check?" Jake reached automatically to unstrap his gun as he headed around the side.

The gate stood ajar, broken. As Jake stepped over a piece of splintered wood, his gaze caught on graffiti. Damn, if the writing didn't look the same as at Macy's house. A sudden clattering sounded. Jake passed a hand over his Glock and moved toward the back.

"Mr. Brown?" he called. "It's the police."

Macy's plan was working. The rental car arrived right after she'd destroyed her second tissue. The assigned agent had been hesitant when she'd appeared at his car looking weepy, bruised, and wearing bunny slippers, but chin held high, she told him she'd been called into work. Baldwin hadn't mentioned her working, the cop claimed. "Things change," she'd replied. "Aren't your orders to follow me?"

His phone rang and he answered it. "Yes. Do we know for sure if it's him? Well, let me know when you do. Do I still need to stay on Miss Tucker? Fine." He frowned.

"What?" Macy asked when he hung up.

He didn't appear happy to share his information, but he finally spoke. "They got a lead on Tanks. About two hundred miles from here."

Macy hoped he was right, but finding Tanks didn't get her closer to her brother. "So you don't have to follow me?"

"Until I get further orders, I'm your shadow."

So he'd followed her to her house. She'd changed into her uniform, slapped on makeup, then headed to Papa's

Pizza, where she purchased—with her employee discount, of course—six cheese pizzas. Pulling out of the parking lot, she watched to make sure he was behind her. He was. Which meant her next stop was the retirement community where Ellie Chandler worked.

"I'm not doing anything stupid, Jake," she muttered.

Macy remembered feeling as if something wasn't right with the information she'd read about Ellie. Maybe someone at the home could shed some light on that. Was Ellie really helping Billy, or was she in cahoots with Tanks? Macy knew her brother believed in his girlfriend, but he'd believed in the tooth fairy until he was nine. Nevertheless, Macy couldn't help but recall Ellie's squeaky telephone message.

I love your brother.

Jake took another step into the backyard. A clanking filled the silence. More as precaution than from instinct, he drew his Glock.

Passing the side of the house, he saw a man standing behind a junked-out Mustang held up on blocks. "Mr. Brown?"

The man turned. Jake raised his gun but didn't point it. The man's hands shot up in the air, clearly showing he had no weapon, but Jake didn't miss the flash of guilt in his eyes.

"I live here," the man spouted.

"You're Mr. Brown?" Jake asked. "I'm with the HPD."

"Yes. I called you guys."

Jake lowered his gun but continued to study the man's expression. Something just didn't feel right.

CHAPTER TWENTY-FIVE

"Any news on Tanks?" Macy asked Agent Adkins as she approached his car in the nursing-home parking lot.

"Nothing yet."

Macy explained that when delivering pizzas to a facility, it usually took a few minutes to find the person in charge to sign off. "Give me at least ten minutes before you freak." The FBI agent didn't look happy, but she also saw the latest James Patterson book beside him and figured he wasn't going to miss her that much.

Inside the old-folks home, she looked for someone who didn't look official enough to throw her out, but with enough snap to give her information. Searching around, Macy knew she didn't have a lot of time.

A man in a wheelchair rolled by. Then she spotted a janitor sweeping out a supply closet.

"Hi!" Macy smiled at the man. "I'm trying to find the hall Ellie Chandler works. She's a nurse's aide, blonde, with a high voice?"

The man, late fifties and balding, looked up from his broom. "Ellie's not working today."

"I know." *Think fast.* "I'm supposed to deliver this to one of her patients, and I forgot which room."

"She works the B hall. But you should check with the nurses. Some of the folks are on restrictive diets."

Think faster, Macy! "Oh. Well, Ellie's ordered pizza for this person before. Mrs. What's-her-name. One of Ellie's favorites." Macy prayed Ellie had a favorite.

"Probably Mrs. Kelly," the man said. "Suite B-15. I know she's not on a restrictive diet."

"Thanks." Macy started to go. Then: "Do you know when Ellie is supposed to be back?"

The janitor frowned. "I heard she called in at the last minute and needed a bunch of time off. It's not like her."

"Not like her, how?" Macy tried to sound causal.

"She cares more about her patients than most of their own families. Comes in on her days off. Bakes them birthday cakes."

"That's Ellie for you." Macy forced a smile.

"Most patients call her an angel. She's damn near it."

"Yeah. Well, I should get this to Mrs. Kelly."

Macy hurried off to find room B-15. *Who are you, Ellie? And who are you to Billy? Friend or foe?*

Jake made sure they had pictures of the taggings. Probably all gang related. They were connected to Tanks—he sensed it in his gut. A feeling of accomplishment stirred in his belly. This was going to help him find his quarry.

While Mark asked Mr. Brown questions in the living room, Jake walked around and listened with a half an ear.

". . . in the billboard business," he heard Mr. Brown say. "They took most of my air brushes and compressors. That's how I make my living."

"What kind of billboards?" Mark asked.

"The kind you see on the freeway," the man snapped. "Do you give me the paperwork to report to my insurance?"

Jake hadn't forgotten the look of guilt the man wore when he'd first stumbled across him in the backyard. Walking over to an entertainment center, Jake studied the area where the TV had sat.

Mark's tone caught Jake's attention. "How did they get the safe open?"

Jake moved forward. This wasn't the MO of the other burglaries. They'd snatched accessible items—TVs, computers, that sort of thing—and left. They hadn't messed with safes.

"I—I don't know," Mr. Brown stammered. "M-my wife could have left it open."

Jake studied the man's expression. "What's missing?"

The man looked over at him. "My wife's jewelry. Family heirlooms."

Jake crossed his arms over his chest. "And where is your wife, Mr. Brown?"

The man's face paled. "She's at the hospital with our daughter. She's heading up our little girl's cancer-fund campaign. She's got a lot on her plate right now. Can't you just leave her out of this?"

"It's our job to cover all the bases," Mark said. He obviously sensed Jake's distrust.

Mr. Brown's shoulders squared. "Our kid is fighting for her life. Can't you cut us a break?"

"I'm sorry," Mark said, but his eyes didn't hold the sympathy stirring inside of Jake. "We've got to do our job."

It was the word *cancer*, used in the same sentence with *little girl*, that got to Jake. Seeing his dad suffer had been hell. He couldn't imagine a child dealing with it. "What kind of cancer?"

"Leukemia."

"Are they doing a bone-marrow transplant?" Jake asked.

The man gripped his hands into fists. "Already tried. Didn't work. There's a new drug, experimental, but the insurance won't pay. So my wife is working with some community leaders. . . ."

Jake glanced out the window to where he'd seen Mr. Brown by the old Mustang. Sympathetic or not, his suspicions deepened.

Macy looked at her watch. She sat in Mrs. Kelly's room discussing sweet Ellie Chandler and praying the FBI agent shadowing her in his car was still patiently waiting. She would have left five minutes ago, but the woman kept talking, and Macy was holding on to each word, praying something useful might be said.

"I hope she's okay." Mrs. Kelly sighed. "It's probably Ellie's brother got himself in some trouble again."

"That's it!" Macy said.

"What's it?"

"I forgot she had a brother." Macy's mind played connect the dots. Jake's file had stated that Ellie was an only child. Macy remembered Billy telling her that the only reason Ellie was involved with Tanks was because of her brother. That might be important.

"Do you know if her brother lives with Ellie?" Macy asked.

Mrs. Kelly picked up her cup of tea. "She says he comes and goes. Sounds as if the boy still has some growing up to do."

Glancing at her watch, Macy stood. "I've got to go. I'm so sorry about Fred." She squeezed the woman's hand in true sympathy for the loss of a friend. "Take care."

"I will." Mrs. Kelly's eyes teared up. "Tell Ellie I said thank you for the pizza. I'll heat it up for dinner."

Yet another lie she'd told. Macy winced. *For Billy*, she reminded herself as she hurried out.

As she passed a phone in the lobby, she considered calling Jake to give him her information. Then again, it might be better to finish her investigation first. It wouldn't help to be giving the police false information. She might be pulling them off the right track.

As she stepped out the door, she saw the FBI agent rising out of his car. She waved and hurried to her vehicle before he had a chance to question her. As she moved, she felt a twinge of pain in her shoulders, a side effect from her accident, but it was nothing aspirin wouldn't cure. Her heart pain was another matter.

Macy headed next to the home of the wife of one of the escaped convicts. Chase Roberts had been David Tanks's cell mate. Macy wasn't sure how this might help her find Billy, but at least she was trying. She checked her rearview mirror for her shadow. Spotting him, she smiled.

How could Jake get mad when she had her assigned body-guard with her?

Jake walked out of Mr. Brown's house. Donaldson met him by his car. "I can't believe you did that," he said.

"Did what?" Jake opened his car door.

"You saw him hide it, didn't you? When you went into the backyard."

"I didn't see anything," Jake answered honestly. "The guy's house was really robbed."

"Maybe. But you expect me to believe that the guys who robbed this place dropped more than fifty thousand dollars worth of jewelry in the backyard? And you just happened to find it?"

Ignoring Mark, Jake pulled out his phone and dialed his house to see if Macy had left yet. His answering machine came on. She had to be at the doctor.

"He was trying to pull off an insurance scam," Mark accused. "He's lying about everything."

"You don't believe his daughter has cancer?"

"Probably not. He made it up just in case you called him on the jewelry. What's the chance of an insurance company refusing to pay for a kid's treatment?"

Jake snapped his phone closed. "This is the real world, Golden Boy. Shit happens that you rich kids never know about."

Mark rolled his eyes. "What you want to bet that, if I check, I'll find out his wife and daughter are in Mexico on some shopping trip? If he even has a wife and kid."

"Fine. You check. But if I'm right, you make a huge donation to his daughter's cancer fund."

"How huge?" Mark asked.

"How much can you afford?"

For a second it appeared as if Mark was going to answer. Then he shook his head. "Fine. If I'm wrong, I'll make a donation. But if I'm right . . . ?"

"You name it." Jake wasn't worried. The pain in that man's eyes had been real. Jake knew—he'd lived through it himself. True, Jake had found the allegedly stolen jewels hidden in the trunk of the Mustang. True, Mr. Brown had been thinking of pulling off insurance fraud, but—

"You bring me breakfast for a year. And no Pop-Tarts without the frosting, either. Deal?"

"Deal." Jake got into his car.

"Billy, wake up."

Billy rolled over to see Andy crouched down beside the sofa. The first thought floating through his mind was that he needed to talk to Ellie. He still needed to find out about the phone call. Last night he'd tried to talk to her, but she'd locked the bedroom door and refused to come out. And while Andy admitted Ellie had used his phone, the kid had cleaned out his messages and erased the memory. How unlucky could he get?

Billy glanced at the clock on the wall. It was almost three in the afternoon. How could he have slept this late? He needed to go back to that house and find Tanks.

"We got trouble," Andy whispered.

Billy saw the panic in the boy's eyes and shot upright. "What—?"

Andy hushed him. "It's the police," he whispered. "They're parked outside."

Macy stepped off the porch when no one answered the door. Her personal guard had parked behind her, and she turned and offered a wave. Right then, a little boy on a bike came pedaling up the drive. His brown skin gleamed in the afternoon sun.

"Did my mama order pizza?" he asked, tossing down his bike.

Macy smiled. "Is she not at home?"

"She went"—the little boy grew quiet—"somewhere."

"Sorry I missed her." Macy spotted the look of longing in the boy's eyes. "You know, I can leave this and get the money later."

"You sure?" He held his hands out for the pizza.

Macy laughed. "Yeah."

She'd started to walk away when he called out, "Wait! She's at my uncle's, down the block. The house with red shutters. She could pay if you need her to."

"Thanks." Macy walked to her car, debating if stopping there would really garner any information. What could Chase Roberts's wife really tell her? But feeling a little Nancy Drewish—hey, she'd already gotten some information that might help—she decided it wouldn't hurt to try.

Pulling over at the red-shuttered house, she grabbed another pizza box and strolled up to the door. Hearing voices inside, she knocked. The sudden silence seemed too fast. Almost eerie. But glancing back at the FBI agent in the car, she reassured herself that he had her back. She knocked again.

"Who is it?" a voice asked from behind the door.

"Pizza," Macy answered. Now, to figure out how—

The door opened, and an older man stared at her. "Come in," he said.

"That's—"

A hand came out and yanked her inside. The door slammed. Macy's pizza fell to the floor.

One look at the man who grasped her elbow, and Macy knew trouble had her number. She'd seen his face on a mug shot.

"We didn't order a damn pizza," Chase Roberts said. "So why don't you cut the shit." He slammed her against a wall.

"I'll not be part of this." The older man who'd opened the door left the room.

"I . . . must have the wrong address?" Macy swallowed hard when the man's other hand came up around her neck. Her eyes shot to the window, then to the man's crotch. She threw her knee but missed, and Roberts's hand tightened around her neck.

"Who the hell are you?"

The escaped convict's face was so close, Macy smelled the onions he'd had with his lunch. She shifted her left hand out toward the table on the wall beside her. She found a smooth, hard surface. A statue.

Buddha to the rescue.

"Fuck!" Billy rolled off the sofa onto the floor. "Are you sure it's the police?"

Andy went to peer out the window. "It's a patrol car. Just one guy. He's just sitting there. Maybe he's not here for you."

Billy took a deep breath. "Go see what he wants. Don't . . . do anything stupid. But if they know . . ." He swallowed. It wasn't supposed to happen like this. "If they know I'm here, I'll turn myself in. I don't want you or Ellie hurt." But even as he said it, he looked at the trailer's back door.

Jake had barely driven off before the desire to check on Macy hit again. He pulled over and went through his phone until he found the number her guard had given him that morning.

"Hey," he said when Agent Adkins answered. "This is Baldwin. Everything okay?"

"Fine," was the curt answer.

Jake settled back in his seat. "She still at the doctor?"

"She didn't go to the doctor."

Jake leaned forward. "Why not?"

"She was called into work."

"Work? She doesn't have a car," Jake said.

"She rented one."

"Why didn't you call me?"

"My orders were to follow her. To look out for any gold Cavaliers. I'm following her and looking out for gold Cavaliers."

"Are you at the pizza place now?"

"No. We're at . . . 1060 Dayton Avenue. She's delivering a pizza."

Dayton? *Dayton?* Warning bells started ringing in Jake's head. He grabbed the escapees' files and scanned the pages.

1042 Dayton Avenue.

It wasn't the same address, but it was too damn close for coincidence. "Do you see her right now?"

"No. She went inside," Adkins admitted.

"Damn it. She isn't supposed to go inside. . . ."

"Shit!" Adkins said. "Was that a Buddha?"

"What?" Jake yelled, but the line clicked dead.

CHAPTER TWENTY-SIX

Jake drove and dialed at the same time. Adkins's phone rang. No answer. Jake turned on his siren and shot out into traffic, putting his emergency light on his dash at the same time. Then he called and requested backup at the Dayton address.

What had Macy done? Friggin' A, when he got his hands on her . . . *If* he got his hands on her. Damn it! He gripped the steering wheel, swerved to miss a car, and for the first time in a very long while, he prayed.

Still fighting a wave of panic, he slammed on his brakes when he passed Dayton Avenue. Doing an illegal U-turn, he drove like a bat out of hell. Finally, he spotted the house. Cars crowded the street: sedans and patrol cars, but no ambulance.

His engine hadn't given its last sputter as he tore out of his Monte Carlo. He hit the porch steps, and glass crunched beneath his feet. The broken window caught his eye. Then he saw the stone statue of a decapitated Buddha laying belly up on the concrete porch.

As he started inside, a uniformed cop moved to stop him. "HPD." Jake flashed his badge and squeezed through the crowd. His gaze zipped back and forth as he moved. Where the hell was Macy?

There! He spotted her curled up on the sofa. Relief washed over him. Now to decide which to do, kiss or throttle her.

She raised her gaze and saw him. Guilt flashed in her eyes.

Adkins appeared. "I figured you'd show up," he said.

"What happened?" Jake spat.

"We got one." Adkins pointed to the handcuffed man in the corner.

Jake recognized Chase Roberts. The convict looked mad enough to kill—and he could have killed Macy. He was definitely going to throttle her himself.

"What the hell were you thinking, letting her come here?" he growled at her supposed bodyguard.

"I did my job. I was supposed to *follow* her," Adkins snapped.

"And you didn't realize this address is right down the street from one escaped convict's wife? What Cracker Jack box did you get your badge from?"

Agent Adkins took a menacing step forward.

Agent James appeared. "Go get some fresh air," he told Adkins. Then he turned to Jake. "You leave my men to me."

Jake gritted his teeth. "You know he screwed up."

"I'd say we've all screwed up." He shook his head. "He just came on the case this morning. He hasn't had time to read the files." James let out a deep breath. "We thought we had him."

"Had who?"

"Tanks. But it wasn't him."

"What do you mean?" Jake asked.

"We got a call that three men were staying at a hotel twenty miles outside the border. They all met the description of our guys. I sent most of my men to bring them in." He passed a hand over his face. "We all let our guard down."

James looked back at the man in handcuffs. "Plus, we have Chase Roberts, which might lead us—"

"Macy Tucker might have been killed," Jake growled.

James's left eyebrow arched. "Well, I have no better luck keeping tabs on my men than you do your *girlfriend*." The Fed's tone was half teasing. Then he sighed. "I won't argue that it was an ideal situation. But it looks like your girl knows how to defend herself. Roberts is only just now able to stand straight again. Buddha didn't fare so well, either."

Jake shot his little ballbuster another look. She stood from the sofa and moved across the room toward them. Jake noticed new bruises on her arms. He reached for her.

"I'm fine," she said, and looked at Agent James. "This is all on me. He had nothing to do with it."

"I don't doubt it," Agent James said. "But I am curious to how you knew to come here."

Macy looked back at Jake. A flicker of guilt darkened her eyes. "I thumbed through a file I found in Baldwin's car. I went to Roberts's wife's house, and her son told me his mom was here. But I didn't know Chase Roberts was."

Agent James shot Jake a hard look.

"It's not his fault," Macy repeated as Agent James walked away.

Jake turned to her. "We had a *deal*."

"I didn't think I was doing anything stupid," she said. "I made sure he followed me." She pointed to Adkins. "All I wanted was to ask the wife a few questions. I thought maybe—"

Jake leaned down until his nose bumped hers. "We . . . had . . . a . . . deal."

"But—"

"Go sit your ass down and don't move until I say so." He pointed at the sofa.

"Fine," she said. "But when you stop being so pissy, I need to talk to you about what I found out about Ellie." She plopped down where he'd told her.

Jake counted to ten and then did exactly what Macy expected. He asked her exactly what information she'd uncovered.

The cops were outside. Billy couldn't believe it. He moved into the bedroom. Ellie rose from the bed where she'd been reading a gardening magazine. "I'm not sure I'm talking to you yet."

He saw the window was open and pressed his finger to his lips to shush her. His heart pounded in his ears, and he remembered he'd left his gun under the sofa. Not that he'd use it, but if he had to run he'd want the darn thing.

"What?" Ellie whispered. Right then, the trailer was jarred by Andy shutting the front door behind him.

Billy stepped to the window, and with one finger he separated the blinds to see out. Ellie moved beside him, and he heard her breath hitch as she spotted the cop car.

As Andy stepped onto the driveway, the patrol officer got out of his car. He brought his radio receiver with him. "Blue van, license number . . ." When the cop finished calling it in, Andy approached.

"Hi," he said. He didn't sound too shaky, Billy hoped.

The officer glanced around. "I'm looking for Mr. Nelson."

Andy grinned. "He lives down the road. Green trailer."

"This isn't 64 Callway?"

"It's 62. What's wrong? Harold not pay his child support again?"

The officer nodded and pointed to Andy's Falcon, which was parked halfway up the yard. "Did you know the sticker has expired?"

Andy tucked both his hands in his jeans pockets. "Yeah, I'm planning on going today and renewing."

"You do that." The officer got back his car and drove off down the street.

The trailer shook as Andy reentered it. "He's gone," the kid called out, laughing.

"I heard," Billy said.

Ellie had tears in her eyes.

Billy went over, wrapped his arm around her, and pulled her against him. And right then, he knew he had to get away from her. He couldn't let her get caught up in this any more than he already had. But first he had to know.

Almost as if she'd read his mind, she looked up. "I never called David, I swear. The only people I called last night were my brother and Mrs. Kelly at the nursing home. And no, I didn't use my phone. I used Andy's."

He remembered he'd never seen who was talking on the phone on that front porch. Then the severity of the situation hit. "Your brother knows you're with me, doesn't he? He told you to get away from me, didn't he?"

"Yeah." Her brow wrinkled. "How do you know what he said?"

Billy raked a hand through his hair. "Did you tell him where you were?"

"No. Why?"

"He's with Tanks," Billy muttered. "Damn it, Ellie! Your brother is with Tanks. And Tanks wants to hurt you, just like he wants to hurt Mace." He took her by the shoulders and gripped her hard. "Would your brother be with him if knew Tanks wants to hurt you?"

"He wouldn't." Her eyes grew moist. "How do you know he's with David? He was staying at a friend's house."

Billy didn't answer. He was too busy playing connect the dots. When he went to get Tanks, if her brother was there and pulled a weapon, Billy might have to shoot him too. That, or take a bullet. Why did things have to be so fucked-up?

Then Billy remembered that the cops had called in their license number. "Who does that van belong to?" he asked.

"My brother," Ellie said.

Billy took two steps and leaned his forehead to the wall, all the while fighting the panic slowly rising in his chest. Could things get any worse? If there were any warrants out for Ellie's brother or if the police suspected him in connection with the breakout, the cops would come back quick.

He looked up. "I've got to get out of here." He raked a hand over his face. "You can't stay, either. Do you have someplace you can go?" He stepped toward the door.

She caught his arm. "I'm not going anywhere without you. You make me madder than blue fire, Billy Moore, but I still love you."

"No, Ellie. You can't come with me." It was time to call it quits.

It was almost seven that evening when Macy and Jake left the precinct to get something to eat. He was still angry at her, she could tell. Though he shouldn't have been. Especially when the information about Ellie's brother—or foster brother, as Jake and the FBI discovered—had turned out to be important. It seemed he had ties to the same gang that Tanks belonged to. After some checking, they'd also learned the phone calls from Tanks to Ellie's house had been made while Ellie was at work. Everyone was back to believing Ellie wasn't involved with the escape, other than probably helping Billy after the fact.

In spite of being sore and chagrined, Macy couldn't help but feel a little heroic for providing the authorities with their new lead, and for being somewhat responsible for catching one of the escapees. Her plans to someday work for the DA's office wouldn't be hurt by this little escapade.

Okay, maybe running across Chase Roberts had been more about luck—both bad and good—than skill, but a girl was allowed to enjoy her accomplishments, wasn't she? And hey, she'd taken on an escaped convict and won. Nan was right: busting balls did give a girl a thrill.

The waitress showed them to their table. Macy picked up her menu. Though Jake hadn't totally gotten over being mad, she could tell he was working on it. Plus, a miffed Jake gave her some insight into him.

She peeked at him over the top of her menu. He wasn't looking at his; he was looking at her. Frankly, she liked seeing how he handled his temper. No way was she getting involved with a guy who—Damn, was she throwing in the towel?

She hid behind her menu. Did she really want to go here? Risk having her heart chewed up? Did she even have a choice?

Hell, yeah, she had a choice, a voice inside her screamed. It wasn't as if she was in love or anything. Love didn't happen in five days. Lust? Yeah. Like? Heck, yeah. Respect, too. But love? That took time to grow.

They hadn't even *made* love yet.

Getting out now would save her, before the lust, like, or respect deepened. But that's where she came to a mental roadblock. She didn't want to be saved. Nope. She wanted to go to the circus. Well, that was something of a metaphor. She wanted to see and experience the sights and sounds of a relationship, to feast on the excitement, even if it meant running the risk of stepping in a big pile of elephant poo.

She glanced over the menu again at him. He was still looking at her.

"Is this place okay?" he asked. "We could find someplace that serves vegetarian food."

"This is fine." She dropped her menu. "If our waitress shows up, order me a Boca Burger." She stood and added, "Without onions." The memory of Chase Roberts's repellant breath lingered.

"What are you doing?" He watched her shoulder her purse.

"Going to the ladies' room."

"Can I trust you to go there and back without getting into trouble?" Frowning, he touched her arm in the same spot where Chase Roberts had bruised it.

"You want to loan me your gun, just in case?" She forced a smile when he rolled his eyes. "Or maybe you'd prefer to come with me."

He grinned. "I'm easy. I wouldn't mind if you came first."

Comprehension struck, and she felt her cheeks redden. "Funny," she said, and walked away.

A short time later, back from the ladies' room and sitting

across from him, Macy was still trying to get the image of her and Jake, all sweaty and satisfied, out of her head. It wasn't working.

Their waitress set two plates on the table. "Two Boca Burgers with fries." The sultry redhead shot Jake a flirtatious smile. "Need another soda?"

He nodded. "Thanks."

Macy glanced at her empty tea glass. She obviously didn't rate. A touch of jealousy stirred in her gut.

Jake motioned to her glass. "And some more tea."

The waitress picked up both glasses and sauntered off.

"Thank you," Macy said. Then she glanced at Jake's plate. "You ordered a Boca Burger?"

He shrugged. "Yeah."

"You like Boca Burgers?"

He eyed the plate warily. "Sure."

She instantly knew he'd ordered it because of her. Warmth swirled in her chest.

She watched him douse the bun with ketchup, retop the burger, and take his first bite. He chewed. His eyes grew round. She bit her lip to keep from laughing.

"How is it?"

"Fine." He continued chewing. The waitress appeared and dropped their drinks on the table. Jake grabbed his and drank half. Then he glanced at her. "What?"

"Just admit you don't like it."

"I didn't say . . ." He looked at the burger, which he held in one hand. "It just . . . needs something."

"Like what?"

He cut his gaze at her. "A pound of ground chuck."

She laughed.

Jake let out a deep breath. "You are so damn beautiful, I can't even stay mad at you."

She popped a fry into her mouth. He made her feel beautiful. He made her feel a lot of things. "Worth eating a Boca Burger for?"

"I ordered it, didn't I?"

She squirted some ketchup onto her plate. "You could have ordered a real hamburger."

He picked up a fry and dipped it in her ketchup. "You won't think less of me if I eat meat?"

"No. I choose to do this, but I don't judge others." Their gazes met. She felt it again—the magical pull, the sizzle. And more. "Besides, I already like you too much."

His smile crinkled the corners of his eyes. "You do?"

She leaned over and kissed him. It was just a simple kiss, but when she pulled back, she saw in his eyes that he thought it meant more. More, as in an invitation to it *all*. Which she wasn't willing to give him yet. First, Aunt Flo's curse had to fully depart. Then there was the issue of not being invited to his grandfather's party. He had three days.

She had three days. Three days before she committed herself. Three days to talk herself out of it—or to convince herself to go for it. The passion. The risk.

The passion.

He ran a slow hand down the side of her neck. "I like you too much, too."

His smile made her insides go mush. These were going to be three very long days.

CHAPTER TWENTY-SEVEN

"Chocolate or strawberry?" Jake looked from his ice-cream selection to Macy. He felt more cold air blowing from her than from the freezer. He didn't understand it, either. She'd kissed him and hadn't pulled away when he'd kissed her back twice at red lights. He'd been so damn eager to get back to his place, so he could concentrate on kissing and not worry about the man in the black sedan behind them enjoying the show, but the moment he parked at his condo, she'd put her guard back up. A guard he was dead set on breaking through.

"Chocolate." She smiled nervously and stroked Elvis, who sat next to her on the sofa.

Jake pulled out the pint-size containers and grabbed two bowls. Shortly thereafter, he put on some soft rock and then settled on the sofa next to her. "What's your *favorite* flavor?" he asked.

"Rocky road. Yours?"

"Depends on my mood. Sometimes nothing will do but chocolate. Then I have my strawberry phases." He scooped a spoonful of pink ice cream from his own bowl and held it out. "Try it."

She did. As her beautiful lips closed around the utensil, erotic images flashed in his mind. He casually adjusted for the tightening in his pants.

"And?"

"It's good. But it's not chocolate." Macy stared at her bowl. "So, your grandpa is really going to be a hundred?"

"Yeah," Jake said. Behind her bowl, he saw her nipples pressed tightly against her blouse. He couldn't help staring. "Give me a taste of the chocolate."

She fed him a bite. He let the cool sweetness melt on his tongue.

"You know, I think I'm in a chocolate mood," he said. He put down his bowl, scooted closer, and eased his arm around her shoulders. Grinning, he used his spoon to steal a bite.

"Hey!" She pulled her bowl closer to her chest.

He scooped another spoonful and held it out. "I'll share." He watched her lips part and accept his offering.

As soon as he drew the utensil back, he went in for the kill. He swirled his tongue around and found the cold chocolate in her mouth. Its dark sweet flavor had him delving deeper. Abandoning her bowl to her lap, she curled warm hands around his neck.

Without ending the kiss, he took her bowl and set it on the coffee table. Then, sliding his arm down between her and the sofa, he pulled her onto his lap, turning her to straddle him. As the V of her legs came against the bulge in his jeans, he groaned. Their kiss went from hot to hotter, sweet to sweeter.

Her hands slid from his neck to his chest as her tongue danced with his. He ran his hands down her back to her hips and tugged her closer to his aching erection. Her sweet pelvic push was all the encouragement he needed. Reaching under her shirt, he touched soft skin that his mouth watered to taste. Moving his hands to her back, he released her bra. Then, slipping his hands around to the front, he moved under the silk material and cupped her naked breasts. Her nipples puckered against his palms.

He moved his kisses to her neck and started working on her shirt buttons. One popped open, and he kissed his way down the exposed skin. Another popped, and he visually feasted. Her breasts were only slightly hidden by the loosened bra.

The need to see all of her had him reaching up to pull down her bra. He'd seen her naked during the towel tug-of-war, but seeing her now was different. Better. This was no accident. This was them sharing their bodies, pleasuring each other. Becoming lovers.

"Perfect," he whispered and leaned in to taste her. He licked her nipple, and she rocked in his lap, pushing her sex against him.

Her last few shirt buttons came undone. While savoring one nipple and then the other, he removed her shirt and bra, and the two pieces of clothing fluttered to the beige carpet. Reclaiming her lips, he settled her back on the sofa. His shirt joined her bra and blouse, and he stretched out beside her. Her eyes stayed closed while he took in her dark-brown hair spread across the sofa's tan leather.

Reaching to the coffee table, he dipped his finger into the melting strawberry ice cream to trace it over one nipple. Her eyes popped open, and she arched up and moaned.

"You like that?" he asked.

A low, shuddering *Yes* escaped her lips.

Coldness tightened her nipple, and unable to resist, he

lowered his mouth and laved it with his tongue. She rubbed her pelvis against his thigh. It was a sure sign that she was his—practically an invitation for complete ravishment.

He slid his hand down to unsnap her jeans and slowly lowered the zipper. His own zipper bulged. He touched the edge of her silk panties. As he slipped one finger under the elastic band, his dick pulsed with the need to find its way inside her, to feel her slick wetness sucking him deeper. He touched the triangle of hair, surprised by its silky texture.

"Soft," he mumbled. His finger slipped lower. "And wet."

"Stop! I . . . we . . . can't."

She caught his hand. He caught his breath.

"We can't."

He heard her words, but they didn't make sense. "We *can*."

"No." She jerked his hand from her jeans and scrambled out from under him. She sat up.

"Why?"

"Because," she answered.

His balls were tight as rocks, his dick so hard he thought it might snap in two. He reached down to reposition himself and managed to sit up. He looked at her, topless, her jeans unsnapped, unzipped, her hair mussed. As impossible as it seemed, he felt himself harden even more. He didn't trust himself to speak, so he concentrated on breathing.

In.

Out.

And when looking at her became too much, he stared at the ceiling.

"I'm sorry," she said. "I should have stopped when . . ."

The sofa shifted as she stood up. After counting to three, Jake dropped his head forward and watched her slipping her arms into her blouse.

"Why stop when you want it as much as I do?" He waited for the answer, afraid of what he'd hear. He could still remember asking what the ex had done. She hadn't answered. Did she still love the bastard?

Damn, he didn't want to hear that. He wanted her in his

life, but he wouldn't play second fiddle to any man. Hell, no! He'd done that with Lisa. God only knew how long she and his brother had been carrying on behind his back.

Macy's fingers shook as she buttoned her shirt over her bare breasts. He spotted her bra still on the floor. She sat back down beside him.

He swallowed. "Is this about your ex?"

Her eyes widened. "No! It's . . ." She pulled her hair back. "It's Aunt Flo."

Inhaling, he studied her. "Your aunt?"

"You know." She waved her hand. "Aunt *Flo*."

Frustrated, he pinched his nose between his thumb and forefinger. "I don't have a friggin' clue how or why your aunt could stop us from making love."

A grin spread across her lips. "No. 'Aunt Flo' is another way of saying my period. Remember the trip we took to the store?"

It took a second for her meaning to sink in. "Oh!" With his dick like petrified wood, it was amazing he could think at all. "That's it? Just that?"

"Yeah." She still wore that damn beautiful smile.

He grinned. "That's the only reason you stopped?"

"Yeeahhh."

It wasn't a *hell, yeah*, but he'd take it. He laughed. "So when does your aunt leave?"

She put a hand against his shoulder. "She'll have overstayed her welcome by Tuesday."

Her palm felt warm against him. Warm and delicious. He wanted that warmth other places. "That long?" More blood rushed to his groin.

"More or less. She keeps her own schedule."

His gaze caught on the open V of her shirt. He could still taste her breasts laced with strawberry ice cream. To hell with her aunt. "And is it a written rule that when she's here, you can't—?"

"Written in stone." She snagged her bowl of half-melted

ice cream from the coffee table. "Just eat some chocolate." She spooned a bite into her mouth then brought another spoonful to his lips. "It's supposed to be better than sex."

He took it and swallowed, and the sweetness slid down his throat. "You obviously haven't had sex with me."

She took the spoon back and licked it slowly. "So, you're that good, huh?"

Images of her mouth on something else flashed through his mind. He gulped. "Yup."

"As good as *really good* chocolate?" Her tongue continued to move over the spoon.

"Better." He snatched the spoon and got more ice cream.

Her eyes twinkled. "You talk big, but—"

"Mr. Dudley isn't all talk." He used the spoon to point to his jeans.

Her gaze lowered to his bulging crotch, then flew back up. "You are *so* crass," she complained. But he thought she was laughing.

"No, I'm honest." He leaned in and kissed her, then deepened the kiss. When he came up for air, his hard-on was even more painful. He stood. "And since your Aunt Flo rule stands, I'm taking—" An idea suddenly hit. "Want to join me? This will relieve at least *some* of our tension."

Billy stepped up on the porch. "You sure no one is here?" he asked.

"I'm sure. I take care of it for her." Ellie opened the front door to the beach house. "Mrs. Kelly's only daughter lives in Ohio, and Mrs. Kelly doesn't want to sell the place yet. I should have remembered. We could have come straight here."

Billy looked around. Everything in the house looked expensive: the furniture, the knickknacks, even the light fixtures. "Does your brother know about this place?"

"No." She dropped the keys in her purse. "He's not good about things like wiping his feet or being careful with dishes."

Billy looked down to make sure he hadn't tracked dirt inside. His shoes were clean. The carpet was the thick, woven kind that sprang back into shape after each step.

"Come here," Ellie said, and led him into the living room. There she opened the curtains and unlatched the windows. The sounds of the ocean and the smell of salt water filtered inside. They watched the ocean, and Ellie laid her head on his shoulder. "Pretty isn't it?"

"Yeah." Billy's chest ached. It ached because even though he'd let Ellie believe he was going to stay here with her, he wasn't. It ached because he felt out of place standing in a beautiful house. It ached because the ocean was so beautiful, and soon—after he tried to take out Tanks—he might never see the ocean again. It ached because Ellie's brother could get caught up in what was going down in all this. Ellie loved her brother. She would never forgive him.

"Make love to me here," Ellie begged. "With the ocean and the moon."

She pulled her shirt over her head and removed her bra. Then she shimmied out her jean shorts and red panties and stood in front of him. The moonlight touched her milky nakedness and he couldn't look away. He didn't want to look away. He wanted to capture this image and burn it into his mind.

Her breasts were *Playboy* beautiful. Her pink nipples reminded him of raspberries. He reached up and touched one, watched it pebble. A soft purring came from her throat and she unsnapped his jeans and wrapped her hand around his dick. Billy knew he should tell her no and leave, but he wanted one more time.

One more time to taste her breasts and her sex, to feel the soft skin pulsing against his lips as he brought her to climax with his tongue.

One more time to feel himself inside her, to pump his hips hard and fast as she wrapped her legs around him and begged him to keep going.

Just one more time.

* * *

While Jake showered, Macy made fast work of finding a set of sheets for the sofa. She'd turned down his offer of relieving their tension. Oh, she'd been tempted. But she'd been scared, too. Today her emotions were all over the place. No doubt, come Tuesday when Aunt Flo had departed, she knew she'd been singing a new tune. But maybe by then he'd have asked her to go to his grandfather's party. Maybe by then she would have stopped doubting and really started believing in happy endings.

Footsteps thumped down the hall. Jake stopped and stood there, wearing nothing but a pair of boxers. His hair shone a dewy black and looked finger combed. A few drops of shower water clung to his chest. She watched one glistening stream spill down his chest and disappear into his belly button.

"What are you doing?" His words drew her gaze to his face.

"Fixing my bed." She looked away and focused on what she was doing.

"Why? We slept together last night."

She gave the sheet one more tuck. "Last night you had doctor's orders." She glanced at him. Another drop of water wiggled its way to the elastic of his boxers.

He ran a hand over his chest. "There's no reason—"

"After what almost happened, I think it would be best."

He ran a hand over his face. "You really don't think I'd try to persuade you to do something you didn't want, do you?"

"No," she answered honestly. "But *I* might."

His blue eyes twinkled. "Then I insist you sleep with me."

As he stepped closer, she put her hand on his chest. A chill from his skin met her palm. He really had taken a cold shower.

"Please, Jake."

He held her waist. "Nothing will happen, I promise. I'll fight you off if you attack me."

"Yeah, but if I sleep in here, I *know* nothing will happen."

"Macy, this is silly. The only reason we aren't making love

in that bed or on that couch right now is because you're on your . . . woman thingy."

"Woman thingy?" She grinned.

He answered her smile with his own. "Hey, if this"—he pointed downward—"is now Mr. Dudley, I can call your time of the month a woman thingy."

Macy laughed. "I guess that's fair. But I'm sleeping right here."

He took her hand and gave a tug. "Let's go to bed."

"No." She dug her heels into the carpet.

When his gaze met her determined glare, he released her and ran both hands through his hair. "God, you are one stubborn woman, aren't you?"

"No." She paused. "Okay. I am stubborn. But you're just as stubborn. And since we're already arguing, I should tell you something else you're not going to like."

"More good news?" His shoulders took a new set, and his eyebrows pinched closer together. Miffed Jake was back.

"I'm going to work tomorrow night."

She watched his body stiffen with anger, but oddly, it didn't make her afraid. Not like she'd been when her father showed signs of temper. Even Tom's fits of anger had given her an uneasy, queasy feeling. But not with Jake. She could stand up to him. Toe to toe. Nose to nose. She liked that.

"Like hell you are," he growled.

"They have a man watching me at all times. Why shouldn't I go to work?"

"They had man on you today, and look what happened!"

She shook her head. "I have to work. I have bills to pay. Heck, I owe you almost a hundred dollars."

"What? Since when do you owe me money?"

"I saw the receipt from Home Depot in your car."

"The same time you were snooping through my files, I guess?"

"Stay on topic," she snapped. "The point is, I know how much you spent. Between the doorknobs and paint, it was—"

"Please! When have I said you owe me that money?"

"You think I'm just going to let you pay for it?"

"I bought it. I didn't ask you if I could. It was a gift."

"Well, it's not my birthday. And I can't just let—"

"Screw the money," Jake hissed. "You think I'm going to let you go put your life at risk to pay me back?"

She matched the stubborn tilt of his chin with her own. If she and Jake Baldwin were going to have a relationship, he needed to understand right off that she wasn't a pushover. "It's not just you. I need to pay my rent."

"I'll pay it." He stormed to a desk and pulled out a checkbook. "How much do you need?"

"Well, darn, why don't you just slap me on the ass, hand over your bank account, and I'll call you sugar daddy?" And with a sigh, she turned her back on him and anything else he could say.

Jake lay on his bed staring at the ceiling and fuming for over an hour. Out of nowhere he remembered a sermon Harry had practiced on him once. The message was one of walking in a man's shoes.

Two new thoughts hit Jake: he still missed his brother and, damn it, if he put himself in Macy's shoes . . . hell, he'd be furious at himself. Handouts were about as welcome to him as a case of food poisoning. He didn't even understand why he'd acted like a jerk, but then that became clear, too. His protective tendency could be a bit overbearing. Yeah, he'd been a jerk.

Not that she wasn't being difficult.

Hardheaded.

Stubborn.

Yet so damn loveable.

Jake shot upright and walked into the living room, prepared to apologize, but also hoping to somehow make her see reason. But she was asleep, Elvis curled up at her feet. A wave of emotion rushed through him, and all he could do was stand and watch her breathe. The way she slept, her hands beneath her face, made her look so young, so innocent, so damn vulnerable.

The memory of her talking about how her father had left on her twelfth birthday flickered through Jake's mind, and he hated the man without ever knowing him. The thought of her ex having hurt Macy, of her brother taking advantage of her, turned his muscles rock hard. The idea of Tanks and then Chase Roberts laying a hand on her made his blood boil.

He wanted to hold her so tight that nothing and no one could ever hurt her again. Which led to his problem. No way was he going to let her go to work.

Right then, he accepted he could not do this alone. He needed help. And while asking for help wasn't easy for him, ask he would. He knew just the person to call.

It was hours before Billy slipped out from under Ellie's soft body. They had made love twice and fallen asleep on the floor. He found his underwear, then his jeans, and dressed.

"What are you doing?" she mumbled, her tone sleepy.

He zipped up his pants. "I've got to find Tanks."

She rose up on her elbow. Sadness filled her eyes. "You're not coming back, are you? This was good-bye, wasn't it?"

A knot formed in his throat. He couldn't answer for fear he'd do something stupid like cry, so he finished dressing. But as he tucked the gun in the waistband of his pants, Ellie sat up. He forced himself to speak.

"I'll let you know where I leave the van."

"Leave it? What are you really planning on doing, Billy Moore?"

CHAPTER TWENTY-EIGHT

"Need some coffee, sleepyhead?"

Macy opened her eyes and stared into a smiling, freshly-shaven face. Steam rose from a cup and billowed deliciously under her nose.

Pulling back so her morning breath wouldn't knock him on his haunches, she sat up. The sofa dipped as he sat beside her.

Once settled, he handed her the cup. "You're really not a morning person, are you?"

She finger-combed her hair, self-conscious. "And I suppose you are?"

"Busted." He picked up the TV remote on the coffee table. "Maybe Saturday cartoons will cheer you up while I get us cereal. It always worked on my brother. You like Lucky Charms?"

She sipped the caramel-colored coffee doused with milk. "Yeah." The brew tasted wonderful. "Thanks." Then his statement about a brother sank in, and she cut her eyes to him. "I didn't know you had a brother."

"Yeah." He leaned in for a kiss, but she covered her mouth. "I've got fuzzy monsters growing on my teeth."

"Then go slay the monsters. I don't serve breakfast without a morning kiss." He stood up, looking content and way too sexy in his faded jeans and white T-shirt.

Her gaze shot back to his smile. She recalled last night when anger had made his eyes dark and his lips tight. "I thought you were mad at me."

"I am." He tugged her upright and gave her a nudge and a pat on the rear. "Hurry."

After brushing her teeth, she sat next to him on the sofa and they ate. He didn't mention their argument about her going to work, and neither did she. One bowl of cereal later, they cuddled together and watched Scooby-Doo. Or rather, she tried to watch, while Jake busied himself nibbling on her neck and that sensitive spot behind her ear. His lips and moist tongue created wonderful sensations that spread to all parts of her body, and Scooby lost all appeal.

"You should stop that," she whispered, and tried to think of a topic to change the mood. "How many sisters and brothers do you have?"

"One brother."

His hand slipped under her pj top, found her nipple, and circled it. Her breath caught. She reached under her shirt and removed his hand.

"Jake, we're just going to get frustrated again."

Shifting, he dropped back against the sofa and pulled at the crotch of his jeans. "I passed that stage about a half an hour ago."

She smiled, secretly loving the fact that she affected him as much as he affected her. Reaching up, she passed a finger across his lips. "You don't have to work today?"

"I'm just going in for a few hours."

The doorbell rang and, pulling at his jeans again, Jake rose and went to answer it. After peering through the peephole, he started back down the hall. "It's your grandma. I'm hiding until Mr. Dudley can behave. Which may not be until Tuesday."

Grinning, Macy went to let Nan in, but right before she opened the door she started to worry. "Everything okay?" she asked as they embraced.

"I can't visit my granddaughter?" Nan came inside.

"Yeah." Macy shut the door. "I just wasn't expecting you." She heard Jake talking on the phone as she poured Nan a cup of coffee and they sat at the kitchen table. "Where's Mom?"

Nan frowned. "At the hospital. Which is odd. She never volunteers on Saturdays. Something's up."

Macy tightened her grip around her warm coffee mug. "What do you think it is?"

"Don't know. But she went shopping again, bought some new underwear. You know what that means."

"A man." Macy remembered thinking last night that she needed new lingerie herself.

"We can hope." Nan sipped from her cup. "She hasn't had any in fourteen years."

Macy rolled her eyes. "Do you really think this is wise? What if she ends up hurt? Do you think she could survive it?" *Do I think I could?*

"Ahh, but better to have loved and lost than—"

"Please!" Macy set her cup down, ready to argue her case, but Jake walked in. One look at him and her argument lost all steam.

He nodded at Nan. "Ma'am." He glanced at Macy. "I've got to go in now." He leaned down and kissed her. Not just a peck, but a serious gonna-miss-you kind of kiss, which was delivered with a touch of tongue.

Macy glanced at her grandma, who beamed as if she enjoyed the show. Then Macy refocused on Jake and what he'd said about going in. "Has something happened?"

"We got a location on some of Tanks's old gang. Donaldson and I are going to talk to them about the robberies." He must have seen her concern, because he added, "I'll be fine." He dipped in for another kiss, squeezed her chin, and said, "I should be home by two. Don't go anywhere until I get back." Turning, he gave Nan a nod.

"I got it," she replied.

Jake had walked out before Macy smelled a rat. She cut her gaze to Nan. Make that *two* rats.

"He asked you to babysit me, didn't he?"

Nan looked around. "Nice place."

"I don't need a keeper." Macy glanced at the clock on the wall and ignored Elvis, who came swaggering into the room. "And you should be teaching."

"Tammy's doing it." Reaching down, Nan petted the cat.

"He let you bring Elvis. He likes your cat? Your cat likes him."

"Elvis hates him. He shouldn't have called you."

"He wants to protect you. And Elvis will warm up to him. You did." Nan's gaze zeroed in on the sofa, which was crowded with blankets and sheets. "So you two aren't serious?"

Macy grabbed her cup. "I haven't known him a week! He hasn't even invited me to . . ."

"To what?"

Macy blushed. "Nothing."

"Sounds like something."

Oh hell, keeping secrets from Nan was about as easy as training a cat to disco dance in the rain. "It's a family party. His mom invited me, but he hasn't extended the invitation. There's only one reason a man doesn't want you to meet his family: he's not really serious."

"You met his mom?" Nan grinned.

"Oh yeah." Macy dropped her forehead onto the table, not ready to tell that story. "I'm going to work tonight," she mumbled, raising her head. "And Monday I'm back in school. Jake is just going to have to deal with it."

Hal heard his door swish open as he splashed the shaving cream off his chin. "You're late," he called out. "That might cost you half a Fig Newton."

"A Fig Newton?" His daughter stuck her head into the bathroom.

"Oh, hi, Melissa." He grabbed his IV pole and wheeled out.

She moved back and let him pass. "Who did you think I was?"

"The nurse." The lie made his shoulders tighten. Even though he'd gotten his child's okay to proceed, it felt a bit wrong. It was wrong to look at his daughter, who was the spitting image of his wife, and tell her he had feelings for another woman.

"You're getting around better," Melissa noted.

"Yeah." Hal slid onto the hospital bed and glanced at the clock. "It's Saturday. You should be home with your kids."

"Did the doctor come in?"

"About an hour ago. Said I might go home this afternoon if the blood work is okay."

"Good. I've got your room set up."

Hal frowned. "My room?"

"Yeah. You're staying at my place for a few weeks until you're back on your feet."

"Nosirree."

"Dad! You're coming home with me and that's that."

"Listen here, young lady—"

"Stop it!" Her lips trembled. "Look, Dad. Mom made me promise I'd take care of you, and . . . and I still miss her so damned much. I can't imagine how I'd feel if I lost you. What am I saying? I *do* know. Because for the last two years, all you've done is bury yourself in your work. You only visit on Sundays. And now this happened." A tear rolled down her cheek.

Hal opened his mouth to speak, but words failed him. Seeing his baby girl hurt did something to a daddy. "Don't cry." He drew her to his shoulder. "Come on, pumpkin."

"I miss Mom," she sobbed. "And I don't want to lose you."

"I miss her, too. And you're not losing me." He put his arm around her back.

The door pushed open. "Sorry I'm late. I brought Fig—"

Hal swallowed hard. Faye came to a quick stop in the doorway. Melissa pulled out of his embrace, her teary gaze surprised.

Something inside Hal froze. His brain, probably. And he didn't have a freaking clue where the defrost button was.

"Hi." Faye's gaze moved from Melissa to him.

Hal managed to nod.

Faye offered a hesitant smile. "You got your lunch?"

He nodded again.

Faye's gaze cut back to Melissa. "I . . . volunteer here."

Melissa nodded.

Faye waited for two, maybe three more seconds, then, damn it, *she* nodded. An awkward, head-bobbing silence filled the room. Faye backed up.

"I—I guess I'll leave you two alone."

The word *no* was on the tip of his tongue. Right on the tip. All he had to do was spit it out. And, by God, she gave him time to say it. She didn't rush out; she walked slowly away. Even looked back.

One word: *No.* Or maybe two: *Don't go.* That's all it would have taken. But he didn't say a goddamn thing. He let the woman who had somehow made living seem so much sweeter walk out of his room. Out of his life.

It was almost three o'clock when Macy got in the shower. Mother Nature was playing tricks on her. Aunt Flo was already gone. Macy had awoken this morning to discover the villainess had flown the coop. The one month she could have used some cooling-off time, some thinking time, and this happened. Now what?

Turning off the shower, Macy rested her head against the tiled wall. *Cook or get out of the kitchen. Jump or get off the trampoline.*

She stepped out of the shower and heard voices. Was Jake back? She cracked open the door, stuck her head out, and let out a low yelp. He stood right nearby.

"Damn!" She jumped back and grabbed a towel.

He looked over his shoulder and pushed his way inside. "Talk about a welcome home!" He glanced at her towel-wrapped body. A devilish grin twisted his lips. "If I remember correctly, the last time you stole my towel . . ."

"You wouldn't."

"Your towel is safe." He leaned in and kissed her. "Did you miss me?"

"No," she said.

"Liar," he pointed out.

"Hey," Nan called, and they both jumped back. "I'll see you two later."

Jake cringed. "I swear she didn't see me come in here."

"She has eyes in the back of her head and ears like a bat."

"I heard that," Nan said. "See you two later."

"'Bye," Macy said, rolling her eyes. Then, glancing at Jake, she remembered she was mad at him. "You asked her to babysit me."

His brows pinched. "I did. I admit it. So, how much trouble am I in?"

She hadn't been prepared for a confession. "Ever heard of Shit Creek?"

"Is that the one where you usually end up without a paddle?"

"Yeah." She glared at him, but didn't have it in her to be mad. Not anymore.

He pulled a wet strand of hair from her cheek. "You wouldn't happen to have a paddle I could borrow, do you?"

"You can't keep doing this. I don't like—"

He cupped her chin. "Only until Tanks is caught. Soon."

Curiosity struck. "Did you find out where he is?"

"Nothing concrete. Donaldson is . . ." His gaze lowered to her body.

She glanced down at her towel, gaping open in the front all the way to her navel. After readjusting, she opened the bathroom door. "Out."

"Why?" His voice was husky. "I'm going to see it all Tuesday anyway."

If I can hold out until then. "Go. I've got to get dressed . . . for work." Maybe a good argument would buy her some time.

Unfortunately, he didn't argue. He just left after another quick kiss.

Twenty minutes later, uniform and makeup on, Macy walked into the living room expecting to find him on the sofa. Returning to the hall, she saw his bedroom door swing open. He stepped out and surprised her.

"What?" He settled a cap on his head.

She stared at him and his Papa's Pizza polyester. "You can't be serious!" She giggled.

"No jokes, sweetheart. It's an honest living. And I hear the tips are good once I get through the training process."

She crossed her arms over her chest. "And I guess you'll be training with me?"

"I told the owner I wanted only the best."

She shook her head. "You're crazy."

"Only about you." He pulled her against him. "Wanna bump uniforms?"

She thumped him on the chest. "You're being crass again. I could have gone my whole life without hearing that line again." Of course, Mr. Prack hadn't looked nearly as good as Jake.

"I'm male. We're all crass." His smile faded. "*Again?* Who said that to you the first time?"

She caught his hand. "You did." She met his frown with her own. "It's not important."

"The hell it isn't! I'm the only man allowed to be crass with you. Remember that."

Hal ground his teeth and looked at the nurse. "No."

"Mr. Klein, the doctor released you."

"Well, call the doctor back and get him to unrelease me."

"I don't get it," the woman snipped. "Are you hurting?"

"Yeah." It wasn't a lie. His heart was hurting something awful. The pain in Faye's eyes kept flashing in his head and sending regret barreling into his chest. He'd called her house and left umpteen messages. She hadn't called back. He wasn't strong enough to go chasing her down, so he'd be damned if he left here before he talked to her.

Macy had just tossed the pizza warmers in the back when Jake crawled into the passenger seat. "How much?" he asked.

"Ten dollars. I told you, he tips big." Macy waggled her eyebrows at him. She'd never had as much fun delivering pizza. They had talked about Billy. Jake had tried to assure her things would work out. They'd teased each other unmercifully about the tips each garnered at deliveries. They had even argued over who would drive. But it was her rental, so she'd won.

"You flirted with him," Jake accused.

"I did not flirt."

"Yes, you did. I heard the way you said, 'Thank you for ordering from Papa's Pizza.'" He put some sleaze into his re-enactment.

She laughed. "I'm supposed to say that! You're just jealous the last delivery only gave you six dollars. And you *did* flirt with her. 'You look nice tonight,'" she mimicked.

"It might have only been six dollars, but she underlined her phone number on her check. You have to count that in the tip."

"So, are you going to call her?" Macy asked, pretending she didn't care.

"No," he said, his tone matter-of-fact. "I'm a one-woman man. And I kind of got my eye on someone special. If her Aunt Flo would get out of the damn picture."

She chuckled and glanced at him as she pulled the Honda out into traffic. "Really, you're a one-woman man?"

"Really. I'm a monogamous sort."

She tapped the steering wheel.

Jake, being typical Jake, had managed to avoid all personal topics. She'd tried to bring up his family, his brother, and his grandfather's party, but he'd dodged those subjects like slow bullets. Not that she was finished firing.

"Have there been a lot of monogamous relationships?"

"A few," he said. "So, how much money do you usually—"

"Don't change the subject. How many?" she pressed.

The silence grew louder, and then she heard him sigh. "Are you asking me how many women I've slept with?"

"No, I'm asking how many relationships you've had."

"And by what criteria do you determine a relationship?"

"Sleeping with them would count." She laughed.

"I thought so." He leaned back against his seat and adjusted his legs.

She tightened her grip on the wheel. "You're not going to answer?"

"Yeah, I'm just counting." He glanced in the rearview mirror, as if to check for the FBI.

She gave the rearview a glance, too. "That many, huh?"

"Well, while I'm figuring it out, why don't you go first?"

She stiffened. "I'm the one who asked you!"

"Yeah, but you can't ask a question you wouldn't answer yourself."

You do all the time. "If I answer, will you promise to tell me?" She cut her gaze toward him.

"Scout's honor."

"Call me paranoid, but . . . were you even a Boy Scout?"

"Got all the badges. When we go to my mom's house, you'll see."

Macy's heart squeezed. "You're taking me to your mom's house?" Was this the party invitation? Had he suddenly decided she was family material?

He studied her. "She really isn't as wacky as she came off. Seriously, she's—"

"I don't dislike her. You . . . just haven't mentioned going."

"Well, now I'm mentioning it. We'll have dinner with her one night."

"Okay." It wasn't the party invitation, but it was something.

"So?" he asked. "How many men have you been with?"

She didn't hesitate. "Two."

"Two?" he repeated. "Seriously, only two?"

"What? You think I'm weird because I don't sleep around, or you don't believe me?"

"No, I . . . Look, you haven't slept with me yet, so I know you don't sleep around. I was just expecting it to be five or six."

"Well, I was married for five years." She paused. "Is that where you're at? Five or six?"

He turned away and looked out the window. "A few more, but I'm older."

"How many more?" When he didn't answer, she said, "If you don't answer me now—"

"Sixteen, more or less. I went a little crazy in college."

"And you were faithful to all of them?" she asked, remembering his previous comment. The pain she'd felt from Tom's infidelity was haunting.

"I never cheated on anyone. And I wouldn't." He stared at her. "Is that why you haven't dated since your ex? You think all men are like Tom?"

"No. I'm not that closed minded. I know all men aren't like Tom." She paused. "They could be like my grandpa, or my father, or maybe Billy. And then there're the Mr. Pracks of the world." She chuckled, thinking that was pretty funny. But Jake didn't laugh, and suddenly the humor was lost to her as well. "We should get back."

They drove back to the Papa's Pizza in silence, the FBI still behind them. The awkwardness of having laid out her fears on a silver platter had her reaching for the door handle as quickly as she parked.

Jake caught her arm. "Tom cheated on you. Billy disappointed you. Your father abandoned you. What did your grandpa do?"

Chapter Twenty-nine

"What did your grandpa do?" Jake repeated.

For a split second, Macy considered taking the Jake Baldwin approach and changing the subject, but the truth spilled out. "He died." She bit her lip. "He was telling me that he was going to take me to the—the circus. Instead, he fell dead right into his spaghetti. Nan swears it was lasagna. But I keep seeing it as spaghetti."

"You saw it?" His tone softened.

She nodded.

"Damn." He leaned over and touched her cheek.

"Yeah. Damn." She tried to swallow the lump in her throat and called herself weak for getting emotional over something that had happened so long ago.

He leaned his forehead against hers. "I don't plan on dying anytime soon."

The lump grew thicker. "You have a dangerous job." That stupid hiccupping happened in her chest again.

"I can't argue with that. But I'm good at what I do." His lips brushed her temple.

Cook or get out of the kitchen. Jump or get off the trampoline. Oh hell, she was headed for the circus and Tuesday wasn't soon enough. She buried her face in his shoulder. He felt so good, smelled so good. Then, remembering the sedan parked beside them, she straightened.

The FBI agent wasn't the only one watching. A frowning Mr. Prack stood at the door to Papa's Pizza.

Macy sighed. "We'd better go in. It's the Prick."

Jake scowled. "What did he do?"

"He's just an ass."

He looked at her, clearly not convinced. "He's the one who asked if you wanted to bump uniforms."

"Forget it."

"Forget it? That's sexual harassment."

"Yeah, but it's my word against his. And he's never touched me. And he's stopped making passes. Now he's just an ass."

"And you let him get away with that?"

"I'd lose my job. You know that. I know that. And I've just got too much on my plate right now for that to happen."

"You're going to start working at the church in a few weeks. Until that works out, I can—"

"I told you, I've still got to work part-time somewhere else. Law school isn't cheap. The job market sucks. And we already discussed you becoming my sugar daddy. Not happening."

He exhaled a deep breath. "Hear me out. I can make it a loan. Shit, you can pay me interest."

She leaned her head back onto the car seat. "Jake, I need to do this myself."

"Why won't you let me help you?"

"Because you're helping too much already. Look at you. You're a cop playing a pizza-delivery person. You fixed my house, saved my life, and I'm staying at your place. I can't handle any more help from you before I . . ."

"Before you what?"

Turn into my mom. Become totally dependent on you. "Go crazy." She got out of the car.

They hadn't yet gotten inside when Jake's cell phone rang. He hung back, and Macy hung with him, thinking the call might be about Billy.

"Baldwin," he answered, giving her a quick glance. Then he handed her the phone. "It's Nan."

"Everything okay?" Macy asked.

"Yes and no," Nan answered. "It's your mom. Can you come by after work?"

"Sure." Macy met Jake's gaze, then said into the phone, "Is she crying again?"

"Not crying." Nan's concern carried over the phone line. "She . . . had her belly button pierced."

"Oh, God." Macy pressed her palm to her forehead. "She's given up crying and taken up body piercing. Can you imagine what she'll look like in a few months?"

"That's why I want to nip this in the bud," Nan said.

"I'll be there as soon as I get off. And for God's sake, hide all the needles from her."

Macy pulled up in front of Nan's an hour later and glanced at Jake. "I wish you'd let me drive you back to your place. I'll be okay. I doubt Tanks was waiting to follow me from Papa's Pizza."

"No way. I'm fine, and I'll wait here in the car. I'll probably fall asleep. I'll be here when you come out. Go." He reached around her to open the door.

She leaned in and kissed him. "Thanks." She tried to shake off the thrill of kissing him.

Inside the house, she found Nan on her yoga mat and her mom in the recliner. "Macy," her mom said. "I didn't know you were coming."

Macy went to sit on the sofa. "Just stopping by."

Her mom frowned. "You told her, didn't you?"

Nan pulled a knee to her nose. "I might have mentioned it."

Macy's mom shook her head. "So I had my belly button pierced. What's the big deal?"

"You're fifty-six. And you're my daughter," Nan snapped.

"Show me the law that says older people can't do this."

Macy tried to understand. "Are you, like, dating some guy who owns a piercing parlor?"

"I'm not dating anyone!" her mother snapped. "You were right the other night. Men are nothing but trouble. They—they lead you to believe one thing and then do something completely different. For God's sake, she was half his age!"

Macy and Nan looked at each other and shared a knowing nod.

"Who did what and who looked half whose age?" Nan asked.

"I don't want to talk about it. Because if I talk about it I'll cry, and I'm not going to cry about another man. Except for my son." Tears filled Faye's eyes. "These are for my son." She pointed to her eyes. "I can cry about Billy. He's my baby boy, and he's God only knows where, and . . ."

Macy moved to sit on the arm of the recliner. She leaned her head on her mother's shoulder. "What happened, Mom? Tell me everything."

Jake opened his condo door and watched Macy walk inside, pick up Elvis, and carry him to the sofa. She looked exhausted and nervous again. She hadn't told him what was wrong with her mom. He'd wanted to ask, but he respected her privacy.

Leaning down, he kissed her. "Want some hot chocolate?"

"You got some?"

He winked at her. "Bought it today."

"You're too good to be real."

He laughed. "I'm not perfect, but I'm real."

After she'd drunk her hot cocoa and he'd had a beer, Jake wondered how to approach the subject of sleeping arrangements. He wanted her beside him, in his bed. He hadn't slept worth a damn last night without her. Of course, he hadn't slept the night before, when she'd been beside him, but he'd much rather have had her close than not. Especially when he was afraid she'd walk out of his life just as quickly as she'd walked into it.

It wasn't as if he thought she might walk out the door. But he'd never had to work so hard to win someone over. And while there were moments when she looked at him and he felt sure she was in this for the long haul, he'd then see a flicker of something else in her eyes, something that suggested she was waiting for the right instant to run.

She sat upright. "I'm going to wash off the pepperoni smell."

He caught her around her middle, leaned in, and sniffed her neck. "I love pepperoni."

"I hope so," she laughed. "Because you smell like it, too."

He raised his arm to his nose. "Yeah, I guess I'd much rather smell you." He slowly kissed her, and when she finally pulled back, they were both breathing hard. They both rose and went to shower—separately, to Jake's unspoken disappointment.

Ten minutes later, he towel-dried his hair and went to find Macy. She was in the hall bathroom, door open, brushing her hair. They had stopped by her house during the night's pizza runs to grab some of her things, and now she wore a different pair of pajamas. They were still cotton, but they were light blue, and the stretchy tank top fit her perfectly. He let his gaze slide down her body, appreciating every dip and curve.

He walked up behind her, curled his arm around her abdomen, and looked at her reflection in the mirror. "You tired?" he asked.

"A little."

He rested his chin on top of her head. "Do me a big favor?"

"What?" She met his eyes in the mirror.

"Sleep with me tonight." He pressed a finger to her lips before she could say no. "I *promise* nothing will happen. I remember Aunt Flo. I just want you there. I didn't sleep worth a damn last night."

She looked as if she were going to argue, then nodded. He laced his fingers through hers and led her to his bedroom before she changed her mind.

He pulled back the covers and watched her climb in. Then he grinned. "You made my bed?"

"And washed your sheets. I didn't want cooties."

"I don't have cooties." Once they both settled in, he was afraid to reach over for fear she'd assume he was trying something. So he opted to get permission. "Can I hold you?"

She rolled closer and pillowed her head on his shoulder. He curled his arm around her back and rested his hand on her hip. "This feels so right," he whispered.

"Yeah," she agreed. Her cat jumped up on the bed and settled in beside her.

He wasn't sure how much time passed, but he could tell she was still awake. "A hundred bucks for your thoughts," he said.

He felt her smile against his bare chest. "I thought a penny was the going rate."

"Inflation."

She chuckled, but the sweet sound came and went too quickly. Then she sighed. "I'm worried. My mom. Mostly Billy. And . . . I feel guilty."

He ran a hand through her hair. The silky strands felt a little damp. "Guilty about what?"

"About having fun tonight with you. Having fun with you since the morning after you showed up."

"You didn't have fun with me the first night." He shifted. The cat hissed.

"No, you were a jerk then. Except when you stood up to Tom." She paused. "And I feel guilty about enjoying being here right now, when I should be worried about my brother. I mean, I *am* worried about him, but this feels good. How can something good be happening when—"

"Don't do this," Jake said. "As far as we know, Billy is okay. And as much as you love him—" He paused, not knowing if he could say what he had to without hurting her. Hurting her was the last thing he wanted.

"What?" She petted Elvis.

He forced himself to finish. "As much as you love him, he brought this on himself. I'm not saying you shouldn't love him. But you can't let his mistakes punish you."

"I know that in my head," Macy admitted. "But he's not a bad kid. He loves me, Jake. And I love him. And . . . he stood up for me." Her breath caught. "He took a beating that should have been mine."

A warm tear fell to his chest, and Jake tightened his hold. "Who did he stand up against?" Jake remembered her mentioning this previously, but she'd never explained. Now he had to know. He wanted to know everything about her: what made her laugh, what made her sad. Everything.

"My dad." Her voice came out wobbly.

Jake's stomach bottomed out. He'd had perfect parents. He might not have agreed with all their beliefs, but he'd never doubted their love. Being a cop, he'd come face-to-face with imperfect parents, but he still couldn't fathom how that happened. "What?"

"He was a mean drunk. He didn't drink all the time. But when he did he'd lose it completely, and sometimes he'd hit my mom. Once, when I tried to stop him, he hit me. And the night before my birthday . . ."

Her voice held so much hurt that Jake's chest felt a lead weight upon it. "What happened?"

"Mom was going to night school to become a nurse. I was

watching Billy." She paused. "My dad came home drunk. I sent Billy to his room and went to mine. Daddy followed me and started screaming. Billy ran in and got between us." She grabbed for the sheet and wiped her tears. For a minute, she didn't talk. Then: "I'll never forget Billy saying, 'You're not going to hurt my sister!'" Her voice trembled. "He hit him, Jake. Knocked him across the room. I thought he'd killed him."

Jake waited a whole minute before he asked, "What did you do?"

"I threw the lamp at him. I called him bad names I didn't even know I knew. He left and I dialed nine-one-one. Mama got home before the ambulance. Billy woke up, but he couldn't remember what happened.

"Mom made me lie," she continued after a moment of silence. "Made me tell them that Billy had fallen out of bed. She said Daddy didn't mean to do it. That he was sick because of his drinking." Jake felt her wad up a fistful of blanket. "I hated her for it. Then Daddy left the next day and Mama fell apart. And I hated her even more because I knew she still loved him."

"Oh, shit." Jake bundled Macy closer, aching for her, wishing he could impart just a little of the normalcy of his own childhood. But he couldn't.

"We moved in with Nan and she took over. Mom cried all the time. Stopped going to school. Stopped working. It took years, but I finally stopped hating her and started hating what she was."

Jake ignored the cat as it moved to lay on the edge of his pillow. "What was she?"

"Weak. Codependent. A victim. I swore I'd never be that. But I am." She sniffled. "I let Tom get away with things. I was so scared of losing him, I made excuses. I was willing to be a victim. I put up with so much because . . . I'm just like her. I suspected he was cheating on me a year after our wedding. I didn't do shit." She sniffled again.

"But you did leave him." Thoughts of Tom hurting Macy dug into Jake's gut. Silence filled the room. "Did he hit you?" He'd kill the asshole.

"No. He'd get grabby and yell. And I would just take it."

"He was an idiot." Jake now understood even more why Macy fought so hard for independence.

She rested her hand on his shoulder, then pulled back. "Ugh! I slimed you." She scrubbed the sheet over his wet flesh. "Sorry."

"You can slime me anytime." He pulled her on top of him. Her weight was the sweetest feeling in the world. He wanted her to lean on him completely, to let him take care of her.

She blinked. Tears pooled in her eyes, but she looked happier. She grabbed the sheet and cleaned his chest again. "I'm going to have to rewash your bedding."

"You can slime my sheets, too. I don't give a damn. As long as you're here."

He brought his mouth to hers. She tasted salty, like tears. He kept kissing her, wanting to chase away the hurtful memories. Tenderness turned to passion, but he remembered his promise not to try anything. "We . . . should stop."

She rolled off his chest. "Bathroom." She and the cat jumped out of bed.

Jake was still talking himself down when she curled back against him. He almost told her to give him a few inches, but he realized he'd rather suffer an endless hard-on than push her away. He wrapped his arm around her and told his libido to go to hell—he'd made a promise, and he'd keep it. It didn't matter how good her soft breasts felt pressed against his side, or how seductively her hair tickled his shoulder.

She snuggled closer. Her hand whispered over his chest. "Your heart's thumping." Her hand whispered lower, all the way to the elastic of his boxers; then it inched back up his abdomen to his chest. "Now it's beating faster."

"It does that." Realizing a part of him was standing at attention, he bent his knee to hide it.

She slowly traced a circle around his left nipple with her fingers. Sweet torture. She scooted closer. Her body pressed firmly to his side. Every inch of him was aware of every inch of her. The arch of her foot climbed his right leg. The woman didn't have a clue what she was doing to him.

Or did she?

Her lips moved against his ear, and her tongue moistened the lobe. Was she purposely trying to torment him?

She started talking. "Last night, when you came in from showering, you had a drop of water that started here and"— she poised her finger at the top of his chest and slid it down— "ended here."

She drew a heart around his navel. He knew it was a heart, because every nerve ending was focused on her finger's path.

"Then . . ." She continued, and so did her finger. "I saw that same drop of water moving down, all the way to—"

"Stop!" He caught her hand.

"Why?" She giggled, a feminine sexy laugh. "Aunt Flo left. My 'woman thingy's' gone. She left late last night. I just . . . freshened up."

It took a full second for the words to register. Letting go of her hand, Jake cleared his throat. "So . . . where did that drop of water go?"

CHAPTER THIRTY

Her cheek against his chest, Macy tucked her fingers under the elastic band of Jake's boxers. His sex, hot and smooth, bounced against the top of her hand. Her insecurities bounced with it. He'd had lots of women. Could she compete? Hadn't Tom's infidelity meant she sucked at this? She glanced up, almost called it quits, but then she saw the way he looked at her. No one had ever looked at her quite like that. A tiny bit of confidence started to bloom.

Turning her hand, she wrapped her fingers around him. He was big, and grew larger and hotter as she tightened her hold. She glided her hand down to the mass of springy curls at the base of his sex, and then up to the tip. Up and over the ridge. His silky length pulsated against her palm.

He sucked in a breath. "I don't know how much I can stand, Macy."

Insecurities forgotten, she wanted to drive him wild. Images of taking that smooth tip inside her mouth filled her mind. Still slowly stroking his sex, she kissed his chest, passed her tongue over his tightened nipple, then scooted down to kiss his rib cage. His navel. Another scoot, and she lowered his boxers. Her hair fell and brushed against his abdomen as she pressed her lips against the swollen tip of his sex.

A deep hissing sound emerged from Jake's throat. "My turn!" He flipped her over.

"I didn't get much of a turn," she complained as she slipped the back of her hand down his belly. "You don't like—"

"Oh, I like. *Really* like. I'm claiming a rain check."

He caught her wrists, leaned forward and placed her hands above her head. "Leave these right here," he commanded.

She extended her hands and gripped the bottom rung of the metal headboard. He gazed at them and then his hungry gaze lowered. "Yeah, like that." He found the hem of her pajama top, and the backs of his fingers brushed against her abdomen as he slowly pulled it up. His gaze stayed on her eyes. "I've wanted you naked since I first landed on top of you." He pulled her shirt over her head. She released her hands from the headboard for only a second, so he could remove it.

"Your hair was the first thing I noticed." His voice was all heat, all sex. Reaching forward, he ran a hand though the curls on her head. "Then"—he pulled back, and his gaze lowed to her breasts—"I saw your shirt open and that blue bra. Your nipples were hard, just like now. And I wanted to do this." He cupped her breasts in his warm hands and pinched their peaks between thumb and forefinger. "And this." He dipped down and took her right breast in his mouth, half sucking, half kissing. Moisture pooled between Macy's legs.

His hand moved to her bare midriff, and he pulled his mouth from her breast. "Then, that day at my office, your sweater came up and I saw . . ." He tucked one finger under the elastic of her pajama bottoms. "All I saw was a little bare spot *here*." He slid a finger across her panty tops. "And all I could think about was running my tongue over it."

With one sweeping motion, he'd removed her pajama bottoms and panties. He repositioned himself down between her knees. "Like this." He slowly licked his way across her abdomen.

As his tongue moistened her bare skin, his fingers moved between her legs. "You're so hot." His fingers separated the lips of her sex and he slid a finger inside her. "And tight." He leaned down, spreading her thighs with his hands.

Macy gasped. "You don't have to do that, I mean—"

"Shh." His tongue moved over her. He found the nub of most sensitive flesh and circled it.

Macy forgot all doubts. She forgot everything but the building pleasure. With two handfuls of sheet bunched in her fists, she started unraveling faster than she'd ever unraveled before. Pleasure exploded within her, and when she realized she was screaming, she slapped a hand over her mouth. "I'm sorry!"

"For what? Scream all you want." He crawled on top of her and positioned himself between her legs. His naked chest met hers. Her nipples, tight and sensitive, pebbled against him. He must have removed his boxers, because his sex rested against her thigh. Hot, hard. Ready.

She spoke breathlessly. "I didn't know I could come so fast. Or that I was a screamer."

"Was it better than chocolate?" he asked. "Really good chocolate?"

His smile was cocky. His sex probed her opening. He pushed his hips forward, and the glorious width of him stretched her. The swirl of sensation, and the hunger to feel him deep inside, had her hips rising off the mattress.

"Look at me." He slowly entered her. "Tell me chocolate can compete with this."

"What's chocolate?" She jutted her hips upward to take him deeper. She wanted all of him, every hard inch filling her, stretching her.

"Damn. I forgot protection," he gasped. "Right back."

She watched him move across the room, his penis so hard it pointed to the ceiling. He yanked open a drawer and dug out a pair of black socks, unrolling them. Several foil packets fell to floor. Catching one, he opened it and sheathed himself.

The bed swayed and he was back. "Miss me?"

She grinned. "You hide your condoms in your socks?"

"Old habits. Mom was a snoop." His brows arched. "Like someone else I know."

He passed a finger over her lips. It smelled musky like sex, both hers and his. He kissed her neck.

But it wasn't her neck begging for attention. "Weren't we further along?" She brushed her knee over his naked thigh.

"Demanding little wench." He rose up on an elbow and ran a finger over her lips. "You want top or bottom?"

"A little of both."

"Hard on a man, aren't you?"

Macy slipped her hand down and cupped his sex in her hand. "Did you say hard?" The condom felt cool compared to his skin. She squeezed.

"You get top first." He pulled her onto him.

Her knees landed on each side of his hips. She shifted until she felt his erection where it needed to be. Where she wanted it to be. Then, as if they had all day, she lowered herself and took him inside her.

His moan brought on a surge of confidence. She pressed her palms on his chest and began rocking, slowly, taking him in an inch, out an inch. They watched each other. Then, reaching up, he brushed a thumb over her lips. She took his finger into her mouth and gently sucked. Their gazes met and locked.

Everything in her mind let go, everything but Jake Baldwin: the way he made her feel, the way he looked at her. His hips moved faster, and she let him set the pace. Sensation exploded.

"Not yet," he ground out. "You asked for both." His words rang deep, and his hips rose to meet hers one more time. "You . . . get . . . both." He flipped her over.

She locked her legs around his waist and he buried himself inside. Deeper, with each thrust of his pelvis he went deeper. Deeper into her life. Into her heart. Into her soul. Her desire built and at last she exploded into a thousand pinpoints of pure rapture. She let out another cry.

She heard him catch his breath, and he collapsed on top of her. The next second, he rolled off but pulled her against him. The sound of their gasping for breath filled the room.

"You okay?" he finally asked.

She nodded against his chest. He pressed a kiss to her temple.

"I knew it'd be good, but I had no idea it would be . . . You're amazing." He rolled onto his side and looked at her. "The way you look. And move." He caught her hand. "The way you touched me." He kissed her palm. "The way you taste. The way your hair feels sliding across my stomach. The way you scream."

She felt her face heat. "It was pretty awesome on this end, too."

His sex, already hard again, bumped against her hip. "I hope you don't like to sleep. Because you're not going to get very much from here on out."

Jake wasn't joking. They made love two more times during the night. Waking up before him this time, she leaned on her elbow and enjoyed the view. This awesome man was an awesome lover. Images of what they'd done filled her head. She remembered screaming. . . .

And instantly she broke out in hives.

How could something feel so right one minute, then so embarrassing the next? Oh goodness, she'd behaved like a wanton little hussy! Like Samantha in the *Sex and the City*. And she was *so* not a Samantha. What had gotten into her?

Her gaze shot to the clock. Almost noon. *Noon?* Oh, crappers. Hadn't she'd agreed to have lunch with Nan and her mom? She hopped up off the bed and started searching for her clothes.

"What are you doing?" Jake sat up, the blanket slipping down to his waist. A sleepy smile pulled at his lips as he stared at her, completely naked. He crooked his finger. "Come here."

Naked. She was completely naked.

Oh, he'd seen it all, touched it all. *Tasted* it all. She still wanted to cover up.

Spotting his boxers at her feet, she snatched them up and held them in front of her. "I'm looking for my clothes. I . . ." She spotted her pj bottoms, but they were too close to the bed—to him. "I told Nan I'd come for lunch."

"Oh." Disappointment filled his eyes.

His disappointment got to her. Still holding his boxers over as much of her as possible, she said, "Nan invited you, too."

"Really?" His eyes twinkled and lowered from her eyes to her body. "You're showing a little something there."

She dropped the boxers a bit to cover herself better. "I'll shower in the hall bath." She set off to do just that.

"You have a gorgeous ass."

She yanked his boxers behind her.

Macy had just gotten the water temperature right, when a naked Jake stepped in. "What—?"

"Mr. Dudley believes in water conservation." Jake pulled her against him. His erection, thick and ready again, pressed against her stomach. He cupped her chin and made her look at him. "Is this the morning-after jitters?"

"No. Well, probably. But we've got to hurry."

As if he had all the time in the world, he soaped up his hands and ran them over her back. "I called Nan. Told her we'd be late."

"You did?"

He didn't answer. Instead, his gaze lowered. "You know the cure-all for morning-after jitters, don't you?" His slippery hands toyed with tight nipples.

"Let . . . me guess. The hair of the dog that bit you?"

His grin widened. "No."

"No? Then what?" She leaned into him. Shameless, she accepted it now—she had no willpower where he was concerned. The sensations were delicious. Warm water hit her back. The warmth of Jake covered her front.

"You do something more embarrassing than the night before."

She rolled her eyes. "I think we already did everything!"

He clicked his tongue. "Sweetheart, I've got a lot to teach you."

The house was filled with the warm scent of Sunday lunch. Macy watched Jake clean up a second helping of pot roast and mashed potatoes, but she just picked at her own food. Her mother had remained mostly silent, still nursing a broken heart.

As the phone rang, Nan snagged it from the bar behind her and looked at the caller ID. "It's him again."

"Don't answer," Macy's mom said.

"Who is it?" Jake and Macy both asked, and Macy suspected they thought the same thing: *Billy.*

"Mr. Klein," Nan said. "For the thirtieth time today."

Macy's mom had confessed everything last night: How

they'd met, had been flirting with each other, how she hadn't told him who she was. Oh, and how she'd caught him with another woman in his arms.

Nan spoke up. "Why don't you see what he wants?"

"Like I'd believe anything he told me," Faye snapped.

Jake let out a breath. "Didn't Agent James suggest you not see him until later?"

Nan spoke up again. "Haven't you figured out by now that none of the women in this family like doing what a man suggests? We pretty much make up our own minds."

Jake frowned. "It might jeopardize—"

Macy's mom spoke up. "I've already told that FBI guy that I didn't have anything to do with the escape."

The phone continued to ring. Nan forked up a bite of mashed potatoes. "He flashed her."

Macy's mom scooped another helping of roast onto Jake's plate. "Let's change the subject."

Macy met her mom's eyes. "Mom, Jake doesn't want any more."

Her mom blinked. "How do you know?"

"Because he didn't ask for it."

"Maybe he's just shy about asking for something he wants," her mother suggested.

"No. He's not. He pretty much takes what he wants." She remembered that morning.

Jake bit back a smile and picked up his fork. "I can handle this. But after that I'm saving room." He pointed to the apple pie cooling on the bar. "And if I haven't said it, I appreciate you inviting me."

"So, have you introduced Macy to *your* family yet?" Nan asked.

Remembering she'd told Nan about the whole birthday-party issue, Macy shot her grandma a warning look. She knew what Nan was up to, and the woman could turn a hard-core conservative into a liberal by way of subtle—or sometimes not so subtle—conversation.

"She met my mom." Jake's smile left no doubt that he was remembering the encounter.

"How about the rest of the family?" Nan asked.

Jake looked suddenly uncomfortable. "I plan on her meeting them soon."

"When?" Nan asked.

The question must have taken Jake by surprise, because he choked on his carrots. When he'd finished coughing, he looked up at Macy. In his eyes, she saw it. Fear. Why didn't he want to take her to his grandfather's party? Jake swallowed so hard that Macy heard it.

"Meeting all the family is important," her mom remarked.

So, her mom was in on Nan's little plan. Macy shot her mother a warning look.

Macy stood and snatched up the silverware. "We're not that serious. We barely know each other."

"Yes we are," Jake argued. "And yes we do."

"He's your boyfriend," her mom said.

Macy rolled her eyes. "He's not officially my boyfriend."

"I think last night makes it official," Jake said under his breath, but Macy felt certain her mom and Nan had heard him.

Macy glanced at him. "We're not *that* serious." But her heart started thumping as if she was telling a big fat lie.

"You invited him to meet us," her mom accused.

Macy ground her teeth. "I didn't invite him. Nan did." *Just like his mom invited me. But I wanted him to come. Why doesn't he want me to meet his family?* She escaped to the kitchen to wash up the dishes.

The bubbles were just rising in the sink when Jake stepped in behind her. This close, she could feel his gun in his shoulder holster. When she'd seen him put it on, she'd asked if it was really needed. He'd kissed her and said as long as Tanks was on the loose, he'd need it. Macy couldn't help but wonder what else would change when Tanks was caught.

"Do me a favor," he whispered in her ear.

"What? Hurry and serve the pie?" She tried to sound casual, tried to pretend that her heart wasn't on the verge of breaking into a thousand pieces, tried to pretend she wasn't already in love with a sexy-as-sin cop who didn't really want to introduce her to his family.

"Go with me Saturday to my mom's. To the party she told you about."

Macy's throat tightened, and she turned around. "What did Nan say?"

Jake blinked. "Say about what?"

Okay, so Nan had used the subtle approach. "Nothing."

He studied her. "It wasn't what Nan said. It was what you said."

"I haven't even mentioned the party."

"About us . . . not being serious." He tapped her nose. "We're serious."

She blinked away several tears threatening to fall. "You don't have to take me. If you don't want to take me, don't."

He looked confused. "I want to take you. It's just . . ."

"Just what?"

"Nothing." He exhaled. "But do me a favor. I want you to dress in something extremely sexy. I want everyone there to know what a lucky bastard I am."

Confused by his statement, she looked up. But his kiss silenced her questions.

"Come on. Let's have dessert!" her mom called.

Macy dried her hands and walked out beside Jake.

Her mom reached for the pie, then pressed a hand to her stomach. "Ouch!"

"It's infected, isn't it?" Nan snapped.

"It's nothing," her mom insisted.

"Nothing?" Nan rolled her eyes and looked at Jake. "Piercing should be outlawed. Can you imagine it? A fifty-six-year-old woman getting her belly button pierced. God only knows why."

Macy's mom scowled. "I'll tell you why: Because my ex-husband would have hated it. Maybe even because my mother would hate it. I did it because I'm . . . I'm rebelling. And if I want to get something else pierced, I'll do it. Maybe my tongue!" She stuck the next-to-be-pierced organ out of her mouth.

Macy looked at Jake. "They aren't always this bad." Then her gaze shot to the screen door and to the woman standing there.

"I might just have my nose pierced, too," her mom was saying.

"Mom!" Macy waved at her mother, then pointed to the door.

Her mom took a step back, bumping into the wall. "Just go away. I'm not fighting you for him. You can have him. All I did was share my lunch. As for seeing him naked, it wasn't my fault. I see a lot of people naked in that place."

"Who is that?" Jake asked Macy.

Macy pressed a hand to her forehead. "I think it must be Mr. Klein's girlfriend."

CHAPTER THIRTY-ONE

"This could get ugly," Jake said.

"I . . . My . . . You saw him naked?" The woman at the door glanced over her shoulder.

Macy fell back against Jake. It was just a little thing, but he really liked how it felt, as if she knew he'd catch her.

"This can't be good," she muttered.

Jake glanced from Macy's mom to the brunette in the door. Then, appearing behind her was a barrel-chested man with salt-and-pepper hair. Hal Klein?

"Can we come in?" the man asked, but he didn't wait for an answer. He stepped inside.

"No," Faye Moore said. "You can't."

"Be nice," Macy's grandma said. "Hear him out, then kick him in the balls."

Klein's eyes widened, but he waved for the brunette to come inside.

Jake, going into cop mode, tried to assess the situation. Klein walked slowly, but not so slowly, considering he'd just been shot in the chest and had his testicles threatened. Jake also noted how the man looked at Macy's mom. Something told him the woman at Klein's side wasn't a girlfriend.

The screen door banged closed behind the woman. Silence filled the small house. Finally, Klein spoke. "Faye, I'd like for you to meet my daughter. Melissa, this is Faye Moore. She's the volunteer I told you I asked out on a date."

Macy's mom sank into a dining room chair. "Your . . . daughter?"

Klein nodded. "It finally occurred to me that you may have gotten the wrong idea. And since I wanted to start dating you, I figured it might need to be cleared up."

Jake, trying not to smile, stepped forward and offered the man his hand. "Jake Baldwin."

"The boyfriend, I assume?" Klein shook Jake's hand and looked at Macy.

Jake glanced at Macy too, and winked. "Yup, the boyfriend."

Jake loved watching Macy sleep, loved the way her head fit into the crook of his arm. He loved the way her nose tilted up at the end, the indentation above her top lip, and the way her hair got messy. He loved her gentle weight against him. It all felt right. As if all his life he'd been waiting for her. It wasn't the sex. Not that the sex wasn't the best he'd ever had. It was. But this was more.

He loved her. The truth had been driven home during lunch. He'd damn near choked on his food when Macy informed her mother that they weren't that serious. It had hit him then that Macy might see his not inviting her to his grandfather's party as a sign that he didn't consider what they had as real. So he'd done it. He'd invited her to his grandfather's party.

His first thought had been, hell yeah, he wanted his aunts and uncles and grandfather to meet Macy. His second thought was that he wanted to rub his happiness into his brother's and Lisa's faces. But now doubt was settling in. Oh, he still wanted his family to meet Macy, and rubbing his good fortune in his brother's face still sounded like a hell of a plan. Even the thought of seeing Harry and Lisa together didn't make him flinch anymore. Well, not as bad as it had. But the last thing he wanted to do was to have to explain to Macy that the woman he'd loved had ditched him for someone else.

He hadn't been asleep for quite thirty minutes when the ring of his cell phone had him bolting out of bed. Remembering his phone was in his pocket and that he'd taken off his clothes in the living room, where he and Macy had made love after they'd returned, he rushed to find it.

"Baldwin," he answered, hoping for a wrong number, because middle-of-the-night calls were rarely good.

"Jake. It's Stan." His friend's tone was grave. "I'm at a homicide scene. It appears it's connected to the Tanks case. I wanted to give you a heads-up."

Jake got images of Billy Moore's mug shot and squeezed his eyes shut as he raked his hand through his hair. Silence filled the line. "Tell me it isn't Billy Moore."

"I'm not sure yet. We're talking two or more shots to the face. CSI is running fingerprints, and they aren't back yet, but the age and height fit. We're taking him to County."

"Shit," Jake said. He heard a shallow intake of air behind him. He turned and found Macy, a sheet wrapped around her, leaning against the wall. "I'm on my way," he said.

Fear glistened in Macy's eyes. "Billy?" she asked.

Jake's throat tightened. "We're not sure." He offered that slightest bit of hope, but she deserved the truth. "A body has been found."

She pressed her hand over her mouth, and her sobs nearly broke his heart.

An hour later, at the county morgue, Jake saw the desperation in her eyes, but no way in hell was he letting her see what he'd just witnessed.

"I want to go in there." Macy tried stepping around him.

Jake caught her, pulling her against him. "The fingerprints will be here soon."

"And I'll know if it's him in two seconds! He's my brother!"

Jake pulled her back into his chest. "They have to prep the body," he lied.

She went to the waiting-room love seat and plopped down. Walking over, he ran his hand over her shoulder, but she pulled back. Well, if being angry with him helped her cope, he'd take it.

The door to the waiting room swung open and Donaldson walked in. Jake had called Mark on the drive over. He figured if it was Billy, he'd have his hands full with Macy and her family and wanted someone here in an official capacity to get the details. Jake stepped beside his friend.

Donaldson focused on Macy. "She okay?"

"She's hurting like hell." And Jake felt helpless to do anything to help.

Mark lowered his voice. "So, it's him?"

"We still don't know. Fingerprints should be here in a few minutes."

"Couldn't she ID him?"

"He's messed up. Bad." Jake blinked, hoping the image wouldn't flash again in his head. "I don't want her seeing that."

"Has Stan arrived?"

"Haven't seen him yet. When he does, get everything he knows. At least, everything he can give you." Jake glanced at Macy, still wrapped in her world of grief. "She doesn't deserve this."

"Life can be ugly, can't it?" Donaldson said. Then: "Oh, by the way, you were right about Brown."

"Brown?" Jake echoed.

"The guy from the burglary. His kid has cancer. She's at M. D. Anderson Cancer Center." Donaldson shook his head. "I made a contribution. Anonymously, so don't you breathe a word."

Jake gazed at him. "I wouldn't have held you to that."

"Why not?" he half laughed. "I would have held you to the bet if I'd been right. I envisioned it chapping your ass every time you had to bring me breakfast." He smiled, but the expression faded as the seriousness of the situation chased away levity. "Besides, it's for a good cause."

He laced his fingers together. "I spoke to Mr. Brown yesterday. He and his brother were hanging a billboard about the cancer fund. It has a before-and-after picture of his kid. Heartbreaking."

"Yeah." Jake made a mental note to send his own donation.

The waiting room doors swung open and Stan walked in. Macy rose up and approached him. "Is it . . . ?"

Jake wrapped his arm around her, prepared for the worst.

"No," Stan said.

Macy collapsed against Jake. Relief shuddered through him, and he tightened his hold on her.

"Have you ID'd the guy yet?" he asked.

Stan nodded. "It's Ellie Chandler's foster brother."

Macy repositioned her head on Jake's shoulder. They'd been home for about an hour, in bed for almost as long, but she couldn't sleep. There was the elation that Billy wasn't the one laying cold in the morgue. Then there was the guilt for being happy that it was Ellie's brother and not her own.

"You okay?" Jake's voice told her he hadn't been asleep either.

"Yeah." She inhaled his masculine scent. "Thank you."

"For what?"

"For everything. Being here."

"I wouldn't want to be anywhere else." He paused. "What's keeping you awake?"

"Pick a topic," she said, putting humor in her tone she didn't feel. "My mom's belly-button ring, her sudden interest in men, my brother the escaped convict, Ellie's brother laying dead in the morgue, my happiness that it's her brother and not mine. Oh yeah, my bills that are due next week and my missed exams." *And the fact that I'm scared about what's going to happen between us.*

"Hmm," he said. "Sort of a long list." He pulled her on top of him, then looked into her eyes. "Let's take one at a time. Your mom's belly-button ring is a nonissue. It's a piercing. It'll heal. And I think her interest in Klein is a good thing."

He rubbed his palms over her shoulders. "I understand why you're worried, but as far as we know, Billy is still okay. And as for the fact that you're happy it wasn't Billy, you wouldn't be human if you weren't relieved." He pushed a strand of hair from her face. "What's next?" He paused. "Oh, the bills? I told you I'd loan you money. A *loan*," he added quickly. "And if they don't let you make up the tests, it's not the end of the world. We'll figure out something."

Macy studied him. "Where did you learn to talk through people's problems?"

"It's inbred. Part of being a preacher's son."

She smiled. "And here I thought all preacher's boys were hell-raisers and lived just to get into a girl's pants."

"I'm that, too."

They both fell silent. Ten minutes later, Jake was still listening to Macy breathe. Sleep eluded them. He had an idea what might help, but he wasn't sure if she'd be receptive. Hell, she'd had a hard night.

"Wanna prove it?" she suddenly asked.

"Prove what?"

"That you can." She suddenly sounded shy. "Get into a

girl's pants, I mean. I . . . heard sex is a good sedative." Her hand shifted down his abdomen, and then up.

He turned to look at her, amused. "I was thinking the same thing."

"Why didn't you act on it?" Her fingers continued to stroke him.

"Because I wasn't sure which head I was thinking with."

She thumped his chest. "You're so crass."

"It's another trait of a preacher's son."

He caught her hand and pushed it into his boxers. She wrapped her hand around his dick. The sweet pleasure of that touch had him catching his breath, but just like that he changed his mind on what he wanted. He pulled her hand out.

"My turn," he said.

"You know," she muttered, as he flipped her onto her back. "It seems my turns are always getting cut short."

He chuckled. "Yeah, well, it's better to give than to receive." He pulled her shirt over her head, then slid off her pajama bottoms. "And tonight you deserve to receive."

He pulled back suddenly. "Something's not right. . . . I know!" He bounced off the bed and turned on the light. By the time he got back, she had the sheet pulled up around herself.

"No."

"Why not?"

"I'm naked."

He grinned. "That's why I want the lights on."

She got up, sheet bunched around her bare feet as she went and switched off the light. Then, with the sheet still around her, she traipsed back and fell into the bed.

He considered his options. After a moment he said, "Okay, we'll compromise." Reaching over, he turned on his lamp, then dimmed it down.

She frowned. "You can still see me."

He leaned down and kissed her. "I *want* to see you."

"You saw me in the shower this morning," she insisted, as if once was enough.

"You think I don't know that's the reason you kept yourself plastered against me?"

"I thought you liked that." She pouted just a bit. And damn, she looked sexy with a pout on.

"I did. But now I want to see. Come on, Macy." He pulled the sheet down. "I promise you'll like what I'm going to do."

She grabbed the sheet back up. "What are you going to do?"

"I'm going to give you a rubdown."

She held the sheet to her chest. "I thought we were going to have sex."

"We're going to do both. Haven't you heard of massages with happy endings?"

"Crass!" she accused.

He laughed. "Yeah, but it's good crass." He reached over for lotion that he kept in his bedside drawer. "Come on." He leaned down and eased the sheet from her fisted hands. "Relax. Let me make you feel like a million bucks. You'll sleep like a baby after this."

She let him pull the sheet off her. He saw her cheeks flush and wanted to laugh. After what they'd done last night and this morning, her blush was unexpected and yet so refreshing. It excited him. She excited him. And he stripped off his boxers so she could see just how much.

Her gaze lowered then bounced back up. He squeezed some lotion into his hands and rubbed them together to warm it, enjoying the view of her naked body stretched out in front of him. "You're beautiful."

"No—"

"Shh. You're not allowed to talk. Just enjoy." He picked up her left hand and rubbed the lotion into her palm. Moving up her arm, he kneaded the muscles, inch by inch. When he was done with that arm, he took the other. She kept watching him, and every now and then he'd see her eyes move down his chest to his sex. Then, aware he might be watching, she pulled her gaze back up.

Hands and arms done, he squirted another handful of lotion into his palm, warmed it, then spread it across Macy's abdomen, moving up ever so slowly to her breasts. He toyed with her nipples until they stood erect. Then he moved to her shoulders, rubbing away the tension, but every few seconds he passed one hand back over her nipples, wanting to keep her mind on the pleasure to come.

She sighed. Her intakes of air became deeper, more relaxed.

"If you think this is good, wait until I move below," he whispered.

After a few more minutes, he inched to the foot of the bed. He picked up one foot, and she squeezed her legs together in shyness. He gently slipped one hand between them. The moment he started massaging the arch of her foot, he felt her relax, and he slowly moved her thighs apart so he could feast his eyes on what lay between.

He finished massaging both of her feet, both calves, and when he got to her thighs, he let his hands occasionally ease inward, toward her moist center. She was ready for him, but he wasn't finished yet.

"Roll over."

She didn't argue.

Slowly, using his hands to relax and arouse at the same time, he worked her over. His hands moved slowly over her perky backside and everything else. Kissing her neck, he told her again how beautiful she was. Then, after rubbing his chest and abs with lotion and donning a condom, he rolled her onto her back.

He covered her body with his. Their bodies came together, sliding, slippery. She wrapped her left leg around him. He brushed her hair from her face. He saw a woman, a purely relaxed woman, but a woman ready to take him into her body. And he was so ready to be there. He slipped into place and entered her.

"Jake," she whispered, raising her hips to take him deeper.

"Yeah?" He set a slow pace.

"You can look at me naked anytime," she said.

"Good."

He laughed, and when she pushed up, taking all of him inside her, he lost it, and the rhythm of their love went from soft to strong, from relaxed to ravenous. Five minutes later Macy fell asleep in his arms, and shortly thereafter he joined her.

Billy sat curled by an oak tree, two houses down from the green-shuttered home where he'd seen Tanks. The only light was a streetlamp down the block, but Billy had been out here long enough that his vision had adjusted.

Closing his eyes, Billy summoned an image of Ellie standing in the moonlight with nothing on. He missed her so much it hurt, but he'd sworn he wouldn't go back to the beach house. It was for the best. He'd almost called her to make sure she was okay, but he'd decided even that might give her a reason to hope. Ellie Chandler needed to know it was hopeless.

Billy ran his tongue over the inside of his lip. He hadn't chewed on it, but the temptation was still there. Old habits, he guessed. Feeling the cold weight of the gun pressed against his side, he pulled it out and set it beside him.

He wondered what it would feel like to be shot, to have a bullet rip through your skin and bone. He'd heard once that it didn't hurt, but after seeing Hal Klein and Brandon take bullets he wasn't so sure. It couldn't hurt worse than losing everyone he loved and staying in prison for the rest of his life, however. There were possibly worse fates than dying.

He picked up the gun. He'd never take his own life. He was too much of a coward to do that. But if Tanks didn't kill him, the cops probably would. What were the odds of him really getting out of this alive? Not good.

Billy's gut knotted, but not as much as the last time he'd

thought about it. Of course, he wasn't getting braver, just more resigned.

The night felt heavy on his shoulders. He blinked. He hadn't slept in days. *So tired*, he thought, but he had to stay awake. He had to wait for Tanks to show up. He had to believe Tanks would show up.

A spray of headlights washed over his hiding place as a car turned onto the street. Billy waited to see where it would go. Slowly, with only the sound of its tires crunching pebbles on the gravel street, the vehicle pulled into the driveway of the green-shuttered house.

CHAPTER THIRTY-TWO

Four days and nights passed without any more dead bodies or attempts on Macy's life, and she took some solace in that. Jake worked those days, went with her at night to deliver pizzas. Not that his presence stopped her from being one baby step away from a panic attack; her worry over Billy never went away. Add her growing feelings for Jake, and Macy wasn't sure how much she could stand.

"Here, try these on." Nan's voice echoed behind the dressing-room curtain, and a hand appeared holding two more dresses. Macy took them.

Shopping was supposed to be fun. Not today. This morning, like every morning when Jake left for work, Macy got a hollow feeling in the pit of her stomach. Not because she was going to miss him, though she did, but because in the last few days, she'd suddenly become aware that every time he left for work he might not come back home. Never had the afternoon news, talking about robberies, shootings, and meanness in general, given her so much to worry about.

Macy slipped off her jeans, her brain playing the what-if

scenarios it did every morning. What if one of the gang members Jake was visiting had a gun? What if he was called to a break-in in progress? What if Tanks decided to come after the cop who'd put him away?

What if Jake died while eating spaghetti?

What if when the case was over he, like Tom, decided that Macy really didn't float his boat and he went looking for another pond?

Macy kicked her jeans into the corner of the dressing room. Of all her fears, the last one was the worst. Wearing nothing but her Skivvies, she stared at her reflection in the mirror. Above her left breast she had a love bite, put there by Jake that morning. Touching it, she remembered his immediate response to seeing her in her blue bra.

Even with the really exceptional sex, these last few days had been hard. Hard not to feel guilty for being happy. Hard not to worry about that happiness coming to an abrupt end. It was like waiting for the second shoe to fall—and to fall right into a fresh warm pile of dog poo. No, make that elephant poo!

She'd tried to lose herself in the make-up work her teachers had graciously allowed her to complete. She'd studied on Monday and taken tests on Tuesday, with a bodyguard waiting in the hall. She'd barely passed the tests. How could she think about constitutional law when it felt as if Murphy's Law was destined to pop up and prove that loving Jake had been a mistake?

"Well? How does it look?" her mom asked, her voice booming into the dressing room. Her mom's voice seemed to boom a lot lately, no doubt a direct result of seeing Hal.

"Just a minute." Macy forced herself to pull one of the dresses from the hanger. She wiggled the slinky fabric onto her body and, taking a deep breath, stared at her reflection.

Too tight. Too low. Too short. Too red.

Dress sexy, Jake had said. Why would he want her to dress sexy at his hundred-year-old grandfather's birthday party?

"Come out and let us see?" Nan called.

Nan had suggested they go shopping for Macy's new party dress. Macy and the FBI agent were the only ones who'd thought it was a bad idea. Macy was certain the Fed standing outside was going to resign as soon as his shift was over. Her mom actually had the man carrying packages, and she'd sprayed him with different colognes, trying to find the one she wanted to buy Hal.

"How long does it take to slip on a dress?" her mom complained.

Macy stepped out and struck a pose. "I look like a call girl who needs a boob job."

"No." Nan reached up and gave her size Bs a lift. "You just need a push-up bra."

"Jake will go nuts," her mom said, giggling. "If he's not in love with you already, he—"

Just like that, with Nan holding up her boobs and her mom giggling about love, Macy started sobbing. And it was more than a two-tissue cry.

Jake parked almost a block away from his mother's house. Cars were lined up and down the street. Holy hell, but he didn't want to do this. He gripped the wheel and stared up at the cloudless blue sky that was the contradiction of the storm brewing inside him.

"So this is it?" Macy shifted in the seat beside him.

He glanced at her and tried masking his frown. "Yeah."

"You okay?" she asked.

"Of course I am." He got out, snagged the necessary items from the backseat: the birthday bag, and the chicken salad he'd picked up from the deli. Taking his first step, he grabbed Macy's arm. "Don't get comfortable. All we're here to do is make an appearance."

"But it's your grandfather's hundredth birthday."

"His birthday was actually Thursday, and I saw him then."

"You did?" She sounded surprised.

"He lives in a retirement home near my work. I see him during lunch at least once a week."

Macy pulled away.

Jake looked at her. "What?"

She shook her head. "It hits me how little you talk about yourself."

"You know the important stuff." And she did. "Come on, let's get it over with."

"You really know how to put a girl at ease." Sarcasm filled her voice.

"Sorry. I'm tired." All week he'd worked like the devil to keep up with his other cases and make up for the time he'd taken off, hoping to get to the bottom of the string of paint-tagged robbery cases, hoping they would lead him to Tanks. But, nothing. Every lead he and Donaldson followed was a dead end. And then yesterday, Agent James had informed Jake that the FBI would be pulling their man off Macy. Everyone was betting that Tanks had left Houston. Macy had even dropped hints about moving back to her place, and Jake was beginning to feel desperate.

Of course, his desperation wasn't just about Tanks and her personal safety. It was about them. He'd accepted he loved her. He hadn't said it, of course; he hoped she'd throw the words out there first. Deep down, he believed Macy loved him. But sometimes she got that scared look in her eyes, like a wild animal about to bolt. And the possibility of losing her opened up a Pandora's box of emotions, a box that still held his feelings about Lisa and his brother.

"Seriously," he said, as they approached the house. "We're in and out of here." He took one deep breath, then reached for the door.

Macy watched Jake take the next step as if he were walking into a prison cell. But contrasting the doom and gloom of his demeanor, they were immediately pulled into a group of happy people—into Jake's world, Macy thought, feeling more than a little uneasy.

"Little Jake. My favorite nephew," someone called, and Jake got swallowed up in a big bear hug by a gray-headed, barrel-chested man with twinkling blue eyes. Jake returned the embrace, a manly hug that included a few hard slaps on the shoulder, and when he was released, he was actually smiling. He introduced Macy to his Uncle Bill, his father's brother.

Bill captured her in a bear hug, too. "We're huggers," he said, his twinkling gaze devouring her white sundress. The dress wasn't as sexy as the little red number her mother had chosen, but it showed off her figure.

The man grinned. "You did good, Jake. Always did have great taste in women."

In a matter of seconds, Macy had been hugged a dozen more times by a hodgepodge of people: cousins, aunts, uncles, and finally Jake's wheelchair-bound grandfather.

Jake's family certainly came in all shapes and sizes. Jake stood close to her elbow, as if he felt personally responsible for her. Then his mom moved in and, after offering her own hugs, stole the chicken salad and Macy's hand, and started for the kitchen.

Macy felt her face heat as she remembered the whole towel fiasco. But something about Jake's mom put Macy at ease.

"Can I help do anything?" she asked.

"Just keep us womenfolk company." She waved around the kitchen, and the introductions commenced.

Macy met Jake's aunt—another hugger—his cousin Ann, and then a beautiful brunette walked into the kitchen through an outside entrance.

"Macy," his mom said, sounding a little breathy. "This is Lisa. She's married to Harry, Jake's brother."

"Hi," Macy said, surprised to learn Jake's brother was married. Though why she was surprised, she didn't know. Jake had kept her in the dark about all these people. And while everyone here was extremely friendly, Macy had this stirring in the pit of stomach, as if she didn't belong.

Lisa smiled. "You look . . . familiar."

"I do?" Macy asked, and oddly felt as if everyone in the room were holding their breath.

"Yeah," Lisa offered. "I could swear we've met somewhere."

Macy studied her face. "You look familiar to me, too. You don't go to Houston Law?"

"No. How about the photography club?" Lisa asked.

"Nope." Macy shook her head.

The same door Lisa had walked through swung open again. Macy saw Jake out of the corner of her eye. She stopped short of speaking when he wrapped an arm around Lisa. But . . . it wasn't Jake.

"This is Harry," Lisa said. "My husband. And this"—she waved at Macy—"is Macy Tucker."

Macy smiled. "You and Jake really favor each other."

Harry stood for a moment, silent, his head sort of cocked, staring at her. "You look familiar."

"I just said that!" Lisa chimed in.

"Have you attended North Baptist Church?" Harry asked.

"I'm afraid not," Macy admitted.

"Wait," Harry said. "Macy *Tucker*. You're from the Community Garden. I've seen you there a couple of times, but your picture in that article about the garden is hanging in the church office. You're the mastermind behind the whole program. Father Luis is always praising you. I'm Pastor Harry."

Macy grinned. "I've heard of Pastor Harry, but I never knew your last name was—"

"They just call me Pastor Harry. Wow. It's an honor to meet you."

Before Macy knew it, Pastor Harry had her in a bear hug.

Macy heard the door swing open behind her. The room became unnaturally silent. Harry's arms dropped away.

Released from the embrace, Macy turned. She saw Jake.

Her breath caught at his expression, which was none too friendly. Not that it was targeted at her—rather, at his brother.

Harry held out his hand. "Jake?"

Macy didn't think Jake was going to shake. Finally, he reached out, but the handshake ended too fast. The door swung open again, and one of the uncles appeared. "Jake, can I get some help getting the grill going?"

Jake walked out so fast that Macy felt the breeze.

"Well, I think that went fine," Jake's mother said.

"Like a fart in church." Harry left the kitchen, followed by his worried-looking wife.

Macy looked back at Jake's mom and didn't know whether to go find Jake or stay in the kitchen, where the awkwardness had arisen.

One by one, the tension seemed to chase people out. Suddenly, Macy realized she was alone with Mrs. Baldwin. The woman grabbed a loaf of bread from the oak table, then slammed it down. She swung around to face Macy, and without any warning collapsed into Macy's arms and started sobbing.

Baffled, but no stranger to sobbing mothers, Macy embraced her. "I'm only good for two tissues," she warned.

Jake picked up the bag of charcoal and swore that as soon he got the fire started, he and Macy were out of there. It had been a mistake to come. He needed to get Macy away before someone let her in on the family's dark, ugly secret.

"Can we talk?" Harry said from behind him as coals tumbled into the grill.

Jake dropped the bag on the concrete patio and faced his brother. Emotion twisted his gut. He'd missed Harry so damn much, but seeing him brought it all back. He raked a hand through his hair and said, "I thought I could do this, but I can't."

Harry grabbed his arm. "We've got to get past this sooner or later."

Jake jerked loose. "Well, maybe if I hadn't walked in and found you pawing my new girl, I might have been a bit more receptive."

Harry shook his head. "I'm not even going answer that accusation."

The hell he wouldn't, Jake thought. He deserved this moment of anger. His hunger for revenge struck hard. For years, he'd imagined hurtful things to throw into his brother's face. Then he recalled himself. "I gotta leave."

Harry grabbed him again. "Look, I know you're hurt, and you have reason. But God knows I'm not guilty of what you think I am. Isn't it about time you hear what I have to say?"

Jake gulped for oxygen and took a step back. "What the hell can you say that will make a difference?"

"I prayed you'd come today."

Did you pray about stealing my fiancée, too? Jake ground his teeth to keep from saying anything. But, by God, he wanted to. Harry had betrayed him, hurt him, and right then more than anything he wanted to hurt Harry back.

His brother continued: "Macy seems . . . I've heard she's a super girl."

The calm in his brother's voice and the mere mention of Macy's name was Jake's undoing. He took a step forward. "So, now you're planning to steal *her* out of my bed? Well, don't waste your time, Reverend. Macy's not my fiancée, so she wouldn't be near as much fun to fuck as Lisa."

A crash sounded behind them. Jake swung around. Macy stood in the open doorway, raw chicken parts and a broken ceramic bowl at her feet. Her new white dress was spattered with meat marinade, and a chicken gizzard lay on the tip of her right white sandal.

Jake's heart landed somewhere beside the chicken gizzard. The words he'd just thrown at his brother ran amok in his head, and instantly he called himself a fool. No, an idiot. A bastard! He would have sent up a prayer that Macy hadn't heard him, but the hurt in her eyes left him with no hope. Zilch.

He raked both hands through his hair, clasped his hands behind his head, and squeezed the back of his neck. An apology lay on the tip of his tongue, but he knew it wouldn't be enough.

Moisture brightened her eyes. She kicked the chicken gizzard from her sandal. It flew up and struck his chest, splattering him with juice. Then she turned and shot back inside without a word.

Macy's silence continued on the ride home, though he'd pursued her and tried to apologize. Jake had turned into his mom: rattling. How many times had he said he was sorry? He'd even told her he loved her. She never responded. With her purse in her lap, she kept her eyes focused on the windshield in front of her. Not one tear slipped down her face. No words, no tears. That told him a lot.

As he pulled up to his condo, he tried to find another way to say how sorry he was. "Macy, I know what I said was cruel and incomprehensible. But I swear to you, I didn't mean . . . I was trying to hurt Harry, and I used you to do it. I was wrong, and I . . . deserve your anger and whatever else you want to do to me."

She looked over at him, her eyes still tearless. "Good. Then you'll understand that I never want to see you again."

She jumped out of his car. By the time he caught up with her, she was in his bedroom tossing clothes into a garbage bag. Elvis, already in his carrier, meowed.

"You can't do this." A knot rose in his throat. He gripped the back of his neck so tight he was certain he'd leave a bruise.

A lump of emotion climbed up to his tonsils and made it hard to talk. "I'll stay on the sofa. I won't talk to you. But you can't go back to your place. Tanks could still be out there."

Macy snatched her pj's from his dresser drawer and added them to her bag. Then, with her garbage bag of clothes in one hand and the cat carrier in the other, she walked past. The front door slammed shut. It couldn't have hurt more if his fingers had been in the jamb. Frankly, it felt as if his heart had been.

And of course he deserved it.

Macy sat curled up on her sofa, wearing her pajamas, staring at the TV. Not that she could remember what had been playing for the past three hours. All that mattered was that she wasn't crying. She wouldn't become her mother. She wouldn't fall apart. She wouldn't quit her job or school. She wouldn't run to Nan to pick up the pieces of her shattered life.

The knock on her door did enter into her consciousness, but she chose to ignore it. Whoever it was would eventually get tired and leave. They had earlier. But then she heard Nan.

Macy unlocked the door, and Nan and her mom rushed in. From their grave expressions, they knew. It was that, or something had happened to Billy. Macy's heart gave a lurch inside her chest. She'd spent the last few hours selfishly thinking of only herself.

"What's wrong?" she asked.

"Jake called us," Nan said.

"About Billy?"

"No, about you," her mom said. "What happened?"

Macy hugged a pillow that she hadn't realized she held.

"What did he do?" her mom asked. "Hal will teach him a lesson."

Macy shook her head and fought the growing lump in her throat.

Nan stepped forward. "She doesn't want to talk about it, Faye." She held up a plastic grocery sack. "Hot chocolate. I'll fix you a double."

Macy nodded, and stared at her mother and grandma. She'd sworn not to go running to them for a pity party. Did it make a difference if they had run to her?

"You know he's out there, don't you?" her mom said. "He's parked right in front of your house. He called us. He said he'd hurt you, that it was his fault, and that he was worried about you."

That piece of news had the lump rising in Macy throat. Crappers! She was gonna cry! She went to the sofa, flopped back against the cushions, and buried her face into the pillow.

Billy was fucking tired of waiting. Tired of waiting for Tanks. Tired of thinking about Ellie. He'd heard on the radio that her brother had been killed. Tanks had done it—somehow Billy knew. He knew Ellie was still at the beach house, too. He'd called the number she'd forced him to take with him, but when she answered, he'd hung up.

Tonight, like the last four nights, the car pulled up in the driveway of the green-shuttered house, and tonight, like the other nights, the guy inside the car was alone. But tonight was going to be different.

Billy watched the guy let himself into the house. "Tired," he mumbled. Then, pulling the gun from the waistband of his jeans, he walked across the street. If this guy knew where Tanks was, Billy was going to find out. He didn't want to hurt anyone, and hoped he wouldn't have to, but he wasn't waiting anymore. He'd find Tanks or die trying.

Taking the porch two steps at time, gun in hand, he knocked.

"Just a minute," a male voice called.

Billy gripped his gun and waited. He didn't have to wait too long. The door swung open and the nose of a sawed-off shotgun jabbed into his gut.

CHAPTER THIRTY-THREE

Jake sat in his car, eyes focused on Macy's house and heart focused on not breaking. He watched Nan and Faye go inside. Macy had opened the door for them, but not him.

"Damn it!" He slammed his palm so hard on the steering wheel that the car shook.

He'd screwed up so bad he couldn't think straight. If he weren't afraid that Tanks would come after Macy, he'd go find a liquor store and buy himself a bottle of something that would numb the ache. He wasn't much of a drinker, not of strong stuff, but right now he was sure he could drink anyone under the table. Weren't all sons of Baptist preachers known for that?

He took a deep breath and fought the urge to run to Macy's door and plead with her to listen to him one more time. Couldn't she hear in his voice how damn sorry he was? Maybe Nan and Macy's mom would convince her to at least let him in.

As he reached for the car door, his cell phone rang. Jerking it out of his pocket, he snapped it open without even checking caller ID. "Hello?" Hope had his chest knotted in one big spasm.

"Baldwin?" a male voice asked.

Jake pushed back in his seat, uninterested in talking to anyone other than Macy. "Yeah?"

"It's Billy."

Jake sat upright. "Yeah?" He held his breath.

"Look, I know where Tanks is. I thought maybe you could be there, too. Help me with him. Then I'll turn myself in." The boy's voice sounded strained, labored.

"Are you okay, Billy?" Jake asked.

"I'm just ready for it to be over." The kid paused. "Is Macy okay?"

Jake forced himself to lie. "She's fine. Where's Tanks?"

Shortly afterward, Jake stood outside his car, parked a block from the abandoned warehouse where Billy said he and Tanks would be. Stan's car pulled up, then Mark's. Because no one from the task force showed up, Jake figured they'd already taken the bug off his line. Sure, he planned to call them, as he would call for standard backup, but only after he got Billy out of this alive. He owed Macy that much.

He grabbed his cell phone and dialed Officer Sala, who'd agreed to watch Macy's house. "Everything okay?"

"I got it covered," his friend said.

Jake hung up and went to meet Stan and Mark.

"Here's what I know, and what I think we should do," he told them. "If that warehouse is like the rest of these, there'll be three entrances, all unlocked. I'll take the front. Stan, you take the back. Mark, you take the side. You two don't come in unless you hear shots fired." He flashed the kid's mug shot. "Let's get this guy out of it alive."

The three of them walked down the street. Each had pulled his weapon. Darkness covered the block. Jake hesitated, having second thoughts about skipping protocol entirely. He took out his cell. "I'm calling Agent James now. That should cover our asses and give us about five or six minutes before they arrive."

Both Stan and Donaldson nodded.

Jake rang James. He was quick and to the point. "I'm at a warehouse. I think Tanks is here." After he gave the address, he hung up.

Nearing the building, Stan motioned to a parked motorcycle. Jake nodded. Their quarry was here.

They all went to their positions. At the front door, Jake heard voices inside, and then—

Gunfire?

"Police! Throw down your weapons!" Jake stormed into the warehouse, his eyes trying to adjust to the darkness. Blinking, he sent up his usual prayer as he raised his weapon, finger on the trigger.

A shadow appeared, swerved to the left. Jake ducked behind some metal shelving. The shadow darted across an aisle. By the man's size and shape, Jake pegged him as Tanks.

"Give it up!" he yelled.

"Fuck you!" Tanks called back. More gunfire rang out. The bullets dinged off the metal shelving all around Jake. Then came silence.

"I'm not going back!" Tanks called out.

More shots were fired from the rear of the building. Was it from Stan, or someone else? It was too dark to tell.

"Billy!" Jake yelled, and heard shuffling where Tanks had been.

Believing Tanks was on the move, Jake jumped up, gun held high, and made a run for an upside-down refrigerator he planned to use as cover. Tanks spotted him. One shot came so close that Jake felt it pass just before he reached his destination.

A shadow moved up from the rear of the warehouse. Stan? He heard a noise directly behind him and swung around, gun aimed, but at the last second he recognized Mark, who was crouching down by a case of wooden boxes.

"You're outnumbered!" Jake shouted, glancing back at Tanks's last known location. "Give up!"

"I'd rather die," Tanks called back. "And I won't die alone."

"Billy, are you here?" Jake yelled. He heard nothing, and remembered the gunfire just as he'd rushed in. Had Billy already bought it?

"Where's Billy, Tanks?" Jake shouted.

Only silence answered.

Then someone bumped into one of the metal shelves where he'd last spotted Tanks. Jake listened, hoping to get a lead on where the convict was heading. From the corner of his vision, he saw Mark. The detective waved toward his right, as if telling Jake where he planned to go, then dashed forward.

Jake heard more noises where he believed Tanks to be. Apparently seeing Mark without cover, Tanks jumped up, gun aimed. Jake leapt up, too. "Over here, you bastard!"

"No!" someone screamed. Shots exploded from all directions. Jake saw Tanks hurtle backward.

"I think Tanks is down," Jake shouted, keeping his eyes on the darkness where the convict had fallen. "Stan?"

"I'm fine."

Jake took a moment to glance toward Mark. He called out when he didn't see the detective, "Mark? Donaldson!" Panic began to buzz within him.

"I'm . . . fine. I think."

"What the hell does *think* mean?" Jake stepped toward his friend's voice, which was tight, keeping an eye and gun on Tanks, who still lay in a heap on the floor. Dead? Maybe not. Jake didn't want to take a chance.

He saw Stan moving in Tanks's direction, and his friend called, "I got him covered." Then: "He's not breathing."

Jake rushed to where Mark's voice had emanated, and he found his friend squatting against a stack of boxes. Even in the dark, Jake saw the blood. It was smeared over Mark's hands. Kneeling, Jake pulled his friend's coat back.

"Where are you hit?"

Mark stilled Jake's hands. "I don't think it's me." He shook his head, as if dazed. He pointed to his right, where another body lay crumpled on the concrete.

"Damn." Jake recognized Billy. "Hey, kid!"

Billy didn't answer at first, but at last he opened his eyes. His features were enough like Macy's that it hurt like hell to see them—and the pain twisting his face.

"Call for an ambulance," Jake yelled to Stan.

"Is Tanks . . . dead?" Billy's voice was a rasp. Blood was

oozing from his shoulder. A lot of blood. Too damn much. Jake put his hand on the wound, praying that it would slow down.

"Yeah," he said.

Mark dropped to his knees beside Jake. "Tanks had me straight on. Kid knocked me out of the way. Took the bullet for me."

Billy's eyes closed. "It doesn't hurt as much as I thought. Take care of—"

Blood oozed through Jake's fingers. "Listen to me, kid. Your sister is waiting for you. I really need for you to be okay."

"I treated her . . . really bad," Billy murmured.

So did I. "I know," Jake said. "But she loves you anyway."

And it was more than he could say for himself.

"Police!" a voice yelled from the front door, a voice accompanied by a figure pointing a gun at Stan.

"*We're* police." Jake stood up. Shots exploded.

Macy sat in the waiting room, Nan on one side, her mom on the other. Macy felt as if she couldn't breathe. Agent James had called, said there'd been an altercation, that Billy was shot. He hadn't said how bad or if anyone else was hurt. Right after receiving the call, she'd run outside to see if Jake was still in front of her house. There was a car, but it wasn't Jake's.

Arriving at the hospital, they'd been told that Billy was in surgery. "How serious is it?" her mom had asked a nurse she recognized.

The nurse shrugged. "I don't know. But I'll get the ER doctor to come talk to you."

Before the nurse walked away, Macy managed to ask, "Was anyone else hurt?"

The nurse paused. "I heard there was one casualty. But he wasn't brought here."

Casualty. The word now bounced around Macy's head.

Jake?

Ten minutes later, a doctor walked in. "Are you the Moore family?"

All three of them bounced up, and the doctor started talking. "Mr. Moore is still in surgery. I won't lie to you, it doesn't look good. But we're doing our best."

Macy's mom dropped back in her seat and started sobbing. Nan stood straight as an arrow and reached out and squeezed Macy's hand. After a few minutes, the doctor left. Macy and Nan sat beside Faye and they held hands in silence.

The waiting room door opened and Mark Donaldson walked in. Macy zeroed in on his face, trying to guess what he was about to say. A knot crowded her throat when she saw the blood on his shirt. She didn't stand up. She couldn't. She couldn't even breathe.

He walked across the room. His gaze focused on her. "How's Billy?"

"Still in surgery." Nan was the one to answer, squeezing Macy's hand.

"J-Jake?" Macy managed to say the name. "Is he . . . ?" Her throat ached. Her chest was an open vat of pain as she awaited his answer.

"He was detained by the task force. He asked me to make sure you guys are okay. He'll be here soon."

Every muscle in Macy's body went limp with relief.

"We heard there was a casualty," Nan remarked.

Donaldson nodded. "Tanks."

Jake is alive. Alive! The knowledge ribboned through her heart, assuaging her fear. But then she remembered her brother.

It doesn't look good. The doctor's voice echoed in her head. A chasm of hurt opened in her chest again. Loving anyone came with a price. A price she couldn't afford.

Jake balanced a Styrofoam tray of hot chocolate in his hands as he pushed open the ICU's waiting-room door. His gaze shot to Macy. She sat between her mother and grandma. She looked up, then away. His stomach filled with a sharp hollowness. He hadn't been sure what kind of a reception he'd get, but when Mark said she'd asked about him he'd hoped for the best.

Macy's grandma motioned to Macy's mom, and they both stood. Nan moved forward and whispered, "I'm giving you a minute, but you're on thin ice."

Then Macy's mom leaned close. "Hurt her again and I swear you'll answer to me. My mom has been teaching me about busting balls."

Jake watched them leave, then sat down beside Macy. "I brought hot chocolate." He held out one of the cups.

She took it. "Thanks."

One word. She offered him the one word, and hope rained down like sunshine. "I would have been here earlier, but James had some questions."

"You don't have to explain."

She didn't look at him. Why wouldn't she look at him?

She continued, "Mark told me what you did, to try to help Billy. Thank you."

He didn't want her thanks, he wanted *her*. "I heard he's looking better."

He reached for her hand. She pulled away, and he closed his hands together, feeling his chest swell.

"I just want to help," he said.

She faced him. Finally. "You want to help me?" There was so much pain in her eyes, he felt certain a piece of his heart had been chipped off.

"I'll do anything. Name it."

"Go." She waved a hand between them. "This hurts. I'm hurting too much for my brother, and I can't handle two different hurts right now."

He inhaled. "I should have never taken you to that party. I—"

Her eyes narrowed. "Maybe you should have told me you were still in love with someone else."

He passed a hand over his face. "Is that what you think? It's not Lisa I love. It's you."

She looked away. "No. You don't mean that. You would have told me. Told me about her."

"I didn't want you to know because . . . because I didn't want you to know someone else didn't want me."

"So your pride is more important than being honest with me?"

"No!" He ran a hand through his hair, remembering how that word popped up a lot. *Pride*. "Maybe," he admitted. "Pride probably did play a part in it." He gripped his hands together. "But I know I was wrong. And for the life of me, I never meant what I said. Can't you forgive—?"

"No, I can't." Her tone was icy. "I can't. And to be honest, I don't even want to try."

He felt that damn lump return to his throat. "You really want me to leave?"

"Please." She turned to stare at the wall.

It took everything Jake had to walk out of the waiting room, but he owed her that much.

The next day, Jake pulled up at his condo, returning from visiting Ellie Chandler. So far, no charges had been brought against her. The boots had proved to be Ellie's brother's, and Ellie had a rock-solid alibi for when the escape went down. There wasn't even any proof that she'd been with Billy. Though Jake felt certain she had, he was relieved at the lack of evidence.

Billy had regained consciousness, and he'd told authorities about the friend of Ellie's brother who'd almost shot him because he was afraid Tanks was going to kill him, too. It had been he who'd led Billy to Tanks. When the cops found the guy, he'd spilled his guts, telling exactly how Tanks had gone wild on Ellie's brother, trying to learn where Ellie was. The confrontation had gotten ugly. Ellie's brother had died trying to protect her.

Ellie had cried when Jake told her. She'd cried again when

she told Jake that Billy refused to see her. God knows, Jake could sympathize. He felt like crying, too, and when he stepped into his condo, the ache in his chest doubled. Everything in his place reminded him of Macy.

His doorbell rang. He hurried to open it, hoping, praying—

"Lisa?" He waited for anger to swell and rise, to add to this emotional maelstrom, but the anger wasn't there—or if it was, it was buried beneath all his misery.

"Can I come in?" she asked.

He stepped back. "Sure," he replied. Sons of Baptist preachers were always polite. Except when it mattered the most. He remembered the horrible words he'd flung at his brother, words insulting to both Macy and Lisa.

"Thanks." She twisted a stand of her hair, a nervous habit. "Look, I'm just going to say what I came to say, and leave."

He didn't speak, so she continued. "Nothing happened between your brother and me while we were engaged. I know that's hard to believe, but it's true."

Jake shook his head. "Doesn't matter."

"Yes, it does." She let out a deep gulp of air. "I know how it looked when we got married, and I know if . . . if we had it to do over again, we'd do everything differently."

"Hindsight is a wonderful thing." Jake left to get himself a beer. He got her one from the fridge, too. When he turned around, she stood in the kitchen doorway. He held out the beer.

She shook her head. "You and I had broken up several weeks before Harry came to see me. When you and I were engaged, Harry and I had lunch a couple of times. I won't deny that we connected, but not romantically. All we did was talk."

Jake set her beer down. "Talking to me wasn't enough?" Okay, so maybe he still felt a touch of the anger. Or was it just curiosity, a need to understand?

"Talk?" she asked. "We never talked. No, let me rephrase that. *You* didn't talk. From the time your dad got sick, you shut me out completely."

"So you married Harry because he talked?" He took a swig of his beer, feeling disgusted.

"No, I married Harry because I love him."

"Correct me if I'm wrong, but I could have sworn you told me you loved me, too."

"I thought I did. Maybe I did. But not the right sort of love."

He took another sip of beer.

She plowed ahead. "This is killing Harry."

"It hasn't been a walk in the park for me, either."

"We didn't plan it. And we tried to explain. You kicked Harry out the day he came to see you. Hung up every time he called."

"What were you going to explain? You were engaged to my brother, a few months after we broke up." He set his beer down on the counter.

"We didn't plan that. We were going to keep things quiet for a year or more."

"That might have helped," he said.

"We couldn't wait." Tears shimmered in her eyes. "I got pregnant. A condom broke. Your brother's a preacher. You know how that would have looked. It was either get married or have an abortion. I couldn't do that."

Jake's gaze dropped to Lisa's belly. No one had mentioned a baby. If they'd had a kid, someone would have told him.

She seemed to guess his thoughts. "I lost the baby on our honeymoon."

Jake remembered how much Lisa had wanted children. And his brother . . . Losing that baby must have killed him.

Jake swallowed. "I'm sorry."

She nodded. "Harry needs you in his life. You can't avoid us forever. We're family."

Jake gripped the beer. "What am I supposed to do? How can I sit across the table from you at Sunday dinners when . . . when we had sex?"

Her eyes grew wide. "If Harry can sit across from you, I'd

think you could stand it." She paused. "Besides, I can't imagine that you'd remember the sex."

"I'm a man. Men remember that."

If Macy were here, she'd call him on being crass. Lisa wouldn't, of course. Lisa wasn't Macy. And right then he accepted that he had never felt about Lisa the way he felt about Macy. Not sexually, not emotionally, not in any way. Marrying Lisa would have been a huge mistake.

"We never meant to hurt you. Harry feels terrible," Lisa was repeating.

Jake drained his beer, then turned around and grabbed the one he'd offered her. He unscrewed the top. "Give me some time, and . . . I'll talk to Harry."

He waited for her to leave—he needed to be alone—but she just stood there. "What happened between you and Macy?" she asked. "After the party."

Jake exhaled. "It's over."

"Why?" she asked.

"Does it matter?" He sipped his beer, wishing it were something stronger.

"Yes, it matters." She stepped closer. "Women don't always remember things like sex, but we remember other things. Like how a man looks at us. I saw the way you looked at Macy. You never looked at me like that. You love her, don't you?"

Jake pressed his beer to his forehead, trying to find solace in its chill. "Yeah, but this isn't my choice. It's hers."

"Have you told her how you feel?"

"In so many words, yeah."

"Then find some other words. And don't think she can read your mind. If you love her, tell her. No, let me rephrase that. Show her how much she means to you. For once, throw your pride aside and just let someone in."

"My pride." He inhaled. "And how do I do that, Lisa? How do I show Macy she's more important than my pride?"

CHAPTER THIRTY-FOUR

The next morning, Jake walked into Mark Donaldson's office and dropped a fast-food bag on his desk. Mark, on the phone, waved for him to sit down.

"Yes, sir," his partner was saying into the receiver. "I understand. I'm sure the Gulf Coast Task Force will back up my story. Yes. Thank you, sir." He hung up.

"Was that about Tanks?" Jake asked.

"No, it was about Billy Moore." Donaldson picked up the bag. "Don't tell me, there was a buy-one-get-one-free breakfast meal deal."

"No, I bought it for you." Jake glanced at the phone. "What about Billy Moore?"

"Just making a few calls." Donaldson pulled out the sausage biscuit with cheese and unwrapped the foil. "You know, the thing I miss most about living the good life is having my meals served to me. Food never tastes as good when you have to fix it yourself—or even buy it for yourself."

Jake leaned forward, his mind still on Billy. "Calls to who?"

"The president." Mark sank his teeth into the biscuit. "Oh, this is good."

"The president of the task force?" Jake picked up his own breakfast bag.

Mark reached for a napkin. "No. Of the United States."

Jake laughed, but Mark didn't smile. "You're joking, right?"

"No." Mark swallowed. "Might as well use my Golden Boy ties." A piece of biscuit dropped to the desk and he grunted, "Next time, could you serve it on a plate?" He grinned.

Jake ignored his friend's remark, his mind still reeling. "What?"

"Billy saved that guard's life. He saved my life. Me, the son of someone who just happens to be buds with the president. Add in the facts that Billy turned himself in and that he only escaped because Tanks threatened the lives of his family. That with the prison corruption he knew about, he couldn't trust anybody at the jail to help him out. I'm trying to push for a pardon. Figured he might give the governor a call."

Jake fell back in his chair. "You really think . . . ? What's the chance that he'll get off?"

Mark shrugged. "Don't know. But the Big Chief really likes my dad."

Jake felt a thrill for Macy. "Damn, you pull this off and I promise I'll never call you Golden Boy again!"

"Can I have that in writing?" Mark laughed, grabbed a bottled water from his desk drawer, took a sip, then got serious. "How are things between you and Macy?"

"The same. But I know what I've got to do. I just have to figure out how to do it."

"Do what?"

Jake started to change the subject, but decided what the hell, he could use the help. "How do you show a woman that she is more important than your pride?"

Mark took another bite of his biscuit and seemed to consider. "You make a fool out of yourself to prove you love her."

"Okay," Jake said. "But how do I make a fool out of myself?"

Mark's eyes brightened. "Rent an airplane to fly a banner that says 'Jake Baldwin was a total full-fledged, major-ass idiot. P.S., I love you,' and have it flown all over Houston."

Jake frowned. "And what if she's not outside when the plane flies over?"

"You have the plane keep flying until she sees it."

"Do you know how much that would cost?" Jake asked.

"You didn't say the idea had to be cheap." Mark took another bite. "Wait!" He grinned. "I know exactly what you've got to do."

Macy walked into Papa's Pizza. It was Friday afternoon, and several of the employees stood at the side door, staring up. She ignored them, heading to clock in and put her purse in the back.

It had been a good day. Because of all the press the story was receiving, one of Houston's best defense attorneys, someone Macy had met while doing a short internship, had offered to take Billy's case. The attorney had gotten a confession from two brothers involved in the robbery, both admitting that Billy hadn't been in the know. The attorney immediately filed an appeal, and after a flurry of legal filings and a few calls from the White House, Billy had actually been moved to house arrest until the legal proceedings could be completed There was a good chance her brother wasn't going to have to go back to prison! It seemed almost too good to believe.

In spite of being thrilled, however, Macy couldn't shake feelings of gloom and doom. She knew what it was about, of course. She missed Jake. But some things were better missed.

She walked to the counter and started counting her bank.

Sandy waved Macy over. "Did you see this?"

"See what?"

"That." Sandy pointed up.

Macy walked over and looked at the sky. "I don't see anything."

"The billboard," Sandy said.

Macy read the large sign:

PIZZA GIRL. WILL YOU PLEASE . . .

Please, what? The sign's message was purposely left incomplete.

"I wonder what that means," Sandy said.

"I . . . don't know." Macy stepped back from the door. It could be anything, like some kind of advertising promotion. Just because Jake had called her Pizza Girl didn't mean . . . He wouldn't do anything so outlandish. It wasn't his style.

She told herself that over and over. So why, on every pizza run, did she keep looking at the sign? And why had whoever paid for the sign chosen to put it here, beside Papa's Pizza? She considered calling Jake and asking, but hearing his voice would have just hurt too darn much.

That night in bed, tossing and turning for several hours, she resigned herself to ignore the sign. It couldn't be from Jake.

Saturday, around noon, as Macy pulled up to her work, there was a television van parked outside. The cameraman leaned against the front, filming the billboard. The female reporter standing next to him spotted Macy and started over. Macy did the only logical thing. She ran.

"Ma'am?" The reporter wobbled on her four-inch heels as she chased Macy inside. "I was wondering if you could answer some questions for the news."

Macy turned. "About what?" Maybe this was about Billy.

"About the sign. The whole city is buzzing about it."

"Why?" Macy asked, playing innocent.

"Radio stations all over Houston have been receiving calls asking about them."

"You mean this isn't the only one?" Macy held her breath.

"No. There're four. But this one is the only one beside a pizza joint."

Four? So, it wasn't Jake. It was some kind of a bizarre marketing gimmick. Next week the billboards would probably announce the name of a new pizza restaurant, or a frozen pizza. Macy let out a deep breath, relieved. But the slightest wiggle of disappointment stirred in her belly.

No, it wasn't disappointment. She didn't want Jake to make some grand play to win her back. Honestly, she didn't.

Her heart hiccupped. Dad-blast that emotional wiggle thing!

On Sunday, Macy turned the TV to the local news hoping to hear the weather. She saw the reporter who'd been at Papa's Pizza the day before, and her gaze instantly glued to the tube. Okay, so maybe it wasn't the weather she wanted to hear.

"Last night the messages on the Pizza Girl signs changed!"

Macy dropped down on the sofa and hugged a pillow to her chest.

The camera shifted off the reporter to the sign.

PLEASE FORGIVE ME, PIZZA GIRL. I . . .

Again, the sentence was left unfinished.

Macy put a hand over her lips. Was it Jake?

The reporter continued talking, "Sounds as if we have a mystery love story on our hands. So, who is this man . . . ? Who is this mysterious Pizza Girl? And who is the man begging for her forgiveness? Perhaps the location of the four signs is a clue."

The woman gave the addresses. Macy's breath caught. One sign was located near Nan's neighborhood. One was located down the street from Macy's school, and the other, right on the corner of the church garden.

Macy's insides started to shake. She went to the bathroom, grabbed a box of tissues, joined Elvis on the sofa, and allowed herself two.

On the Wednesday of the next week, Macy went to Nan's for a visit. She found everyone sitting in the living room, eyes locked on the midday news. Macy's gaze dropped to Nan's shirt, which read, LET'S MAKE THIS EASY. JUST TELL ME I'M RIGHT.

"Who do you think those signs are for?" Nan asked.

Macy shot her grandma a silencing glare. She'd expected

Nan to have figured it out—nothing got by Nan—but her mom and Billy were another story.

"I think we all know who they're for," her mom said.

Okay, Macy was going to have to rethink her mom's intelligence. Maybe her IQ had increased since she'd stopped soddening her brain with tears all the time.

"The question is," Billy said, "what is Pizza Girl going to do about it?"

Macy sashayed over and clicked off the television. "Can we change the subject?"

"Why?" Billy sat up without flinching. He was looking better every day. Enough that his comments about her refusal to see Jake had passed the stage of just annoyance and arrived on the doorstep of pissing her off.

Reaching for a glass of tea, Billy studied her. "What did he do to cause all this?"

Macy fired back before she could stop herself. "What did Ellie do that was so bad?" When Ellie had shown up at the hospital, her brother had refused to see her.

Billy frowned. "That's mean, Sis."

"Yeah, but it made my point."

"Did you read the sign coming into our neighborhood?" her mom asked. Then, oblivious to the tension, she sat down beside her son, who wore an ankle bracelet that would have brought sweet memories back to Martha Stewart.

"No, I didn't look at it." It had taken everything Macy had in order not to look, but she had managed to keep her eyes down. She wasn't giving in to Jake. How could she? She had too much to risk.

The screen door swung open and Hal Klein walked inside. "I just read it, and it says, 'I need you in my life.'" He looked at Macy. "That boy has it bad for you. Sounds as if he's in a world of hurt. It takes a lot for a man to confess his love and mistakes publicly."

Macy's mom went to kiss Mr. Klein. Their relationship had advanced with hurricane speed. Nan had proudly informed Macy that her mom hadn't come home the night before last. Which didn't make sense. Nan was proud of her daughter for having sex, but she'd threatened to throw her out of the house if she didn't get rid of the belly-button ring? Dysfunctional didn't begin to describe this family.

"I've been trying to tell her he cares about her," Billy said.

Macy turned for the door. "I just remembered I need to go watch my toenails grow."

"Sit down," Nan said. "You're not going anywhere. Everybody drop the subject. Macy will do the right thing. She always does. She's a smart girl."

Nan cut her eyes to her daughter. "She never puts holes in her body where holes don't belong."

Macy's gaze shot to Nan, ignoring the "hole" comment and going straight to her own concerns. "What do you mean, I'll do the right thing? I'm doing the right thing."

"I don't mean crap. Now come help me in here." Nan grabbed hold of Macy's ponytail and pulled.

Macy followed her into the kitchen. Not that she had much choice when Nan had a hold of her hair. Letting out a frustrated breath, she jerked her ponytail free. "You always say I'll do the right thing when you think I'm doing the wrong thing. But this isn't wrong."

"Are you sure?" Nan reached for the salt and pepper.

"Yes, I'm sure." Wasn't she?

Nan turned around. "What did that boy do that was so bad?"

Macy dropped into a kitchen chair. "I don't want talk about it." She hadn't told Nan or anyone what had happened at Jake's party. It hurt too damn much.

"I think the billboard idea is romantic." Nan added salt to the four pots boiling on the stove. One of them would be something vegetarian. Nan was the only person who respected her eating preferences.

Except Jake. The meat-loving, bullheaded, closed-mouthed lover boy had accepted Macy for what she was. He'd even filled his freezer full of veggie burgers and his cabinets full of hot chocolate, and had gotten takeout menus from all the vegetarian restaurants in town. She missed him. She missed him so bad her toenails ached.

Before she realized it, she was crying, Nan shoved a box of tissues at her. "You're reminding me more and more of your mama, girlie. Before she wised up, of course. Took that woman fourteen years. I sure hope it's not going to take you that long. But come hell or high water, don't you even *think* about getting anything pierced!"

Thursday night at nine, Macy made hot chocolate and settled on the sofa in front of the TV. She'd managed not to drive by any of the signs today, but she couldn't help but watch the local news. It was, after all, about her.

Or at least she was 99 percent sure it was. Just as she was 99 percent sure Jake had something to do with the owner of Papa's Pizza's sudden decision to send Mr. Prack packing. Not that she felt sorry the guy was gone. Jake was right—what Prack had done was sexual harassment. He deserved to be fired.

The news came on. The familiar reporter filled the screen and held up several letters. "These are addressed to the Billboard Mystery Man, in care of me. I've read a few, and I have to tell you, Pizza Girl, if you don't want your man . . . well, a hundred other women do. At least forty of the letters included proposals—some a little more explicit than the others." The reporter grinned.

Macy didn't grin. She didn't think it was funny at all.

CHAPTER THIRTY-FIVE

Jake was sitting at his desk trying to focus on his cases and not the empty hole in his heart and life, when Mark rushed in.

"Come here. The news is on in the lunchroom. You're not going to believe it."

Jake burrowed back in his chair. "I'd rather not."

He'd stopped watching the news when they started reading letters from possible replacements for Macy. One woman had written how she wanted to *lick him like a Popsicle*. He only wanted one woman messing with his Popsicle, and he wasn't sure how or when he should make his move to approach her.

"Hey, Preacher Boy," Mark said. "Get off your ass and come here! This is good. I promise you. It'll put a smile on that ugly face of yours."

Jake followed his friend into the lunchroom. A crowd circled the TV, which flickered with images of the billboard signs. Good Lord, when the truth came out, everyone at work—no, everyone in *Houston*—would be privy to the sad state of his love life. He fought a wave of grumpiness, because he knew if it won him Macy back, it'd be worth it. If it won Macy back, he'd let the story go national.

The screen flashed and the blonde reporter appeared. "We're at M. D. Anderson Cancer Center, where we finally located Mr. Brown of Brown Billboard Company. He's the man responsible for the Pizza Girl signs. Mr. Brown, can you tell us the identity of man behind the signs, and what he did that needs forgiving?"

"Of course I can't." Mr. Brown looked offended.

"How long does he plan to do this?" the reporter asked.

"If I was a betting man, I'd say he'll do it until his woman forgives him. When a man loves a woman that much, he'll do just about anything. And if she'd take my advice, she'd take that boy back. This isn't an ordinary guy. He's what you women would call a keeper."

"We're told that you've taken about a dozen other orders for signs like these now."

"It's communication," Brown said. "I have to be careful of regulations, but nothing is better advertising than billboards."

"Is that why you advertised about your daughter's cancer fund?"

"Yes, it is," Mr. Brown continued, and told his daughter's story. Before it was over, they showed the man's daughter. "She's a fighter," the man said, and his voice shook.

The reporter looked into the camera, her tears evident. "Another love story," she said. "If anyone would like to donate to this fund, contact . . ."

Mark elbowed Jake. "Talk about something good coming out of all of this!"

"Yeah." And maybe it was time his story was put to bed and Mr. Brown got all the media attention. Jake just hoped both love stories had happy endings.

Billy had called Andy and asked him to come over. While he'd never told the police about the teenager who'd helped him, he'd told his mom and grandma. Andy seemed happy to visit, and they spent several hours just talking, Nan and his mom included.

When Andy left, Nan called Billy and his mom to the kitchen/boardroom. Any serious talks were held at the kitchen table. Billy, secretly smiling, knew exactly what this talk would be about.

"The boy needs a home," Nan said. "He can't continue to live on his own like that."

Billy feigned innocence. "Maybe he could hang out here."

Nan cocked her head to the side. "Well, it depends on

how much of a pain in the ass you plan on being. I sure as heck wouldn't want two hell-raisers living here."

Billy grinned. "If I actually get out of this mess. I'm going back to school. And getting a job. My hell-raising days are over. And Andy doesn't come off as much of a hell-raiser."

"We'd have to do it legal-like," Nan said. "Things like this can get messy if you don't."

Billy's mom piped up. "Hal's daughter works for the Children's Advocacy. I'll bet she'd help us. She likes me better now that I got rid of the belly ring." She shot her own mother a smile.

Nan gave Billy a questioning look. "Do you think Andy would go for it?"

"Yeah." Billy sipped his tea. "He's hungry to have someone in his life. He took to me. What does that tell you?"

"It tells me he's smart," Nan said as a knock sounded on the front screen door. "Coming!" She popped up and went to answer it.

"Faye?" Nan called out a moment later. "Can you come here?" Billy's mom got up and left him alone.

Billy rose slowly. It still hurt if he moved too fast. Leaning against the kitchen counter, he put his glass in the sink. His back was to the door when he heard footsteps behind him. "Who was at the door?" he asked, turning around.

His breath caught. *Ellie.* She stood at the door of Nan's kitchen wearing a green scrubs-like nurse's uniform top and not a stitch of makeup. She appeared more than a little uneasy. He let himself just look at her. God, she was beautiful.

She fidgeted with the hem of her uniform top. Finally, she raised her gaze. "I'll leave if you want me to."

He didn't know what to say. Ever since he'd heard her brother was killed, he figured she'd hate him. No, he hadn't done the killing, but it was because of him, because she'd gotten involved with him, that her brother was dead.

She looked away. "I guess I shouldn't have come. I just

wanted to see you, to make sure you were okay. But I'll go. I'm sorry." She turned to leave.

"Wait."

She swung back around. Her soft green eyes met his and his chest grew tight.

"It's not that I didn't want to see you. I—I thought you'd blame me for your brother."

Her eyes washed with tears. "At first, I blamed *myself* for getting involved with you, but then I got to thinking about how he was. He was always getting himself into trouble. He wasn't a bad person, but he was always making bad decisions."

"Sort of like me," Billy said.

She shook her head. "We all make mistakes. Maybe you made some bad decisions in your past. But you saved two people's lives, Billy. You were willing to die to save that cop."

He hated hearing all that crap, and he blurted out what he hadn't been able to say to anyone else. "It's not like I thought about it or even meant to do it. I just reacted!"

Her eyes widened. "Yeah, but not everyone would have reacted like that." She stepped closer. "That's what I saw in you. Even in the beginning, in your letters, you were kind and good. You owned up to what you'd done. You're not a bad person. And sometimes I got the feeling you felt like you were. People make mistakes, but it's not so much our mistakes that make us good or bad, but how we clean up the messes and what we learn from them."

His chest filled with a lightness he hadn't felt since he'd left her at the beach house. Not even learning that he might not have to go back to prison felt this good. "My lawyer says . . . she really thinks I won't have to go back to prison." He moved away from the counter and pressed his palms on the back of a chair. "I want to go to school. I've got a lot of plans."

She looked at him. "That's good."

"I need to get my life together. It could take some time."

"I understand." She started backing out of the kitchen, hurt in her eyes, and Billy realized Ellie didn't understand. Her next backward shuffle took her farther away from him. Leaving. She was leaving.

"Would you help me?" His words came out fast.

She bumped into the side of the door frame. Her gaze shot up. "You want me to?"

"More than anything in this world."

They met in the middle of the kitchen. And when he stood directly in front of her, he thought he'd die if he didn't touch her. So he reached out and placed his hands around her waist. Pleasure that bordered on pain flowed from the touch and filled his heart.

She leaned in and placed a hand on his chest. Her soft mouth came so close that what came next was as natural as breathing. He kissed her. Drank the sweet taste of her lips and swore to himself that he'd become the man Ellie thought he was.

"You kids, don't get too carried away in there!" Nan called.

Billy laughed and pulled back. Then he brushed the soft blonde strands of hair from her cheek. "Have I told you I love you?"

Later that afternoon, Jake got the courage to just do it. He checked to make sure Macy wasn't working, then called Nan to make sure she was at home.

"She's home. Just talked to her." Nan paused. "You're gutsy. What do you have up your sleeve now?"

"Just watch the news." Jake guessed that Nan was smart enough to have figured he was responsible for the signs.

"Will do. By the way, you owe me and my daughter."

"For what?" He liked this woman and hoped he could call her part of his family soon.

"Do you know how many love letters we wrote to the news station saying we'd marry your sorry ass? We figured it might help if Macy thought somebody else wanted you."

Jake laughed. "Which one of you wanted to lick me like a Popsicle?"

Nan giggled. "Got that out of a romance novel."

"Okay," Jake said. "I owe you. Name your price."

"How about making my granddaughter happy?"

"I'm hoping I get the opportunity."

An hour later, Jake pulled up at Macy's house. He waited until the two news vans pulled in behind him to go to the door.

He knocked.

Macy's voice sounded through the door. "Who is it?"

"It's Jake. Let me in, please." His request met silence. His heart ached and he sent out another prayer. "Please, I've got all sorts of media right behind me. I'd rather say what I have to say to you in private. Unless you want it on tonight's news."

Her front door opened. She stared out in horror at the reporters approaching her front lawn.

"Crappers!" She motioned him inside, then slammed and locked the door.

Once he was in, she glared at him. "I don't know why I rescued you. You did this to yourself."

"Guilty as charged." He half smiled, hoping to put her in a good mood. God, it felt good to see her.

She rolled her eyes. "Why would you do something so . . ."

"Public?" he finished for her. He took a step closer and ached to touch her.

"Yeah, public." She took a step back.

That little step hurt. He fought to hang on to hope. "I thought you'd figured that out by now."

"Well, I guess I'm not as smart as you think."

He heard the reporters nearing the front door. "I did it to show you that my pride isn't as important as you are. *Nothing . . .* is as important as you are."

She took another step; then, swinging around, she walked into the living room. At least she hadn't told him to leave.

He followed and watched her drop on the sofa. Elvis

scurried over and did figure eights around his ankles. Kneeling, he petted the feline. "Your cat's happy to see me."

"And his rations will be docked for it, too." She glared at Elvis.

Jake rose, then moved to the sofa and sat beside her, careful not to touch her too soon. This might be his last chance. That thought had all kinds of emotions racing around his heart.

"Macy—"

"Don't." She pressed a finger to his lips, then jerked away. "I can't do this, Jake."

The weight of her words burrowed into the pit of his gut. "Do what? Forgive me? Do you really think I don't love you? I was so angry for so long at my brother, I wasn't thinking straight. Do you really think I meant what I said?"

"It's not just that."

She closed her eyes. Her dark, thick lashes rested against the tender skin beneath. The bluish circles told him she hadn't slept well. He liked thinking she'd missed him, but knowing she'd been hurting, that he'd been the one to cause that pain, only deepened his guilt.

"Then what is it?" he asked.

She opened her eyes and looked right at him. The vulnerability and fear he saw pooling there had his mind reeling. And just like that, everything made sense.

"This isn't about what happened at my mom's, is it? This is about your dad, and you not trusting men in general." When she didn't answer, he knew he was right.

He stood up and paced across the room. "What do I have to do to prove to you that I'm not your dad, Macy? I'm not going to walk out on you. I'm not Billy, who took you for granted. And I sure as hell am not like that asshole of an ex who had a slice of heaven and didn't know it."

She blinked, and her baby blues filled with tears. "You're still like my grandpa. You could get killed. You put your life on the line every day. You get shot at. You shoot at bad guys.

On the day Billy was shot, I thought you were dead. They said there was a casualty. I thought it was you. I can't take that. I can't take losing someone else."

He watched one of her tears slip down her cheek. "Well, I wasn't killed. I'm right here. I'm alive."

"But you *could have been* killed."

He gritted his teeth. "What are you saying, Macy? You want me to give up my job? Is that what you're saying?" The thought sent a bulldozer through his life plans. He'd never wanted to be anything but a cop. But if it meant—

"No. I wouldn't . . . I don't . . ."

"Then, what?" He dropped down on his knees in front of her. "I love you, Macy. I love you so much that I can't imagine my life without you."

She blinked, and a couple more tears fell from her eyes. "I'm scared. I'm scared you'll get killed. I'm scared you'll start cheating on me. I'm scared that I'll fall so deeply in love that I couldn't handle losing you. Then you'll leave me and I'll be . . . I'll become my mom."

He took her hands in his. "I'll never willingly leave you. Never cheat on you. Damn it, Macy, you can't go through life not trusting anyone because they might die." Right then Elvis skittered past. "You love the cat right? But you damn well know it's going to die before you. It doesn't stop you from loving it."

Macy blinked, and it appeared as if he was actually getting through to her. But just in case, he kept going. "Besides, even your mom has dealt with this, and she's letting herself give love a shot. And to be honest, I'm scared, too! I think that's part of the reason why I didn't tell you about Lisa and Harry. I thought if you knew one person had dumped me, you'd think twice about wanting me. I felt as if you had one eye on the door at all times, waiting for me to make a mistake."

"You did make a mistake." She said the words as if it were her last stand.

"I know, and it was a champion of mistakes, too. Which is

why I did the whole billboard thing, to show you that—that I'm sorry. That you're more important than my pride."

She let go of his hands. "You should have told me about Lisa and your brother." She released a shaky breath. "And the things you said, they—"

"They were horrible. I know. And I'll regret that all my life. Just don't make me have to live that life without you." Their eyes met and held, and he'd never been more certain she loved him. His chest swelled with hope. "I need you in my life."

A knock sounded at the door. Macy glanced up and then shot him a panicked look. "What do they want?"

He leaned in and pressed his forehead to hers. "A fairy-tale ending?"

"I'm not sure I believe in fairy-tale endings," Macy said.

"Then I'll have to spend the next forty to fifty years proving you wrong." He leaned in and kissed her softly. "Marry me, Macy Tucker."

"If I say no, will you keep posting billboards?"

"Probably."

"Will you end up marrying the woman who wants to lick you like a Popsicle?"

He laughed. "Sorry, but Nan doesn't do it for me."

Macy's eyes widened. "She . . ."

"Yeah."

Macy shook her head, then focused on him, but the look in her eyes told him everything was going to be okay. "You're a lot of trouble," she said.

He arched an eyebrow. "So are you."

"Oh, pleeaase! What did I do?"

He held his hands out to count. "One: you messed with the family jewels. Two: you told the FBI I was a dirty cop. Three: you convinced me you were about to become a nun. Four: you made me go with you to buy tampons. Five: you wouldn't admit I was your boyfriend. Six: you don't eat bacon. But remind me to tell you that I found some vegetarian bacon I bought at the specialty grocery store. Seven: you stole my towel and my mama saw me naked . . . with a stiffy! Eight: you made me fall in love with you."

He touched her face. God he loved touching her. "Nine, and this is a biggy: you named my penis Mr. Dudley!"

She leaned against him and laughed. "So I guess we're both trouble, and that makes us perfect for each other, right?" She sat up.

"Right." He studied her. "Is that . . . a yes?"

"What do you think?" she asked.

"I think I gotcha." He smiled. "But I need to hear you say it."

"You got me, Jake Baldwin," She leaned in and kissed him.

He pulled her onto his lap and kissed her to show her just how right he and Mr. Dudley thought they were for each other.

ICE

SOMEONE IS WAITING

Most people find beauty in Alaska's austere mountains. To Kaylie Fletcher, there is only death—her whole family gone after a disastrous climbing expedition. Then again, maybe not. A raspy call in the middle of the night leads Kaylie to believe her mother might still be alive. For now…

SOMEONE IS WATCHING

A strange message in a bar. A bloody knife. A fiery explosion. There's a killer inching closer, but Kaylie has nowhere to run. Except straight into the arms of Cort McClaine. The rugged bush pilot is too much of an adrenaline junkie to be considered safe, but Kaylie can't resist the heat of his touch amid the bitter cold.

SOMEONE WILL DIE

Caught in a high-stakes race against a murderous madman, Kaylie and Cort know that with one wrong step they'll be…iced.

STEPHANIE ROWE

ISBN 13: 978-0-505-52775-2

ELISABETH NAUGHTON

Antiquities dealer Peter Kauffman walked a fine line between clean and corrupt for years. And then he met the woman who changed his life—Egyptologist Katherine Meyer. Their love affair burned white-hot in Egypt, until the day Pete's lies and half-truths caught up with him. After that, their relationship imploded, Kat walked out, and before Pete could find her to make things right, he heard she'd died in a car bomb.

Six years later, the woman Pete thought he'd lost for good is suddenly back. The lies this time aren't just his, though. The only way he and Kat will find the truth and evade a killer out for revenge is to work together—as long as they don't find themselves burned by the heat each thought was stolen long ago . . .

STOLEN HEAT

ISBN 13: 978-0-505-52794-3

To order a book or to request a catalog call:
1-800-481-9191
This book is also available at your local bookstore, or you can check out our Web site **www.dorchesterpub.com** where you can look up your favorite authors, read excerpts, or glance at our discussion forum to see what people have to say about your favorite books.

COLLEEN THOMPSON

"[Thompson] more than holds her own in territory blazed by Tami Hoag and Tess Gerritsen."

—*Publishers Weekly*

In Deep Water

Ruby Monroe knows she's way out of her depth the minute she lays eyes on Sam McCoy. She's been warned to steer clear of this neighbor, the sexy bad boy with a criminal past. But with her four-year-old daughter missing, her home incinerated and her own life threatened by a tattooed gunman, where else can she turn? Drowning in the flood of emotion unleashed by their mind-blowing encounters, Ruby is horrified to learn an unidentified body has been dredged up, the local sheriff is somehow involved, and Sam hasn't told her all he knows. Has she put her trust in the wrong man and jeopardized her very survival by uncovering the secrets...

BENEATH BONE LAKE

ISBN 13: 978-0-8439-6243-7

EXTRA, EXTRA!
Read all about the hot new
HOLLYWOOD HEADLINES series
from GEMMA HALLIDAY

The *L.A. Informer* is Los Angeles's premier tabloid magazine, reporting on all the latest celebrity gossip, scandals and dirt. They're not above a little sensational exaggeration and have even been known, on occasion, to bend the law in pursuit of a hot story. Their ace reporter, Felix Dunn, has just been promoted to managing editor. Now, he's got his work cut out for him, keeping the magazine running smoothly while keeping his staff in line…

Coming in November

Scandal Sheet

Tina Bender is the *Informer*'s gossip columnist extraordinaire. She knows everything about everyone who's anyone. And she's not afraid to print it. That is, until she receives a threatening note, promising, If you don't stop writing about me, you're dead. And when her home is broken into the next day, she realizes they're serious. Teaming with a built bodyguard, a bubbly blonde, and an alcoholic obituary writer, Tina sets out to uncover just which juicy piece of Hollywood gossip is worth killing over.

JOY NASH

When a girl with no family meets a guy with too much…

For Tori Morgan, family's a blessing the universe hasn't sent her way. Her parents are long gone, her chance of having a baby is slipping away, and the only thing she can call her own is a neglected old house. What she wants more than anything is a place where she belongs…and a big, noisy clan to share her life.

For Nick Santangelo, family's more like a curse. His *nonna* is a closet kleptomaniac, his mom's a menopausal time bomb and his motherless daughter is headed for serious boy trouble. The last thing Nick needs is another female making demands on his time.

But summer on the Jersey shore can be an enchanted season, when life's hurts are soothed by the ebb and flow of the tides and love can bring together the most unlikely prospects. A hard-headed contractor and a lonely reader of tarot cards and crystal prisms? All it takes is…

A Little Light Magic

ISBN 13: 978-0-505-52693-9

☐ **YES!**

Sign me up for the Love Spell Book Club and send my
FREE BOOKS! If I choose to stay in the club, I will pay
only $8.50* each month, a savings of $6.48!

NAME: _____

ADDRESS: _____

TELEPHONE: _____

EMAIL: _____

☐ I want to pay by credit card.

☐ VISA   ☐ MasterCard.   ☐ DISCOVER

ACCOUNT #: _____

EXPIRATION DATE: _____

SIGNATURE: _____

Mail this page along with $2.00 shipping and handling to:
Love Spell Book Club
PO Box 6640
Wayne, PA 19087
Or fax (must include credit card information) to:
610-995-9274

You can also sign up online at **www.dorchesterpub.com**.
*Plus $2.00 for shipping. Offer open to residents of the U.S. and Canada only.
Canadian residents please call 1-800-481-9191 for pricing information.
If under 18, a parent or guardian must sign. Terms, prices and conditions subject to
change. Subscription subject to acceptance. Dorchester Publishing reserves the right
to reject any order or cancel any subscription.